Praise for Catherine Bybee

Wife by Wednesday

"A fun and sizzling romance, great characters that trade verbal spars like fist punches, and the dream of your own royal wedding!"
—Sizzling Hot Book Reviews, 5 Stars

"A good holiday, fireside or bedtime story."
—Manic Reviews, 4½ Stars

"A great story that I hope is the start of a new series."
—The Romance Studio, 4½ Hearts

Married by Monday

"If I hadn't already added Ms. Catherine Bybee to my list of favorite authors, after reading this book I would have been compelled to. This is a book *nobody* should miss, because the magic it contains is awesome."
—Booked Up Reviews, 5 Stars

"Ms. Bybee writes authentic situations and expresses the good and the bad in such an equal way . . . Keeps the reader on the edge of her seat."
—Reading Between the Wines, 5 Stars

"*Married by Monday* was a refreshing read and one I couldn't possibly put down."
—The Romance Studio, 4½ Hearts

FIANCÉ BY FRIDAY

"Bybee knows exactly how to keep readers happy . . . A thrilling pursuit and enough passion to stuff in your back pocket to last for the next few lifetimes . . . The hero and heroine come to life with each flip of the page and will linger long after readers cross the finish line."
—*RT Book Reviews*, 4½ Stars, Top Pick (Hot)

"A tale full of danger and sexual tension . . . the intriguing characters add emotional depth, ensuring readers will race to the perfectly fitting finish."
—*Publishers Weekly*

"Suspense, survival, and chemistry mix in this scintillating read."
—*Booklist*

"Hot romance, a mystery assassin, British royalty, and an alpha Marine . . . this story has it all!"
—Harlequin Junkie

SINGLE BY SATURDAY

"Captures readers' hearts and keeps them glued to the pages until the fascinating finish . . . romance lovers will feel the sparks fly . . . almost instantaneously."
—*RT Book Reviews*, 4½ Stars, Top Pick

"[A] wonderfully exciting plot, lots of desire, and some sassy attitude thrown in for good measure!"
—Harlequin Junkie

TAKEN BY TUESDAY

"[Bybee] knows exactly how to get bookworms sucked into the perfect storyline; then she casts her spell upon them so they don't escape until they reach the 'Holy Cow!' ending."

—*RT Book Reviews*, 4½ Stars, Top Pick

SEDUCED BY SUNDAY

"You simply can't miss [this novel]. It contains everything a romance reader loves—clever dialogue, three-dimensional characters, and just the right amount of steam to go with that heartwarming love story."

—Brenda Novak, *New York Times* bestselling author

"Bybee hits the mark . . . providing readers with a smart, sophisticated romance between a spirited heroine and a prim hero . . . Passionate and intelligent characters [are] at the heart of this entertaining read."

—*Publishers Weekly*

TREASURED BY THURSDAY

"The Weekday Brides never disappoint and this final installment is by far Bybee's best work to date."

—*RT Book Reviews*, 4½ Stars, Top Pick

"An exquisitely written and complex story brimming with pride, passion, and pulse-pounding danger . . . Readers will gladly make time to savor this winning finale to a wonderful series."

—*Publishers Weekly*, Starred Review

"Bybee concludes her popular Weekday Brides series in a gratifying way with a passionate, troubled couple who may find a happy future if they can just survive and then learn to trust each other. A compelling and entertaining mix of sexy, complicated romance and menacing suspense."

—Kirkus Reviews

Not Quite Dating

"It's refreshing to read about a man who isn't afraid to fall in love . . . [Jack and Jessie] fit together as a couple and as a family."

—RT Book Reviews, 3 Stars (Hot)

"*Not Quite Dating* offers a sweet and satisfying Cinderella fantasy that will keep you smiling long after you've finished reading."

—Kathy Altman, USA Today, "Happy Ever After"

"The perfect rags to riches romance . . . The dialogue is inventive and witty, the characters are well drawn out. The storyline is superb and really shines . . . I highly recommend this stand out romance! Catherine Bybee is an automatic buy for me."

—Harlequin Junkie, 4½ Hearts

Not Quite Enough

"Bybee's gift for creating unforgettable romances cannot be ignored. The third book in the Not Quite series will sweep readers away to a paradise, and they will be intrigued by the thrilling story that accompanies their literary vacation."

—RT Book Reviews, 4½ Stars, Top Pick

NOT QUITE FOREVER

"Full of classic Bybee humor, steamy romance, and enough plot twists and turns to keep readers entertained all the way to the very last page."
—Tracy Brogan, bestselling author of the Bell Harbor series

"Magnetic . . . The love scenes are sizzling and the multi-dimensional characters make this a page-turner. Readers will look for earlier installments and eagerly anticipate new ones."
—*Publishers Weekly*

NOT QUITE PERFECT

"This novel flows extremely well and readers will find themselves consuming the witty dialogue and strong imagery in one sitting."
—*RT Book Reviews*

"Don't let the title fool you. *Not Quite Perfect* was actually the perfect story to sweep you away and take you on a pleasant adventure. So sit back, relax, maybe pour a glass of wine, and let Catherine Bybee entertain you with Glen and Mary's playful East Coast–West Coast romance. You won't regret it for a moment."
—Harlequin Junkie, 4½ Stars

NOT QUITE CRAZY

"This fast-paced story features credible characters whose appealing relationship is built upon friendship, mutual respect, and sizzling chemistry."
—*Publishers Weekly*

"The plot is filled with twists and turns, but instead of feeling like a never-ending roller coaster, the story maintains a quiet flow. The slow buildup of a romance allows readers to get to know the main characters as individuals and makes the romantic element more organic."

—*RT Book Reviews*

DOING IT OVER

"The romance between fiercely independent Melanie and charming Wyatt heats up even as outsiders threaten to derail their newfound happiness. This novel will hook readers with its warm, inviting characters and the promise for similar future installments."

—*Publishers Weekly*

"This brand-new trilogy, Most Likely To, based on yearbook superlatives, kicks off with a novel that will encourage you to root for the incredibly likable Melanie. Her friends are hilarious and readers will swoon over Wyatt, who is charming and strong. Even Melanie's daughter, Hope, is a hoot! This romance is jam-packed with animated characters, and Bybee displays her creative writing talent wonderfully."

—*RT Book Reviews*, 4 Stars

"With a dialogue full of energy and depth, and a twisting storyline that captured my attention, I would say that *Doing It Over* was a great way to start off a new series. (And look at that gorgeous book cover!) I can't wait to visit River Bend again and see who else gets to find their HEA."

—Harlequin Junkie, 4½ Stars

STAYING FOR GOOD

"Bybee's skillfully crafted second Most Likely To contemporary (after *Doing It Over*) brings together former sweethearts who have not forgotten each other in the 11 years since high school. A cast of multidimensional characters brings the story to life and promises enticing future installments."

—*Publishers Weekly*

"Romance fans will be sure to cheer on former high school sweethearts Zoe and Luke right away in *Staying For Good*. Just wait until you see what passion, laughter, reconciliations, and mischief (can you say Vegas?) awaits readers this time around. Highly recommended."

—Harlequin Junkie, 4½ Stars

MAKING IT RIGHT

"Intense suspense heightens the scorching romance at the heart of Bybee's outstanding third Most Likely To contemporary (after *Staying For Good*). Sizzling sensual scenes are coupled with scary suspense in this winning novel."

—*Publishers Weekly*, Starred Review

FOOL ME ONCE

"A marvelous portrait of friendship among women who have been bonded by fire."

—*Library Journal*, Best of the Year 2017

"Bybee still delivers a story that her die-hard readers will enjoy."

—*Publishers Weekly*

HALF EMPTY

"Wade and Trina here in *Half Empty* just might be one of my favorite couples Catherine Bybee has gifted us fans with so far. Captivating, engaging, lively and dreamy, I simply could not get enough of this book."

—Harlequin Junkie, 5 stars

"Part rock star romance, part romantic thriller, I really enjoyed this book."
—Romance Reader

FAKING FOREVER

"A charming contemporary with surprising depth . . . Bybee perfectly portrays a woman trying to hold out for Mr. Right despite the pressures of time. A pitch-perfect plot and a cast of sympathetic and lovable supporting characters make this book one to add to the keeper shelf."
—*Publishers Weekly*

"Catherine Bybee can do no wrong as far as I'm concerned . . . Passionate, sultry, and filled with genuine emotions that ran the gamut, *Faking Forever* was a journey of self-discovery and of a love that was truly meant to be. Highly recommended."

—Harlequin Junkie

SAY IT AGAIN

"Steamy, fast-paced, and consistently surprising, with a large cast of feisty supporting characters, this suspenseful roller-coaster ride will keep both series fans and new readers on the edge of their seats."
—*Publishers Weekly*

My Way to You

First Wives Series

Fool Me Once
Half Empty
Chasing Shadows
Faking Forever
Say It Again

Paranormal Romance

MacCoinnich Time Travels

Binding Vows
Silent Vows
Redeeming Vows
Highland Shifter
Highland Protector

The Ritter Werewolves Series

Before the Moon Rises
Embracing the Wolf

Novellas

Soul Mate
Possessive

Erotica

Kilt Worthy
Kilt-A-Licious

My Way to You

CREEK CANYON, BOOK ONE

CATHERINE BYBEE

 Montlake

Published by Montlake, Seattle

www.apub.com

Amazon, the Amazon logo, and Montlake are trademarks of Amazon.com, Inc., or its affiliates.

ISBN-13: 9781542009805
ISBN-10: 1542009804

Cover design by Caroline Teagle Johnson

Printed in the United States of America

This one is for Paul Melillo.
You told me it was all going to be okay . . . and it was.

PROLOGUE

Parker peered into the mirror, closed one eye, and swiped a perfect cat shape eye line over the lid. She fanned the wet makeup before opening her eye completely. She stood back and moved her head side to side to check out her skills.

Her roommate, Suzzie, stood beside her, competing for space in their tiny apartment bathroom. "I wish you didn't have to work tonight, Marcus said the party is going to be the memory of the summer."

It was late August and the fall semester was already a week in. At twenty-four, Parker had spent more time with people like Marcus on the beach with bonfires than in the classroom, and her parents had put their foot down.

She had one year to finish her classes and earn a degree. All doable if she skipped a few tequila-induced sunsets and worked her ass off. Saturdays and Sundays were her only days to work, and since she made the best tips on the weekends, that's what she was going to do.

"Time for you to grow up, Parker. Your dad and I have been patient, but enough is enough." Her mother and father sat across the dining room table making her feel like she was the target of an intervention.

Her parents were skimming their early fifties . . . and kinda free thinkers. "We were fine with you taking a couple years to figure out what to do. When you started college at twenty, we were happy to make it happen. But four years and you aren't taking it seriously."

"It's because I don't know what I want to do," she told them.

Her father smiled, patted her hand from across the table. "We figured that out when you changed your major for the third time. We also know that San Diego State is a party school, and we were young once."

She wanted to argue that many students change their majors, and that she didn't party as much as they were implying, but held her breath.

Her mom released a long-suffering sigh and looked her straight in the eye. "Mallory was accepted to four UCs, and the reality is we can't afford to pay for both of you to be in college at the same time for more than a year. We'd planned on you being out by the time she was in, and Austin is three years from going off to school, too. And you know how much it cost us last year before Nana passed away."

Their grandmother had lived in their guesthouse before she suffered a stroke and her care became simply too much for her mom to take on. Assisted living was not cheap.

Parker looked around her family home, a sprawling ranch style that sat on over five acres in an upscale part of the Santa Clarita Valley. It was the closest to country living one could get while living less than forty minutes from Los Angeles. She'd grown up with everything she needed and many things she wanted. But that didn't mean her parents were floating in money. Her dad yelled at them as kids to turn off lights, and they weren't allowed to be wasteful when it came to throwing food away.

In the end, Parker didn't argue. Her parents were right . . . it was time for her to start adulting, and that began with her finishing college and getting a real job.

Parker twisted the cap off her lipstick and applied it in three gentle swipes. "Tell Marcus that if I get off early enough I'll drop by."

She slid behind Suzzie and exited the bathroom. After grabbing her apron and a hair tie, she tossed her cell phone in her purse and ran out of the apartment. San Diego was unusually warm, even for August, and she secretly hoped that she wouldn't be put on the patio for the night's shift.

She plugged her phone into the aux cable and flipped through her playlist for the short drive.

It rang and flashed her sister's name.

Parker silenced it and continued with her playlist.

She put the car in reverse and backed out of her parking spot.

Her sister called again.

Instead of ignoring her a second time, Parker picked up the phone and kept her foot on the brake. "I'm in the car on the way to work, can I call you later?"

"Parker!" Mallory screamed her name, hysterical.

Everything inside Parker froze.

"What is it?"

"It's Mom and Dad. Come home right now."

"What is it, Mallory?"

Her sister started sobbing, and panic tore every cell in Parker's body in two. "Oh, God . . . What is it? What happened?"

There were shuffling sounds, and an unfamiliar voice sounded on the line. "Hello, is this Parker?"

Tears already threatened. It was like everything started moving in slow motion and she couldn't stop what was about to happen. "What's going on?"

"I'm one of the nurses at Henry Mayo. There's been an accident."

TWO YEARS LATER

CHAPTER ONE

"We're going to be late."

"Trust me. This is the third time I've done this." Parker waited patiently for the gate on their property to open and let them out. "It doesn't matter when you show up, we're going to walk into a tiny room with a bunch of kids from your school. When you get there, your name goes on a list and you wait. The appointments are a joke."

They passed through the gate and drove down the private road shared by seventy of her neighbors. She turned the air conditioner on high, hoping to combat the ninety-degree heat radiating through the windows.

"I hate being late."

Parker glanced at her seventeen-year-old brother, who was staring out the window. He looked like their dad more every day.

"You could have just driven yourself," she reminded him.

He shrugged.

He was starting his final high school year in a month, and it was time for senior portraits, hence the rush to the tiny room filled with pimply-faced kids on the cusp of starting a new future. Sure, Austin could have driven himself, but he wanted her there. She wasn't a substitute for their mom, but she was the next best thing.

Of the three of them, Austin had the hardest time after their parents' accident. His grief came in the form of rebellion that lasted six months and almost forced the courts to take him away. Parker pushed the memories aside and focused on what was in front of her.

"I made Mom get there almost an hour early when she took me," Parker said as she turned off the private road and onto the one major street that traversed their neighborhood. "We ended up waiting an hour and a half."

"I hope it doesn't take that long. I told my friends I'd meet them at In-N-Out at two."

They drove past the burger joint in question and onto the highway.

"You might be late."

"I hate being late," he muttered a second time.

Parker glanced in the rearview mirror as she merged onto the freeway and saw a plume of smoke in the sky behind her.

"Oh, no."

Austin turned in his seat. By now Parker had eased into her lane and was searching the landscape behind her.

"That looks close."

She focused on the road. "Someone probably tossed a cigarette out the window. Assholes." Southern California was in its seventh year of severe drought. The hillsides were nothing but dense vegetation too starved for water to even scream anymore. "I wouldn't worry. The Santa Anas aren't blowing."

They'd had plenty of experience with wildfires in the canyons surrounding their family home. Some had come close enough for the authorities to close the one major street in and out, but all were put out before any homes or properties were touched.

Austin turned back around and put his nose in his phone.

Forty minutes later, Parker sat tapping her foot against the air while she waited with her brother. The photographers provided a dress shirt and tie for pictures. Around them, boys sat in formal attire from the waist up with shorts and flip-flops waist down. The girls had these drape type things that offered the same effect.

She snapped a couple of pictures of the crazy scene for Mallory to see later. Her phone buzzed with a text from her sister. Did you see the fire?

We noticed it as we were leaving. Is it close? Parker felt her heart skip a beat just asking the question.

I think it's in Acton. I'm not sure. You guys should get home before they close the road.

Parker snuck out of the studio and shuffled through the lobby over-flowing with teens, and out the door. She looked up to the eastern sky, saw only a puff of smoke from her vantage point. Then again, they were miles across the Santa Clarita Valley.

I'm sure it's fine. Parker quickly walked back into the studio.

Austin still sat on the bench waiting for his turn.

She glanced at the time on her phone.

Minutes clicked by.

If the fire was close, she wanted to be home. The last time they closed the canyon road it was off limits for anyone coming in for four days. The fire hadn't come that close, but the authorities asked for an evacuation. Only half the residents left. Her parents were alive when that had happened. Her father had loaded their horses onto the trailer and told her mother to take the animals, Parker, and her siblings out of the neighborhood. Dad had stayed behind. He promised that if things got hairy, he would leave.

Nothing happened. Not even a layer of ash. For three nights and four days they were kept from going home.

Austin's name was finally called, and Parker released the breath she didn't realize she was holding.

She smiled at her brother as he took his seat and grinned for the camera.

9

Much like an attraction at a theme park, the wait was much longer than the ride. Once Austin was out of the hot seat, she rushed him along. "Mallory thinks the police are going to close down the canyon."

"The fire?"

"Yeah. She thinks it's in Acton."

The silent drive home buzzed much faster than the one out. The small bursts of smoke in the sky had been replaced with huge mushroom clouds in less than an hour. When she passed the point of entry where the authorities would close down the road, she sighed in relief.

They both exited the car with their heads craned toward the sky.

Mallory met them at the bottom of the driveway. "What do you think?"

It was close.

Too close.

"The wind is blowing the opposite way. If the sky wasn't blue above us, I'd be worried." Her insides quivered, but she wasn't about to show her siblings that.

"What do we do now?" Austin asked.

"You skip burgers with your friends. If they close the road, you're not getting back in. And if we have to leave, I'd want to pack your car with as much stuff as we can."

Their property sat on the edge of the Angeles Forest. It was one of the best parts about it. The ten acres that they called The Sinclair Ranch had the illusion of being even bigger without neighbors on one side of them. The house itself had been engineered by the previous owner to withstand a California wildfire. Stucco walls, tile roof. Their father had planted ice plant all around the back hill. Although a freeze one winter and then multiple summers of zero rain and water rates as high as they were . . . yeah, most of that had died off. The neighbor directly above them did a crappy job of clearing their brush. Parker had hopped the fence many times in the past two years with a Weed Eater to knock down the vegetation close to their fence line.

She turned without comment and started down the long driveway. "Where are you goin'?" Mallory asked.

"To open the gate so the fire department can get in." If there was one thing that was consistent with fires in the neighborhood, it was the fire department using their property to stage. The land was flat, with the exception of where the house was perched, therefore the fire engines could easily turn around.

The three of them ate dinner in front of the TV, the news all competing for the best angle of the fire. Thankfully none of them were on her street or in her yard, which gave Parker some semblance of safety. And the sheriff wasn't going house to house asking for evacuations either.

They'd gathered the photo albums and put them by the stairs leading down into the garage. It was all they had left of their parents, the pictures and the memories. One sparked the other and it's all that really mattered.

As much as Parker hated to admit it, she worried. It was hard not to when darkness replaced the sunset and the glow in the east was easy to see.

Austin stood by the big bay window overlooking the property. "The fire department is here."

Her chest squeezed.

Parker stopped doing the dishes and walked outside. Lights flashed from the engine slowly rolling toward the house. Austin shadowed her down the driveway while Mallory hibernated in her room. Scout, their black lab, ran circles around them with the excitement of a nighttime walk.

"Good evening," she greeted the firefighters, who were standing beside their engine looking at the glow.

"Hello. You the homeowner?" one of the men asked.

"I am." She reached out a hand. "Parker. This is my brother, Austin."

"I'm Captain Moore. Thanks for opening the gate."

11

"Of course. Anything to make it easier for you guys to put this out. How far away is it?" she asked him.

"Miles. We're just keeping a watch on it tonight."

"No evacuations?" Austin asked.

"No, not yet. If the wind keeps going the way it is, it won't get here. Don't worry. If something changes in the night, we'll wake you up and get you out of here. Do you have livestock?"

She shook her head. "Just chickens."

"Good."

Scout pranced around the captain, looking for attention.

"We'll probably be in your yard most of the night."

That was a relief. Not that she thought any of them would find any sleep. "Good by me," she told him. "If you need anything, please just ask."

"We're pretty self-sufficient."

Parker noticed a couple of her neighbors at the edge of the property looking in. She left Austin talking with the fire guys to chat with her neighbors.

She walked just outside the gate and put on a fake smile. "Shit gets real when the fire department camps in your yard," she said with a nervous laugh.

"What did they say?" Lori asked.

"They're just watching right now. No need to panic."

"It's not coming down here," Mr. Richards said. "I've seen this a dozen times. I remember sitting on your porch with your dad the last time, drinking beer and listening to the quiet before they opened the canyon back up." Mr. Richards had to be in his early seventies. His property didn't touch hers, but his home was tucked higher on the hill. If anyone needed to worry, it was him.

"I wouldn't stress, Parker." Susan and her husband, Ron, shared a fence line with them. "Your dad would be kicking back a beer."

Susan's words were meant to comfort her. Instead they fell flat.

"I feel better with the fire department here." She glanced at the flashing lights of the fire engine. Wished her dad were here instead. That thinking would paralyze her, so she pushed it aside.

"Are the De Lucas still in Hawaii?" Lori asked, changing the subject.

"Yeah. I'm sure someone is watching the house." The De Lucas traveled a lot and always had someone behind watching over their home.

"I suggest you all get some sleep. Tomorrow this place is going to be crawling with flashing lights," Mr. Richards said.

"Let's pray the wind doesn't shift," Susan said.

Parker ignored the looks of sympathy, the ones that accompanied every conversation since her parents had died and she'd taken over their life. She said her good-nights and walked back toward the house. When she reached the crossing at the dry creek, she paused. The glow in the distance was brighter there. No flames. Not that she could see, anyway.

She shivered.

Hot July night and she was cold.

~

The morning air was still. The wind chimes didn't bother to move.

Parker managed a few hours' sleep and woke before the sun or Bennie, their rooster, had a chance to do the job.

Sliding into a pair of shorts and a tank top, Parker followed Scout out the door. The fire truck had left the property. Haze shadowed the blue sky as the sun started to rise.

Mallory joined her, a cup of coffee in her hands. "What do you think?" she asked.

"Hard to say. According to the weather report, the wind is supposed to shift." She waved a hand in front of her face. "Hence the crap in the air."

"Dad would be telling us to relax."

"And Mom would be freaking out."

Mallory put an arm around Parker's shoulders. "I wish they were here."

Parker really didn't want to stroll down that rabbit hole. She had enough to think about. Sweating in sorrow had no place in her day. She broke out of her sister's arm and marched away.

"What are you doing?"

"Turning on the sprinklers. Rolling out the fire hose." There was a hydrant in the middle of their yard. A five-thousand-gallon gravity tank fed it from up on the hill behind the house. It wouldn't save it, but it might help. Until it was empty. Then there was the pool. But she hadn't replaced the pump her father had set up to pull water from it in situations like this. Avoiding that bill had seemed like a good idea at the time.

I should have replaced the pump.

By ten o'clock, helicopters were buzzing over the neighborhood in regular succession. The firefighters parked in the yard and the air was full of hot ash.

The stillness of the morning shifted, and the wind started pushing the fire in their direction. Slowly, the blue sky disappeared behind smoke plumes that hovered overhead. The wind chimes kept a steady, pleasant beat to the movement of the air. Not like a Santa Ana, Parker thought. Where she would come out in the dead of night and take the chimes down because their frantic movement would keep her from sleeping.

All Parker and her brother and sister could do was watch the sky and the silhouette of the hillside. Standing beside one of the half a dozen firefighters, she started asking questions. "Will the air attacks put this out before it can get here?"

"They're going to try, but those mountains aren't easy to fly in with this much smoke."

She grew up on those hills, understood firsthand just how steep they were.

"Bulldozers?"

"If there's time."

What did that mean?

The thirty-something-year-old firefighter must have sensed her worry and smiled. "I'd pack your cars and be prepared to evacuate if this gets any closer."

"Is there an evacuation order yet?"

"Voluntary. Many of your neighbors are moving their livestock, just in case."

Parker hadn't left the property all day and had no idea how many of her neighbors still hung around.

She ran a hand over her face, felt a fine layer of dirt on her palm after she did.

Not dirt, she corrected herself.

Ash.

She motioned for Mallory to join her as she walked back up to the house. "Let's load the cars . . . just in case."

Parker looked into the same blue eyes that she saw every day in the mirror. A gift from their mother.

"I'm scared."

"They always put it out before it crests the hill," she assured her sister.

"Yeah, but it's always been on the other side of the canyon. Never from this side."

Her sister was right, but she wasn't about to feed into her panic. "You grab the photo albums, yearbooks . . . clothes and fill your car. I'll get Mom and Dad's stuff."

Still, as Parker packed she told herself it was a wasted precaution.

Nothing was going to happen.

She loaded up her father's gun collection in the trunk of her car along with all the ammo she could find. The last thing she wanted was to have bullets flying if the house did catch fire. She wasn't sure if that was possible, but it seemed like the right thing to do. Her hands shook even as she told herself that she'd be unloading the car without leaving the property.

"Did you pack Mom's china?" Mallory asked.

Parker looked around the space left in her car. "We don't have room."

"I don't like this." Tears blossomed in her sister's eyes.

Parker started to choke up. "I don't like it either, Mallory. Let's keep it together, okay?"

"Okay." Her sister took a gulping breath.

The helicopters had stopped buzzing overhead. Not one water drop or plane filled with Phos-Chek graced them with any relief.

The smoke thickened and so did Parker's nerves.

At one point she looked around all the first responders and didn't see her brother. "Where's Austin?"

Mallory pointed toward the neighbors. "At the De Lucas' helping Lynn." Lynn was the De Lucas' adult daughter, who was watching the house.

"Did he pack anything?"

"I don't think so," Mallory said.

Parker ran back to the house, went into her brother's room, and took inventory. It didn't appear that he'd packed a single thing. She grabbed his hamper, the clothes he obviously wore, and headed to his car.

Mallory ran into the house, the fear Parker felt rising shined in her sister's eyes. "We see flames."

Everything chilled.

Hair stood on end and the thud of Parker's heart was loud enough to hear.

She dropped the basket on the floor and rushed out the door.

They both ran to the dry creek bed and stared at the path the fire was taking. A clustering of flames flickered up the hillside.

Parker marched up to the hotshot crew that had staged in the middle of the property. "Where is the other crew?" she asked, looking for the truck with hoses.

"One of our guys just left to get them."

Her heart wouldn't work for long at this pace.

The sky went from hazy to gray. White ash started to fall.

She turned to her sister. "Go get Austin."

Without question, Mallory ran to the neighbors' house.

Parker removed her phone from her back pocket and started to record. A habit from when she was in college and recording life events was a part of her daily life. "I don't like this," she said to her recording. Her video caught the way the sky started to move from gray to black and the wind started to pick up. The view landed on the barn that only housed a half a dozen chickens.

The guesthouse stood several feet from that, her father's flags waved proudly in the wind.

Shoving her phone back in her pocket, she ran to the barn and opened the chicken coop door. She wouldn't try and gather the birds. If the fire moved in, they would just have to run for themselves.

From across the property, the sound of wind chimes slamming against each other screamed like an omen in her head.

Still, denial sat in a far corner of her brain.

This isn't happening.

The desire to sit idle and cry was huge.

Back inside the house, she grabbed a quilt her grandmother had made and ran down the hall removing family photos from the walls, dropping them on the blanket until it was too heavy to pull.

She filled the back of her brother's car.

Scout ran beside her, smart enough to stay close. The same couldn't be said for the family cat.

Sushi, the cat, was nowhere to be found.

Austin ran into the house. "Parker! You have to see this."

She hadn't been in the house ten minutes, yet walking outside was like walking from daylight to midnight. Air swirled like a hurricane. The noise the fire was generating was deafening. They ran down the driveway and took in the ridgeline.

It was as if someone had poured a massive spray of accelerant and a wall of fire exploded as a result.

The captain of the fire department she'd spoken with most of the morning stood looking at the flames. "You have a defendable house," he told her.

"That doesn't look like a fair fight," she told him.

He looked around with strange excitement in his eyes. "Now would be when I need to tell you to leave."

Not that they had much of a warning.

"Would you? If this was your home?" Austin asked.

The captain blinked. "I'm a firefighter."

She saw her father's fighting look in her brother's eyes.

Mallory appeared more like their mother, ready to flee.

"The road leaving the neighborhood is already backed up," the captain told them. He stared directly at Parker. "I'm going to save your house."

Bits of hot ash started to rain down on her skin. "What's going to happen now?" she asked.

The firefighter looked to the streaks of flames that started to surround them. "It's going to get really interesting, really fast." His crew had already backed their truck up the driveway and were running around laying out hoses.

The three of them moved back into the house and watched the fire as it crept closer, for less than a minute.

"I want to stay," Austin told them.

"And do what?" Mallory yelled at him.

"Dad would stay."

"Dad isn't here." Parker kept her voice even.

"I don't want my car to fry," her sister told them. The cars were outside the house and filled with anything worth saving.

Scout barked at their feet as if adding his two cents.

Leave or stay?

Outside, the flames crept closer. The hillside next to the barn was starting to go up.

Before she could make a sound, the fire alarm in the house went crazy. Without thought, Parker ran through the house to see if the fire had somehow gotten inside.

The phone rang. She knew without looking that it was the alarm company calling to ask about the fire alarm.

There was nothing in the house worth their lives. And the path for them to exit the canyon was starting to catch fire.

Parker grabbed the leash for the dog and hooked him in. "We're leaving."

"I want to stay," her brother argued.

She grabbed her sister's hand, stared her brother down. "We already lost Mom and Dad. And none of us can do anything to save the house."

He blinked. The boy he once was, looking more like the man he would become. "Okay."

Parker sighed in relief as they fled the house.

Outside was a war zone. Flames were so close that the heat of them was a sunburn on her bare arms. Smoldering ash dripped from the sky, making it impossible to breathe without coughing.

Scout jumped in Austin's car and one by one they drove down the quarter-mile driveway as they exited their family ranch.

The last thing Parker saw before leaving her childhood home was an orange glow of flames catching one of the heritage oaks on fire.

CHAPTER TWO

Parker rocked, her phone in hand, while the news slowly revealed the fire coverage as it happened.

It had taken over an hour and a half to leave the canyon. The captain hadn't been kidding when he said the exit was congested. A standstill would be a better definition.

Now she and her siblings were with friends across town, but not too far that they couldn't see flames in the distance.

Slowly, one text at a time, Parker watched as the alarm system at their home pinged on her phone.

Front door intrusion.

Glass break living room.

Motion detection family room.

Glass break dining room.

Parker rocked.

This wasn't happening. She'd taken care of their family home every day since her parents' death. Keeping it together so that once Austin graduated from high school she could sell the ranch and they could all start a new life.

Two days ago that's all she had wanted.

A new life. One without the responsibilities of raising her siblings and taking care of all the bills her parents left behind with the money that came with their deaths.

A life where she could return to school herself, instead of keeping the go-nowhere job she'd taken, to follow a traditional school schedule so she could be there for Mallory and Austin.

A new life where she might even try and go out on a date.

Only now, none of that mattered. Parker watched her phone as their home presumably exploded, until the alarm system finally gave out and stopped texting her altogether.

"That's the house above us," Austin exclaimed, pointing at the TV.

Parker glanced up, her friend Jennifer kept her arm around her.

The home above theirs flashed on the screen.

It was entirely engulfed.

The pilot in the news helicopter said the smoke was too thick to reach the other side. At the same time, he told the people watching that several structures in the area were complete losses.

Parker stared at her phone and the alerts from the system at the house.

The system that had stopped talking to her.

She thought of her mother standing on the porch of the house, waving them in for dinner. Her father digging a hole for yet another tree he wanted to plant.

Gone . . .

All her denial that this was happening started to take hold, and her eyes swelled with unshed tears.

"Do you think it's still there?" Mallory asked.

Parker couldn't say yes, wouldn't say no.

By now, it was all over . . . one way or the other.

The fire had moved in so quickly that they either had a home to go back to or they didn't.

"I can't sit here," Sam said as he stood. "I'm going in to see if the house is still there."

"The canyon is closed," his wife told him.

"I'll take the Jeep to the wash and walk over."

Austin stood up. "I'm going with you."

Sam stood beside Parker, placed a hand on her shoulder. "I won't let you sleep tonight not knowing," he told her.

Tears rolled freely down her cheeks. The house was all they had left of their parents. A big gaping hole that hadn't had a chance to heal since their deaths was punched back open and left her bleeding out.

She nodded.

Mallory sat curled up on the couch, two out of the four Chihuahuas on her lap. The other two were curled up next to Scout on the floor.

"C'mon," Jennifer said. "Help me with dinner."

They moved into the kitchen and Jennifer handed her a beer. "You doing okay?"

Parker shook her head. "I'm a mess."

"It's going to be okay. Whatever happens."

"What if it's gone?"

"You have insurance."

"To what, rebuild?" The thought made her ill. "And where would we live in the meantime?"

"You can stay here."

Yeah, right. Sam and Jennifer had two of their own kids, four dogs, and two cats. There was no way that was going to happen.

"Mom, Samson won't let me play." Jennifer's eleven-year-old daughter ran into the kitchen to tattle on her brother.

"I'll be right back."

While Jennifer left to deal with her children, Parker looked out the kitchen window. The sun had set and she could still see the glow of the fire in the far distance.

Breathe . . .

Just breathe . . .

Thirty minutes later her phone rang.

Austin's name popped up on the screen.

Her hands shook.

"Tell me," she demanded while holding her breath.

"My hand is on the house. It's still here."

Her chest shook with the force of tears that took the place of worry.

"It's a mess, Parker. The barns are gone. But the house is still here."

"Oh, thank God." The first smile that split her lips in two days told everyone in the room watching that everything was okay.

~

A mess.

Understatement of the year.

Even as Parker stood in the center of their charred property, three-hundred-year-old oak trees, gone, her mother's small fruit orchard, gone, the barns, gone, the wood fence only six feet from their home . . . gone . . . Even then, Parker counted her blessings.

All she had to do was look up on the hill, to the home above them, the one where the neighbor did a piss-poor job of clearing his brush every year . . . the house that was reduced to smoldering timber.

Gone.

The neighborhood was quiet. Even the sound of the wind chimes didn't fill the air.

She managed to sneak back into the canyon by way of driving through the wash where the authorities weren't monitoring.

They had a generator and food. And now that she knew they had a home, Parker wanted to stay. And thankfully, Sushi had hid somewhere in the house during the whole thing and hadn't so much as charred one hair on his feline back.

Sam walked up the side of the hill that Parker had climbed to take in the damage from above. The ground was black and warm under her feet. Once at her side, he draped an arm over her shoulders. "We tapped the sprinkler lines that were melted."

They'd arrived early and found two lines that were spraying water everywhere. Though the power was off, the water flowing to the house was not. And the fire had melted the PVC pipes that rose from the ground.

"Thank you."

"You coming back to our house?"

She shook her head. "No. We can stay here. But thank you."

Leaving the canyon meant not coming back without the same she-nanigans to get back in. Much as she appreciated the favor, she didn't want to keep asking for help. "I'll come for the cars as soon as they open everything up."

Sam stared up at the hills. "Looks like moonscape."

She turned to the blackened forest behind them. "I never knew these bowls were here."

There were three bowled-out stretches of earth, hidden by fifty years of brush, now exposed with nothing but charred sticks where plants and trees once stood.

"Looks different, that's for sure."

"Feels different."

That night as she sat on the porch, the hillside above the house and up the canyon was a speckled glow of smoldering fire that burned roots deep in the ground and was kicked up by a small gust of wind.

The fire still blazed in a remote part of the canyon, and every once in a while the sound of someone's propane tank exploding would catch them off guard . . . but for the most part it was quiet.

No coyotes.

No shaking of a rattler's tail.

Nothing.

~

Soot and ash coated her throat and skin as Parker walked over the remains of what once were the estate barns. Three hens and Bennie managed to escape the flames and return once the dust settled. The others weren't so lucky.

"I have pictures of what it looked like before the fire," she told Andrew, the insurance adjuster. "It once housed three horses, two goats, and these guys." She pointed to the remaining chickens with a huff.

The past three weeks had been a blur.

It took four days for the canyon to open up. In that time, she had just about every fire marshal, county, city, and forestry department official or advocate on their property. At one point they brought in a real-life chain gang. As in inmates to draw a line between the dark soil and the light where the fire had been put out, as a containment line. Parker thought the firefighters that told her that were kidding.

She'd watched as the orange-suited men filed in a straight line and marched up her driveway and around her house like they were just another crew.

"They're inmates," the firefighter she couldn't name told her.

"Ex-inmates?" she assumed.

"No . . . as in right now. Guys on good behavior and all that."

With that tidbit of information, Parker had raced up to the house to cover her father's gun collection she'd tossed on the floor after their return, and locked the doors.

Never in a million years did she think she'd have criminals on the family property, good behavior or not.

Nothing unexpected had happened, and the inmates did the job they were commissioned to do and moved on.

Now Parker stood ankle deep in what the fire left behind.

"Pictures help, but I can get a pretty good idea of what was once here."

They walked out of the small barnyard, past the horse barn and charred fencing.

"Somewhere in all the mess, someone ran into the gate entering the property. My guess is the power blipped and the fire department had to force it open. And the split rail fences didn't survive the fire or the trucks," she pointed out.

Andrew smiled at her as he wrote down his notes. His accent was pure midwestern. "What about the house itself?"

"The fire wrapped around the back, took out a few trees, the fence, but overall it didn't seem to damage a lot."

"Does the home smell like smoke?"

"Everything smells like smoke," she told him.

"We'll get a professional cleaner in to do a number on the air vents."

Parker led him around to the pool, or the black pond that once was a swimming pool.

"I don't think we're going to get away with not draining it," she told him. Summer water rates wouldn't make it cheap to fill back up.

He motioned toward the guesthouse. "Any damage there?"

Parker shook her head. "The crew that was here the day of the fire returned and told me that the roof had caught on fire, and once they saw the flags waving they pointed their hoses at it. They thought it was an outbuilding and weren't supposed to make it a priority, but the flags made them think twice."

"That's a blessing," Andrew told her.

"Yeah. I'm going to need to rent it out after all this is said and done," she said.

Andrew tucked his pen away in his shirt pocket and smiled. "You're going to be covered, Miss Sinclair. Your policy has a cap on outside structures and landscape, but I think you're going to be okay. I'm going to spend some time taking measurements and pictures for the next couple of hours."

It was in the triple digits and walking around in ash didn't sound like a good time to her.

"Thank you," she told him.

He smiled. "No problem."

Parker looked up at the hillside and found her smile fading. "What can the insurance company do about keeping that hillside from sliding onto my yard?" Because after fire . . . floods happened. All California needed to do was add rain.

"Nothing," he said, deadpan.

"What about those concrete barriers you see lining the freeway?" The name for them escaped her.

"K-rails?"

"Right, those. Or that green spray stuff to get vegetation to grow and hold the soil down? Anything?"

"Preventative isn't covered."

Parker's heart started pounding. "That's stupid. All this is going to be a bigger issue once it starts to rain," she told him.

He paused, looked her straight in the eye. "Then you call me back. Everything that happens because of the fire is going to be covered too."

"Are you sure?"

He reached into his pocket and handed her a business card. "I'm sure."

"Can you do me a favor?" she asked him.

"What?"

"Before you leave, can you tell me if the coverage I have for the house is enough? My parents set up the policy and I never really looked at it." She huffed out one side of her lips. "Not that I would know what I was looking at. But I want to know that if everything had burnt to the ground, would we really have enough insurance to rebuild."

Andrew smiled, nodded. "Of course. I'll look at your policy and the going rate to build in the area and let you know."

She reached out, shook his hand. "Thank you."

Parker paused and peered at the looming mountainside.

Her smile fell. A shiver crawled up her spine.

"You're going to be okay," Andrew told her.

She couldn't find the assurance he was offering.

CHAPTER THREE

Colin stood on the peak of the charred remains of what was technically the Angeles National Forest, but in reality was someone's backyard. Several someones.

Grace stood beside him, her hand sheltered the glare of the sun as she studied the landscape before them.

"What do you think?" he asked his younger sister.

"It sucks."

"Beyond that?"

"I think you're going to be stupid busy and I'm going to be happy I work in city development and not in mopping up this crap."

Colin smiled, despite the dread he felt. His sister was an engineer with the City of Santa Clarita and he recently acquired the supervisor position for the LA County Public Works Department.

He rolled out a map and spread it over the hood of his county issue truck. "There are two places the majority of the water sheds off the hills." He pointed at the largest one. "The wash here is wide enough to take it. There are a couple places that will likely cut off access for a few homes."

"What about damage?"

"Backyards, landscape, erosion. But there isn't anything we can do to slow it down in this path." He pointed to Creek Canyon. "That one is the trouble spot."

Grace pointed at the red on the map. "Burn area?" she asked.

"Yeah."

She blew out a breath. "How narrow is this canyon?"

"I haven't been on-site yet."

"Why not?"

"It's private property."

She pointed at the green line. "This is the forest, isn't it?"

He pointed to a property on the map. "Forest that butts up to someone's home."

"Looks like you have some room to work with."

He shook his head. "Not enough."

At five foot three, his sister was a tiny powerhouse of piss and vinegar when cornered, yet incredibly kind and optimistic at the same time. "What are the chances of the forestry department working with you?"

"When has that ever worked?"

"Maybe when Noah built the ark."

They both snickered.

"You have your work cut out for you, brother. I don't envy you."

Colin glanced up at the ash blowing off the hills. "I just hope the homeowner cooperates." He needed the project to go smoothly. His mentor had retired the year before and recommended Colin to take his place. At thirty-three, he was the youngest head supervisor in the department, and the man he reported to made sure Colin knew he didn't think he was experienced enough to do the job. Even though his probationary time in the position had passed, Ed made sure Colin knew who the head boss was.

"If they don't, the homes downstream won't stand a chance."

Yeah, he knew that.

"Maybe we'll have another dry winter."

"We can hope," he said, even though Southern California really needed the rain.

Creek Canyon didn't need any.

~

"This is stupid," Austin whined and dragged a hand through his pillow-brushed hair.

"Which part?" Parker reached into the pool with the vacuum hose and attached it to the suction.

"The part where I'm out here before nine o'clock in the morning doing this."

The *this* he was referring to was their normal Saturday routine. Except since the fire, once a week turned into every other day. Parker scowled at the two inches of soot that sat at the bottom of the pool. Once the insurance money came in, she had drained the pool and acid-washed the damage. A month later, the Santa Ana winds made it look like they hadn't touched it.

"Would you rather come out here when it's a hundred degrees of stupid later on?"

Her brother nodded and offered a hopeful smile. "I would."

She nudged the skimmer his way. "No, you won't."

"Hire a pool man."

"Once you're both back in school," she said. "Until then, we're the pool man."

Austin snatched the skimmer and plopped it in the pool. "And the gardener, and the maid, and the plumber, and the—"

"I get it, Austin." And she did. Their workload had tripled. The inside of the house never stayed clean. Between Scout going in and out and the entire property covered in ash and a hillside that blew dirt with every gust of wind, it was impossible to keep up.

The damage to the sprinkler system had been unreasonably crazy. From all the trucks that had run over risers and the fire melting the pipes on the perimeter, Parker had become exceptionally efficient with PVC pipes and Red Hot Blue Glue.

She had sat down with her sister and brother and talked about how to best spend the insurance money. Much as they hated to see the barns gone, none of them wanted to rebuild them. Not when they had no intentions, or ability, to own a horse to live inside them. By the time Andrew had cut the checks, Parker had lived with the mess long enough to realize they were going to need outside help. At least once they were all back in school. Austin in his senior year, Mallory in her third year of college, and Parker working as an aide at the very elementary school they'd all attended. "I put an ad in to rent out the guesthouse. The extra money will help pay for that kind of help."

Her brother frowned. "I hate the thought of strangers here."

She pointed to the pool. "More than you dislike a three-hour job of cleaning the pool every time the wind blows?"

He dragged the skimmer filled with leaves from the trees that didn't burn and muttered something she didn't hear.

"That's what I thought."

"I should have got a job like Mallory. Then I wouldn't be out here."

Parker flipped on the pump to the pool and talked over the noise. "You're right, you'd be at work. Stop bitching and let's get this done before it's too hot to breathe out here."

~

Too hot to breathe descended upon them by noon. With Austin mumbling the whole time, she sent him inside and grabbed a long extension tree pruner and a pair of gloves. Hot or not, there was still some green at the top of a dozen trees on the far end of the property that she wanted desperately to save.

So while her brother showered and bellied up to the TV in his bedroom, Parker kept working. Every hour she spent doing the job was one less that she needed to pay someone else to. She pulled a couple of green waste cans and went to work.

Within an hour, she filled the two barrels and rolled them outside the automatic gate where the trash collectors could pick them up on Monday. She had no less than six cans on the private street each week.

An easy task when she needed to remove over thirty dead trees, some of which were nothing but black sticks with no life in them. Half a dozen barrels a week would take a few years to remove all the debris.

She'd have to cave and hire someone eventually.

Right now, she felt the need to move. Cut dead branches, clean swimming pools, fix sprinkler lines. Anything to exhaust herself and make it easier to sleep at night.

"Excuse me?"

Parker turned toward the sound of the male voice and brushed aside hair that had fallen out of her ponytail. The sun glared in her eyes, making it difficult to get a clear picture of the man standing on the other side of her gate.

"Hello," she greeted him.

"Do you live here?"

Probably a neighbor, she thought to herself. They'd shown up constantly after the fire to see how close the flames had actually come to their homes. Many of them invited themselves in without knocking. That was until she paid to have someone come in and fix the broken gate and stop the trespassers.

"I would hope so," she said, waving the pruner in her hands. "I don't think I would take this job for actual money." The closer she got to the gate, the better the features of the man came into focus. He stood at least three inches taller than her, no easy task when she was five nine. Broad shoulders and arms that didn't look like they slaved in an office all day. He wore jeans. It had to be over a hundred degrees, and the man wore jeans.

And filled them out nicely, if she wasn't too tired to notice.

Parker forced her gaze back to his face, his eyes hidden by his sunglasses; his thick brown hair wasn't covered by a hat.

She stopped in front of him, the gate to the property a clear division. The intense set of his jaw softened slightly. "Is your, ah . . . husband here?"

Three years ago, in a bar . . . or while out with friends, she would have instantly denied a lack of a husband. Out here, with a stranger . . . even an attractive one standing at her front door, she wasn't about to correct him. "Who's asking?"

The man's smile fell and he quickly removed his sunglasses. "I'm sorry. My name is Colin Hudson. Colin to my friends."

"What can I do for you, *Mr. Hudson*?" She wasn't about to call him by his first name.

"I work with the Public Works Department and wanted to see if you'd let me take a quick look at the wash that runs through your property." He reached into his back pocket and removed his wallet. Out came a business card that he handed her through the bars of the iron gate.

She had to move close enough to take the card, but retreated once she had it in her fingertips.

He instantly shoved his hands in his front pockets and took a step back.

The card looked legit. Parker reminded herself that anyone with a computer could make a business card. "Does your department work on Saturdays, Mr. Hudson?"

"All the time."

She peered beyond the gate, didn't see a car. "Did you walk here?"

Mr. Hudson looked over his shoulder, pointed his thumb down the street. "I have a company truck. I parked around the corner."

"Ah-huh." She wanted to believe him. His caramel brown eyes looked kind enough. "Even Ted Bundy was good-looking," she said loud enough for him to hear.

Parker looked up to find him staring, his mouth gaped open. "That's a first."

"Sorry." *Not sorry.* "By-product of being a lone woman on a large piece of property with a stranger asking to come in. Business card aside, you could be anyone."

He lifted his hands in the air. "Very wise. I hope my sister would do the same. I was just hoping to get an eye on the canyon before Monday's meeting. But I can wait."

She relaxed her grip on the tree pruner. "What meeting?"

"The city and county are meeting to discuss the concerns of the watershed after the fire. We're developing a plan to preserve property during the winter. If I could take a quick look, it would help."

"You mean prevent mudslides?"

"*Control* mudslides," he corrected her.

She shifted from foot to foot. "You can do that?"

"It's a big part of our job." He smiled, looked over her shoulder. "I can wait. I don't want to make you uneasy."

Parker looked back toward the house. "Tell you what. You go get your company truck and I'll grab a snake fork and show you the wash."

His eyes narrowed with an unasked question.

"It's summer. Rattlesnakes are a thing," she explained.

"You sure?"

Yeah, she was sure. "I'll open the gate. You can park inside."

"Thank you." He turned around and Parker marched double time down the driveway, through the wash crossing, and up to the house.

The minute she walked in the door, Scout jumped to his feet. Parker retrieved her "snake fork," checked to make sure it was loaded, and walked back out the door. Scout bounced at her side.

With a shotgun over her shoulder, she walked the long path to the other side of the property and used a remote to open the gate so Mr. Hudson could drive inside.

The white public works truck had a light bar on top and all the fancy stickers on the door.

If Colin Hudson was a Ted Bundy wannabe, he was going through some serious effort to appear otherwise.

He stepped out of his truck and lowered his sunglasses enough to look over the rim. "I can come back later," he said, looking at the gun. Scout ran around his feet demanding attention.

"It's for snakes, Mr. Hudson. Are you a snake?"

"My junior high school girlfriend said I was."

Parker tried not to smile.

The grin on his face said she'd failed.

"We kill five or six rattlers every year. A requirement of living this close to Mother Nature."

"You shoot them?"

"I usually use a flat head shovel, but that's a little harder with the rocks." The wash was littered with them.

"*You* use a shovel?"

"If you tell me you're one of those 'save the snake' people, I'm gonna have to ask you to leave."

He shook his head, amusement danced in his eyes. "Nope. Hate snakes. Shoot 'em. Have fun."

He was teasing her.

Parker called the dog and turned and walked away, confident that Mr. Hudson was following her. "You can see the burn line," she started.

"That's your house?"

"Yeah." From the midpoint of the wash, they were still five hundred yards from the base of the driveway and slope of the actual house.

"Looks like the fire came close."

"Took out the fence six feet from the east side."

"Were you here?"

She blinked, picturing the flames, felt the heat of them, the smell of them. "We were."

He was quiet for a minute. When she looked up, those kind eyes searched hers. "The house doesn't look to be in any danger of taking on mud."

Parker pushed away memories of flames. "I'm not concerned my house is going to float away. It's the damage to the property, the lack of being able to get in and out." She pointed to the culverts that were under the Arizona crossing through the wash. "I've seen these culverts fill up. When they do, it takes a lot of work to get them clear. We park a car on this side of the wash and use the footbridge, but doing that for long periods of time is a royal pain."

He cocked his head to the side and stared at her. "How long have you lived here?"

She opened her mouth to answer and saw Austin driving his car down the long drive. He rolled down his window as both she and Mr. Hudson stepped to the side.

"Where are you going?" she asked.

"Will's house."

"When are you coming home?"

Austin looked at the man standing beside her. "I don't know. Who's this?"

Parker didn't bother with his name, Austin wouldn't care. "He's with the city—"

"County," he corrected her.

She waved him off. "He's here looking at the wash."

Her brother gave a single nod. "Cool." He switched his eyes to hers. "We haven't seen a single snake since the fire."

Parker moved the weapon to her other hand. "Doesn't mean they're not out here."

"Whatever." He started to roll up his window.

"Call if you're staying the night."

"I will."

"If you're drinking, stay there or call me."

Austin rolled his eyes. "Yes, *Mom*."

She laughed. Austin didn't drink all that often, and when he did, he told her about it. The courts would take custody away in a heartbeat if Austin started getting in any trouble. None of them wanted that. Especially this close to Austin's eighteenth birthday.

She stepped out of the way of his car as he drove past.

"He's not really your son . . . right?"

His question made her pause. "I'm pretty sure I look like crap right now, but I doubt I look old enough to be his mother."

"He called you Mom."

It was her turn to roll her eyes. "Older sister."

"So this is your parents' home?" He seemed relieved with the information. Like a weight had lifted from his brain.

"Was. Our parents died two years ago. So if I seem a little paranoid"— she lifted the gun as if *paranoid* was written on the barrel—"it's because I'm responsible for taking care of him and my sister." And that's all she wanted to say about that. "Now tell me about the wash. What can you guys do to *control* the mud?"

CHAPTER FOUR

Annie Oakley.

No makeup.

Soot smudged on at least three places on her face.

Light brown hair sticking out of a half-cocked ponytail and a gun slung over her shoulder as if that were a thing.

Colin followed her across the dry creek and past the fenced portion of the property.

Annie was tall.

Long legs, short shorts.

He tore his gaze away. "I'm sorry, but I didn't get your name," he said, distracting himself.

"Parker."

Was that her first name?

"Parker Sinclair," she told him as if she knew he was about to ask if that was her last name.

The shotgun moved from her shoulder to her hand as she jumped down into the wash and started to march. She was girl-next-door beautiful despite the messy state she was in.

"How long have you lived here?"

"As long as I can remember. Minus a couple years of college." She hiked a leg up onto a rock and kept moving along the blackened path the fire had ravaged. "My parents moved here when I was two."

He was trying to calculate her age in his head but he couldn't quite figure it out. "I can see why. It's beautiful."

She huffed a breath. "It was."

Colin looked at the blackened hillside . . . the soot. "It's peaceful."

Parker glanced over her shoulder, didn't meet his eyes, and said nothing.

He felt, more than saw, the weight of the property on her shoulders. He couldn't imagine how anyone kept their crap together after losing their parents. Yet she was marching around, jumping off rocks, and juggling that shotgun as if it were second nature. Whoever Parker Sinclair was, she was the most atypical California girl he'd ever met.

Several yards away, she paused. "This is where our property ends."

Colin looked behind them, confused. "The fence is back there."

"Yeah, well. My father bought this piece of land years ago and left it undeveloped. He didn't like neighbors."

In front of them stood a massive debris basin that appeared as if it had been constructed forty years ago.

"There's a plaque on the wall that says this was a project back in the seventies. My guess is it was a way of slowing down the flow of water back when the neighborhood was being developed. At one point there were vineyards up and down the street."

Colin marched past her and up to the plaque she described. Only now it was too charred to read. He peered up at the hillside, the V of the canyon. Yeah, engineers back in the seventies would have wanted to do something to slow down the force of water to save homes downstream.

"The forestry department owns the property beyond this point?" he asked, already knowing the answer.

She nodded. "My parents used to tell me about the first year they lived here. People would drive onto the property and up the creek and camp."

Colin watched her eyes narrow as she looked up the canyon.

"Camp. As in campfires and tents. Mom told us that my dad fenced the property in the space of one weekend after he realized that people thought they could trespass to get on forest land."

"I would imagine that would be difficult." He'd never lived on a property this large, and didn't really know what it would feel like if he had. Yet from the look on Parker's face, she understood the full extent of the difficulties.

"Ever since the fire, neighbors and lookie-loos have felt free to march right up the creek or through the open gate as if this isn't private property. I completely understand why my dad fenced the place the way he did." She jumped up on a rock and kept moving beyond the structure. Parker stopped only once they were in the center of the dry creek bed and surrounded by steep hillsides.

Colin turned around and looked behind them. He knew as they walked on forest land that there wouldn't be anything the county or the city could do at that point. Their jurisdiction ended at Parker's property line. And even then, they would need her cooperation to do anything.

"With this much privacy surrounding you, I'd take offense to strangers trespassing, too." He pictured his crew, their equipment . . . and so much more invading this gunslinging woman's space. The weight of her stare caught his attention before he turned to look at her.

"What is it going to take to hold all this back?"

"A lot."

"I have a feeling that's an understatement."

He noticed her shiver.

"We may have another winter of drought." It had been over seven years since Southern California had a decent amount of rainfall.

"You wanna make a bet on that?" There wasn't an ounce of humor on her face.

He shook his head. "No."

Miss Sinclair released a long breath, and Colin wanted to put an arm over her shoulder to tell her everything would work out. Even though he wasn't sure it would.

~

The cork released from the bottle with a refreshing *pop*.

Mallory walked around the corner and tossed her purse on the island in the kitchen and an overnight bag on the floor.

"Where are you off to?" Parker asked.

"I already told you. Tricia's parents are letting us use their place at the beach."

Parker poured a generous portion of wine in her glass. "Oh, right. I forgot."

Her sister regarded her with a frown. "It's Saturday, you should be out."

The energy it would take to put on makeup sounded exhausting. "Maybe next weekend."

"You say that every weekend."

Parker tilted the glass to her lips. "I'm fine. Go, have a good time."

"Come with me."

She set her glass down. "And who would feed Scout in the morning?"

Just the mention of their dog's name had him lifting his snout from his paws to look at them.

"Austin can do it."

"Austin is with friends. He already called to say he's staying the night."

Mallory opened her mouth to argue.

Parker cut her off. "I'm exhausted. I appreciate the offer." Though partying with her sister's friends sounded more like babysitting than a night off.

"I feel bad."

"Don't. I'm going to toss some chicken on the grill, make a salad, and go to bed."

"You're working too hard. Why don't we use the insurance money to hire some guys to take off some of the load?"

"We've already been over this. We need to save as much as we can now so we can fix the place up after the winter."

Mallory opened her purse and removed her car keys. "I don't know what you're worried about. We haven't seen runoff in the creek for years."

"And if winter comes and goes and nothing happens, all the better."

"You'll hire help then?" she asked.

"I will."

Mallory shouldered her bag and waved with her purse. "I'll be home Sunday night."

Parker buried the jealousy sneaking up her spine. "Have fun."

From the expansive porch off the family room, she watched the taillights of her sister's car as it made its way down the driveway. The car paused at the gate and the alarm sounded in the house through the speakers. "Driveway gate operating."

Scout moved to her side and sat.

"Just you and me," she told the dog.

Scout looked at her as if he understood and lowered the rest of his body to the ground.

After tilting one of the outdoor dining chairs over, and pounding off the ash, Parker sat for the first time in hours.

The sun was starting to set, and the temperature had finally dropped under ninety.

The hillsides she'd stared at her entire life stood in blackened silence. Her ears strained for the sound of wildlife.

Nothing.

All she heard was the beat of her own heart in her head. She never thought she'd welcome the call of coyotes, or the scurrying of bunnies that destroyed the lawn.

Colin Hudson's conversation rolled in her head as she sipped her wine.

He'd told her about the upcoming meeting of department heads that would determine if there was anything the city or county could do in the limited time they had before the rainy season began. Then, of course, someone needed to find the money to fund the project. Colin made it clear he had nothing to do with that. His job was to manage a team to do the work the engineers designed.

When Parker had asked what kind of design, Colin had been vague.

"Containment structures."

"What does that mean?"

"Basins."

"Like a ditch?"

"More like an empty lake."

Only the space he pointed out wasn't anything like a lake. It wasn't deep, it was filled with rocks, and it funneled right through her property.

Before he left, he shook her hand and said the people above him would be getting in touch with her once they had a plan.

"And if they decide they can't do anything?" she'd asked him.

"Then I'll come by and tell you." His assurance calmed her, or maybe it was the man. Either way, it was soothing to hear someone else talk about preventing a problem before it happened. For weeks she felt as if she was the only one thinking about the *what-ifs* of winter. Then TDH—tall, dark, and handsome—showed up and reaffirmed her fears and offered solutions at the same time. It felt good to know she wasn't crazy.

It felt even better that the person telling her wasn't thirty years older than her and condescending. So many people she'd come across since her parents' death had been just that. *You don't understand. You're not old enough to get it. Don't worry your head. We'll take care of it.* Yeah, no one had come in and taken care of anything.

It scared her to think that nothing was going to happen, and now it appeared as if something might. If she had any energy at all, she'd be down at city hall during their meeting to advocate for her neighborhood. Instead, she'd use her time trimming trees and digging wells around them. What she really needed was a chainsaw and a chipper. Maybe she could rally a few of her friends with the promise of a free workout, pizza, and beer.

But her college friends were long gone. She'd dropped out of college and moved back home the day her parents had died. The friends she'd had then were around for the funeral but not the life she had to adopt to keep their family together.

That's when Parker met Jennifer and Sam, and her circle of friends was less about happy hour and more about sippy cups for their kids and going to bed by ten.

She shook away the memories of her shared apartment in San Diego and a time when she could study TDH's butt as he walked around her yard instead of concentrating on what he was saying.

She found a half smile on her lips. Colin did have a nice butt.

Parker opened her mouth wide with a yawn.

The wind chimes gently started to sway as a breeze moved through the air.

The last rays of sun shifted over the western sky leaving bright purple streaks on the horizon.

It really was peaceful, just like Colin had said.

Almost too quiet.

Even Bennie and the three remaining hens that no longer had a proper shelter were quiet.

The breeze picked up, which on any other day would be welcome.

Parker blinked away the dust flying through the air.

Ash, she reminded herself.

Almost two months after the fire, and she could still smell smoldering embers.

Or maybe that was her memory playing tricks on her.

Either way, the wind was making her relaxing evening on the porch uncomfortable.

She called the dog in and closed the sliding glass door behind them. Knowing sleep was necessary, Parker turned on the air conditioner and prayed the bill wasn't going to be as bad as it had been the month before.

Skipping the chicken, she threw together a salad and finished her wine. After washing the soot and grime away in the shower, she fell into bed at half past eight. When had she grown so old that she was in bed, fighting to keep her eyes open, before nine?

Heaviness sat in her throat.

This isn't supposed to be my life.

The thought brought moisture to her eyes. Instead of giving in to tears, she closed them and rolled to her side.

She fell asleep hard and woke up with a jolt.

Her heart was pounding, her body on edge.

The fire dream fled from her head when she opened her eyes to the hazy morning sun.

"Just a dream," she told herself.

Her wind chimes crashed together, and the wind outside howled like a frustrated wolf separated from his pack.

Not wanting to get up, Parker rolled to her side and felt the cold, wet nose of Scout pressing against her arm. "What are you doing up here?" she asked him as if he would answer.

That's right, Austin wasn't home.

Scout normally slept with her brother.

The dog whimpered.

Parker grumbled.

Another gust of wind and she heard something on the patio scrape against the side of the house.

She gave up.

Tossing aside the covers, she climbed out of bed and walked barefoot to the kitchen and turned on the coffee maker.

She rubbed the soreness in her shoulders and peered out the front window of the house. Everything was brown, the air, the hills, the trees. The Santa Ana winds were in full force. Branches from the dead trees littered what was left of the lawn. At least she wouldn't have to trim them before tossing them in the trash.

Parker fortified herself with a cup of coffee before going outside to check out the pool.

Black.

The top was covered with leaves; the bottom had two inches of soot. She wanted to cry.

CHAPTER FIVE

"It comes fully furnished. Utilities included."

Parker walked around the nine-hundred-square-foot one-bedroom guesthouse.

"It's cute."

"My grandmother lived here before she passed."

The woman she showed it to was only two years older than Parker. Single. No kids. Shoulder-length red hair that she couldn't tell was natural or store-bought.

"She didn't die in here, I hope."

Parker shook her head. "Oh, no. She had a stroke and died in an assisted living facility."

Erin Fleming turned a full circle before ducking into the bathroom.

"I can't offer garage parking, but it's safe to say no one will break into your car on the property. You have full use of the pool and the outside deck, barbeque . . . whatever you need."

"It feels like the right fit."

Parker shuffled from one foot to the other. The next thing she had to mention had scared off every prospective tenant she'd shown the space to. "Do you like to entertain?"

Erin tilted her head to the side. "What do you mean? Have parties?"

"Guests?"

"I'm new to the area. It's hard to party when you don't know anyone."

"What about where you're from?" Parker looked at the rental application she held in her hand. "Tacoma?"

"I'm an introvert," Erin told her.

That sounded promising. "I hate to ask . . . it's just that my brother is still in high school and the courts are strict about the kind of environment he's exposed to. He turns eighteen in six months."

Erin waved a hand in the air. "I'm looking for a quiet place to start a new life."

"Right. About that." She looked at the glaring empty space on the application under employment. "How do you plan on paying for the space?"

Erin moved to the front door and looked outside. "You can see on my application that I have plenty of finances to pay the rent. I'll sign a lease and pay you six months in advance. If I haven't found a job by the fifth month, I'll give you notice and leave."

Parker calculated the rent in her head. "Six months up front?"

"If you'll rent to me."

It sounded too good to be true.

"You only have one personal reference and no previous rental history."

"I moved from my parents' home, to college, to my boyfriend's place." She looked away and continued to talk. "My name was never on the lease."

"The application doesn't give me a lot to go on." And from Parker's research on renting out property, Erin was a risk. At least on paper.

Parker's gut said she was fine.

"Does the pool always look like this?" Erin asked.

Looking at the thin layer of soot she hadn't gotten to that morning made her cringe. "It's a constant job since the fire. I can't guarantee it will always be usable until after the wind gives us a break."

"Sounds like it's been difficult."

"Understatement. Renting this space will offset some of the costs of hiring help for these things."

Erin smiled. "I definitely want the space. I hope you'll consider my application. I know it's thin on details. I'm not a felon, I won't throw parties. You'll hardly know I'm here."

"I wonder if a felon would admit they were?" she mused aloud.

Erin chuckled. "Probably not."

Parker walked past her and out the door. "We have a shed to put any personal belongings, or some of the furniture in here if you want your own things."

"Are you saying we have a deal?"

Parker shook her head, lowered her hand holding the application. "I need to talk to my sister and brother."

Erin smiled through thin lips. "I understand."

They walked out of the guesthouse and across the lawn to the main drive where Erin had parked her car. "If you'd be kind enough to let me know that you're passing and not leave me hanging, I'd appreciate it. The seclusion of this space feels perfect for me."

"I need to check on a few things with this." Parker waved the application.

"Of course." Erin opened her car door, stepped around it. "You have my number."

~

"I don't care," Austin said around a spoonful of chili. "If renting the place means I won't have to muck out the pool every weekend, I say move her in tomorrow."

Parker shifted her gaze to Mallory.

"Was she nice?"

"Perfectly. A little quiet. The best part is she's going to pay six months in advance."

"Then why are you hesitating?"

"Because she just moved to the area, doesn't have a job or any local references. I spoke to one friend with a Washington State phone number."

Mallory shrugged. "You have to have credit to get credit. We all have to start somewhere. Besides, it isn't like we have people rushing the gate trying to rent the place."

No, they hadn't.

"What would Dad have done?" Austin asked.

"Dad wouldn't have had this problem."

Mallory pushed her bowl of chili aside, half-empty. "If Dad had died and Mom had survived, she would have rented the place by now."

Their mother had been the practical one.

Parker picked up her spoon. "I'll call her in the morning, tell her she can move in."

"Your second call is for a pool man," Austin demanded.

"And someone to set up some rat traps," Mallory suggested. "The De Lucas are killing almost one rat a day over at their house. It's only a matter of time before they get into our cars."

Yeah, the rats survived the fire and were relocating to the first available homes. Parker was surprised they hadn't found theirs yet.

"Pool man, exterminator . . . anything else?"

"I could use a new spoiler for my car."

Parker rolled her eyes at her brother. "Then get a job."

He shoveled in a bite. "I had to try."

Classes for both her brother and her sister had started the previous week, so their conversation switched gears. While Austin pissed and moaned about school, her sister seemed excited. Even though Mallory had been accepted to colleges outside of the area, she picked Cal State Northridge so she could live at home and commute. Unlike Parker,

Mallory declared her major before the first semester was even over. Psychology had sparked her interest after they'd all attended a few grief counseling sessions the court had mandated before Parker got custody.

Mallory never took for granted that she was able to go, especially in light of the fact that Parker had needed to drop out in order to get custody of both of them after their parents died.

In midconversation about school, Parker's cell phone started to ring.

She didn't recognize the number when she answered the call.

"Hello?"

"Miss Sinclair?"

The man's voice sounded familiar, but she couldn't quite place it.

"Who's calling?"

"This is Colin Hudson . . . with the county."

She immediately matched his voice with his face. "Oh . . ." She wiped her mouth and pushed away from the table.

"Ted Bundy?" he clarified.

Okay, that made her smile. "I remember you."

"Good. I told you I'd call if I had any news."

"And do you?" She pictured his dimpled easy smile and the way he looked at her when she walked up to him carrying the shotgun. Unease and amusement all rolled into one.

"The city and county are working on emergency funding to help with the situation there in Creek Canyon. I wanted your permission to give your phone number to the people in charge of permits and access paperwork."

She shook her thoughts away from TDH to his words. "I guess."

He hesitated. "They can go through other channels to find your number, but that may take some time. I didn't think you'd like strangers in suits showing up at your gate."

"I'd rather not have that. Go ahead and give them my number."

"Perfect. You should hear from them in the morning."

"That fast?" He moved quick.

"Rainy season starts in November. That doesn't give us a whole lot of time."

Parker moved to the panoramic window and looked down at the property. All images of the man talking vanished. "They're going to need my permission to do anything, aren't they?"

"The space we need to work on is on your land."

"Will they want to do something up in the forest?"

TDH paused. "I haven't seen the engineer's plans."

She closed her eyes and lowered her head. "Oh, boy."

"I know it's uncomfortable, but when the rain comes, you're going to want us there."

She knew that.

"Your neighbors need your cooperation."

"I know that, too."

He paused and then said, "Expect a call tomorrow. My guess is they will want to set up a meeting by the end of the week."

Her aide work at the elementary school was starting on Thursday. "I need to arrange time with my job."

"They'll work around you."

"How many of *them* are there?"

"Half a dozen or so."

"A room full of suits." Probably all older men who would look down their noses at her and tell her how it needed to be. Dealing with the estate attorneys had put a bad taste in her mouth.

"They don't all wear suits."

"You know what I mean. Will you be there?" The stranger she knew versus the six she didn't.

"Not normally."

Disappointment released in a sigh.

"I can be."

Her head was starting to ache. "It's okay." *Put on your big-girl pant-ies, Parker!*

"I'll be there," he told her, switching gears.

"You don't have to." She sounded pathetic. One-on-one she felt strong enough to deal with . . . this, not so much.

"No, no . . . I should be. Sometimes the guys in the office can be . . . intimidating. Unless you're used to this process, you may not know the kinds of questions to ask. And honestly, they may not be able to answer all of them."

"You sure?"

"I'm sure."

"Okay. Thank you." Parker knew her voice shook.

"Parker?"

"Yeah?"

"It's going to be okay."

That wasn't what her gut was saying.

"I'll see you at the end of the week," she said as a goodbye.

"Have a nice evening."

Parker held her cell phone in her hand and stared out the window once she disconnected the call.

"Who was that?" Mallory asked.

"The guy from the city . . . ah, county," she corrected herself. "They want to have a meeting and talk with me."

"That's a good thing, isn't it?" Austin asked.

"I guess we're going to find out."

CHAPTER SIX

"I'm telling you, the less people in the room the better." Colin stared at Ed, the principal engineer, and glanced at the dozen people in the meeting room behind them.

"We need to impress upon Miss Sinclair the need to move on this."

"So you have a lawyer at the table?"

Ed stood an inch taller than Colin, and looked down on him. "If we meet with resistance, there might be a need to emphasize the weight the city can bring."

Colin felt his chest tighten. "That won't be necessary."

"I know you think you know these things, Colin, but you're never on this end. Half the people we deal with are utterly opposed to disrupting their life to help others. It's a *fuck them, screw you* world out there. If we need to drop words like *eminent domain*, we will."

"That's not who we're dealing with."

"This information is based on what?"

"I've been on the properties talking with the neighbors with every project long before Paul retired. I know people. Parker Sinclair isn't the kind of person to turn her back on others."

"Then a room full of brass isn't going to hurt." Ed appeared done with the conversation with a turn of his shoulder.

Colin stepped in front of him.

"She will cooperate, but this"—he indicated the room behind them—"this will scare her. Did you look at the property profile? Parker is the executor of the estate her parents left after they died."

"So?"

"This is all new to her. You have enough people in that room to go after the property rights of the Vargas family." The Vargas family had a steep investment in the Santa Clarita Valley and would never come to a city meeting without a team of their own at their side.

Ed looked like he was swaying in Colin's direction.

"Clear out the room. You, me, one of your civil engineers, and Grace."

The last name put a roll in Ed's eyes. "Your sister has nothing to do with this department."

"You're right. But Grace is a woman. As much as I'd like to say that isn't a factor, we both know it is. Women speak a different language . . . sometimes." And his sister had a way with her soft strength when needed.

Colin knew he was winning when Ed's shoulders slumped. "I'll send the lawyers into the other room."

That was only two people. "And the geologists and design staff."

"You're pushing me, Colin."

"Tell them to go grab a coffee. You can bring them back in if things get hairy."

That's what Ed needed to hear. At the same time the receptionist told him Parker was there, Ed ducked into the conference room, said something, and over half the room filed out and moved back to their respective offices.

Colin doubled his steps leading to his sister's office and knocked on the open door.

Her face lit up. "Hey. What are you doing here?"

"Answering later. I need you to come with me."

"I'm kinda in the middle of something."

She was alone in her office and not on the phone. "It can wait. C'mon."

Grace pushed away from her desk and unfolded from her chair to follow him down the hall.

"I need your estrogen factor," he said under his breath.

"I try to downplay that around here."

"Then you might try wearing flats." The sound of her heels accompanied her wherever she walked.

"I'm vertically challenged. I need all the help I can get."

Colin opened the conference room door for his sister and waited for her to pass. "Have my back," he whispered in her ear.

Her response was a smile.

Colin took a chair on the opposite side of the table as his boss. He didn't want Parker coming into the room and having a panel of people staring at her from the opposite side of the table.

His butt barely hit the chair before the door opened and Parker stepped into the room. Unlike his sister, Parker didn't seem to have any problem playing up her femininity. If not for the similar deer-in-the-headlights look she sported on her face when she'd been walking her property, he may not have recognized her. Her hair was down, brushing just past her shoulders, sun-kissed highlights framed her face. Her eyes were highlighted with makeup that accentuated the piercing blue of them. She wore a white billowy blouse and a knee length pencil skirt and shoes that should have been impossible to stand in. Colin found a strange knot in his throat that squeezed tighter when he realized she walked in the room and stared directly at him.

He extended his hand and walked toward her. "Parker, it's good to see you again."

While her shoulders were pulled back and her chin was up, her hand was cool and clammy. He squeezed it in hopes that it would relay to her that she was going to be okay.

"Thank you," she said before her eyes took in the rest of the room.

He stood beside her during introductions. "This is Ed. He's the head of engineering for this project."

"Thank you for coming in so quickly, Miss Sinclair."

"Of course."

"I believe you spoke with Raul Mendez."

Parker moved to the next man. "City planning and contracts?" she confirmed.

"That's right." Raul shook her hand and moved to his seat on the other side of the table. "This is my assistant . . ." Raul introduced the other three people on his team.

"This is Grace, also part of our city development."

He noticed Parker try to smile for the first time when Grace shook her hand.

"Shall we get started?" Ed asked, indicating a chair for Parker to sit in.

"Can we get you anything to drink first?" Colin asked.

"I'm fine, thank you."

She set her purse on the floor and sat rod-straight in her chair. Colin took a seat beside her.

"Colin explained to us that he's already been on your property and you're aware of the problem your neighborhood is facing this winter." Ed sat forward as he spoke.

"I am."

Ed tilted his head. "The magnitude of the problem?"

Parker sighed. "I understood the danger the moment I stepped back on my property after the fire. I've lived there my whole life and vividly remember a winter about eight years ago when the boundaries of the dry creek bed overflowed. I can only imagine what will happen when it starts to rain."

"Have you ever experienced a flash flood?" Ed asked.

"Not outside of Universal Studios or the evening news."

Ed moved a map around on the table and pointed out landmarks. "The Creek Canyon fire removed fifty miles of vegetation, dense vegetation, surrounding your entire canyon."

"I live there. I'm aware of that."

"Right. However, you may not know the sheer amount of debris that will funnel through your property, and likely take out many of your neighbors' homes downstream."

Parker looked at Colin. "Are there any other stress points up and down the canyon?"

Colin was actually impressed that she called the areas in question stress points. She'd either listened very intently when he was walking with her on the property, or she had done some homework before coming in. "There are, but none that we have any hope of controlling." Colin pointed to the map. "There is a debris basin here that we will spend some time in, but the wash spreads out here and will contain much of the runoff until it empties into the river. This water flow doesn't directly impact your street."

Ed tapped his finger on the map. "But this does. Steep mountains on all sides will give the volume significant power if we get any real rain."

"It won't take much to cause issues," Raul stated.

Parker looked up from the map, her hands wringing in her lap. "So what is the plan?"

Colin saw Raul reach for the paperwork Parker would need to eventually sign, and cut him off.

"The engineers are working on details, but basically, and correct me if I'm wrong here, Ed . . . basically the goal is to build structures, two of them here and here. The one closest to the mouth of the canyon will be somewhere around the space of three football fields long and two wide. And deep. The second about half that size." He pointed to a second map that they pulled off of a Google aerial. "Behind the structures we will excavate the site to provide debris to pool and slow down the flow."

Parker leaned forward and stopped wringing her hands together long enough to pull the map closer. "This is the original dam?"

"Yes."

"And you want to build these structures here and here?"

Colin nodded.

"Why not go above the dam? There's a lot of space there."

Ed shook his head. "That's the forest. Not our jurisdiction."

"We can't touch that land," Raul offered.

"Why not? There's nothing there now."

"That's just not how it works. We've attempted throughout the years to get the forestry's cooperation, but they believe the forest shouldn't be touched for any reason."

Parker's brows furrowed. "But someone built the dam at some point and didn't maintain it. It's been full for as long as I can remember."

"These structures were often one-time projects designed to put America to work during times of recession or after wars. The departments that created them never had contractual need to go in and maintain them. Our only place of impact is where Colin has pointed out. Now our emergency team is working on permits and funding somewhere to the tune of thirty-five million to fund this—"

"Thirty-five million?" Parker's jaw dropped.

"We're looking at removing thirty thousand cubic yards of material on-site, shoring up the sides with boulders to help with erosion, building the temporary 'dams' as you're calling them," Colin explained.

"Cubic yards?" The deer-in-the-headlights look was back again.

"It's a lot."

"Define *a lot*." She looked him in the eye.

Okay, no simple answers for Annie Oakley. There was no way to sugarcoat this. "A dump truck will haul anywhere from ten to fifteen cubic yards in each load."

Parker paused. "That's a lot of loads." She moved her gaze away to stare at the map.

"What we're doing here today, Miss Sinclair, is obtaining your permission to use your property to address this problem that will impact your community." Ed nodded to Raul.

Raul pushed a paper across the table. "We need you to sign these so we can keep moving forward."

Parker reached for them and started to read.

The room fell silent as she did.

"When do you need this by?"

Raul's assistant tapped on a binder at his side. "I can notarize your signature today."

Colin watched her rubbing her thumbs on her forefingers. "I need to have my attorney look these over."

"You'll find this is just an ingress and egress and temporary-use contract. We will return your property back to its current state in five years," Ed said.

"Five years?"

"The amount of time it takes for vegetation to grow back after a fire and the threat of erosion passes." Colin kept his voice soft. He could tell by her expression the full scale of what they were asking was settling in. "Once the retention basins are built, we will need to be able to access them to remove debris buildup between storms."

"I-I need to talk with my lawyer." Her voice wavered.

"We need your cooperation," Ed said again.

"She didn't say no, Ed . . . she said she needed her attorney to look over the contract." Grace reached over and patted Parker's arm. "It's a reasonable request. One everyone at this table would make if they were in your shoes."

Ed sat back and narrowed his eyes at Colin.

"When did you want to start this . . . project?" she asked.

"As soon as possible," Ed muttered.

"Realistically, we will need to come on-site in the next couple weeks with the engineers and survey team and devise a solid plan. We will rush the permit process and the city will find the money." Colin wanted to cover her shaking hand with his. "Mid-October is my best guess."

"And how long will it take? The first round?" Parker met his eyes.

"Six to eight weeks."

"Our rain usually starts in mid-November."

"Let's hope we have another year of drought."

Ed sat forward and tried again. "We could expedite if you sign this today."

Parker shifted her gaze and narrowed her eyes. "I will sign your papers. But not until the estate lawyer looks them over. I can't imagine there is anything here that goes against what my parents left me in charge of doing. But since they're not here and I didn't go to law school, you're going to have to wait." Her voice was firm and direct, even if her hands shook as she folded the contract and reached for her purse. "It sounds like you have a lot of work to do, so I won't keep you from it." She pushed out of her chair.

Grace moved to her side. "I'll show you out."

Colin wanted to follow but held back. Once she exited the room he rounded on Ed. "Smooth, Ed . . . really smooth."

"You said she would cooperate."

"Would you let your kid sign a contract without someone looking it over?"

Ed gathered his papers off the table and waved them at him. "If we don't hear from her within the week, we're going to talk eminent domain."

Colin ran a frustrated hand through his hair and watched the brass file out of the room.

Asshole.

CHAPTER SEVEN

Friday nights in the Sinclair household were either stone-cold silent or filled with loud music and tons of testosterone.

Parker listened to a soft rock radio station and enjoyed the calm. Football season would end before she knew it, and Austin would be inviting his friends to tear apart the engines of their cars in their massive garage. Even Mallory was out with friends. She mentioned a football game at the college, but Parker knew the game was an excuse for a Friday night party.

With Scout panting at her side, the tennis ball in his mouth, Parker utilized the last rays of daylight to run the dog. After retrieving the ball from Scout's slimy mouth, she stood at the railing of the patio and tossed it over the slope of the house and watched it bounce in the yard. Scout shot down the stairwell, across the driveway, and searched for the bouncing ball. By now it had settled, so he was nose to the ground to look over the acre of lawn in search of a prize.

Activity coming from the guesthouse had Scout forgetting about his ball and bounding in that direction.

Erin stood on the edge of the covered deck and bent down to greet the dog.

Parker walked down the path and started talking when she came within hearing range. "I hope you like dogs."

"Love 'em." Scout's tail wagged as he leaned into Erin's leg.

"He loves people. Barks when he doesn't know ya, but runs up and licks you just the same."

"Not a very good guard dog then," Erin said.

"I wouldn't say that. He barks at strangers, but never growls." Parker sat in one of the patio chairs. "It's going to be hard keeping him locked up," she mused out loud.

Erin stopped showering the dog with attention and took a seat opposite Parker. "Why do you have to lock him up?"

Parker sighed and leaned back in her chair. For the next fifteen minutes she explained what Colin and the city people had told her. "I have my attorney looking over the contract. I need to put a clause in there that whatever damage the trucks do to the property they are mandated to fix. Make sure I'm not liable if anyone gets bit by a rattlesnake or anything like that."

"Sounds like a lot of people coming in and out."

"I know. Can't say I'm happy about it, but I don't really have a choice. If I say no and neighbors downstream lose their houses, they will come after me. If I say yes, we all have to deal with whatever traffic and noise comes with the trucks and workers."

Erin ran a hand through her hair, looked out over the lawn. "And here I thought this would be a quiet, private place."

Parker cringed. She didn't want to lose her tenant this soon. "I didn't see this coming. I'm sorry. I knew the wash would pose a problem, but the amount of money the county is talking about dropping on this project is huge. They're obviously worried."

Erin met her eyes. "Are you worried?"

"I'm just tired." She huffed out a laugh. "I feel like I'm twenty years older than I am. I have an itchy feeling things are gonna get worse before they get better."

Erin stood. "Do you drink white? I'll open a bottle."

"You sure? I don't want you to feel like you have to—"

"I try not to drink alone so . . ."

Parker smiled. "In that case . . . white sounds fabulous."

~

Parker stood beside six of her neighbors while a team from the city and county descended upon the property. It was the first time the engineers were getting sight of the landscape after the attorneys gave her a green light and she'd signed the contracts with a couple of revisions. Two of the faces were familiar . . . Colin and Ed. Everyone else, the whole dozen of them, were strangers.

Tracy, one of her closest neighbors, leaned in. "Are they all engineers?"

"I know Colin isn't, but other than that . . . your guess is as good as mine."

The pocket of men and women walked down into the empty wash and hiked up the canyon.

"I don't see why they don't dig behind the old dam," Susan said.

"That's forest land. Apparently they won't sign off." Parker told those listening what she'd heard. Her eyes tracked Colin as he walked ahead with the team. Every once in a while he'd look over and offer a smile.

"It sounds like they're gearing up for a really big project," Mr. Richards added. "Rightfully so. I remember back in the seventies when this whole area was underwater after an unprecedented winter. That was before half the street was developed."

"And without a fire," Susan reminded them.

"We've been in a drought for years," Parker said.

Her neighbors agreed and continued to talk about storms in the past, and times the wash had overflowed and caused problems for people who had to cross it in order to get to their homes. As they did, they kept several yards behind the engineering team, who pointed and scribbled inside their notebooks.

Slowly the crowd made their way back to where they'd parked their cars and Parker's neighbors walked home.

Colin approached as the last of his people funneled out.

"Did they get everything they needed?" Parker asked him.

"I think so."

"What happens next?"

He leaned against the side of his truck, his eyes hidden by his sunglasses. "They come up with a plan, the city gathers the permits . . . and I assemble the on-site team."

"Sounds easy."

He laughed, flashing his dimples with enough charm to make her push a lock of unruly hair behind her ear. "I wish it was. The good news is, there is a time limit, so there won't be a lot of back-and-forth before things are finalized and moving."

"I'm glad they understand the urgency."

"Let's hope it's not needed. Ideally, it would be nice if we build all this and none of it fills up due to a lack of rain."

"Then what happens?"

"We come back in, empty the basins, and wait for next winter."

Parker looked up, but couldn't see his eyes because of his glasses. "And if things aren't ideal?"

"Then I bring the team in and empty the basins throughout the winter to keep them clear and functioning."

She placed her hands in the back pockets of her shorts and looked up the canyon. She was grateful that Colin didn't treat her as if she were too young to be handling things on her end. "This group of people that was here today, will they be around?"

"Not really. Only during inspections and even then, maybe two of them."

"Ed?"

Colin nodded. "Yeah."

She scowled. "I don't care for him."

Was that a grin on Colin's face? "He, ah . . ."

She lifted a hand. "You don't have to say anything. I'm just putting it out there. I'm not a fan. He might be doing his job, but being a used car salesman and strong-arming me wasn't necessary."

Parker was pretty sure the look on Colin's face said respect. "I heard it took a week for the contracts to come back in."

"Yup. Made sure there were a few things in writing ensuring this property was going to look the same, if not better, when your team is done. If someone hits the gate, or the driveway gets torn up, I want them replaced. And my family needs to be able to get in and out . . . always," she told him.

Colin removed his sunglasses and met her eyes. "I'm going to make sure you're okay, Parker. You have my word."

"Thank you."

He pushed away from the truck and opened the door. "You're going to like my crew. Great group of guys who go above and beyond."

"I'm counting on that."

"And not one of them wears a suit."

Those dimples were starting to put a flutter in her belly. "Don't trust men in suits."

"Good thing I only wear them on rare occasions."

The image of him in a suit had her biting her lip. Maybe she could trust him in a tie. Parker closed her eyes, briefly, tried to get the thought to go away. There was no time in her life for butterflies and dimples.

He reached in and turned over the engine. "Next time you see me, I'll be here with my on-site supervisors before we bring in the equipment. You'll meet them, and they you."

Her head was swimming and she felt heat prickle under her skin. "Okay."

He placed a hand on her shoulder and the undercurrent snapped.

Parker paused and looked up, fairly certain he could see her blood churning for all the wrong reasons. She had no business feeling this way. For all she knew he was married. Just because he didn't wear a ring didn't mean he didn't have a Mrs. somewhere.

"You have my number. If you have any questions, don't hesitate to ask."

He squeezed her shoulder before he let her go.

Yeah . . . he saw it all right. "I'm holding you to your word," she said, trying to keep her voice even and firm.

"Good. Have a nice evening, Parker."

~

Twice a month, typically on a Sunday, Colin joined his parents and siblings for a family dinner. His mother insisted. Actually, *insisted* might be too delicate a word.

Demanded.

Right out of high school, Colin had landed a job with the county as a laborer. His parents had made sure he and his brother and sister had all they needed growing up, but not all they wanted. Great parenting, as he saw it. He liked the money, took night classes at the local community college, but decided quickly that studying subjects that didn't interest him was never going to get him where he wanted to be in life. He liked working with his hands. Liked organizing and motivating people. Sitting behind a desk would result in a potbelly and a weekend alcohol problem in ten years. Or so he thought.

By the time he was twenty-three, he was making good money and socking it away. About the time he moved out of his parents' home, his younger brother, Matt, was putting out fires with a shovel as a hotshot up in Northern California. Grace was in her senior year of high school, and their mom, Nora, was feeling the empty nest.

Hence the demand to see her children all in the same house twice a month. The date rotated around Matt's schedule since he worked twenty-four-hour shifts at the firehouse.

His dad, Emmitt, sat in his lazy chair in the family room with a baseball game plastered on the big screen. Matt argued a call the umpire made while their father told him how wrong he was.

"Hand me the cheese," Grace told her mother from across the island in the center of the open kitchen.

"Do they always argue over the game?" Robert, Grace's latest boyfriend, asked Colin.

"It's half the fun," he explained.

"If you say so." Robert didn't look convinced.

"Do you watch sports?"

"Not even when I was in school."

Before Colin could comment, Matt jumped up from his seat, clapping for a Dodgers base hit.

"We're just about done here, Colin." His mom caught his attention. "How much more time on the meat?"

He took the hint and headed back outside to the grill. "Not much longer."

Grace followed behind him with a marinade they'd deemed a secret family recipe.

He opened the lid on the grill and sat his beer to the side. He slid a knife into the ribs . . . almost done.

"So what do you think of Robert?" Grace asked him under hushed tones.

He glanced over his shoulder, made sure the boyfriend wasn't close by. The man was leaning against the island with his cell phone in his hand. More than once Colin had caught him playing some kind of video game or texting someone. "He seems fine."

Grace handed him the barbeque sauce. "Fine? Ugh . . ."

Using a brush, he slathered on the marinade. "You're not serious about him, are you?" Robert had been to two family dinners, this being the third over the course of five months.

"You don't like him." She scowled.

"I think you can do better," he told her honestly. "He sits behind a desk, Gracie." He was some kind of computer analyst or some such thing Colin couldn't remember. Parker's comment about men in suits popped into his brain.

"So do I."

Colin shook his head. "You stand behind a desk, work with men twice your size, and push them around to your way of thinking. You're a powerhouse and he's a . . ." Once again he took in his baby sister's boyfriend. "He's not." And for good measure he added, "He doesn't even like sports."

Grace sighed. "Dad doesn't like him either."

Their father was a retired sheriff and didn't hide his views well.

"The fact you're asking my opinion means there's something not working for you."

She reached for his beer and took a swig. "I thought it would be great. We work similar hours, he has his own home, never been married."

"Uh-huh . . ." Colin retrieved his drink before his sister could finish it and continued to listen.

"But he's boring. And the sex isn't even all that good."

Colin squeezed his eyes shut. "This is not what you tell your older brother about."

"Well, it's true."

He finished his beer and turned a deaf ear. "Talk to your girlfriends about that. I don't share my sex life with you."

"You told me Rebecca was crazy in bed."

The mention of his last somewhat girlfriend made him grin. "I said she was wild, I never mentioned the bedroom."

Grace nudged his side with her shoulder. "It was implied."

"Still. I won't tell you about my sex life, you tell your friends about yours."

"I work with men in the field and old women in the office. There aren't many ears to choose from."

"That sounds like a personal problem." He moved the ribs around on the grill as if doing so was going to speed up the cooking. "*Your* personal problem."

"You need to find a girlfriend so I can have someone to confide in."

"I'm too busy for a relationship." Although with the mention of female companionship, the image of Parker with a gun slung over her shoulder emerged in his head.

Grace silently watched him.

"What?" he asked.

"What was that smirk for . . . or should I ask, *who* was that smirk for?"

He closed the lid on the grill. "No one."

"Liar."

"Would I lie to you?"

"Yes."

He smiled.

She made a gesture with her fingers inviting him to talk. "C'mon, give it up."

Their family didn't hold secrets from each other. "Remember Parker Sinclair?"

Grace's smile spread from ear to ear. "The Creek Canyon project?"

"Yeah."

"I knew there was a reason you wanted me in on that meeting. Are you seeing her?"

He quickly shook his head. "No, nothing like that. I just . . . I don't know. I think about her."

"Uh-huh . . ."

71

"She's gorgeous, right? Not in a dressed up, high heels, night-on-the-town kind of way, but more subtle." She was the right mixture of the girl next door and sexy he liked.

"Not that you've given that any thought," Grace teased.

Colin shook his head and told his body to calm down with the image of her in his head. "Whatever. She hasn't looked at me twice." Except for the *Ted Bundy was good-looking* comment.

"You're smiling again."

"She has a full plate."

"And if she hasn't noticed you, it's because of that. You turn on the Hudson charm and she'll see you."

"Is that dating advice from my little sister?"

Grace picked up the empty bowl and licked some sauce from her finger. "It's all about me. The sooner you bring a woman around here, the sooner you can stop hearing about my sex life."

He leaned in, wiped his finger inside the bowl, and brought it to his lips. "So what, you can talk to her and learn about mine? That's twisted, Gracie."

She winced. "I didn't think about that angle."

"That's what makes me the big brother."

CHAPTER EIGHT

The permits were signed, the engineers had drawn up their plans, and it was time for Colin to do his thing. That started with an on-site walk-through with his team. And in this case, it started with him calling Parker a few days before and setting up the date and time for the walk-through. She'd sounded nervous. He knew there wasn't a thing he could do to calm her fears until he was on-site and working with his men to assure that she and her brother and sister were going to be taken care of.

The impact on her life was going to be significant. He knew from experience that the homeowners thought they knew what they were in for, but never really saw the scale until the trucks started to arrive. The last thing Colin was going to do was describe that. She'd figure it out soon enough.

He drove up to the Sinclair home at eight in the morning. The gate was open as she said it would be, so he drove in on the south side of the property and parked. What he really wanted to do was drive up to the house and see if she was there. But that wasn't what he'd normally do on a job where the property owner wasn't someone he was attracted to. So instead, he sat in his truck until three more trucks filed in behind him. He jumped out and tucked his cell phone in his pocket.

"This is some place," Fabio said. His name wasn't actually Fabio, but he'd been called that for years because his hair ran down the length of his back and the crew loved giving him shit about it.

"I wonder what it looked like before the fire," Glynn said.

"Green," Colin told them.

Ron pulled up in his welding truck. He wasn't a supervisor, but one of Colin's main men for the actual structures, and he wanted to see the scale of the project so he could calculate the time needed. He slid out of his truck, ditching his cigarette in an ashtray before closing the door. "Hey," he greeted them.

Colin shook his hand.

"So this is where we're staging the equipment?" Fabio asked.

The property was set up in four quadrants. The dissecting points were the driveway down the middle running north and south and the creek bed running east to west. They were in the southeast corner, which took up a little less than an acre of property.

"We're going to try and keep the entire operation on this side of the wash."

Fabio snorted. "Yeah, right."

"Try." Colin put up his hand. "I know. You don't have to say it." The likelihood of keeping anything contained was slim to none. The magnitude of water that could come off the canyon didn't hold to any contract or boundaries. It was going where it wanted to, and it was up to him and this team to do what they could to contain as much as possible.

For twenty minutes, he pointed out the areas of immediate need to prepare for the excavation and trucks, which were arriving within the week. But before any of that, they needed to prep the area and set up shop.

They walked across the wash and stopped at the site of the second structure. This one sat on the edge of the fenced portion of the Sinclair property.

They were deep in conversation about the engineers' plans when Glynn said, "Is that the homeowner?"

Across the manicured section of the lawn, Parker emerged with her black lab on a leash. She marched toward them, a nervous smile on her lips.

"She doesn't look old enough to be the homeowner," Glynn pointed out.

"It was her parents' place," Colin said before she was close enough to hear. "She's holding it all together for her brother and sister after they died."

"Oh, damn."

Colin wasn't sure who muttered the words. His eyes were focused on the woman marching toward them.

"Good morning," she said once she stopped at their side.

"Good morning, Parker," Colin said. He took a minute to introduce the men. "I was just showing everyone around and explaining the layout."

Her lips were a thin line. "I wanted you to meet Scout. He's big and loveable, if not a tad stupid. I'll keep him tied up when I'm at work, or inside. But if he gets off the leash, I hope one of you can bring him back up to the house so he doesn't get run over by the trucks."

Scout sniffed the bottom of Glynn's shoes.

"He won't run off?"

"No. With the activity, he will just get underfoot."

"Good to know," Colin said.

"We'll be pulling equipment in on Monday," Fabio told her.

She nodded. "What are the hours you guys will be here?"

"Monday through Friday. We will start as early as seven thirty in the morning and likely be out of your hair by five."

Colin sat back and let Fabio talk. He would be the main man on the site, outside of him, and Colin needed Parker comfortable with him.

"And weekends?" she asked. She held Scout's leash firm, even though the dog looked like he wanted to jump on anyone willing to hand him attention.

"No. Not until the rain comes. Then we can be here at any time, day or night."

The smile on Parker's face fell. "Excuse me?"

"We stage on-site during the storms. It's not out of the question for us to show up at two in the morning."

"You need to call me first," Parker told him.

"That's not always going to be possible."

Parker squared her shoulders, turned to face Fabio. "You're going to call anytime you come onto this property outside of the hours of seven thirty to five."

Fabio shook his head and laughed in dismissal of her words.

Colin opened his mouth to assure her but she cut him off.

"I have an AK, an AR, a shotgun, a nine-eleven, and a forty Glock, and I'm a really good shot. I'm responsible for my teenage brother and college-aged sister. The only time that gate opens at two in the morning is if someone is sneaking in or sneaking out. You *will* call me if you're coming in."

Colin had to turn to keep her from seeing the smile on his face.

Glynn flat-out laughed, and Fabio lost his smirk and replaced it with admiration.

"Well, okay then, young lady. I guess I need your phone number."

She smiled, stood taller. "Great. Now that we understand each other, what's happening next?"

~

Parker sat in the faculty break room that was overrun with cookies and cake due to a popular teacher's birthday. Just walking into the room made her feel like she gained five pounds. It was noon and her one-on-one student she sat with during the day didn't need her during her lunch. Jennifer walked into the room shortly after Parker removed her lunch from the staff refrigerator and set it on a table. Like Parker,

Jennifer worked as an aide at the school. But she had a full-time position, where Parker had only been there two years and was still considered per diem. The district avoided hiring full-time aides for special needs students who were close to graduating. She didn't argue. It wasn't her dream job by any stretch, and she didn't see herself working at an elementary school once she finished her own education. Not that she knew what the dream job was. She was no closer to determining what she wanted to do with her life than she had been two years earlier when she'd finalized her major in business with an emphasis on marketing. Now that sounded like a job this side of hell.

"Wow, you look like crap," Jennifer said once she sat down.

Parker regarded her friend with a frown. "With friends like you, who needs enemies?"

"Seriously, are you sleeping?"

She shook her head. "Not enough. This whole thing is making me crazy."

"I can't imagine." Jennifer picked up her sandwich, took a bite.

"They start pulling in trucks on Monday." She lowered her voice. "I'm going to have to call in sick. Janice gave me a hard time when I asked for a day off this week."

"Do you have to be there?"

Parker nodded, then shook her head . . . settled with a nod. "Maybe, yes . . . no. But I'm going to be. I need the crew to know who I am. Demand respect. One look at me and most of them think I'm a kid."

"You *are* a kid."

"I'm twenty-six going on forty."

"Which may be true, but from the outside . . . you look like a kid. Certainly not someone old enough to be dealing with your crazy life."

It was nice to have her feelings validated. "It is crazy, isn't it?"

"Nuts. But you're strong. You've been through worse."

Yeah . . . the months following her parents' death were horrific.

"Are you taking night classes this semester?"

"No," Parker said. "I'm barely keeping it together as it is."

Jennifer's sympathy was written on her face. "You keep putting your life on hold."

"It's not forever. Erin, my new tenant, is working out. The extra cash is really helpful. I'm hoarding the insurance money from the fire to help make up for the time off I need to take. I have to get through the winter and assess where things are then." Saying the words made her feel them a little deeper.

"That's a great attitude."

Parker bit into an apple and closed her eyes.

"You know, maybe having your property swimming in testosterone will be a good thing."

She smiled, thinking of how she'd set Colin's men straight. "So far Colin is the only one I truly trust."

"Colin?"

"Hudson. The head guy I told you about."

Jennifer grinned. "When did he become Colin and not Mr. Hudson?"

Parker paused, looked at the ceiling. "I'm not sure."

"Hmm . . . and ah, how old is this Colin guy?"

"I don't know, midthirties maybe. Seems young for the position, so maybe he's older. I couldn't tell you."

"Married?"

Parker narrowed her eyes. "I don't know, maybe. I didn't ask."

"Good-looking?"

Holy cow, she was slow on the conversation. "Okay, I get it . . . Yes . . . he's attractive." Really attractive, if she were honest with herself. "But no. I don't know if he's married, and can't even think about going there. I haven't so much as texted someone outside of my platonic circle of friends in two years."

"Which is a damn shame. Prime of your life and you're not out living it."

"Hard to do when I'm treading water."

"Well, pull your head out of the water once in a while and look around. You never know who might show up."

~

She couldn't breathe. Everything was dark. She couldn't see them, no longer heard their voices calling out to her.

If only the smoke would lift so she didn't have to crawl.

She coughed and sputtered the ashes that fell into her mouth. Austin, Mallory . . . Where are you?

Her mouth moved but nothing came out.

She crawled as fear took over logic.

Austin!

Mallory!

Her hand landed on an arm.

The arm didn't move.

She needed to look away, knew what was there and tried to focus on anything other than the cold dead arm touching her.

Slowly her head moved with a will of its own.

Her parents lay there motionless, their eyes blankly staring at her.

Parker jolted awake, her heart in her throat, her breath labored.

She sat up and forced her breathing to slow. The clock said it was just past three in the morning. "Damn it." Right after the fire she'd had the same nightmare. Each time she woke thankful that it was just a dream and Mallory and Austin were still alive.

Each time she woke she was reminded her parents were gone.

A single tear fell down Parker's cheek.

~

Parker stared down at her second cup of coffee long before the first truck arrived. Her sister had early classes on Monday and typically spent Sunday night with a friend who lived closer to campus to avoid traffic. Austin had a 7 a.m. class and was already out the door. Most Mondays, Parker was right on his heels.

Her call in to work that morning started with her pinching her nose and purposely coughing into the phone. Much as she didn't really like her job, she didn't want to lose it either.

"Driveway gate operating." The voice alarm inside the house signaled the end of her peace.

She looked outside and saw two white trucks, the kind Colin and his men drove, pull inside and park. Scout put his nose up to the sliding glass door and barked. "I know, right?"

Parker watched the first semitruck pull in with a tractor on a flatbed. "Here we go."

She brushed her hair, pulled on a pair of shorts and a T-shirt, and walked out the door. Scout tried to follow, but she brushed him back inside.

By the time she made it down the driveway and across the wash, no less than a dozen men with an equal number of vehicles were buzzing around. Everyone wore hard hats and vests. All of them were men.

Colin met her in the driveway, a smile on his face. "Good morning."

"Good morning." She tried to smile.

The intermittent beep of a tractor backing off a truck filled the air. "How many tractors are you bringing in?"

"They're actually called skip loaders. And quite a few. We're throwing a lot of people on this project to knock it out as fast as we can."

"Before it starts to rain."

"Right."

Colin pointed to one of his men at the gate. "That's Ray. I have him on the gate. The first few days on-site we get a lot of lookie-loos wanting to see what we're doing."

"Good. I'll introduce you to my immediate neighbors since they're going to be impacted the most. Everyone else I'd just as soon keep outside the gate. I'll invest in some 'No Trespassing' signs."

"Good idea. I already met the De Lucas and the Sutters."

Her neighbors were all decent people. "We're a little concerned about the runoff from the canyon above their homes." She pointed out a flash point that often caused runoff during heavy rains.

"It's already been brought to my attention."

"Any mud flow from that direction might keep you guys from getting in here."

Colin smiled, all dimples and charm. "We have big toys. We'll get in. And more importantly, we'll make sure you and your brother and sister can get in and out."

She liked the sound of that.

Two men started unrolling heavy sheets of plastic and laying it down. "What are they doing?"

"Laying the foundation for the trucks."

No sooner did the words come out of Colin's mouth than a dump truck started backing up, and tons of tiny rocks released from the back. "Oh."

Everything moved at a breakneck pace from that point on.

"I have an arborist on-site today. The heritage oak trees need special attention."

"Those trees have more rights than people," she said. According to her father, back when he was alive, they were supposed to get a permit for trimming a branch more than three inches thick. Not that her father played by the rules.

He laughed. "Tell me about it. While he's here, I'm going to have him look at the other trees on your property."

Parker swatted at an ant that had crawled up her leg. "I trimmed most of them down hoping to save them. A couple of the cottonwoods have been struggling from the drought."

"*You* trimmed them?"

She rubbed the back of her neck and thought of Jennifer and Sam. "Me and a few friends. We rented one of those chippers and made a weekend out of it during the summer."

"That's a big job." He looked impressed.

"What, you don't think I have it in me?" she teased.

Colin lifted both hands in the air, his eyes crinkled at the corners. "Everything I've seen so far says you are capable of just about anything."

She lifted her chest a little higher and teased, "You'd do well to remember that."

He laughed.

"Besides, renting the chipper was cheaper than hiring it out." It had been a bitch of a weekend, but they'd managed to get a lot done for a fraction of the price.

Colin kept nodding, then pointed to what was once a thriving manzanita that framed the entry of the driveway. "How do you feel about that?" It had been reduced to blackened wood with only a few green leaves at the very top after the fire. She'd trimmed half of it away, hoping it would come back.

She watched the trucks trying to maneuver around the dying plant.

"It's in the way, isn't it?"

He nodded. "The arborist already confirmed it was past saving."

She moaned. "Okay, fine. Take it out."

Without delay, Colin signaled someone over. "Let's get this out of here."

"You got it."

Parker didn't catch any names. She stood back and watched as three men worked together to guide the driver of the skip loader. The beep of the machine made it hard to hear. The driver kept backing up, his eye on the tree and not the chain-link fence behind it.

The fence started giving way while three men yelled at the driver to stop.

Parker's heart leapt in her chest, her mouth opened.

Colin leaned over and calmly said, "We fix fences, too."

She backed up and bit her lip while activity exploded around her. Within minutes, the base of the manzanita was pulled out by its roots and taken to a pile.

"Walk with me," Colin told her. He pointed to several pepper trees that were completely charred.

"I know they're dead. But the tree guy wanted three hundred bucks a tree to cut them down."

"They're in our way so we will take care of them. We're going to pull this fence back and put in a gate to give our trucks room to get up into the wash."

"Okay." Her head was spinning.

"Hey, Colin?"

Someone called to him from across the wash. He looked at her. "I've got to . . ."

"Go. I'm around all day. If I have questions, I'll ask."

He patted her shoulder, looked her in the eye, and then turned and left her side.

As she headed back toward the driveway, the Porta Potty truck arrived and unloaded one big blue toilet next to her garbage cans.

"Oh, God . . ."

CHAPTER NINE

Austin came home from school and brought a friend so they could gawk at the scene in the front yard.

The crew had set up an E-Z Up canopy with park benches under it to take their breaks and kept any trash they created cleaned up.

Still, it was chaos. Organized chaos, but madness nonetheless. One by one, the loaders, backhoes, long reach excavators, water trucks, and graders were lining up and had parked for the night. They'd managed to take down no less than a dozen dead trees, two of which were cottonwoods that lined her driveway and had died prior to the fire because of California's lack of rain. Colin asked if she wanted them gone and she couldn't nod fast enough.

Now she sat on a rock and held Scout by his leash while the men slowly peeled off for the night.

She watched as Colin shrugged out of his safety vest and tossed his hard hat inside the cab of his truck. He closed the door and angled her way.

"Well, what do you think?"

"I think I'm in for a crazy ride."

He leaned against the remains of a split rail fence that was charred but not destroyed by the heat of the fire.

"I'm not going to argue that."

"I know you guys didn't have to take down all my dead trees."

He shrugged. "I'm all about the good neighbor policy. It's not going to be easy having us here. A couple extra trees and any debris you need to get rid of doesn't cost anything for us to do."

She doubted that, but was grateful for it.

"Would you be able to clean up what's left of our barns?" She was half teasing.

He looked behind him and up toward the house. "Absolutely. I'll have one of the guys take care of it tomorrow."

"Seriously?"

He nodded. "I would imagine you get water runoff from the back of your house."

"We do, but it's usually diverted around the barn."

"The barn that isn't there anymore."

"Right." She hadn't thought about that.

"The last thing we need is that debris ending up down here and clogging up the wash and creating a bigger mess."

She found herself smiling. "That's how you'll spin it if anyone asks."

"I speak the truth."

She called bullshit on that. "Well, thank you."

"No, thank you."

"I know I busted your guys' chops last week. I'm not normally that bitchy."

"You're giving them boundaries. Nothing wrong with that."

She rubbed the back of her neck before taking Scout off his leash. The second he was free, he darted over to the parked equipment.

"So this is what it's going to be? Day in and day out?" She took in the sheer magnitude of equipment sitting on her property.

"Give or take."

"What does one of those things cost?"

"Depends. Anywhere from a hundred grand to half a million new."

She knew her jaw slacked. "That's a lot of money."

"They do the heavy lifting."

She shook away the enormity of what she was looking at. "Well, I should let you get home to your wife." Where had those words come from?

His silence made her look him in the eye.

"What?" she asked him when he didn't say anything.

"Is that your way of asking if I'm married?"

Even though the sun had dipped over the mountain, she felt sweat start to pool on her neck. "No . . . I just assumed."

Now he was grinning.

A flutter stirred low in her belly.

"Why would you assume that?"

She shifted her weight, looked at the ground. "I don't know. It's just, ah . . ." She started mumbling. "You seem like a decent guy. Old enough to be married. Maybe even have a kid of your own."

"You've given this some thought."

She shot her eyes back to his. "What? No! Absolutely not."

"Right."

She stood from her perch on the rock and dusted off the back of her shorts. "Fine. Whatever. I don't want to keep you from *whatever* . . ."

"How old are you, Parker?"

"It's not polite to ask a woman's age." And why was he looking at her like that . . . all smug and happy with himself?

"Twenty-five?" he asked.

"Twenty-six," she said a little too quickly. "How old are you?"

"Thirty-three." He leaned in a little closer. "And I'm not married."

He was onto her. Parker didn't know what made her want to run more, the fact that he wasn't looking at her like the county contractor guy only interested in the property but instead a thirty-three-year-old trying to figure out his next move. "It's none of my business." And before he could comment further, she called her dog.

"We'll be back in the morning."

"I'll be at work." Her tone was defensive. "I get home at two thirty."

"I'll see you tomorrow afternoon."

"Fine."

She walked away and heard him chuckling.

Halfway up the drive, she felt some of her defensiveness fade. Replacing it was a smile. TDH was single!

~

Colin had grinned like a cat with a mouse in its paws all the way home. He took a quick shower, scrubbing the dust from his hair, and flopped on the couch with a beer in his hand.

His phone buzzed at his side with a text message from Matt. You home?

His response was a thumbs-up.

I'm on my way over.

Colin didn't ask why. He pushed his ass off the sofa and unlocked the front door. Everyone in his family had a key to his house, and always knew they could come by anytime they wanted. Their family's open door policy was one of the things he loved the most. Only once had his brother shown up when Colin was entertaining a woman, and from that day on, he always sent a text before coming over. Kinda like a one-knuckle knock on the door before flinging it open when they were still living with their parents.

Colin opened up the pictures app on his phone and scrolled through the Creek Canyon project. Twice he might have *accidentally* taken a picture of the homeowner when she wasn't looking. While everyone else ran around with hard hats and long pants, she strolled about in shorts and a tank top. Her hair was in a loose ponytail all day, straggly bits all over the place. No makeup. Only the sun on her skin to brighten her cheeks. Not to mention dirt. When she'd asked him about a wife, he was having a hard time not staring at the smudge of dirt across her chin. She probably didn't even know it was there. Obviously, she didn't care. Somehow that was endearing to him.

He was halfway through his drink when the sound of Matt's motorcycle signaled his arrival before he walked in the door.

"Over here," Colin yelled from the back of his house where the family room and kitchen lived.

His brother strolled in dressed in a T-shirt and shorts. He placed his helmet on the kitchen island before beelining to the refrigerator.

"Nice safety jacket and leather pants you're wearing there," Colin gave his brother hell.

"You live less than two miles away." Matt flashed the smile he and Grace had inherited from their mother and twisted the top off his beer.

They had their mother to give him trouble, so Colin left it alone. His brother took risks every day in his job, a couple of miles on a bike was the least of them.

"So what do you think of Robert?"

"Gracie's Robert?" Matt asked.

"Yeah."

"He's a putz. Not sure what she sees in him." Matt toed off his shoes and tossed his feet up on the coffee table.

"I think she's going to dump him before our next family dinner." Colin flipped through the pictures on his phone.

"That's a relief. Talking to him is like talking to a wall. And what's up with the video game on his phone? Texting, sexting, or hooking up on Tinder I get . . . but a video game at a family dinner?"

Colin looked up from his screen. "You still using that app?"

"It was a phase. I'm over it." None of his Tinder dates ever made it to Sunday dinner. Which was probably a good thing.

"I can't see why you ever needed it. You're the hero. Every single panty in the valley throws themselves at you."

Matt smiled because he knew it was the truth. "I'm more than just a piece of meat."

That had them both laughing.

"Seriously, though . . . I'm over the whole scene. The bar scene, the singles scene. Half my friends are married. Most of the guys at the station have families. I'm the third wheel they invite out to the desert when we wanna go riding."

"Someone is feeling sorry for himself."

"Really, Colin . . . don't you ever get bummed sitting at home alone at night?"

"You mean like right now?" With his family, he was never home alone for long.

Matt tilted back his beer again. "Maybe I'll try Match."

Colin shook his head.

Before he could offer his brother a suggestion, he heard his front door open and close.

"Hello?"

It was Grace.

"Back here," both he and Matt said at the same time.

Her heels clicked on the tile as she walked through the house.

Colin glanced over his shoulder while she made the same circuit as his brother.

"No call first?" Colin asked.

"I saw Matt's bike, figured it was safe." She made an attempt to open her beer, gave up, and handed it to Colin.

He took care of it for her and handed it back.

"So, you're having a party and didn't invite me?" she asked with a grin.

"Not a party, just happy hour."

She lifted her beer in the air. "Cheap drinks."

Matt did an "air cheer" from across the room and they both drank.

"We were just saying how much we don't like Robert."

Gracie did this squishy lip thing she did when she wasn't happy with something. "I know. I'm cutting him loose this Saturday."

"Dad will like that," Matt said.

Her shoes met Matt's on the floor and she tucked her feet under her on the couch.

"How did today go?" Grace asked Colin.

"It went well. The equipment is on-site. The ground is staged. I have everything lined up for the week. Not one hitch." That was a rarity in his world, but necessary since he was new in the position.

"And Parker?" Grace said her name with a lift at the end and suggestion in her tone.

"Who's Parker?" Matt asked.

"Just the single, sexy homeowner that our brother has the hots for."

"I never said I had the hots for her."

Grace pointed the neck of her beer in his direction. "You didn't have to. Your smile said it all. Kinda like the one you're wearing now."

Colin forced the grin from his lips.

"She noticed you today, didn't she?"

Colin took his empty beer and unfolded from the couch. "Your interest in my love life is a direct reflection on yours being a mess."

"No denying that," she said. "Now answer the question."

He opened his fridge, snagged another beer. "She asked if I had a wife."

Matt made a sound somewhere between a moan and a hum.

On second thought . . . "Not asked . . . more like assumed."

"And you denied that." Grace was like a dog with a bone.

"Not immediately. I called her on it. Asked if that was her way of finding out if I was single."

Matt gave him a thumbs-up. "Good for you."

"Wait . . . what? That's rude."

"How?" Colin asked.

Grace set her beer aside, sat taller. "If a woman subtly asks about a wife, it's her way of testing the water."

"Yeah, I know. I think I suggested it to you at one point."

She shook her head. "But you don't call her out. That makes her defensive."

Now that he thought about it . . . "Yeah."

"Defensive is not how you turn on the charm, Colin."

He paused for a minute to see if his sister had a point. "Too late now."

She shook her head. "Men can be so stupid sometimes."

"This from the woman dating the twenty-five-year-old gamer . . . Does he even shave?" Matt didn't hold back any punches.

"He's twenty-seven, and . . ." She grabbed her beer and scowled. "Only every third day."

CHAPTER TEN

Janice called Parker into her office before the school day started.

As Parker looked down, her palms started to sweat. The look on her boss's face suggested she wasn't happy.

"Sit, please." Janice took her seat behind her desk and waited.

"Is everything okay?" Parker asked as she perched on the edge of the office chair.

Instead of answering the question, Janice offered, "You look like you're feeling better."

Okay . . . so this was about her calling in sick. "Yes, thank goodness. Yesterday was awful."

Her boss wasn't buying it. "Right. I like you, Parker, I do. I know you're going through a hard time, and the last thing I want to do is add to it."

She felt a *but* coming.

"However, as you know, dealing with our special needs students requires continuity. When the parents of those students come to me with concerns, I cannot ignore them."

"What kind of concerns?"

"Behavioral problems at home, lack of attention in the classroom. These students need consistency to trust and grow."

Parker had some backpedaling to do. "I know. I'm sorry. I shouldn't need to take any more time off—"

"You do know that Mrs. Fields lives right down the street from you." She was one of the third grade teachers.

"Yes." Her heart was beating way too fast, and way too loud.

"She informed me about the magnitude of the activity going on at your house."

"Yes, but—"

"I think it's safe to say that you're going to need to call in sick several more days this year in order to manage everything going on."

"We don't know that," Parker argued.

Janice waved a hand in the air, cutting her off. "None of that really matters. I need to make sure Molly has as stable a school experience as the district can give her. And right now, I don't feel that is you."

"You're firing me." She felt tears in her eyes.

"No. I'm reassigning you. I'm putting you on yard duty before school starts, and during recess and lunch, relief help in the classrooms."

The same job she'd gotten when she first started with the district right after her parents died. She managed to get up to full-time work and per diem pay last year, now she would be cut back to part time with no guarantee.

"I'm sorry, Parker. I think this is for the best. It will give you more flexibility and not leave the district in a bind every time it rains this winter."

She couldn't stop the tears from rolling down her cheeks.

"Go ahead and take the morning. Let this sink in and come back at ten thirty for the first recess."

Parker ignored the looks she received while she walked down the short hall to the teachers' lounge where she kept her purse locked up.

"You okay, Parker?"

She didn't even look to see who asked. "I'm fine." Her voice shook and the tears were only going to flow faster if she talked to anyone. She dug in her purse, slid on her sunglasses, and exited the building. Only when she had skirted past the morning drop-off and climbed behind the wheel of her car did she lower her head and sob.

~

Parker's car pulling into the driveway and past the trucks stuck out like a lake in the desert. Colin felt a smile in his chest knowing she was home. He looked at his watch, was it two thirty already?

No, it was only half past one.

He could have sworn she said she worked until two thirty.

Ray brought his attention back to the job. For the next hour he worked with the building crew on the first structure. Every once in a while he'd pop his head up to see if Parker was meandering around the yard like she had the day before.

It wasn't until her brother came home from school that Colin saw any activity up by the house. He noticed Scout running around the yard, chasing a ball, and Austin standing there watching at a distance.

Maybe Grace was right. Maybe his calling Parker out on the wife question made her defensive enough to pull back.

"Hey, Colin . . . you with me here?"

"Sorry, yeah." He forced his attention to the work in front of him.

By four thirty Austin was sitting in their break area with Scout on a leash lapping up the attention of some of the men on the team.

Colin made his way over and knelt down to pet the dog. Scout licked his face in approval. "It's Austin, right?"

"Yeah."

"See ya tomorrow, Colin." One of his crew waved to Colin as he headed to his car.

"What do you think of all this?"

He shrugged. "Not sure. Weird seeing everyone here."

"I bet. It's probably pretty quiet around here most of the time."

"Not since the fire."

If Colin hadn't been looking at the kid, he would have missed the flash in his eyes that said those words had a deeper meaning.

"Were you here? During the fire?"

"Yeah. We all were. I thought the house was gone. Fire was everywhere." And to help his point, Austin pulled his phone from his pocket and pulled up a picture.

Colin stood up from where he was with the dog and sat beside Parker's brother and looked at his cell phone.

"I recorded this right as we were leaving."

The sky was black; flames licked the side of the hills and surrounded the Sinclair home to where you couldn't see the structure. The video stopped right as Austin had crossed the dry creek bed.

"That's, ah . . ." He had no words.

"It sucked."

"Yeah. I can't imagine."

"We didn't die, so . . ."

Jesus . . . Colin never thought about that angle.

"You had time to get out, right?"

"The fire took a while to get here, but then it exploded. I've seen stuff on the news and always thought that people could just get out. We did, but I get why some don't. One minute it was over there." He pointed to the V in the mountain range where the dry creek bed lived. "The next it was hopping trees and cutting us off."

"I'm glad you got out."

The kid shrugged. "Yeah."

There was more there, but Colin didn't feel like it was his place to ask. "I thought I saw your sister pull in a while ago. Is she here? I had a question for her."

"She's here. She was in bed."

"Bed? Is she sick?"

Austin shrugged again. "I don't know."

Colin wondered if he had ever been a teenager as he stared into one in Technicolor.

"It can wait."

But Austin was putting the phone to his ear after pressing a few buttons.

"Hey, Colin has a question for you . . ."

He wanted to stop the kid. If Parker wasn't feeling well, he didn't want to wake her up.

"Okay." The kid hung up. "She's on her way down."

"You didn't have to. It can wait."

Austin patted Scout on his neck. "It's okay. She's a control freak. The more she knows about what's going on out here, the easier it will be for her."

Suddenly the teen was gone and the adult he would become made a peek.

"It sounds like you know your sister well."

"I guess." The teen was back.

"I'm going to make this as easy on you guys as I can," he assured him.

"That's what Parker said."

Colin watched while Austin looked at his phone.

Yeah . . .

He didn't talk teenager.

Once he saw Parker walking down the drive, he excused himself and abandoned the kid.

He could tell something was off several yards before Parker reached him. She wasn't smiling, sunglasses hid her eyes, and the confidence she normally carried in her stride had been replaced with a slow pace and slumped shoulders.

"Hey." He kept his voice even and measured. "Austin said you weren't feeling well. This can wait."

"It's okay."

He doubted that, but kept talking anyway. "We're going to be bringing in K-rails that we'd like to set on this side of the wash."

"All right."

He kept waiting for her to look at him.

She didn't.

He pointed to two posts that were once part of a split rail decorative fence. "Did you plan on fixing this?"

"I don't know. The fire trucks knocked them down. I'm waiting until after the winter to see what damage we take on." There was very little emotion in her voice.

"You sure you're okay?"

"I'm fine." But her declaration was met with a sniffle.

He couldn't stop himself. She was upset, not sick. And he had a hard time not probing. "When a woman says *fine*, she's never *fine*."

"Who told you that, your mother?"

"My mother showed me. My sister told me."

"Did your sister also tell you that when a woman says she's *fine*, it's her way of saying she doesn't want to talk about it?" Her head swiveled his way, he felt her eyes on him through the sunglasses.

"Yeah . . . she did."

Parker lifted her palms in the air. "Well?" She was getting more annoyed and less sad as the conversation progressed. At least anger had energy, which he always thought was a better emotion than depression.

"Right. Okay, so these posts make it hard for the trucks to turn into this part of the property."

"You want to take them out?"

He nodded, but jumped right back into their other conversation. "I'm really good at fixing things, maybe if you told me what was wrong, I could help."

She angled her body toward him, removed her sunglasses, and pointed her tear-swollen eyes his way. "Can you fix my job? Can you turn back time and make it so this fire never happened? Can you magically make it so that no rain comes and none of this is necessary?"

He pulled out the only part she had any control of. "What happened at work?"

"I was demoted."

"You're a teacher, right?" Something with the school district.

And the floodgates opened. "No, I'm not a teacher. I had to drop out of college when my parents died. I'm an aide for special needs kids at the elementary school. *Was* an aide. Which wasn't much in the way of pay, but at least I worked full-time hours. Now I'm back to playground police and yelling at parents talking on their cell phones in the drop-off line." She ran both hands through her hair and accidentally dropped her glasses.

Colin reached down to grab them before she could beat him to it.

"Thank you," she said when he handed them over.

"I'm sorry." And he was. The stress she was carrying for her siblings couldn't be easy. "I'm guessing that means a cut in pay."

"Yeah. It does. I didn't make a lot, but it helped. My mother didn't work, but my father was still pulling in money when they died. There's social security and a pension. Separate college funds for all of us, thank God . . . but there's cars and insurance and gas and cell phones." She covered her face with her hands. "Never mind. None of this has anything to do with you. I'm sorry. I'm just having a bad day."

"Sounds like more than one."

"Whatever." The sunglasses went back on her face. "So, you want to get rid of these poles."

"Yes."

"Fine."

"Fine?" he asked with a lift to his voice.

There was a slight grin on her face. "No, really. I don't care. It's all messed up anyway and looks like crap."

"I might be able to swing replacing them when we're all finished."

She shook her head. "No. No reason for both of us to have problems with our bosses. I saw you took care of the barns today. Thank you for that."

"You're welcome." Colin really wanted to pull her into his arms and hug away her pain.

She shuffled her feet and looked around with a sigh.

"My mom is retired now, but she worked as a bookkeeper for years. She's all about budgets and planning. Maybe she can help."

"I wouldn't want to—"

He placed a hand on her arm, tried to push aside the shiver on his skin with the contact. "It would make her day to help. My dad is a retired cop and makes her crazy." Not really true, but Colin felt he needed to add that in to make Parker say yes. "Another set of eyes on the books may help."

She was wavering. "I don't know . . ."

"Look at all the people you're helping by allowing this. Let someone else help you. Maybe she can't help, maybe she can." He squeezed the arm he held.

Parker released a long breath. "Fine . . . I mean, okay," she clarified. "Only if it's not a bother."

Colin patted himself on the back. "Not a bother at all. I promise."

"You sure?"

"Parker."

"Fine." The coy smile she sent him made him think some of the weight had been lifted from her shoulders.

CHAPTER ELEVEN

"Come on in." Parker opened the door and held Scout back at the same time.

Colin had texted her the night before, after their conversation, to say his mother was dropping by once Parker was home from work the following day.

"You must be Parker."

"I am." Scout tried to jump. "I'm sorry. He's not used to being cooped up all day." The sound of all the heavy equipment drifted in from the open door.

"It's okay. I love dogs."

Parker dragged the dog out of the way and scolded him before he settled enough to let him go.

She stood up straight and took a good look at Colin's mom for the first time. She was slender, but not frail . . . probably in her late sixties, although it was hard to tell. Her hair was a sandy brown, cut short but not overly curled. Colin had her eyes. Warm brown, almost a copper color to them. "Thank you for coming. I'm really not sure if there is anything you can do."

Mrs. Hudson followed her into the oversize dining room where Parker had opened up a laptop and brought out her files of monthly expenses.

"Colin told me your hours were cut. If we look at everything and there is nothing to be done, well, at least you know. Besides, I'm never too old to meet new friends."

Her kindness struck a chord in Parker's chest. "I like that. Can I get you something to drink?"

"Water is fine." Mrs. Hudson looked around the family room. "You have a lovely home."

"I can't take credit for it. This was my parents' doing. Well, except for the TV. I had to replace that a few years ago."

"Colin said your parents had passed and that you've been caring for your sister and brother."

Parker grabbed a cold bottle of water from the fridge, gave it to her. "We look out for each other."

"Hmmm. How long has it been?"

"Two years."

She shook her head. "I'm so sorry."

"It's okay. I've had some time to adjust."

Her kind smile turned to pity. Something Parker had seen every time she told someone about her situation. "It can't be easy. And you're so young yourself."

"I don't feel young lately."

"No. I imagine you don't." She swiveled to stare out the window looking down over the property. A parade of trucks was hauling debris and excavating the site while separate crews were building the structures five hundred feet from the house. "Colin said this was a big project."

"I didn't really know what to expect."

"It probably wasn't this."

Parker found her gaze fixated outside the window, her stare blank. "No."

Mrs. Hudson placed an arm over her shoulders and brought her out of her daze. "Well, young lady, let's see what we have here."

For the next two hours Parker sat beside Colin's mom and disclosed every source of money coming in and expenses going out. She opened up the bank site and looked at all the accounts her parents had set up. Everything was still in the name of the trust except the personal accounts for her and Mallory.

"These are the college accounts?"

"Yes."

She clicked around the website. "There is still money going into your brother's. And yours is almost empty."

Parker shrugged. "Mine was fully funded by the time our parents died. Austin was fifteen. I didn't think it was right that I was the only one who could afford to go to college. I kept funding Mallory's and Austin's out of mine. I figured by the time they were in college, maybe we could sell the house and I could use that money to go back." That had been the grand plan, anyway.

"Then where would you live?"

"An apartment . . . I don't know."

Mrs. Hudson pointed to a number on the screen. "This is your mortgage, right?"

"Yes."

"You do realize that is less than what the average apartment is in this valley."

"That might be, but without the capital I'm not going to be able to go to school and get a job to pay for all this. My dad's social security will run out once Austin is out of high school."

"I see the problem."

The door downstairs that led into the garage slammed shut and footsteps followed as someone came in.

Mallory tossed her backpack on the couch and said hello.

"This is Mrs. Hudson, Colin's mom. She's helping me with the books."

Her sister smiled and waved. "Hey."

"You can call me Nora. Mrs. Hudson is a mouthful."

"Did you find the pot of gold yet?" Mallory went straight to the fridge, pulled out the milk.

"We're searching for the rainbow first."

Her sister laughed, moved into the walk-in pantry, and came out with a box of cereal. "Tell her to use the insurance money and stop stressing."

"Insurance money?" Nora asked.

"It's in a separate account. It's meant to fix the damage from the fire, not live off of," Parker reminded her sister.

"How much money are we talking?"

"A lot," Mallory exclaimed.

"It's not as much as you think and it won't go far when we start making repairs. And we don't know what's coming with the flooding, or if the insurance will cover it if new shit happens." Parker argued with her sister, realized she cussed, and said, "Sorry . . . *stuff* happens."

Nora patted Parker's hand and didn't call her on her bad language.

"Do you have a file from the insurance company, what they paid for, so I can take a look at it?"

Parker nodded and scooted back her chair. "I'll go get it."

As she walked out of the room, she heard Nora talking to her sister. "Is that your dinner?"

Parker cringed.

~

Parker sat in bed . . . the house was quiet. Austin had come home right as Nora was leaving with the promise of coming back the next day. She wanted to look at her parents' books before their deaths and compare them with what Parker was doing.

She wasn't sure what the woman was going to find any different.

Money came in and money went out.

Simple as that.

But she liked her. Even if Nora couldn't find a way to make money spread, it was nice to know Parker was doing everything in her power to make it all work.

So she sat in her bed with her cell phone in her hand.

Her finger hovered over Colin's name. She pressed it and typed in a text message. Your mom is wonderful. Thank you.

She watched her screen for a full minute before setting her phone aside. It was late . . . well, only nine thirty, but she was already in bed since she needed to be at the school thirty minutes earlier than normal because of her reassignment. Line duty and yard duty. She dropped her head on the back of her headboard and closed her eyes. Maybe she should go back to waiting tables. The money would be better. The hours would suck.

Twenty-six and waiting tables.

How is this my life?

Before she could answer, her phone rang.

She saw Colin's name and picked it up.

"Hello."

"It's Colin." The timbre of his voice soothed her.

"Hi, Colin."

"I figured you were awake."

"Not for long. I have to yell at moms early in the morning."

He laughed. "I won't keep you, then."

She snuggled a little deeper in her bed. "You got my text."

"Yeah. My mom couldn't stop talking about you."

"I'm not sure if that's good or bad."

He coughed. "Are you kidding? Look what you're holding together over there. She's impressed."

"I'm keeping it together with bubble gum and not duct tape. Your mom is wonderful. Unfortunately, she didn't see anything obvious to hang hope onto."

"She told me she needed more time."

Parker wasn't holding her breath. "She's coming by tomorrow when I'm at work so she isn't distracted and will explain everything to me when I get home."

"For someone who was so anxious about strangers on the property, I'm surprised to hear you're okay with my mom there when you're gone."

Parker grinned. "Well, she's your mom. Which innately means she's vetted."

"Is that right?" She heard laughter in his voice.

"Yeah. Besides, I'm getting better about allowing people into my personal space." The words no sooner left her mouth than she realized how they might be construed.

"Who else are you allowing in your personal space?" he asked.

"No one," she quickly said. "You know what I mean."

"I'm teasing you."

She couldn't stop smiling. "I can tell."

"Are you feeling any better?"

"A little."

"You *sound* better."

It helped that she had stopped crying. "Thank you for offering solutions. Sometimes my blinders are on and I only see what's right in front of me. The other day all I could see was the unemployment line."

"Which is worse than the DMV," he said with a laugh.

"True. I appreciate you checking on me. I'm pretty sure that's not in your job description."

"It could be."

She paused, not really sure what he meant by that. "I'm not following you."

"You're right. As the supervisor on the project, it's not necessary that I check on you unless it's raining or something is wrong with the project. But as a man who doesn't have a wife, checking on a woman who doesn't have a husband . . ."

Her breath caught and words failed her.

"Unless you'd rather I—"

"You're flirting with me." She leaned into her phone, hanging on what he was going to say next.

He chuckled. "Yeah. You could say that. Is that okay?"

Parker smiled . . . full-on ear-to-ear smile and did a hand pump in the air. "Wait, why?"

"Why am I flirting with you?"

"Yeah?"

"Let's see. You're attractive, hardworking, intelligent . . . that lack of a husband thing is a plus. You're confident and self-aware, care about others . . . Do I need to go on?"

"Maybe," she teased. She pulled her knees into her chest and enjoyed the warmth his attention was putting in her belly.

"Okay, the guys on the team respect you, my mother and sister like you—"

"I haven't met your sister."

"Yeah, you did. In the meeting with the city. Grace."

"I thought she was a project person." Parker tried to remember the woman's face. She vaguely remembered her being short.

"She is, just not on your project. I thought she'd help counter Ed's bulldozing personality."

"He *was* pushy."

"So . . . is it okay?"

"Okay for what?"

"That I'm flirting with you."

It took her a minute to respond. "I'm a hot mess, Colin."

"Yeah, I know. I like that part, too. Unless you're not interested. In which case I'll need to turn up the charm." He was doing that smile with his voice thing again.

By now Parker was cradling the phone and remembering what it felt like to be a girl talking to a boy. "I didn't say I wasn't interested. Although I'm tempted to see what *turning up the charm* looks like."

His throaty laugh had her giggling along with him. "We're getting somewhere."

"I'm rusty at this," she warned him.

"Then we move slow."

"We're going to have to."

"Well then, Parker. I'll let you get to bed now since you have to yell at moms first thing in the morning." The man had heard everything she'd said. That was a first.

"Good night, then."

"Good night." She tossed the phone on the bed after he hung up and hugged her knees hard. God, it felt good to have a man flirting with her.

CHAPTER TWELVE

Parker drove through the long line of dump trucks that Ray waved back once she was spotted. She rolled down her window as she pulled in. "Thanks, Ray."

"No problem."

She peeked out her window in hopes of spotting Colin. Half a dozen trucks that looked just like his were parked side by side. Much as she wanted to see him, had thought about him most of the day, she wasn't about to go search him out. She'd be subtler than that.

Nora's car was parked to the side of the driveway.

Parker walked into the house from the garage. The minute she opened the door the scent of something savory cooking stopped her. She closed her eyes and took a deep breath through her nose. Pot roast . . . or something similar.

The garage was situated under the main living area of the house, so she had to take a flight of stairs before the full force of smells hit her. She turned the corner to see Nora sitting at the dining table they'd been perched at the day before.

The morning chaos had been cleaned from the kitchen and a vase of fresh flowers sat on the kitchen island.

"What smells so fabulous?"

Nora looked up, set her reading glasses to the side. "I thought I heard someone come in."

Parker glanced inside the oven. "You cooked?"

"I hope you don't mind. I thought you might need some comfort food after everything."

"You didn't have to—"

"I know. I wanted to." Nora walked over to her. "I found a few ingredients, bought a couple others. One of the things I miss most about my children growing up and leaving the house is cooking big meals."

"I don't make the time for big meals," Parker told her.

"We get together at least twice a month so I can get my fix. I'd have them over every week or more if I could."

"This is because of Mallory's cereal dinner last night, isn't it?"

"I'm not judging, sweetheart. I understand what it was like to have teenagers running in all directions. I think Colin lived on frozen pizza for three years."

"Austin's favorite."

Nora tilted her head. "What you may not realize is how much more expensive that kind of eating is in the long run." She waved Parker over to the table. "There was a time when my husband and I were struggling. My mother had been declining in health and we eventually had to move her into a home. It was expensive and I needed to make the grocery budget stretch."

Nora handed her a notebook full of recipes and discussed the art of cutting coupons. Next she handed her a spreadsheet. "For someone so young, you really do have a handle on your budget. I can see where you used your father's life insurance policy to pay the mortgage, taxes, and insurance."

"But it's running out."

"I see that." She pointed to a column. "This is from your renter. Is there a reason you didn't rent the guesthouse out sooner?"

Parker nodded. "Mallory and Austin were both under eighteen when our parents died. Taking guardianship at twenty-four came with supervision from the courts."

"Do they still watch you?"

"Not really. I mean, the high school knows about our situation and I'm aware that they could report it if there were any real problems. I thought it was best to avoid any potential for issues with a tenant."

"And when Austin turns eighteen, you no longer have that hanging over you."

"No. We also lose our parents' social security checks once he's out of high school. I've already filed for the three-month extension after his eighteenth birthday."

"Like we figured out yesterday, all this is working but obviously not for long since the accounts are running low, less than two years with your current expenses. Even with the tenant."

"Unless I got a better job."

"Which is going to be key if you're staying in the house."

For the next ten minutes, Nora talked to her about the pros and cons of moving out of the family home and into an apartment. She talked about equity and the economy . . . things Parker hadn't spent a lot of time considering. While Parker realized the fire would stop potential buyers and lower the overall sale price of the home, she hadn't considered the whole picture.

"What if I can't afford to pay all the bills here?" Parker asked.

Nora lifted a finger before slipping her glasses over her eyes. "The insurance money. They paid you for the loss of your barns, but there is nothing here that says you need to rebuild them."

"I would think the property would be worth more with a barn."

"Maybe. But do you need them?"

"Not anymore. The first thing we did after the accident was sell the horses." A hundred dollars a month per horse to feed was out of their budget.

They mulled over the spreadsheets of damage and moneys collected from the insurance company, and Nora had added a column for estimated cost of repairing the damage with a do-it-yourself budget.

"I have no trouble doing any and all of the work that I can, but I don't know the first thing about fixing shingles on a roof or building a fence," Parker told her.

Nora's kind smile helped ease the tension building in Parker's shoulders. "That's where you ask for help, m'dear. A barbeque dinner and cookies goes a long way with some of your new friends in your front yard right now."

The thought made her uncomfortable. "I couldn't do that."

"Why not? People like to help." Nora kept going. "I'm not suggesting you won't have to hire a few things and pay the inflated price for it. But on a few of these things, you won't have to hire anyone. The mom in me wants to tell you not to stress about the money. But I realize that's not possible when you're sitting on so many unknowns this winter. I am going to tell you to try not to stress, Parker. Mainly because you're too young for wrinkles."

Parker tried to smile.

"Work the hours the school district gives you. Encourage your brother to get a part-time job. All my kids worked when they were in high school." Nora placed a hand over hers. "This is temporary. A new job may not be as forgiving of the interruptions that you may not be able to avoid right now. Colin and his crew are doing all that out there, but you have a lot going on in here. And that's personal and emotional. It would have been difficult on your parents if they were here, and doubly hard on you."

"I'm afraid of it all falling apart. This house is all we have left of them."

Nora squeezed her hand. "I know. I can see that. I recommend you cut coupons, skip frozen dinners . . . bake cookies and do some of the labor yourself to stretch the insurance money out. Then in the spring, after the winter does whatever it's going to do and Austin is out of high school, you and I can sit back down and reassess."

It all felt too easy. "You really think this is the best thing to do?"

"It's what I'd advise my daughter if she were in the same situation." Nora sat back, removed her glasses. "Have you even thought about what it is you want to do with your life? What you'd go back to school for?"

She rubbed the ache behind her neck. "That's changed three times in the last six years. I keep waiting for some kind of inspiration to spark."

"That hasn't happened yet."

She shook her head.

"Not surprising. You're too busy living someone else's life to plan one for yourself."

The door to the garage opened and slammed shut. "What is that?" Austin called as he ran in from outside. He shot around the corner, backpack slid to the floor.

"Mrs. Hudson made us dinner."

"I only got it started," Nora told her. "Austin?"

"Yeah?" He was looking inside the oven.

"There is a bowl of cut-up vegetables in the refrigerator. I need you to put them on top of the roast at four. Everything will be done by five."

"I can do that. Smells amazing."

Nora leaned over and whispered, "Delegate whenever you can."

Austin moved from the oven to the fridge. "Someone went shopping." He reached in and grabbed an apple.

Parker wanted to ask if he was feeling well. "You didn't have to buy us food," she told Nora.

She stood and started gathering her things. "Accept when others want to help, my dear."

Parker glanced at the bouquet on the counter. "You have to admit, the flowers are over the top."

"Oh, they absolutely are." She headed toward the front door, opened it. "But they weren't from me."

Parker lost her smile, doubled a look over her shoulder.

"I'll call on you on Monday. Bring over some of my family-approved Crock-Pot recipes."

They stepped out the door and onto the covered porch. Across the yard, Erin was getting out of her car with an armload of groceries. "Is that your tenant?"

"Yes. She's nice. Quiet. I couldn't ask for a better person to rent the place."

"Good. I feel better knowing there's another adult here with you. Even if it's in the guesthouse."

"I do, too, actually."

Nora turned and opened her arms for a hug.

Parker happily returned the gesture. "Thank you so much."

"Anytime."

Once Nora was down the steps and to her car, Parker walked back into the house and straight to the flowers.

She found a card with her name on it. On the other side all it said was *This is what "turning up the charm" looks like.*

It wasn't signed.

It didn't have to be.

CHAPTER THIRTEEN

Colin waved at his mother as her car passed through the line of trucks.

Fabio stood beside him, arms crossed over his chest. "Was that your mom?"

"Yup."

"Did she drop you off food or something?"

"Nope. She's helping out Parker." Saying her name had him smiling.

"Is she the *only* one helping out Parker?" He met Fabio's leading question with silence. His phone buzzed in his back pocket.

A text from Parker showed on his screen.

The flowers are charming.

Points for me.

"Ah-huh."

"What?" When Colin looked, Fabio was walking away.

He rocked back on his heels, a grin plastered on his face. Maybe by the following weekend, he could get her to go out with him.

~

Parker invited Erin up to the house for dinner since Nora had cooked a roast that would feed ten. For the first time in months, she set the table and made a salad to go with the meal.

She'd gone out on the property trying to locate Colin earlier, only to find out he'd been called away to another project in a different part of the city. She considered texting him but decided against it. He'd given her flowers and she'd thanked him. The ball was back in his court. Besides, going slow meant she didn't need to talk to him all day long. That would be the opposite of slow. Much as she wanted to.

The weather had cooled enough for her to open up the house and let in some fresh air. The trucks had stopped for the night, and in the absence of the backup beeping noise, the crickets and nightlife started to come alive.

"Knock, knock," Erin said from beyond the screen door.

"Come in," Parker called from the kitchen.

"I brought wine."

"Good."

"It smells fabulous."

Erin wore a sundress, her hair bounced around her shoulders. In her hand was a bottle of red. Parker didn't know a lot about wine outside the two-buck variety at Trader Joe's. It seemed Erin had much better taste. And the budget for it.

"I'd love to take credit, but it was Colin's mom. I think she feels sorry for us."

Erin walked in behind her. "Everyone on the street feels sorry for you." She shook a small red can she held in her hand. "This is the gravy stuff I was telling you about."

Parker read the label. "Bisto?"

"I came across it when I was in London. Never clumps, always spectacular."

"You were in London?"

Erin opened her mouth, paused, and turned away. "Yeah, uhm . . . backpacking trip. Years ago."

"That must have been amazing."

"Yeah . . ." She looked around the kitchen. "Do you have a small saucepan?"

Parker pointed to the cabinet where the pots and pans were stored. "In there."

While Erin rummaged through, it seemed she had no intention of talking about London. If she were reading the woman right, it appeared she wasn't happy about mentioning it. Parker wanted to ask, but dropped the subject.

She removed a wine opener from a drawer and proceeded to uncork the bottle.

"Is it done yet?" Austin walked into the kitchen.

"Yes. Go get Mallory."

Go and *get* didn't register in her brother's head. "Mallory! Dinner's ready," he yelled across the house.

She shook her head. "I could have done that."

Erin laughed while she mixed the gravy.

They all worked together and brought everything to the table.

"So what did Mrs. Hudson come up with?" Mallory opened the conversation.

Plates moved around the table as they all dished up what they wanted. Parker explained what she was going to do. ". . . by summer things should even out and I'll look for a better full-time job."

"What about school?" Mallory asked before putting a forkful of pot roast in her mouth.

"If I find a direction, I'll look into more online schools. Maybe a trade school."

Austin set his phone aside. "I've been thinking about trade school."

That was a surprise. "What kind?"

He thumbed toward the window. "Do you know what those heavy-machine operators make? I looked it up."

"If it's that good, maybe I should look into it." She was only half joking.

Austin frowned. "You're a girl."

Mallory nudged her brother with her elbow. "Hey."

"Seriously, do you see any girls out there?"

Now that he mentioned it . . .

"That doesn't mean a woman can't do the job." Mallory was the liberal free thinker in the family.

"Didn't say *can't*," Austin talked around his food. "It's dirty and greasy. Not something I see *you* doing," he told Mallory.

"I see Parker doing it," Mallory said.

"Me? Why me?"

"You could see Colin all day, every day." Mallory and Austin exchanged smiles.

"What are you talking about?" Parker glanced at Erin for support. All she found was a sideways glance.

Austin rolled his eyes. "Oh, c'mon. It's obvious you're into him."

And here she thought she'd been hiding her attraction.

Mallory pointed her fork in her direction. "Just talking about him and you're blushing."

Austin chewed his food with his mouth half-open. "The flowers are a pretty good sign it's not just you," he told her.

Parker glanced at the flowers and back to Erin.

"Don't look at me."

"Fine. He has his shit together and he isn't married."

Mallory snickered. "You're leaving out the good-looking part."

"And tall," Erin added.

"Tall, good-looking, has a job . . . So when are you going out?" Mallory asked.

Parker reached for her wine. "Aren't we jumping here?"

"No." Austin shoved more food in.

"We're not there yet. He hasn't asked."

"So ask him," Mallory suggested.

Now Erin chimed in. "No . . . let him ask you. It's better that way."

"Archaic tradition. Waiting on a man to ask you out, or asking you to marry him . . . any of that sets women back centuries."

Austin shook his head. "Decades maybe. A century, arguably . . . but not more than one."

"I'm glad your history class is sticking. Maybe that should be your major in college." Parker tried to move the conversation off of her and Colin and back to school.

"Nawh, I like the idea of trade school."

"Mom and Dad wanted us to get a degree from a university," Mallory interjected.

"Mom and Dad wanted us to have the option. If Austin wants to go to a trade school and leave with an education that can make him a living, that's all any of us can ask for."

"A lot of people out there have a college degree who aren't using it for their employment," Erin added.

"I guess." Mallory took another bite.

"What about you, Erin? Do you have a degree?" Austin asked.

She sipped her wine. "A bachelor's degree in communications and liberal arts."

"Where did you graduate from?" Parker asked.

"Small college, back east."

"I thought you were from Washington State," Mallory pointed out.

She set her glass down. "A lot of people move away for college."

Austin reached across the table, grabbed the salt and pepper. "I'm going to ask Keith to show me how to run his loader. Half the guys out there own their own equipment. Did you know that?"

And the conversation moved on to Austin's new passion.

Parker found herself smiling, laughing, and enjoying her brother and sister more during that meal than she had in months. Maybe it was because she had decided to take Nora's advice and let go of some of her work stress. Or maybe it was the comfort food in her stomach and the reality that they were talking about their parents without the empty pit that often gnawed in her stomach with the loss of them. Whatever the reason, Parker enjoyed the moment and dedicated it to memory.

An hour later, once the dishes were done and Mallory and Austin were off in their corners of the house, Erin and Parker sat outside on the porch and watched what remained of the sunset. Scout bounded around the yard, happy with his freedom. They sipped the rest of the wine and chatted.

"I consider myself the lucky one," she told Erin. "I can remember sitting on this porch with my mom watching the sunset. I didn't appreciate it until I was in college and home that summer before the accident."

"I don't know how you managed. You were only twenty-four?"

"Yeah. Mallory was just starting her senior year and Austin wasn't even driving yet."

"So young."

Sorrow started seeping back in, a feeling Parker didn't want to address, so she shifted the conversation off of her. "What about you? Are you close with your parents?"

Erin hid behind her wineglass. "Not that close. We, ah . . . we talk once in a while." She looked away.

Yeah . . . there definitely was something Erin wasn't telling her. She'd let it go for now, and hopefully Erin would trust her enough to share more soon.

"What about your job hunt? Find anything yet?"

Her eyes lit up. "Actually I may have found work online."

"What do you mean?"

"I studied journalism in college and never did anything with it—"

"Wait, I thought you said you have a communications degree," Parker interrupted her.

Her mouth opened, closed, and opened again. "Right. Which included journalism." She shook her head. "Anyway, I found some editorial work online. Something I might be able to build."

"That sounds promising."

"Right now it's articles, but there is a lot of demand for fiction editors."

"As in books?"

She nodded. "Yeah. You wouldn't happen to have any editing skills, would you?"

"I wish. I'm lost without my Word program."

"You need to be able to see what Word doesn't. It's perfect for me. I can work from home, enjoy the quiet . . ."

"When the trucks aren't here."

"They won't be here forever."

"I keep telling myself that." Parker emptied her wineglass and set it aside.

The sound of an owl called from a nearby oak tree.

Parker smiled.

"You know what I find strange?" Parker asked.

"What?"

"That you and I aren't even thirty and we're sitting on a porch, drinking wine, and watching the weather like we're in our sixties."

"It's called maturity. We don't have to hang out in a bar to have a good time." Erin held her glass with both hands.

Parker turned to look at her new friend. "See . . . I understand why I'm the way I am. Raising my siblings for the last two years, keeping my parents' life together. But how is it that you're so mature? Even my friends that are my age that are married still have a wildness that makes them want to go out on Saturday nights and find a weekend concert venue in the desert during the summer. Or are you naturally an introvert?"

Erin set the rest of her wine aside. "I wasn't always, but we all have things in our past that make us grow up."

Parker looked away, didn't pry. "If you ever need someone to talk to about those things, I'm a good listener."

Erin sighed. "I'll remember that."

CHAPTER FOURTEEN

Just like when she'd first gotten into her job with the school district, Parker received early morning phone calls either telling her she wasn't needed or telling her she was. Every night she'd go to bed early anticipating the need to work the next morning, and half the time she'd end up staying at home until eleven.

So when the text came through calling her off until ten thirty, Parker was already up and on her first cup of coffee.

She stared at her phone, read the text again, and closed her eyes. "This is temporary."

Nora's advice rolled in her head like a script. *Real food, not frozen. Bake cookies, cut coupons. Ask for and accept help from others.* That was the hard one. Help had flooded in the first few months after her parents' death. The occasional holiday or birthday card would come from her aunt on her mother's side who lived in Florida. Almost nothing from her father's brother, who lived in Alaska. He lived on propane and food he shot himself, so he didn't even learn about her parents' death until they'd been buried. She didn't ask for help often. It wasn't in her nature. Depending on help you didn't get was worse than not depending on it at all.

"What are you staring at?" Austin asked as he walked by and saw her peering out the window.

"The lack of trucks."

"Give it thirty minutes."

He opened the fridge, grabbed the milk. "I take it you're not working this morning."

She stood in her bathrobe. "Not until recess."

"Then can you toss my clothes into the dryer for me?"

"Sure."

He stopped what he was doing and ran downstairs to the laundry room. Within a minute, she heard water running through the pipes in the house.

It was nice that they could count on each other. Every day she was thankful that Austin hadn't reverted back to the mess he was after their parents died. She'd like to think she didn't worry he would relapse, but she'd be lying. The closer he came to his eighteenth birthday, the better adjusted he became.

Austin ran back up the stairs. "So what are you going to do with your mornings now?"

She finished the last of her coffee, smiled. "I'm going to get donuts."

"What?"

She sat her cup down and walked toward her bedroom. "Donuts. For the guys." Everyone loved donuts. Which was like cookies for breakfast.

Yoga pants and a T-shirt later and she was in her car and driving down the street.

She didn't make it back before the first of the trucks started rolling in, but she did manage to pull out three pink boxes and set them up on the break table as the bulk of guys parked.

If there was a universal language of food, it was pink boxes in the morning and large, flat, square boxes filled with pizza at lunch. Years of working in an elementary school taught her that.

She was sitting on the edge of one of the benches, holding Scout back from jumping up to get a sugar high, when Colin stepped out of his truck.

This was the first time she'd actually seen him since they agreed to flirt and flowers had become a thing. She was debating sprinkles or no sprinkles with one of the guys when he walked up.

"Who brought the donuts?" he asked.

Ray directed a chocolate-tipped thumb toward Parker. "This one."

"You didn't have to do that," he said, yet he was reaching into the box.

"I wanted to."

"And we're glad you did." The voice was behind her.

Scout barked and then sat and panted with his tongue hanging out of his mouth. "None for you."

The welder, his name escaped her, grabbed two, waved, and walked away.

It was nice watching them dig in like it was something special. Less than thirty bucks and the crew's morning had been made.

"I appreciate the extra help around here," she told them. There was the little issue of needing a trench dug behind the fence to help channel water that flowed off the back hill. But instead of asking right then, she tabled that for a day or two.

Ray popped up when the sound of the first dump truck driving through the gate alerted him. "It's time to get going."

"We need to hustle. The extended forecast is showing it clear, but I don't trust the weatherman," Colin told the men in earshot.

"You got it, Boss."

The crew worked their way to their respective equipment or task, leaving Colin standing beside her, one foot up on the bench, him leaning on his knee while he devoured a maple bar. "Was this my mom's idea?"

"She suggested cookies."

He waved the uneaten half of his donut her way. "Chocolate chip. Oatmeal doesn't go over well with this crew."

She smiled. "Noted. I should have thought of it myself. I've been a little self-absorbed."

He dropped his foot, sat beside her. "I think you're allowed. This is a lot to take for an outsider."

She looked around, confirmed none of his men were close by. "Thank you for the flowers."

He presented his fully dimpled smile. "My pleasure."

The fluttering in her belly was starting to become a regular thing when he was smiling at her. "You sure it's not some kind of conflict of interest . . . you giving me flowers?"

"The only conflict is if you didn't want me to give them to you."

"Won't the guys give you a hard time?"

He finished the donut. "Undoubtedly. But probably not in front of you."

She ran a hand over Scout's head. "They won't give you too bad a time, then."

"No, I expect nothing less than a dump truck full of hard time. But I think you might be worth it."

"Might?" She grinned, stopped petting Scout's head.

He pushed the pink box aside. "Depends on the cookies." He winked.

"I see where this is going."

His eyes found hers and held. The smile on his face matched the warmth in her cheeks. That smile slowly slid and his eyes traveled to her lips.

It dawned on her then, how close they were sitting to each other. The heat of his thigh met hers even though they weren't touching. Men buzzed around them, but for the first time in weeks, she didn't seem to notice.

His lips were full, the kind that promised they knew how to kiss. That single thought had her mouth open and she moved in an inch.

When one of Colin's fingers grazed her thigh, she stopped staring at his lips and found his eyes. The humor was gone, replacing it was a heat she hadn't ever seen in a man's eyes.

"What are you doing Friday?"

She swallowed. "This Friday?"

He dropped his gaze to her lips again. "Yeah. Two days from now. I want to take you out."

She dropped her hand to her thigh, touched his pinky that reached for her. "Well . . . if I wasn't so rusty, I'd say Friday is too short a notice for me to be available to do anything."

He slowly smiled.

They stared at each other.

"Six thirty?" he asked.

"I can clear my schedule."

"You do that."

She bit her lip as he walked away.

He asked me out first!

~

"I want you to invite her and the kids over for Thanksgiving." Colin had his mom on speaker as he walked around his bedroom getting ready. He'd cut out at four thirty that afternoon, but then got called into the engineering office in the city to discuss a change in the structures. Now he was rushing.

"It's a first date, Mom. A family holiday dinner is a little soon, don't you think?" She'd seen the flowers and called him on them the day she'd been at Parker's helping with her finances. Then Grace opened her trap, and now his mom was running with the information.

"I'd ask you to get her over here even if you weren't dating her."

He ran a belt through his slacks. "I'll see how things go tonight."

"Thanksgiving is in two weeks."

"I know, Mom."

"Hmmm."

He paused. "What?"

"Where are you taking her?"

"Out."

"Fine, fine . . . don't tell me. None of that *modern woman, she pays half* stuff. She doesn't have the extra money."

He rolled his eyes. "You do realize we had this conversation when I was seventeen, right?"

"She's a sweet girl."

He picked up his phone that was sitting beside him on the bed. "Maybe you should go out with her and I'll watch baseball tonight."

"I get the hint. Have a nice time."

His finger hovered over the end button. "I love you, too."

"Call me tomorrow."

He rolled his eyes and hung up.

Even with the route to her house being cluttered with traffic, he managed to arrive at her gate with two minutes to spare. He rolled down his window to punch in the code to let himself in and hesitated.

He pressed the call button instead.

It rang twice before he heard Parker's voice. "Hello?"

"It's me."

"You know the code."

"It's after five. It would make for a really short date if you accidentally shot me," he said.

He heard her laugh and then heard the tone that signaled the gate to open.

He maneuvered down the driveway, past the equipment, the Porta Potty, and benches. Erin's car was in front of the guesthouse. He couldn't tell if Austin and Mallory were home.

Colin pulled up the steep drive and parked in front of the closed garage doors.

He walked up the steps and was greeted by Scout. "How you doin', boy? Enjoying your freedom?"

The dog answered with a wagging tail and a stretch.

Colin knocked on the front door and waited.

He felt his hands needing to move. Nerves. That was new. He'd seen Parker earlier that day in passing, had teased her about picking her up in a dirt truck. He shouldn't be nervous.

His palms started to itch.

The click of the door had him lifting his chin.

When the door opened, Scout ran inside.

Colin stood there speechless.

She wore a cream colored dress that ended midcalf. Her hair fell around her face, not something he'd seen very often since she wore it up in a ball cap or ponytail most times. Her skin was kissed by the sun with only a hint of eyeliner, and a rose pink lipstick made her lips even more kissable.

Simply gorgeous.

He couldn't stop smiling.

"Is this casual enough?" she asked.

"Perfect. You're perfect."

Her cheeks grew even redder.

"Did you wanna come in? I need to grab a sweater."

"Sure." He closed the door behind him. "Where is everyone?"

"Austin said he was out with his friends. Mallory likes spending her weekends on campus."

"So you're here alone on the weekends?"

She walked away and it took everything in him to not watch the sway of her hips. Okay, he noticed, but didn't stare . . . much.

"Austin eventually comes home. When he doesn't, he calls or texts."

She disappeared around a corner he assumed was her bedroom. He took the moment to look around the house. Fully furnished with all the things people collect over the years. It reminded him of his parents' home.

Above the fireplace was a family photo.

For the first time, he saw Parker's parents. She looked like her mother.

Parker walked up behind him and stopped. "That was taken a year before the accident."

"They were so young."

"They were."

He looked at her, then back to the photograph. "Well, Mr. Sinclair. I promise to be respectful and bring your daughter home at a decent hour."

That had Parker laughing.

"Shall we?"

She turned off lights as they made their way to the front door. When they passed the house alarm, he pointed and asked, "Are you going to set it?"

"It's been messed up since the fire. I've been meaning to get someone out here to look at it."

"You live out here next to the forest, your nearest neighbors are five acres away, and your alarm doesn't work?" That didn't sit well with him.

She tugged on his arm. "We've never had a problem."

He shook his head and tabled the conversation for another time.

"Where's the truck?"

It took him a minute to react. "It's a county truck. The Jeep is mine." He skirted around her to open the door. He'd had the four-door Jeep since they came out with it. He'd sometimes drive out to the desert with his brother to spin around in the sand and build a campfire. Lately he'd been too busy to do even that.

He closed the door and walked around the car before settling behind the wheel.

Parker fidgeted with her dress and then buckled in. "So where are we going?"

"Someplace I think will take your mind off your troubles." With that, he turned down the driveway and away from his day job and her life.

CHAPTER FIFTEEN

Colin drove them out of the suburbs and into the heart of West Hollywood. Lights shined up into the palm trees and people filled the sidewalks.

"I don't think I've been down here in three years," she told him.

"That's a shame. There's a lot of life in LA."

She smiled as he turned onto the Sunset Strip.

Colin found a parking garage and made a point of opening the door for her before she could do it herself.

She took the hand he offered when she stepped out of the car and smiled when he didn't let go.

Colin led her to a building and into an elevator that opened up on the top floor to a restaurant. "Have you been here before?" he asked.

"I haven't been anywhere other than the tourist attractions in Hollywood."

He let go of her hand only to place his on the small of her back as he led her into the restaurant. His simple touch along with the soft glow of lights in the space had her in a daze.

"You said casual," she whispered when they were being escorted to their table.

"Look around, no one is dressed up."

She did, and he was right. Some of the patrons wore jeans, and most of the women wore California casual attire. The place felt fancier than that. Or maybe she was so far out of the loop she'd forgotten what fancy was.

Colin pulled her chair out.

The little scoreboard in her head kept racking up the Colin points.

He smiled across the table, flashing the dimples that probably had gotten him plenty of dates in the past.

Damn, he was sexy.

"Does this feel like a first date for you?" he asked.

"Yes . . . no." Parker made a fist in her lap and tried to find the right words. "Most of my first dates in the past were with guys I didn't really know. So when compared to that, no. But . . ."

"But?" he asked as he sat back and seemed to enjoy the way she squirmed under his gaze.

"Oh, no . . . you answer."

He leaned forward and lifted his palm up over the table in a silent request for her hand.

She shook out her fist and placed her palm in his. Slowly he traced the back of her hand with a thumb for several seconds. The slow, mesmerizing motion was impossible to pull her eyes away from. Everything inside her, from her breath to the way her nipples constricted, sparked to life with such a little touch. Colin stopped moving his thumb and she looked up.

"That feels like a first date to me," his voice promised what his touch had started. Chemistry and fireworks and all the tingles that went with it.

"Yeah . . . that definitely feels like a first date."

"Good. Let's eat a great meal, talk about whatever comes up. Phase two of our date is at nine thirty. But if we want to skip that, we can."

"Phase two?" She figured dinner and conversation and that was it.

He pointed out the window and down the street. "We have reservations at the comedy club. I thought a good laugh might be exactly what you need right now."

She couldn't stop smiling. "I've never been to one."

"They're a lot of fun."

"That's really thoughtful, Colin."

"That's me, Mr. Thoughtful. Maybe I'll have some T-shirts made." He squeezed her hand.

"I was thinking some TDH T-shirts."

He questioned her with a narrowing of his eyes. "TDH?"

Did she say that out loud? "Tall, dark, and handsome."

He laughed, squeezed her hand. "Only if you get a shirt that says TTD."

Okay . . . The first *T* for *tall*, but what were the other letters? "I give up."

"Tall, tan, and dangerous."

"Dangerous?"

"The first day I met you there was a shotgun slung over your shoulder like it was normal."

She laughed. "I guess I deserve that, then."

The waiter walked up to the table in that moment and Colin gave her back her hand. She ordered a fruity martini and Colin ordered a whiskey she'd never heard of. When she opened the menu, her eyes grew large with sticker shock. Suddenly some of the lightness in her chest started to thicken.

The last date she'd been on, the guy had met her at a popular chain restaurant and expected her to split the bill. Something she'd done more than once in her life. And since she and Colin hadn't talked about who was going to pay . . . she didn't know what to expect. At least she had a credit card in her purse.

Maybe she'd just have a salad.

"What are you going to get?" she asked.

When he didn't answer, she lowered her menu and looked at him.

He was grinning ear to ear.

"What?"

"Grace told me there are two types of women out there. The kind who ask their date what they're ordering so they make sure to not order anything more expensive than the guy, and the kind of woman who orders what she wants with no regard for her date's wallet."

She folded the menu and placed it in her lap. "Grace forgot about the third kind of woman."

"Who is she?"

"The kind who doesn't assume her date is picking up her meal and realizes the only thing on the menu she can afford is the salad."

Colin slowly nodded. "Ahhh, right. I forgot about that woman. I haven't met her."

"Yeah, you have." Parker pointed to her chest.

"I'm not that guy. I asked you out, took you to a place I can afford, and don't expect you to do anything but have a good time."

That was a relief. "You sure?"

He reached over again, rubbed his thumb against the back of her hand. "My mother would disown me."

The muscles in the back of her neck started to relax. "I like your mom."

Colin lifted his menu again.

After twenty seconds Parker asked, "So what are you having?"

~

She'd finally settled on the ahi and didn't leave one vegetable on the plate. She ohh'd and ahh'd and thanked him more than he felt comfortable accepting. They talked about the project and Austin's interest in the big machinery. He talked about his family and the recent in and out of Grace's latest boyfriend. "So your family brings all the boyfriends and girlfriends around your parents?"

"Yeah. From the beginning, my mom insisted that family dinners included whoever we were dating from the get-go. None of that *bring a woman around only if you're planning on a trip down the aisle* nonsense."

"Why?"

By now they were sharing a dessert he insisted on but Parker was enjoying even though she said she was full.

"My dad will tell you it was so we could do something if Grace started dating some ass. He didn't want to find out too late that his future son-in-law was wrong for her."

"Isn't that for her to decide?"

"Ultimately. So far she's quick to beat us to the relationship dump. We don't have to do much more than ask a few questions and she sees what's not ever going to work."

Parker was scooting the crème brûlée around with her spoon. "It must be nice to have two older brothers looking out for her."

"Her high school prom date dumped her at an after-party and she ended up having to call home to get picked up. My dad was still working at the time, so our mom called Matt and me. We showed up, tucked Grace in the car, and then found her boyfriend."

Parker stopped smiling. "You didn't—"

"No. We didn't. Her feelings were hurt, but he hadn't crossed the line and gotten physical with her. Which was good for him and my brother and I. Especially since he was seventeen and we were both adults. That wouldn't have gone over well."

"You're a good big brother."

"I try." He set his spoon down, let her enjoy the rest of the dessert. "Which brings me to a question."

The tip of the fork sat on her tongue and suddenly his mind jumped right in the gutter.

"What's that?" she asked, oblivious to the scene that had flashed in his head.

He closed his eyes, told his body to calm down. "Thanksgiving. My mom wants you and your brother and sister to come over."

"Really?"

"Yeah. I was talking to her this afternoon. I told her I thought it might be too soon to ask, but now I'm not so sure. As first dates go, I think this one is working out pretty well. Besides, you know half my family at this point, and I know yours."

"Part of the reason this isn't a typical first date."

He liked her smile. The one she wore now . . . the one that wasn't forced or fake. The one that reached her eyes.

"Can I think about it? I'd have to ask Austin and Mallory."

"Yeah." He placed his napkin on the table. "You have two weeks."

Parker sat taller, pushed the dessert toward him. "I can't eat any more."

He picked up his spoon and finished the last bite.

Ten minutes later they were walking down the Strip and Colin slipped her hand in his as if to say, *This is where you hand belongs when you're with me.* The way she smiled at him said she got the message.

Phase two . . . he wanted to see what made Parker laugh.

~

Parker couldn't remember the last time she felt this good. She'd had two drinks during dinner, and that had certainly helped. The meal had been to die for. The view was perfect. Above and beyond all of that was the man she was with.

Colin kept ahold of her one way or another as they maneuvered through the Friday night crowd. It was as if he couldn't stop touching her, and she ate it up. There was an awareness of him like this that she didn't feel when they were in her yard talking about dirt and trucks. This was all man and woman and pheromones. Maybe she needed to change her major to chemistry when she went back to school. Colin was emitting something that made her want to curl into him and never leave.

They found their seats a few rows back from the small stage and ordered sparkling water. Colin told her to feel free to order another drink, but he was driving and had his limit.

"I hope this is okay."

She glanced around the compact audience and took in the people. Most were in their age group, many were already several glasses into whatever they were drinking. There were a couple of groups of women, but most looked like they were with a date or with a significant other. "I haven't been out this late in a long time," she confessed.

"It's not even nine thirty."

"I know. Sad, isn't it?"

He leaned over, laced his fingers with hers. "Hopefully this is good enough to keep you awake."

Him touching her was enough to keep her eyes open.

The show went for an hour and a half. The first two acts had her and Colin both in stitches. One was a woman talking about her experience in a sex shop, and the second was an older man talking about the difference between teenagers now and teenagers thirty years ago.

Act three was when the happy tears started flowing down Parker's cheeks.

The comedian started talking about first dates and then asked if there was anyone in the audience on one. Parker squeezed Colin's hand and shook her head.

Too late. The heavyset comedian caught her denial and zeroed in. On the other side of the room was another couple that had pointed out they were out for the first time, too.

The comedian talked about how the man picking up the bill on the first date was all about his desire to get laid. When Colin shook his head, the man onstage jumped on him, making him the butt of the joke. "C'mon, man, look how you two are holding hands. You totally picked up the bill. Unlike Fred and Ethel over here . . ." He pointed to the other couple. "He made you pay for your ticket coming in here, didn't he?"

Parker couldn't see the other couple's response, but some in the audience did and laughter erupted. For fifteen minutes Parker and Colin found themselves referred to during the whole act with half the audience staring at them. When the show was over and the lights came on, a few sideways glances connected their way.

"I had no idea that was going to happen," Colin said once they were back in his car and headed home.

"It was hysterical. I haven't laughed that hard in forever."

They talked all the way home, and it wasn't until they reached her gate that Parker considered how their date would end.

He parked the car and held his hand up, asking her to wait when she moved to get out.

She felt silly waiting for him to round the car to open the door for her.

The air was cool, and the sweater she wore wasn't doing a good job of keeping her warm. They walked up the steps together and she fished in her purse for the keys. "I had a really good time," she told him. The comedian's synopsis of how first dates end sounded in her head, and she found herself saying them out loud to calm her nerves. "So how should we end this? Is it a kiss? An invitation inside? Breakfast in the morning?"

He knew she was joking, she saw it in his eyes.

Instead of answering, he stepped closer, brought the palm of his hand to her cheek.

She held her breath and the smile she'd worn all night slid, replacing it was a measurable tension that poets try to articulate and singers hum to. TDH was going to kiss her. Those lips parted and she leaned in just enough for him to know she wanted to sample him as much as he appeared to want a taste of her.

"It ends like this," he whispered before lowering his lips to hers. He was warm and soft and oh so very smooth. Parker closed her eyes and stepped into his arms and let herself feel. She'd missed this . . . arms circling her back and the first taste of a man. One swipe of his tongue against hers and she knew what else her life was missing. He held her like he needed her, and made anything cold inside of her melt.

Like everything she'd seen from this man, he executed a good-night kiss as if he were born to it. Parker leaned in and felt his breathing shudder. She placed a hand over his chest, felt her fingers curl like her toes were doing. All her girl parts stood at attention and waved frantically while cursing her for being left dormant for so long.

Colin kissed her like he had nothing better to do, and ended with a tiny bite of her lower lip.

Parker licked her lips before opening her eyes. "That was, uhm . . ."

"Yeah, it sure was." His hand lingered on her face.

"I'm changing your nickname." She finally looked in his eyes, saw the passion swimming inside of her looking back.

"Oh?"

"TDY. Tall, dark, and yummy."

"I'll change the T-shirt order."

She lifted her chin again. "Just a little more."

He kissed her again, this time his hand swept around her waist and pulled her flush to him from knees to lips. Open mouth and hungry, she kissed him back.

Tall, dark, and holy shit, this was getting really hot, really fast.

Colin pulled back, rested his forehead to hers, and caught his breath. "So did I pass for a second date?" he managed to ask.

Her whole body shook with quiet laughter. "I hope so, otherwise it would make the next few months incredibly awkward."

She heard Scout jump up on the window from the inside to look out.

"That is the equivalent of someone flicking on and off the porch light," Colin said, giving her some space.

Her fingers shook as she attempted to twist the key in the lock. When it clicked, she sighed. "Thank you again." She turned back to look at him.

All confidence and grins, Colin rocked on his heels, tucked one hand in his front pocket as if he didn't trust himself not to touch her again. "Good night, Parker."

"'Night, Colin." She slid behind the door and closed it once he was halfway down the stairs. From the window, she watched the taillights of the Jeep moving down the drive. When the gate opened, the house system told her he was gone.

She fisted both hands, pumped them in the air, and did a little dance.

CHAPTER SIXTEEN

Parker knocked on Austin's bedroom door. "Family meeting in fifteen minutes."

She moved on to Mallory's door now that she was home. "Fifteen minutes."

Austin poked his head out of his room. "What's going on?"

She marched by. "Finish up the game or put it on hold."

"Just tell me."

She waved a hand in the air and ignored him. He'd stay in his room and play video games until two on a Sunday if left on his own.

Fifteen minutes later Austin flopped on the sofa, clearly irritated that he was called away from his fun.

"What's this all about?" Mallory did some flopping of her own.

Parker sat cross-legged on the oversize ottoman in the middle of the sectional that dominated their den. "I wanted to talk about some of the things Mrs. Hudson and I discussed."

"You already said you weren't looking for another job until spring."

"We talked about more than that, Austin. We talked about long-term with the house."

That got their attention.

"Okay . . . what about it?"

"She brought up what we kinda already knew about the condition and the optics of selling since the fire."

"You said we were going to wait a year," Austin said.

"I think we're going to need more than a year. The county has a five-year agreement to come in and empty the basins once they're filled whenever it's needed during that time."

"You wanna wait five years to sell?"

Parker shrugged. "It's not only my decision. The trust clearly states that unless things weren't financially sound, we were to keep the house until Austin is out of high school. Then at that point if we decided to sell, both your shares go into a trust until you're twenty-two. We knew Mom and Dad's money would peter out by next year at this time, so it made sense to consider selling."

"What's changed?" Mallory asked.

"Other than the fire dropped the value of the house by fifteen percent, nothing."

"That's a lot."

"I'm not getting any money for five years, so the answer is easy. Keep the house until then," Austin said.

"Sure, Austin . . . but the money to pay for it is going to be gone in a year, am I right?" Mallory asked.

"It's a little longer than that, but yeah."

"We're screwed either way." Scout jumped up on the couch and laid his head in Austin's lap.

"Maybe not. But it's time we start working together to keep things going. I can't do it all." Like she had been for two years.

"You want us to start paying our own bills, split the household expenses?" Mallory's voice pitched.

Parker saw the worry on her sister's face. "It's the social security money that has kept us floating. In July, that's gone. I suggest we divide that cost up and each month put it in the account to keep the bills paid."

"Are you telling me I have to get a job?" Austin's question sounded like an accusation.

"I'm saying we can't keep pulling money out of the general pot for the fun things in life like extra gas for unnecessary trips and In-N-Out burgers."

"That sucks."

"I had a job when I was your age," Parker told him.

"I bet Mom and Dad paid for your gas."

They did. Much as it pained her to say it, she did anyway. "They're not here."

Austin rolled his eyes and put on a great impression of a mistreated teen.

"Having Erin renting the guesthouse is a huge relief. And Tracy suggested we let the studios know about the house and property. They pay a premium for parking when they're filming on the street. We may be able to make some extra money doing that, Austin."

Mallory nodded. "What else can we do?"

Parker unfolded from where she sat and grabbed a notebook from the kitchen counter. She handed it over and sat back down. "That's been our grocery bill for the last six months. What we don't spend, we make."

"We need to eat." Yeah, Austin was butt hurt with the whole conversation.

"But we're all guilty of not cooking and grabbing what's easy. I'm not suggesting we completely change everything, but let's each take one meal a week and make dinner from scratch. Mrs. Hudson's pot roast lasted for two meals."

"I can't cook," Mallory whined.

"I don't think Hamburger Helper counts either, but we could all put in some effort. I pulled out Mom's recipe box. I'll do the shopping, you guys just tell me what you wanna cook each week. And since we're all working, we all have to chip in."

Austin handed the notebook to Mallory. "This all starts in July?"

"The bulk of it, yeah. I'm not saying you have to get a job until high school is over, Austin."

"I guess that's fair," Austin said.

Mallory stood, ruffled Austin's hair like she had when they were kids.

"Hey!"

"I can't believe you're almost eighteen."

"I'll take fourteen back with no bills any day."

They were all silent for a few seconds, all thinking the same thing. When Austin was fourteen, their parents were still alive. "I would, too, Austin," Parker told him.

The moisture in his eyes sparked hers to well up.

"Mom and Dad would want us to keep the house," Mallory said.

"Lots of things can change in a year. Maybe we can rent out one of the rooms downstairs. Set up some RV parking for a neighbor. I don't know. We'll figure it out."

Austin sighed, put both hands on his knees like he was going to leave.

"One more thing? Mrs. Hudson invited us over for Thanksgiving."

"One less meal we have to pay for." Her brother gave two thumbs-up.

Mallory was a little more real. "You've only had one date with Colin, you sure you want to go over to his parents' house for Thanksgiving?"

"Colin is awesome, and Mrs. Hudson can cook. What's to think about?" Austin jumped off the couch, Scout followed.

"You sure?" Mallory asked Parker again.

"I'm sure."

"Okay, but if you change your mind, our loyalty is with you."

Her sister's words warmed her heart.

"Speak for yourself. I need some testosterone in my life. A house full of chicks is getting old."

"Hey!" Parker chided.

"Kidding . . . I'm kidding. We done here? I wanna get back to my game."

She waved him off.

When he disappeared around the corner, Mallory muttered, "He's totally not kidding."

~

We are a go for Thanksgiving. Parker texted Colin later that day.

She watched her phone, waited to see if he was going to respond right away. Then remembered that he was watching the game with his dad. What game, she didn't know.

The Sunday *Times* was spread out in front of her, the coupon section in her hands. Never in her life had she cut a coupon.

Her phone pinged.

You've made my mom's day.

Parker sat back, phone in hand. Just your mom's?

Three dots flashed on her screen. My dad's too.

She was fairly sure he was teasing her, but she dug in a little more. Only your parents?

The rest of the family doesn't know yet. But I'm sure they'll be happy.

Was he really that clueless?

Okay. She texted and put her phone to the side, facedown. That voice of doubt whispered in her head. Doubt was a troublesome bitch.

Parker picked up her scissors and started cutting. Her phone buzzed, but she didn't turn it over to look at it. When it buzzed a second time, she dropped the coupons and pushed her chair back. She returned to her perch a minute later with a bottle of water in her hand.

Her phone rang the second she sat down. Colin's name flashed on her screen when she picked it up.

"Hello?"

"The person who is the most excited would be me."

And just like that, her doubts shattered. "I hope so."

"I was teasing. Didn't you get my last text?"

She waved the water bottle in her hand as if he could see it. "I walked away to get a water."

"Oh. So you weren't upset?"

A white lie sat on her lips. "Maybe a little. I told you I'm rusty."

"I'll be more careful, then." The sound of a TV in the background filled the silence.

"I don't want to interrupt. Go back to your game."

"It's football. There's a time out and five minutes of referees disagreeing with the coaches. What are you doing?"

"Cutting coupons."

"That sounds . . ."

"Boring," she finished for him. "But a new skill set I need to embrace."

"I'll leave you to it, then. Will I see you in the morning?"

Parker put the phone down, put him on speaker. "We have teacher conferences this week so I'll be in early and stay late to babysit the classrooms."

"More hours for you. That's good, right?"

"Yup." There were cereal coupons. That stuff was expensive. She started cutting.

"My plan is to be on-site early, but then I'm being pulled over to Sylmar. I won't be around as much as normal. If you need anything, call me. If it's immediate, Fabio will be on-site."

"I doubt I'll need anything."

The background noise of the TV faded. "Anything?"

"Anything that *Fabio* can offer." Her voice said she was teasing.

Was that a hum? "I dreamt about you last night."

"You did?" The coupons went back on the table.

"Oh, yeah. You were wearing a dress and on the back of a horse."

"No one wears dresses while riding horses anymore." She certainly never had.

"In my dream you did. Your skirt was hiked up on your knees. Very sexy."

Parker was all smiles and staring at her phone while they talked. "So that's it, I was on a horse in a skirt and you were turned on by my knees? That sounds like a historical romance novel." Something she hadn't read in years.

He laughed. "Except you were holding that shotgun and yelling at my men to hurry up. I was fascinated by the fact the horse in my dream didn't move . . . even when the trucks rolled by."

"Please tell me there wasn't a Porta Potty in your dream." She couldn't stop laughing.

"Can't say there was."

"Thank God for small favors."

"But that knee peeking out from the dress . . ."

"You've seen my knees."

"That was before I kissed you. Your knees have changed now."

It was nice to flirt and know the person on the other end of the line was just as into it as you were. "I promise you, they're exactly the same."

"Not for me."

Without thought, Parker rubbed one of the body parts in question. "Is that a thing for you?"

"Knees?"

"Yeah."

"No. You're a thing."

Okay, all the teasing earlier was completely wiped clean. "You're not being overheard right now, are you?"

"I stepped outside to talk to you."

"I don't want to pull you away from your fun."

"You're not. I walked away voluntarily."

Even that made her want to squeal. "You know what I mean. Go back and enjoy. You can call me tonight and flirt and we can talk about knees then."

"You sure?"

"Go. I have things to do and money to save."

"Okay."

"Oh, be sure and ask your mom what I can bring for Thanksgiving."

"She's going to say nothing," he told her.

"Ask her anyway, please."

"I'll call you tonight."

"I'll hold you to it."

CHAPTER SEVENTEEN

The week passed with a lot of texting and late night conversations, but it wasn't until Friday that Colin walked up to the house once the men were gone for the day.

"Can I convince you into happy hour?" He waved a six-pack of beer in one hand and a bottle of wine in the other.

"That looks like more than an hour."

He climbed the stairs up to the porch to stand beside her. "Here. Hold these." He handed her the beer and the wine. Once her hands were full he cradled her face in both of his hands and kissed her without warning.

"Oh . . ." It took serious concentration to not drop the liquor while he took full advantage of the fact her hands were full.

She'd thought about kissing him all week and secretly hoped he would have found an excuse to come up to the house so she could take a liberty of her own or two.

He pulled away and she stumbled toward him.

"I've been wanting to do that all week."

"You and I have very similar thoughts."

His fingers trailed down her arms and he transferred the beer and wine back to his hands.

He followed her inside where they uncorked the wine and poured a glass.

They settled outside on the porch to take advantage of the last rays of sunshine before it set behind the horizon and the air chilled.

"I should have planned something for this weekend with you," he told her.

"You told me last week you planned on helping your brother build a fence or something."

"Right. His shifts at the fire station don't always afford him the same days off as me."

She sipped her wine. "I understand. It's okay. Besides, Thanksgiving is Thursday. And Erin and I are going to do the *girls' night in* thing once she gets home."

Parker sat with one leg under her beside him on the loveseat.

"Yeah, but I hardly saw you all week."

"And a month ago you barely knew me."

"True. You were Annie Oakley on the ranch."

She did a double take. "Ha, I'm a what?"

He shifted to his side, placed his arm over hers on the back of the loveseat. "C'mon, that first day when you shouldered the shotgun and led me up the creek. I dubbed you Annie Oakley then, and I think it still stands."

"So that's where the dream of me on a horse wearing a dress stems from."

"You might be right about that." His gaze traveled to her lap, and his free hand touched her knee through the jeans she wore. "Still sexy."

Before they could elaborate on her knees, the front door opened and Austin walked out.

Colin's hand fell to the side.

"Hey," Austin said, lifting his chin.

"Where are you off to?" Parker asked.

"There's a car thing. A bunch of us are getting together. Figure I need to enjoy my freedom while I have it."

Parker rolled her eyes.

"What's that mean?" Colin asked.

"Austin got a job at the Christmas tree lot," she told him.

"Yeah, my buddy worked there last year, said he made like a thousand dollars in tips between Thanksgiving and Christmas. But that means I'm going to work after school and every weekend."

"Sounds like a good gig."

Austin shrugged. "Gotta start somewhere."

"Have fun tonight," Parker told him.

"See ya later, Colin." Austin started down the stairs.

"Remember. Make good choices and if there's any drinking—"

"Stay there or call you. Yeah, I know, Parker." Austin kept walking toward the car as he spoke. "Colin, tell my sister she's paranoid for nothing."

She yelled after him. "Teenagers drink. I'm not stupid."

"I'm not going to. And if I did, I'm not stupid enough to drive."

That made her smile. "Love you."

"Love you, too."

And he was in the car with the engine fired up.

"Does that happen every time he goes out with his friends?"

She nodded. "Yup . . . just about."

"Has he ever called you to pick him up?"

"No."

"Has he ever come home drunk?"

They both watched as Austin's car rolled down the drive. "No. He has stayed over at his friends', though."

"Can't ask for more than that."

"I know. He's a good kid. My parents would be proud of him and Mallory."

Colin gripped her arm until she looked at him. "Your parents would be especially proud of you."

"You didn't know my parents."

"I don't have to. Not too many twenty-four-year-olds would have given up their life to raise their siblings."

"More like watching out for them. They were both teenagers."

"You know what I mean."

"You saying you wouldn't have done it?" She could tell by his expression she was right. "The alternative would have been them going into foster care. I just did what had to be done. Kinda like when your tire goes flat. You have to fix it."

Colin frowned. "Did you just compare raising your brother and sister to fixing a flat?"

She found her hand playing with his. "I know it's more than that, but those are the kinds of things I would tell myself every step of the way. When people die, you need to bury them. When bills need to be paid, you need to get a job, write a check. When a kid needs to go to school, you drive them. When they need to learn to drive, you teach them. You can't stop to think about it or you go a little crazy."

Worry sat between his eyes. "So that's how you did it. One task at a time?"

She had to look away. "In the beginning it was one minute at a time, one hour, one day. Now here we are. I keep believing I can stop thinking like that, then this happens." She waved a hand at the charred landscape. She was depressing herself. "I'm sorry."

He reached over, lifted her chin so her eyes met his. "Please don't ever apologize for telling me how you feel. I can't read your mind, and can't begin to understand if you don't talk to me."

Most guys she'd tried to find a connection with over the years would run in the other direction after what she just said. "What planet are you from?"

He grinned. "Those early years were a blur, I'm not sure."

She laughed. "I have a lot going on, you sure you want to date me?"

"I'm seven years older than you, you sure you wanna date me?" he countered.

That made her smile. "Women mature faster than men."

She noticed Erin's car pull up in the drive.

Colin must have noticed, too. He stood and pulled her to her feet. "I'm going to leave you to your girls' night and dream about you when I go to bed."

She moved closer, enjoyed the feeling of his arms as they circled her back. "All of me, or just my knees?" She lifted her lips.

He bent close, spoke over them. "I haven't seen *all* of you."

"We could probably arrange that."

"One body part at a time." He kissed her and stopped her brain from functioning. For some women, it took a half a bottle of tequila to make them want to get out of their clothes. For Parker, it took less than a glass of wine.

The man was intoxicating, and the way he kissed gave her all kinds of hope for other talents he might have up his sleeve.

"Mmmm. I like the way you taste," he said.

She hummed and opened her eyes. "You're really good at that."

He wiped her bottom lip with his thumb. "And you're not as rusty as you think."

"Knock, knock . . ." Erin announced her arrival as she walked up the stairs. "Oh, sorry. I can come back."

Colin took a step away. "No, I was just leaving." He turned to Parker. "You guys have fun, and if Austin calls, and you need me to pick him up because the wine was good, call me."

Her jaw dropped. "You don't have to . . ."

"I want to. Call, okay?"

She had no words. "Okay."

He jogged down the steps and to his truck, waved before he got in and drove away.

"That looked awfully cozy," Erin said beside her.

Parker turned and bit her lip. "He is pushing all the right buttons."

Erin laughed. "I can tell by the smile on your face."

"And he's a good guy. The kind parents approve of."

Erin looked across the property and hummed. "There has to be something wrong with him."

Parker nudged her with her shoulder. "That's what I keep thinking."

"Well, when you figure it out, tell me."

She shivered. "Let's go inside. It's getting cold out here."

They had all the right ingredients for a girls' night. Chips and salsa, chocolate chip cookies, wine, and a salad just to say they ate dinner.

"It's been a really long time since I've been kissed, let alone had sex," Parker confided once she and Erin were working on their second glass of wine.

"I'm sure you'll remember how."

"My body is on autopilot when Colin's around." She tossed a chip in her mouth. "I like it."

"I like to think there are good ones out there." Erin nursed her wine while they talked. "Lord knows there's a lot of crappy ones."

Parker couldn't tell if Erin was trying to open up, so she asked a fun question. "Okay, worst date?"

"Mine?"

"Yeah. Who was your worst date?"

The question seemed to push Erin off-center. "I don't date a lot."

"But you have. So you have to have a bad date story."

She scooted around on the couch in thought. "Okay . . . It was high school, and my date had to bring his younger sister with us to winter formal."

"Why?"

"His parents insisted since her date canceled last minute."

"So what, you danced with the two of them all night?"

"We didn't dance at all. He was mad, got drunk with his friends, and I ended up walking home in heels." Erin sat her glass down. "What about your worst date story?"

"That's easy. First year of college, which I didn't start until I was twenty . . ."

Erin frowned.

"I know, I know . . . I was late to the game. Anyway, I was in San Diego where good surf days meant the classrooms were almost empty. I skipped class with a guy who was going to teach me what it felt like to live by the beach."

"That doesn't sound like a bad thing."

Parker snorted. "Have you ever tried to surf?"

"I barely swim."

"Really? Never mind. I can swim, but standing on a board in the ocean while the sea is trying to fold you in is no easy task. By the time we paddled out to where the waves were, I was exhausted. My date tried to give me a lesson while we were out there but I just didn't get it. Every time I tried to stand, I fell. Each time I fell, more parts of me hurt. Stan, that was the guy . . . He was so frustrated as he saw wave after wave go by without him, he finally gave up and started doing his own thing. Next thing I know, he's riding the tide in and I'm stuck out there floating on a piece of fiberglass and freezing my butt off. I got caught in a rip current that kept pulling me out while he stood on the beach waving his arms at me like an idiot."

Erin's eyes widened. "What did you do?"

"I paddled parallel to the shore for-freaking-ever and eventually managed to get to where I could touch the bottom, only to step on a stingray, which scared the shit out of me."

"Oh my God . . . It didn't sting you, did it?"

"No. But I jumped back on the board until a middle-aged, pot-bellied man walked out to me and showed me how to shuffle my feet in the sand to push the creatures away."

"That sounds awful."

"It was, and when Stan finally found me all he did was laugh. Such a jerk. Needless to say we never went out again."

Erin leaned back. "I'll take my bad dance to being stuck out in the ocean."

Sushi made a rare appearance and jumped up on the couch asking to be pet. "Do you have plans for Thanksgiving?" Parker asked, changing the subject. "I'm sure Colin's parents won't mind one more if you don't."

"No, no . . . I'm leaving town. I have plans."

Parker wasn't convinced. "You sure? I'm betting it's not a problem—"

"I'm sure."

"Okay. Maybe you can help me pick out a good bottle of wine to bring over."

Erin smiled. "That I can do."

CHAPTER EIGHTEEN

The Hudsons lived across town, which like anywhere in the valley meant you could get there in fifteen minutes or forty depending on traffic. Much as she liked to think that was an exaggeration, it wasn't.

Colin's Jeep was parked in his parents' driveway, telling her she undeniably had the right house. Beside it was a motorcycle. She pulled in behind the Jeep, pretty sure he wouldn't leave before she did. Austin held a bouquet of flowers in his lap. He insisted, and Parker wasn't about to tell him he didn't have to. She liked to think she mentored where her parents had left off with him. As much trouble as things were in the beginning, he seemed to be past it all now.

"If anyone feels uncomfortable, we make excuses and leave," Parker reminded them.

"All for one," Mallory said.

"One for all," Austin chimed in.

Noise from inside the house drifted out. The door was open and a screen separated them from inside.

Parker rang the bell, stood back.

Colin's family . . . the whole family.

Yeah, she was nervous.

"I got it."

Parker glanced at her siblings.

A petite woman walked around the corner. "Parker."

Parker had only met Colin's sister the one time, and her head hadn't been all that clear to remember much about the woman.

She opened the door and waved them in. "Come in."

"Hello. You're Grace, right?"

The woman was all smiles. "That's right. And this must be Mallory and Austin. I've heard a lot about you."

No handshakes, just a wave through the door and Grace yelling throughout the house. "Colin! Parker is here. C'mon in."

They walked through a foyer with what looked like an unoccupied formal living room to one side before emptying into the great room.

Colin met her with a dishtowel in his hands. "Sorry, I was helping." His smile seemed only for her. His eyes sparkled at the corner, and her heart reminded her it was in her chest and alert.

"It's okay."

Colin leaned down and kissed her briefly.

The room was filled with people. Several men. A couple of youngish adults. A boy close to Austin's age, maybe a little older. She couldn't tell.

Nora and another woman similar in age were buzzing around the kitchen. When Nora noticed them, she stopped what she was doing and wiped her hands on her apron. "You made it."

Colin took the wine from Parker's hands before his mother reached her.

She hugged her. "You look lovely." Nora moved on to Mallory with a hug.

Austin handed her the flowers. "Thanks for having us."

Was it right for Parker to swell with pride for her brother? Didn't matter, she was. "These are beautiful. Thank you, Austin." She took the flowers and placed an arm around his shoulders. "Emmitt, come here and meet Colin's girlfriend and her family."

With the title, Parker shot a look at Colin.

He rolled his eyes and added a silent laugh.

Grace leaned over. "Don't worry, she does that to anyone we bring over."

One date and two kisses didn't really qualify her as a girlfriend, yet it thrilled her to have the title.

Parker was introduced to Colin's father and brother and then moved on to an aunt, two uncles, and three cousins. As it turned out, one of Colin's cousins was only a year older than Austin, and the two of them started talking within minutes of arriving. It helped that there was a game on, and conversation circled around that while the finishing touches on dinner were happening.

Nora waved Mallory over and asked her if she had ever made deviled eggs. After a shake of the head, Nora went into teacher mode.

"White or red?" Grace asked.

"White is fine."

"So you're Parker," Emmitt said once Grace walked away to pour a drink.

"I am."

"She's pretty," he said over his shoulder to Colin.

"*She's* standing right there, Dad."

Parker laughed.

"Not like that redhead you brought over a couple years ago." Colin got his height from his father, but hadn't yet developed the belly. Emmitt leaned in as if no one else could hear him. "Her eyes were too far apart."

Parker looked at Colin. "Is that right?"

"Yeah. None of us liked her."

"You can say that again." This from Matt. "She had cats."

Emmitt narrowed his eyes. "You don't have cats, do you?"

"One," she confessed. "But he lives outside most of the time."

He winked. "Well, that's okay, then. What about dogs?"

"They have a black lab, Dad."

That seemed to do the trick. Emmitt was all smiles.

Grace arrived with the wine. "Enough with the twenty questions."

"I guess I should have warned you," Colin said.

"Maybe." The whole conversation was both overwhelming and strangely charming at the same time. More importantly, she felt completely at home with the Hudsons.

Mallory stepped up, a plate of deviled eggs in her hand. "Try one."

~

Colin wasn't sure what was going through Parker's mind, but her wide eyes and laughter put him at ease.

The smile that hadn't left her face since walking in the door did something to him he couldn't quite name. Even the conversation about his ex he let continue, and allowed himself to be the butt of the joke since it seemed to delight Parker to hear.

She and Grace hit it off.

Grace was only two years older than Parker, and it turned out that they had similar memories of crosstown rival games while in high school.

Still, Colin didn't mind taking the back seat for the day. He'd get his time.

When dinner was ready, the TV was put on pause and the game suspended until after the meal. Like many family tables, there was an adult table and a kid table. The youngest at the kid table was Austin, but it seemed he was finding something in common with Colin's youngest cousin. Mallory might have been flirting with Jase, his middle cousin, who had just celebrated his twenty-first birthday.

Colin sat beside Parker and inched his hand toward hers throughout the meal. Every once in a while he'd reach with his little finger and make contact, and she'd look up at him with a blush in her cheeks. It was a look he could get used to and wondered how long he could keep it there.

Once dinner was done, the kid table, and everyone at the kid table, had to help clean up.

The game was turned back on, but by now the tryptophan in the turkey had taken over, and the score was a sideways glance and not the main focus.

The back door to the patio was wide open and Southern California did what it did.

Years ago his father had installed mounted gas heaters that forced heat onto the patio and made the space comfortable for all but a few months out of the year. Most of the time, Mother Nature took care of it for them.

"It's a rare holiday that we have Matt with us and we're not taking food to him," Nora told Parker at one point.

"I get Thanksgiving or Christmas off, but not usually both," he told her.

"Last year you worked both," Grace reminded him.

"Paying my dues." Matt stretched out, his long legs ate up space between him and the rest of the group scattered around the outdoor living space. "Eventually I'll have a family of my own and want to see my kids on Christmas morning."

Nora spoke up. "And when is that gonna happen? I'm not getting any younger."

Matt did what any younger brother would do and pointed at Colin. "Talk to the oldest."

The statement would have been met with conflict if not for the fact that Parker was sitting right next to him.

Luckily, Grace kicked in. "There's nothing that says Colin needs to procreate first."

"Great! You have the uterus . . . you're up!"

And then his aunt asked, "So how are things with Robert?"

Both his mother and father moaned.

Colin pulled Parker away an hour later when his mom and sister went into the kitchen to start the next round of food featuring every form of sugar possible. "My family is more open than Denny's on Christmas."

"They're delightful."

"Even the part about Matt's ex that burped like a trucker?"

She skipped a beat.

"See, TMI."

"They're not bad. You don't even have a family drunk."

"That was Grandpa Larry. He's been gone five years now."

Some of the smile slipped from Parker's lips. "This is the third holiday season without our parents. The first one we didn't bother to celebrate."

"Not even Christmas?"

She shook her head.

He couldn't imagine life without his family. Just the passing thought made his gut ache.

"Last year sucked, but it wasn't as bad. It helped that Austin had straightened out."

"What happened with Austin?"

"Do you have an hour?" she asked with a grin.

"You have as long as it takes."

"He struggled the most. He skipped school more than he went. Mouthed off to his teachers. Started hanging out with the wrong crowd. His grades were so bad he was almost held back, and the court threatened to put him in foster care."

Colin glanced back toward the house. "I had no idea."

"I came home early one day and found him with a friend smoking pot in the garage. I snapped."

He knew lots of kids who did that when he was in high school. "What did you do?"

"Called the other kid's parents and waited until one of them came to drive him home. He was older, had his own car. His parents were never around and spoiled their kid. They seemed annoyed that I involved them."

"That's messed up."

"The thing is, I wasn't pissed that he was smoking pot. I was ticked that he was skipping school and hiding it. I'm the older sister, not the parent. At least that's what I kept telling him. I kept with the *let's all work together and make this happen*, and all that did was take even more away from him. It was a court counselor we were mandated to see who told me that if I wanted my brother to be shipped off to foster care, or worse, end up in juvenile hall, then I should continue to be a big sister instead of his guardian. He needed rules and boundaries. I took away his cell phone and dropped him off and picked him up every day from school. I spoke with each of his teachers and we made contracts for his work that I had to see and sign every Friday. He spent every Saturday available in Saturday school, and only once he was passing did I give him back his phone."

No wonder Parker seemed older than her years. "He's obviously earned your trust."

"Yeah. He changed. Gave up the new friends and found his old ones. I taught him how to drive and reminded him that if there were ever issues like before, I'd take the car without blinking. We'd lost our parents and it wasn't fair for us to lose each other."

Colin ran his hands up and down her arms. "I'm not sure what to say."

She lowered her eyes and shook her head. "Sorry. I don't mean to be a downer."

He placed a finger under her chin. "You're not. I'm glad you told me. It helps me see the sides of Parker I don't know yet."

They stood at the far end of the backyard and she started to shiver. The right thing to do was take her back inside the house, but he wasn't ready to share her again quite yet. "I'm glad you came."

"You and me both. It looks like Mallory and Austin even made some friends."

He looked toward the house. "Did you notice Mallory and Jase? Or more importantly, the way Jase was making eyes at your sister?"

"Yeah . . . I'm not sure what that's about."

"She just turned twenty and he's twenty-one. What's to figure out?"

Parker gave him a look way beyond her years.

"Oh, you're good at that."

"At what?"

"The mom look."

She did it again.

Colin laughed. "I'll talk to him. Make sure he knows to behave."

"Good." She shook her head. "I know Mallory has already gone there . . . but."

"She's your little sister."

"And more."

He figured that out, too.

She shivered and he ran both hands up her arms and pulled her close. "I don't know if I'm going to be able to do this before you leave without an audience."

Parker lifted her chin. "You pulled me out in the yard to make out?"

He wiggled his eyebrows. "That wasn't quite what I was thinking," he lied. "But if you insist."

"Never mind." Parker turned away.

Colin caught her and pulled her back.

"Okay fine."

He captured her playful smile on his lips, both of them smiling a little too hard to kiss properly.

She started to laugh. A belly laugh that made him laugh right along with her.

Still their lips stayed touching, even when she tried to talk. "This isn't working."

He pulled back half an inch. "Stop laughing and it will."

They both took a deep breath and came together again.

This time he started to chuckle, and the next thing he knew, her head was buried in his shoulder and her body shook with giggles.

Even laughing in her arms was worth the effort. "We're hopeless," she said after a full minute had lapsed.

"I'm not sure about that." He drew back just enough to see her eyes. "I like hearing you laugh."

"I'm out of practice. Maybe that's why I can't control it."

He placed a hand to the side of her face and waited for her to look at his lips. He didn't wait long.

This time, there was no laughing.

No, Parker slid in closer and he tilted her back to take a long, satisfying taste.

Her hand clenched his shirt, his semiaroused state bucked against his sanity.

Only Parker tilted her head just enough for their kiss to settle in for the long haul. Her laughter was replaced with tiny hums and sounds of approval.

He could kiss her all day. The cold was no longer a factor.

The tip of her tongue played with his, and her arms slid around his back.

Everything south of Colin's beltline came to a full strut. Damn it, he wasn't wearing jeans. He had to stop.

Didn't want to stop, but he'd embarrass both of them if he didn't. "Parker . . . ," he whispered right as her teeth nibbled on his lower lip.

"Damn . . ." Never mind. Maybe just a little more. He let his hand drift to the small of her back; his fingers reached a little lower.

She moaned and slid her hand down his chest.

He caught it before she discovered just how ready he was for more than a stolen kiss in the garden. "We have to stop . . ."

Was she laughing again?

"Sorry."

"Bite your tongue," he said against her hair.

"I'd rather bite yours," she teased.

Her words made his cock jump.

When she tried to pull away, he held her steady with his hands on her hips. "No, no . . . I need a minute."

Parker tilted her head, looked down. "Oh."

"Yeah . . ." He tried not to think of the subtle woman in his arms.

"Shall we talk about Grandpa Larry again?"

The image his name created in his head definitely helped. "He was a happy drunk. Gave away all the family secrets when he had a new audience. Told terrible jokes."

"Like what?"

"I don't remember. Most of the time the punch line was off." Okay, blood was easing away from his groin.

She looked down again. "Is that helping?"

"Not with you looking at it," he scolded with a growl.

Yeah . . . her laughter wasn't helping either.

CHAPTER NINETEEN

The Santa Ana winds started blowing the day after Thanksgiving, making everything a complete and total mess. The swimming pool looked like a swamp. All the walkways and stairs leading up to the house carried a half an inch layer of ash and dirt. And the county crew's picnic area was subject to overturned tables, and the E-Z Up rolled through the property before getting caught in a pepper tree.

But that wasn't the part that worried Parker all that much. It was the shingles flying off the shed and guesthouse, and the massive limbs dropping from the damaged trees. Even the evergreen bottle trees that didn't take on any fire damage appeared to teeter under the force of the gusting winds.

Colin arrived at the house to take them on what was supposed to be a date to Ventura to enjoy the salt air of the Pacific. But there was no way she was leaving.

"Santa Ana winds go hand in hand with wildfires."

"I didn't see anything in the news about a fire." He looked up in the sky as if looking for smoke.

"It only takes a spark." She was sure she sounded paranoid, but didn't really care. "A fire could come from the other side," she told him. "I can't be gone if something started."

"You do know there is nothing left to burn and the wind isn't blowing in that direction."

Didn't matter. "The power could go out. One of the trees could go down in the driveway. I can't do it. Leaving isn't an option." Her hands shook with the memory of the hillside on fire.

Colin smiled understandingly, and tossed his car keys on the kitchen island. "Okay then, what can I do to help?"

He was dressed for a day out, not work. "You don't have to."

"I don't have to do a lot of things. But since I'm going to spend the day with you one way or the other, you might as well put me to work." He leaned down, touched his lips to hers, and stood back up. "Direct me."

"You sure?"

Parker wasn't positive he rolled his eyes . . . but yeah, he rolled his eyes.

"Okay, fine. Can you check how much gasoline we have for the generator? There are cans in the generator room and some down in the garage. I'm just not sure how many of them are empty. I'll go down to the pool and bungee cord the patio furniture together so it doesn't get tossed all over the yard."

They went in opposite directions. Unfortunately, she was one gust too late for the pool furniture. Three out of the six chairs were already in the water.

She'd lugged one of the chairs out of the pool by the time Colin found her.

"I'm going to the gas station to fill two cans."

The ash flying through the air made it hard to keep her eyes open. "Thank you."

"Leave this, I'll get it when I get back."

"I got it."

"Parker."

She smiled at him, waved him along. "Thanks for the gasoline."

It took less than half an hour to drag everything out of the pool and tie it all together to keep it from taking a second swim. She turned off the pool pump to save the thing from overheating when it went on. Her weekend workload just tripled. And since both Austin and Mallory were at their part-time jobs, she had only herself to depend on. She blinked with the thought. And maybe Colin.

Erin met her halfway up the steps to the house. "This is crazy."

"Welcome to my life. Come inside."

Scout met them at the door.

"Where is everyone?" Erin asked.

"Work. Colin went to fill the gas cans for the generator. We lose power a lot when it's this bad," she explained. "You should take the guest room if that happens."

"I'll be okay."

"I insist. The noise alone in that place with the wind this crazy will even scare Freddy Krueger. It gets cold in the guesthouse without power to run the heater this time of year." The main house had three fireplaces and a generator if needed. The guesthouse didn't.

The wind rattled the windows as if it were emphasizing her point. "Besides, I'm not a superfan of being alone when it's like this." Even though the fire hadn't hit when the wind was this bad, thank God, the reality was, it could. Even a house fire in these conditions could spread into a neighborhood disaster. She realized her fears may be edging on PTSD, but Parker didn't care. The wind was not her friend.

"You'll have Colin here."

"Then he can keep us both safe. Please. I wouldn't be okay with you down there, in the cold, dark, wind-ravished space."

Erin was grinning. "Fine. I'll go grab my laptop and try and get some work done while we still have the internet."

"Solid plan."

Erin disappeared back down to the guesthouse and Parker pulled out the Crock-Pot, a pork roast that had been on sale that week, and followed a five-ingredient recipe Nora had given her. She was putting the lid on when Colin knocked on the front door.

"You don't have to knock," she told him.

Scout lifted his head long enough to see who it was and went back to his nap.

"I put the cans by the generator."

He walked over to the kitchen sink and washed his hands.

"I told Erin to come up and join us. I hope you don't mind."

"Of course not."

She paused in the middle of the kitchen and looked up at the ceiling. "I didn't hear the gate."

He grabbed a towel and dried his hands. "When I came in?"

"Yeah. Did it open like normal?"

"I didn't notice any problem."

One more thing to look into once the wind stopped.

Erin rapped on the front door. When Parker pulled it open, she gave her the same line she'd given to Colin. "Just come in."

Once they were both in the kitchen chatting, Parker went over to the refrigerator. "I have a roast cooking for dinner, but who wants lunch?"

Before long, she and Erin had tossed a salad and made turkey sandwiches with the leftovers Nora had sent home with Parker.

Colin turned on some music, and it was like a post-Thanksgiving party without pie.

They were finishing their lunch, not quite as stuffed as the day before. "So what are we going to do while we're waiting for the sky to fall?" Colin asked.

"I should probably get some work done," Erin told them.

"That sounds boring," Parker teased. "How about a board game?"

Erin shrugged and Colin pointed at a couple of boxes of Christmas decorations that Mallory had pulled down the day before. "What are those?" he asked.

"Two of the million boxes of decorations we have for the house."

"A million, huh?" he asked.

"My parents loved the holidays."

He pushed back from the table. "A million boxes must require some serious effort to put up."

"You want to help me decorate the house?"

Colin smiled at her. "I suck at Monopoly."

Next thing Parker knew, Colin was schlepping decorations from the garage up into the house, and the place became a holiday explosion.

Parker pointed where the decorations went while the three of them transformed the house for the season.

At one point, once the garland was up on the walls and white lights were adding that extra spark, Parker felt her throat thicken with emotion. Memories of her parents working together to make the house festive surfaced.

Colin came beside her and placed an arm over her shoulders. "You okay?"

"It looks beautiful. My parents would approve."

He kissed the top of her head. "It has to be hard without them."

"This is the third Christmas without them. The first we didn't bother with anything. Last year we put up a few decorations and forced ourselves to celebrate at least a little."

"I'm sure your parents would want you to move forward."

She leaned into Colin's side. "They would."

Erin called out from the living room. "Why are we not listening to Christmas carols?"

Parker smiled. "Good suggestion."

Hours later, when the sun was setting, the winds picked up as they often did at dusk. Deep into the twelve days of Christmas, with all of them singing in their own key, the power blipped once before completely cutting out.

"Oh, man!"

Colin moved to the window, looked out.

"Let's give it a few minutes, see if it pops back on," Parker suggested.

"I'll open the wine," Erin said.

Dinner still had another hour, and since the house ran completely on electricity and not gas, they would have to run the generator if they wanted to eat.

"That's pretty handy," Erin told her when Colin went outside twenty minutes later to fire up the generator.

"So is he," Parker said before Colin returned. "It could be really easy to start depending on him."

Erin huffed. "Be careful with that."

"Depending on him?"

"Yeah—"

Colin walking back in with his cell phone in his hand interrupted Erin. "Looks like a transformer blew. They're estimating six hours before the power is back on."

"Good thing you filled the gas cans."

Colin went over to the stereo and turned their entertainment back on.

Parker grabbed the master key ring to the house, the one that held every key for every lock on the property and headed for the front door.

"Where are you going?" Erin asked.

"I have to turn off power to the gate and open it. All these blips screw it up. I don't want it shutting on Mallory or Austin's cars when they come in."

Colin opened his palm. "Give those to me."

"I can . . ."

"And take my man card? I don't think so. Pour yourselves some wine and talk about me when I'm gone."

She smiled and lifted her lips to his.

He winked after he kissed her, and called the dog. "C'mon, Scout. Keep me company."

After he walked out the door, Erin turned to her and said, "I didn't know men like that existed."

"Me either."

~

Austin and Mallory both walked in the door after nine, ate dinner, and went to bed.

Erin excused herself to the guest room, and Colin finally found some alone time with Parker.

"Alone at last."

They curled up on the couch, full from dinner and warm from the wine. The generator still ran, the noise hummed behind the music.

Parker tapped her fingers on his thigh. "What should we do?" she asked, a lift in her voice. ·

"Spin the bottle or three minutes in the closet are my best games."

"You need more than two people to play spin the bottle."

Colin stopped her hand and brought it to his lips. "Three minutes in the closet it is."

She leaned her head back on his arms and he took the offering of her lips.

Kissing her was becoming an addiction he was fast learning he couldn't do without. They started out lazy . . . a slow languishing of lips and tongues until he felt Parker's hand land just shy of his groin while she repositioned herself.

Colin pulled her up against him and captured her sexy little hand before she could move it away.

"You're bad."

He nodded. "You found my fault."

He pressed her hand dangerously close to his erection and watched her eyes widen.

"Colin, I . . ." She looked away, her palm squeezed his hip. "I've never done anything in this house. With a man . . ."

It took a second for her words to catch up to his brain. "What about a woman?" he teased to try and ease what he felt were her nerves speaking for her.

His goal was achieved with her laughter. "It's just that, Austin and Mallory are in the other room, Erin . . ."

"You don't have to explain, Parker. I understand."

Her eyes narrowed. "I took over my parents' bedroom, so that just feels weird."

He placed a finger over her lips. Sure, he was disappointed, but he completely understood. "Shhh. Let's just make out on the couch," he said before kissing her again.

Parker pulled away, smiled. And the fist next to his goods relaxed and grazed his cock. "Maybe some heavy petting?" she asked.

He pulled her higher on his lap, kept one palm firmly on the cheek of her ass. "Until one of us cries uncle."

The sweetest torture of his life commenced and ended with an awkward walk to his car an hour later. He placed the cold water bottle she'd given him for the drive home between his legs to calm his hormones and pulled out of her driveway.

He drove through the neighborhood, where not even the streetlights shined.

It was dark and unsettling. In neighborhoods where the houses were closer together, power outages didn't feel so empty. But out here in the middle space between big cities and rural countryside, it was like a dark vastness of quiet. It was then Colin understood Parker's father's desire for fences and gates, shotguns, and "No Trespassing" signs. It wasn't that he felt threatened, but he didn't want some opportunistic criminal to see a dark house at the end of the road and take advantage.

It was also at that point he was happy that his little Annie Oakley could be a serious ballbuster when she wanted to be.

But he still worried.

~

The problem with the big box stores is you go in to get one thing, leave with twenty . . . and forget the one thing you went in for. But Parker was learning to buy in bulk.

She was on her third trip up the stairs with armloads of groceries when Erin poked her head into the garage. "Want some help?"

"Absolutely."

"So how is the world of editing?" Parker asked while pivoting around the kitchen putting groceries away.

"Strangely satisfying. I'm reading more books than I have in years."

"I don't remember the last time I read for pleasure. It's always school or how-to manuals on fixing something here." She shuffled through the produce, putting it away and tossing stuff that was growing the wrong shade of green.

"I have some great recommendations once your time frees up."

She peeked around the open door of the refrigerator to look at her. "Like that is ever going to happen." They'd spent three days power washing patios, furniture, and swimming pools.

Scout let out a bark while staring out the sliding glass door.

Parker stopped what she was doing to investigate. Her eye traveled to the far end of the property. The last of the heavy-machine drivers was climbing on the back of his loader. The men who worked directly for the county had all left. It wasn't uncommon for the subcontracted men to stay behind to oil their rigs and repair any issues before they left for the day. "What's got you excited?" She reached down to pet the dog.

He barked again.

One of the large oak trees at the bottom of the driveway cut off her view from a large section of the property, the part that once corralled the horses when they had them. After the fire, there wasn't anything left of the fences to contain anything. Parker opened the door and Scout darted out.

"Hey!"

He ignored her and ran off.

"What is it?" Erin asked.

Parker walked to the far end of the patio and spotted a small convertible parked in the center of the field away from where the construction workers parked. Then she saw another dog running around.

What she didn't see was the person who drove the car in.

It wasn't completely uncommon for one of the office engineers to make an appearance, but most of the time they came with one of Colin's people in the middle of the workday. Not after everyone else had left for the day.

"I don't know," Parker told her. "I'll go find out."

She trekked down the stairs and driveway and cut across the yard. The closer she got to the car, she was able to make it out. A Mercedes. Not the kind of car anyone had driven in before.

Scout had run up on the hill outside of the chain-link fenced portion of the property. The gates had been open since construction had started. No need to shut them when no one other than her family and Colin's workforce walked up there.

Scout and another dog were dancing around each other, playing. At the top of the hill stood a man she didn't recognize. She made it halfway up before the man turned, smiled, and waved.

"Hello," she greeted who she assumed was a county employee.

He peered over the work in progress, hands on his hips. "This is some project."

That sounded odd.

"Yeah, it is."

"Looks like they're expecting some serious flooding."

Okay, not an employee. Parker's guard went up.

"They're not taking any chances."

The dogs started barking, and it looked like Scout was getting a little too friendly with his companion.

"That your dog?" the man asked.

"Yeah."

"Is he fixed? Cuz I breed mine. I wouldn't want any mutts."

Parker's jaw dropped. "I'm sorry, who are you?"

"Oh, I'm one of your neighbors, Bill . . . I live down the street. I thought I'd drive up here and take a look."

Her heart rate started to pick up speed. "Did you miss the 'No Trespassing' signs . . . all five of them?"

The blank look on his face suggested he didn't get it. "I wanted to see what the big deal was."

By now Scout had jumped on the back of Bill's dog that kept trying to sit down to avoid being violated.

"Let me get this right. You drove past the 'No Trespassing' signs, pulled your car in the middle of my yard, parked . . . let your dog out, and walked around like you had the right. Did I get that straight?" Her hands shook with anger. Where was her shotgun when she needed it?

He had the nerve to look offended. "I'm your neighbor."

"What's my name?" she yelled the question at him.

"Sinclair, I think."

She pointed down the drive. "Get the hell off my property."

"Excuse me?"

"Now!"

"I didn't mean to upset you."

"Too late."

The man finally got the hint and started to walk back to his car. He called his dog, who shook off Scout and trotted with her owner.

He slid behind the wheel and started his car while glaring.

"Don't come up here again."

No apology left Bill's lips.

For good measure, Parker placed a hand on Scout's head. "By the way, my dog isn't fixed." A complete and total lie, but the horror on the man's face was worth it.

She waited until his car left the property before marching back up to the house.

Erin met her at the door. "What was that all about?"

Anger fueled her as she walked into her bedroom and dropped to her hands and knees. "Son of a bitch thought he could just come in here. Brings his dog and has the fucking nerve to ask if my dog is fixed? Who the hell?" She grabbed the shotgun under her bed, checked to make sure it was loaded. It was, she knew, but the habit was there.

Erin's eyes widened as Parker stormed past her.

"What are you doing?"

"Closing the gate and daring that ass to come back."

Livid wasn't a strong enough word.

Scout found her energy addictive and ran around her as she burned some of her anger with a stroll to the gate. The last worker of the day called out to her as she passed him. "Everything okay, Parker?"

She walked past the gate to the keypad, punched in the code to shut the gate, and walked back in while it closed behind her.

She'd calmed enough not to center her anger on the guy hanging off the loader. "Let's keep the gate closed once the trucks stop rolling, okay?"

"Did you know that guy?"

"No." She waved the gun. "He couldn't read the 'No Trespassing' signs. I hope he reads twelve gauge."

"I'll let the guys know," he told her.

"Thanks."

"Sorry. I thought he was a friend or something."

"I wouldn't expect you to think otherwise. Fancy car and a dog. Asshole." She called Scout. "The gate will open when you drive up to it," she reminded him.

"Okay. Really sorry. I would have yelled at the guy for you."

She smiled. "I'm pretty good at yelling. But thanks."

By the time she made it inside the house, her adrenaline was back to normal. She rested her gun beside the door and went to the sink to wash her hands.

Erin stood there staring at her. "That was . . . you're . . . I don't know what to say."

"Nothing pisses me off more than when someone feels entitled to invade our space because they exist."

"That was something else. I can't believe you marched out there with a gun."

"I should have done that to start with. My mistake." *Won't happen again.* "I thought it was someone with the county."

"You're a little badass."

She shook her head. "No, just pissed." Parker placed both hands on the side of the sink and sighed.

Erin glanced at the gun leaning against the wall. "I've never shot a gun."

"Really?"

"Never. Maybe you can show me."

"I'd love to. Maybe when things calm down."

"I'd like that."

CHAPTER TWENTY

Colin ducked into Ed's office midweek for their weekly update on the projects he was in charge of.

"Where are we at?" his boss asked.

"We're finishing up the Creek Canyon project next week."

"Right on schedule, then."

Colin sat across the desk from Ed, leaned back in the chair. "I'm not convinced the structures are going to hold."

"We had a whole team engineer the hell out of them."

"Did that team walk up the canyon and see what's lying in wait for a little moisture?"

Ed propped his feet up on his desk, never really happy when someone questioned his work. "You know the answer to that."

"Well, I have, and I gotta tell you, the amount of material teetering on the sides of those hills is impressive." And not in a good way.

"We took into account the last time that area burned. The structures will hold. Especially given the amount of rain we've been averaging the last seven years."

"The reports are showing rain in two weeks."

"And in one week that rain will turn into partly cloudy skies with a high of sixty-three." He dropped his feet to the floor. "How is the mouth of the river looking?"

"We've done what we can." They talked about the other projects Colin was in charge of. "A lot of the guys are taking time for the holiday. Let's hope there isn't any rain until after the first."

They finished up the weekly report and Colin made his way out. "Before you go . . . rumor has it you have a thing going with the homeowner."

"Circulating the water cooler buzz, Ed?" His private life was just that.

Ed tapped a pencil on his desk. "I find it convenient that Miss Sinclair had her lawyer draw up several contingencies mandating that the county pay for what Mother Nature delivers over the next five years."

The hair on Colin's arms prickled. "What are you suggesting?"

"I'm not suggesting anything. I'm saying for a woman so young and without any experience, she certainly knew what to ask for." Ed narrowed his eyes. "You wouldn't happen to know where she obtained her education in flood management, would you?"

Colin tried not to let his building frustration show. "Parker is highly intelligent, especially in regards to what happens on her property. I can't take credit, or blame, for what she had her lawyers draw up."

"I didn't say you could."

Colin's lips were a thin line. "No. You implied."

Ed tossed the pencil in his hand on the desk and sat forward in his chair. "Be careful, Hudson. We don't need any misconduct accusations or false promises haunting this department."

"Understood."

Colin pulled onto Parker's property with Ed's words chirping in his head. It was obvious Ed had a steady eye on everything Colin was doing . . . and assuming a hell of a lot. The fact he was underestimating Parker was a testament to the fact he didn't know the woman. She controlled her world with a tight fist.

As for the misconduct concerns, Colin supposed if it was any one of his men in the same situation he might have the same conversation, so it shouldn't have come as a surprise that his boss had it with him.

But this was Parker.

If there were going to be any misconduct accusations, it wouldn't be by her. She'd take care of anyone's transgressions head-on.

That fact was confirmed within thirty minutes of stepping out of his truck. Apparently Parker had run a trespassing neighbor off her property at gunpoint. At least that's how Colin heard it.

I hear you've been gunslinging. He sent a text to Parker, unsure if she was up at the house or at work.

When she didn't respond right away, he assumed she was at work and pocketed his phone.

Nearly an hour went by before she replied. Don't you have better things to do than talk about me at work?

Colin stood at the mouth of the canyon looking over the gaping hole his men had created to collect debris. Why didn't you tell me?

It just happened yesterday. I haven't seen you. I was going to talk to you about it on Saturday. Their dinner date over at his place.

When are you coming home?

He glanced at Parker's reply. Kids Christmas thing tonight at the school.

I'll call you later. He sent his text and pocketed his phone. He tried to shake off his irritation but realized he'd failed when the men on his crew went out of their way to avoid him.

~

Parker went straight from the school to the Christmas tree lot where she promised Austin she'd pick out a tree. Most years they picked up something cheap at Home Depot, but Austin insisted the trees at his lot were fresher, and his boss was going to give them a great deal.

Christmas music played through the speakers surrounding the lot, and kids ran in and out of the rows of trees playing tag and getting ramped up on the free candy canes being handed out at the entrance. She saw Austin right away and waved. He was talking with a couple and holding on to a tree while the woman walked around it.

Parker pulled in the fresh scent of pine through her nose and walked around. She hadn't so much as bought a single Christmas present. She'd baked cookies and set them out for the guys, but that was about it when it came to giving for the season.

When her phone rang and Colin's name came up, some of her seasonal blues lifted. "Hello."

"Hey."

She stopped walking. "Is everything okay?"

"Yeah." His voice said no. "Are you around? I wanted to stop by."

"I'm at the tree lot. Austin's going to help me pick out a tree. You don't sound okay."

"You're picking up a Christmas tree?"

Why did he sound surprised? "It's that time of year. Although these are not really in my budget."

"How are you getting the tree home?" He sounded miffed.

"On top of my car like everyone else. What's the matter, Colin?"

She heard his sigh through the phone. "I'm on my way."

"What? I can—"

"Don't leave. I'll be there in ten minutes."

He hung up.

She looked at her phone as if it had grown horns. What the hell was up with him?

Parker watched Austin from a distance as he helped the couple with the tree, took it over to the guy with the chain saw to give it a fresh cut, then shoved it through the net thingy that cost an extra buck. He then picked up the tree, and walked it out to the parking lot and out of sight. By the time he returned, Colin was at his side and he was tucking something in his pocket.

"Sorry that took so long," Austin said. "Women can't make up their minds."

Colin let out a short laugh.

"Hey!" She tapped his arm as if offended.

"Have you picked anything out?" Colin asked.

"No. I was waiting for Austin."

Colin looked at Austin as if she'd just confirmed her brother's words with her statement.

"He told me he knew where the freshest ones were." She returned Colin's glare. "Don't look at me like that."

Austin started walking away. "They're over here."

Colin placed a hand on her back as they walked through the lot.

Austin stopped and made a sweeping motion with his hand. "I put all these out today from this morning's shipment."

Parker ran a hand along one of the branches. "These are the Douglas firs. The expensive trees."

Austin shot a quick look at Colin, then back toward the booth where they collected the money. "I told you, I get a deep discount. I'll tell them to take it out of my check."

"Which is more than you make in a day," Parker argued.

"Just pick one out. I got ya covered. It won't cost me hardly anything. My boss loves me."

She tilted her head. "Austin. Don't lie to me."

"If he says he has it, he has it," Colin said.

Her brother stared at her. "I have it."

Parker let her shoulders relax. "All right."

Austin looked up, grinned. "I see new customers. Pick any one of these. I'll be back." He rubbed his hands together. "They look like big tippers."

She watched him walk away and glanced at the first tree on her right.

"You were really going to put a tree on the roof of your car?"

Parker wasn't sure it was an actual question. "That was the plan."

"Why didn't you ask me?"

She walked around the tree. The shape was right . . . not too fat, not too skinny. "Ask you what?"

"To help with the tree."

"And put it on the top of your new Jeep?" How was that different?

"My Jeep is four years old, but I have the truck."

"I thought you said it was a work truck." Not that she considered him using it to help with a Christmas tree.

"Parker?"

His tone made her stop examining the tree and look at him. "What?"

Two kids ran by . . . "You can call me. I want you to call me."

"I didn't think to." She turned back to the tree.

He stepped in front of her. "Well, think to."

His words shifted her thoughts from trees to the man. She was tired and more than a little overrun, but she just figured out what was going on. "You're mad at me."

Colin slapped his lips shut, took a deep, audible breath, and blew it out like he was taking down a hundred birthday candles. "Irritated. No, frustrated that you didn't think to ask for my help."

"I'm not used to asking for any help."

Before more could be said, Austin appeared at their side, ear-to-ear smile. "Did you pick one?"

Her eyes plastered on Colin, she pointed to the only tree she looked at. "This one."

Austin hesitated. "You sure?"

"Yeah."

"Isn't it a little bare on this side?"

"Fine, you pick."

Austin moved trees around at her side while she and Colin stared wordless at each other.

"What about this one?"

Parker stopped staring long enough to glance at the tree. "It's fine."

"You sure?"

She forced a smile. "Perfectly fine."

Good with that, Austin lifted it from the tiny water bowl and carried it to the front of the lot.

For the next ten minutes, Parker watched Austin as he trimmed and bagged their tree. All while glancing at Colin from the corner of her eyes. His frustration seemed to wane, and replacing it was something softer.

Austin introduced her to his boss, who then didn't charge her. She still wasn't completely comfortable with that. But she let it go and walked beside her brother and Colin as they carried the tree to the parking lot.

Austin tossed it in the back of the work truck. "I'll see you at home."

Parker hugged her brother. "Thanks."

She stood back while Colin and Austin shook hands. "I got it from here."

Austin waved them off and returned to the lot.

It took twenty minutes to make it home. Twenty minutes of Parker rolling over how she managed to frustrate Colin for not asking him for a favor. How was that even a thing?

Colin followed her through the gate and up the drive. She pulled into the garage and met him by the side of the truck when he stepped out. He didn't even make it around the back of the truck with the tailgate down before she flat-out asked, "Exactly what did I do again?"

"Never mind, just drop it."

"No."

"It's not important."

"Are you miffed or not?"

"Yes." He pulled the tree out of the back of the truck.

"Then it's important."

With one hand holding up the bound tree, and the other resting on the side of the truck, Colin had the nerve to look indignant with her. "You ran a man off your property with a shotgun yesterday and didn't tell me."

"That's not exactly how that happened."

He rolled his eyes. "Was there a guy on the property that didn't belong?"

"Yes, but—"

"Did you not storm the property and close the gate with a gun in your hand?"

"Yes, but—"

"I rest my case."

"He had already left! I was pissed and felt violated that he had the nerve to waltz in here uninvited, so I grabbed the shotgun on the off chance he could see me from down the street."

Parker noticed Colin's hand grip the side of his truck. "*Violated* is not a word I want to hear the next day. *Violated* is the kind of thing you call me for as soon as your cell phone will allow so I can be here."

He picked up the tree with what looked like angry energy and started up the stairs toward the front door.

She chased after him. "And do what?"

"Be the guy who makes assholes like him know you're not back here alone."

"I'm not here alone."

Colin put the tree down on the patio, wiped his hands on his jeans. "And where is everyone?"

"You know where Austin is, Mallory's at work. Erin might be home, I'm not sure."

"Alone. With an alarm system that isn't set and a dog that would just as soon lick you than bite." His words snapped at her, accusingly.

"You don't think I can take care of myself."

"I didn't say that."

"You didn't *not* say that."

"I know you're a self-reliant woman, Parker."

Her frustration was starting to reach his level. "You make that sound like it's a problem."

"No. It's not a . . . Can we go inside to have this argument?"

She was half tempted to tell him to give her the tree and go home. Instead, she opened the door and let him in.

"It's not locked?"

Apparently she couldn't do anything to please him tonight.

She walked in before him and pointed to the corner of the family room they had always put the tree. "That's where the tree goes. I'll grab the stand from the garage."

"Fine."

He was soooo not fine.

She dug in the back of the storage closet and found the stand. The sound of her own footsteps said Colin's irritation had transferred to her.

She climbed the stairs and put the stand where she wanted it.

Scout stood beside Colin, sniffing the tree and wagging his tail, oblivious of the tension in the room.

They went through the motions of putting the tree in the stand. Their conversation consisted of "A little more to the right" and "That's too much" before the tree was as vertical as it was going to get.

He removed a pocketknife and sliced away at the netting, and the tree sprang free.

"Thank you," she said . . . leaving out the part where she could have done that all by herself. Or waited until Austin came home to help her.

Colin walked over to the sink and washed his hands while Parker glared.

He held on to the counter as if he were searching for control. "I know you can take care of yourself."

"Good."

He lifted his chin and looked at her from over the island in the kitchen.

"I want you to know you can lean on me."

"Why?"

Colin blinked . . . twice. "What do you mean, why?"

"I mean, why? Why do you need me to lean on you?"

"So I can take some of the stress off your shoulders."

Parker let his words tumble around in her head. "Picking out a Christmas tree is not stressful. Depending on someone else to do it for you is."

"Damn it, Parker. Let me help around here."

She looked at him as if he were crazy. "You have helped around here. Inside my home and out."

"I want to do more." His voice was tight.

"And I'm used to doing it all alone."

He ran a hand through his hair. "Why are you fighting me on this?"

"I'm not fighting you on anything. You created this drama. As far as I see it, you're arguing with yourself. I just went about my day doing what I had to do." As she had every day since her parents died. She reached for the towel he'd tossed to the side to wipe some of the tree sap from her hands. "I have to tell you, if you're going to be ticked every time I do something for myself, this might not work out." As the words left her lips, her throat clenched in denial.

"Parker . . ." The anger in his voice mellowed and he reached for her hand.

She wasn't sure if she should pull away or apologize.

He turned her around, placed his hands on her hips, and lifted her onto the island. The movement was so swift, it took her by surprise. Then he caged her in, a hand on each side of her, and looked her straight in the eyes. "I was worried. Okay? Scared after the fact about the guy on the property. Upset I wasn't here to run him off myself. I left here the other night, after the power outage, and realized how isolated it is here, and if I'm honest, it scares the crap out of me."

The concern in his voice and look in his eyes pulled at her resolve to stay angry with him. "I've been back here all my life."

"I know that. But that was before I was in your life. Now that we're dating, I'm allowed to be concerned."

"I'm not used to someone caring enough to fight to help me."

He placed his forehead on hers. "I'm not used to someone fighting off my help."

"I guess we both have some room to grow."

He kissed her forehead with a nod.

She placed both hands on his arms, felt him trembling. "I know how you can help," she said, smiling.

"Anything."

She wrapped one of her legs around his and pulled him close, reaching for his lips.

The man was accommodating and open to suggestions. She sat on the kitchen island, legs spread while he stepped into them and kissed her senseless. It was as if the tension he'd kept inside of him released, and he pulled her hips flush with his, the contact ignited some serious heat between them.

His lips traveled to her neck and Parker's head fell back. "Oh, yeah."

"Let me be here for you," he said right before his teeth grazed her skin.

"Do that again."

He did, and her entire body heated with the need for more.

Parker dropped her hands down his chest and lifted the edges of his shirt as her fingertips grazed his skin. "This looks uncomfortable," she said as she pulled it up.

He lifted his arms and his shirt fell to the floor.

She ran her fingernails over the defined muscles of his shoulders and arms.

For a moment, Colin watched her exploring his body and held perfectly still. She leaned forward and teased one of his nipples with her teeth.

He groaned and pushed even closer.

Her hips bucked with the contact and searched for more friction. She wanted him inside of her, needed to know what it felt like to have him push all her control away until she screamed his name. If Colin wanted control, in this, she would happily give it to him.

She raked her fingers over his ass and he hissed her name. "Parker?"

Instead of answering, she leaned back far enough and started unbuttoning her shirt.

Thankful she had picked out a lace bra that morning with no intentions of anyone seeing it, she admired the clouded look in Colin's eyes as her shirt slid down her arms right before she brushed it to the floor next to his.

Colin's choppy breath and parted lips told her what she was doing to him. He placed his hands on her bare waist. "What are you saying?"

"Do I need to spell it out?" she teased.

"But we're here, your parents' home."

"And alone." She leaned close, felt her breasts press against his chest through her bra. "I don't want to wait." It was time to chase away the concerns of her parents and move on with her life.

His tongue ran across his lips. "You sure?"

Instead of answering, she wrapped her legs around his waist and lifted her arms to his neck. "My bedroom is that way." She nodded toward the door.

Colin wrapped one arm under her butt and the other around her waist and picked her up.

This was what she needed him for, at least at that moment.

He kicked the door closed behind him and set her on her feet beside her bed. This time his kiss was tender, accepting, and it went on until she needed to breathe. Colin turned her around and brushed her hair off one shoulder and kissed the back of her neck.

With eyes closed, her head rolled to the side. Colin's hand circled her waist and traveled across her flat stomach. When his fingers pushed into her bra and found the tight nubs of her breasts, her knees gave way.

His soft laugh in her ear said he was satisfied with her reaction to his touch.

"You're torturing me."

"That's the plan."

She lifted her arms over her head and leaned back against his chest, giving him all the surface in the world to torture and please. "Getting back at me for making you worry?"

He squeezed her breasts through her bra as he nibbled the side of her neck. "That would take hours." Hands traveled down her hips to the tops of her thighs with only a feathering touch against her sex.

Parker rocked against him, felt his erection through his clothing. Two could play at this game. She reached behind her, let her thumb trace the outline under his jeans. "Challenge accepted."

He chuckled, unbuttoned the snap of her jeans before dipping inside.

Sweet Jesus, his hand felt good against the folds of her sex. No matter how many times she'd done this to herself, there was no substitute for Colin's exploration and learning what she liked.

One minute they were playing a game of touchy-feely and the next he was pressing her back against the bed and sliding on top of her with his knee spreading her open. She captured his lips with open mouth kisses that left her panting and riding his leg for the joy of the friction it created. The tight bud of an orgasm started to build, her hips took on a life of their own, only she couldn't quite get there with so many clothes on.

"Don't stop now," he murmured.

"I need more."

He reached between them, cupped her sex through her pants.

"Yeah, that."

A tug of her zipper and his hand slid down her clothing and his fingers were sliding inside of her.

"God, yes."

Her head fell back as sensations danced around her in bright, shiny sparkles.

Colin's mouth found a nipple. He'd somehow discarded her bra without her noticing. Between his mouth and his hand, she was having a hard time controlling her body. He seemed content having her half-clothed as his fingers slid in and out of her, catching her clit and pressing hard, then soft.

She wanted to come, needed the orgasm more than taking her next breath. "Too many clothes," she moaned when her release was chased away a second time.

Colin took his hand away and slid off the bed. His hands gripped her pants and pulled them off, her panties gone with them.

She opened her eyes long enough to see him toss his wallet onto her nightstand before shedding his clothing to the floor. His erection jutted out, just as impressive as the man himself. Colin walked both hands up her thighs, pressed his thumbs over her clit. "Is this better?"

All she could do was nod and close her eyes.

"You're so beautiful," he told her. "All of you."

She arched into him as he leaned over and replaced his fingers with his mouth.

The intensity of the feeling was so instant she yelped and gripped his shoulders. Everything he promised with his fingers, he delivered with his tongue.

"You need me for this," he said before adding his teeth to his torture.

She placed a hand on the back of his head. "I will return the favor."

"Ladies first," he muttered before going back to the task at hand. Parker may not have had many lovers, but she knew what she liked, and Colin learned her desires in a few strokes of his tongue, teeth, and lips.

So much desire stormed over her, his relentless pursuit of her pleasure kept him at the exact spot she needed him while her orgasm built. Soft, hard, fast, slow . . . damn, he was good. He added a finger, then two, and turned up the heat until her orgasm bucked inside her and spilled out.

When she finally opened her eyes, Colin was staring at her from between her legs. Embarrassment slowly flooded in. Was she loud? Demanding?

No, Colin was smiling from his eyes.

"Now that I know what you sound like when you come, I'll always know if you fake it."

She chuckled. "I wouldn't know how to fake that hard of an orgasm."

He reached for his wallet, removed a condom. "Let me show you some more."

~

Colin wasn't sure what he loved the most . . . hearing Parker come, watching her come, or making her come. He couldn't get the condom on fast enough, and she was rolling him onto his back and straddling his hips. It took biting the inside of his lip until there was actual pain to keep from exploding the moment she opened her body and let him in. She'd been tight and hot, wet from her own release.

And if she was rusty, he'd found the oil needed to limber her up. They teased and fondled for some time before he caught his name on her lips with open mouth kisses. Her breath caught again, and he felt her body squeezing and milking his cock until he couldn't hold back any longer.

He held her until their breathing returned to normal. Colin snuck away long enough to get rid of the condom and returned to find that she'd tossed a blanket over her hips. There was a siren quality of her like that, breasts exposed, half of one leg . . . a satisfied smile on her face.

"That was incredible," she said after he'd taken his place beside her.

"It doesn't get better." Not in his memory at least. "But we can try. We're both overachievers."

Parker snuggled her head onto his shoulder and laid a lazy arm over his stomach. "I don't think I have it in me tonight."

"I could be talked into round two, but I don't want you sore."

"And I don't want my brother or sister to overhear anything."

He kissed the top of her head. "Then we'll save the next round for the weekend."

She tangled one of her legs with his. "At the risk of sounding like an insecure woman . . ." The pause was long enough for him to think she wasn't going to say whatever she was thinking.

"What?"

"Was it . . . I mean, were we . . ." She looked up at him. "It's been a while, for me. I've had sex before, but I don't think I've had anything like that."

There was nothing she could have said to make him happier. He pulled her up to him for a kiss, stopped with only that. "It was, and we are. That wasn't *just* sex, Parker."

She was slow to smile as his words sunk in. He wasn't ready to put labels and words to what they were doing, or the relationship they were embarking on, he didn't want her believing she was feeling those things alone.

"Okay . . ." She returned to the crook of his shoulder and sighed. Less than five minutes later, they both heard the house speakers announce that the gate was being opened.

Parker sprang out of bed. "Someone's home."

CHAPTER TWENTY-ONE

"That's it?"

"Yup. We're all done."

Parker, Colin, Fabio, and Scout stood on the high hillside on the north side of the project looking down. The first basin looked big enough for the foundation of a twenty-story high-rise. Boulders lined the south side at the mouth. The earth had been compacted and sloped where the water had no choice but to funnel by the slatted structure that was designed to hold back debris, but allow water to sift through. The second basin was much smaller, but still gave up a lot of space to fill with material. K-rails were then placed on the shallow north side just above the next structure, but then things got tight. They'd cleaned out a lot of overgrowth that managed to make it back from the fire, but the depth through the fenced portion of Parker's land hadn't changed . . . couldn't without undermining the concrete covered culverts that made up her driveway. The dip in the driveway was there to funnel water if the culverts filled with rocks and dirt. Which had happened at least twice that Parker remembered, which was why there was an elevated footbridge on the downside of the driveway so they could get past any flooding nature tossed their way.

"What happens now?" Parker asked.

"We're pulling out tomorrow."

She looked over at where the loaders and excavators were parked. "Are you leaving anything on the property during the winter?"

Fabio shook his head. "We'll bring them back if we need them."

Strange how she didn't really like the sound of that. "They're predicting rain by the end of the week."

"We'll keep an eye on it, Parker."

Colin had made good on keeping an eye on almost everything. Only now he wouldn't be there every day for work.

"No more trucks beeping as my alarm clock," she teased.

"Can you handle it?" Fabio asked.

She grinned, despite the trepidation she was feeling. "I'm sure there's a ringtone I can download from the app store if I miss it enough."

They both found that funny.

Slowly, they trekked down the hill and onto the field portion of the property.

"What about the toilet?"

"That's the last to go. We scheduled pickup on Friday."

"Good. I could go the rest of my life without seeing men emerge from that thing while they're zipping up their pants."

"Sorry," Colin apologized.

"Par for the course. I expected nothing less. But I won't cry when it leaves."

She walked them to their trucks. Some of the men were taking down their break station and loading picnic benches and tables into the backs of trucks.

"I won't be here tomorrow," Fabio told her. "I'll see you when we come back to clean out when these fill up."

Which she'd already been told was likely to be at the end of winter at the latest. Their optimism was just that. Parker was a realist. Fifty miles of burned-up forest being funneled into a neighborhood, even with the structures they built, was right up there with placing a Band-Aid on a hemorrhage. Maybe she was wrong.

Parker opened her arms to hug Fabio before he left. "Thanks for everything."

"Just doing my job."

No. None of them *just* did a job. They cared about what they were doing, and the people they were doing it for.

It showed.

He drove off, leaving her and Colin standing there. It was then that he placed a hand on her arm. Even though Colin's team knew they had something going, he didn't go out of his way to flaunt it when they were around. "You okay?"

"Nervous."

"Your house is going to be okay."

"I know."

"The guesthouse should be fine." It sat low on the property and had been surrounded by sandbags. The surviving shed as well. Colin had directed one of the guys behind the burned fence to shore up a path to give the runoff a place to go. All the normal ditches on the property had been etched as well as they could be.

"I can't afford to run off my renter."

"Anything that happens, we can fix."

She really hoped that was true.

Colin's phone rang and pulled his attention away. "I have to take this." Parker smiled. "Go to work. I have stuff to do."

He tucked a strand of hair behind her ear as he lifted his phone.

She blew him a kiss and walked away.

～

The first media van of the winter showed up as the last truck pulled off the property. Reporters searched for places to film weather stories in Southern California, and the best place was in narrow canyons scorched by summer wildfires. Parker had expected them. A woman about the size of a pencil stepped out of the van before the driver had a chance to pull inside the gate.

"Are you the homeowner?" She was all smiles and lipstick.

"Yes."

"Would you mind if we came in and talked to you?"

Parker thought about the neighbor down the street, and how others were probably keenly interested in what was going on. Maybe if the news broadcasted what the county was doing, for those who didn't go to the meeting in late summer to discuss it, her neighbors would heed the "No Trespassing" signs.

"Sure, come on in."

The van pulled in and lifted their antenna.

Parker stood back and took a photo of the news van and then texted it to her brother and sister. Guess we're going to be on the news.

She tucked her phone in her pocket and wondered what she looked like. She hadn't bothered with makeup that morning and put her hair in a ponytail. The fleece holiday print jacket was a step away from an ugly Christmas sweater, but it kept her warm.

Whatever . . . anyone who saw her on the news and knew her, understood she wasn't a slave to fashion.

The news lady introduced herself . . . Lisa something or other, Channel 2.

"My cameraman is making sure we have a solid uplink," she told Parker.

"Okay."

"So who did all the work here?"

Parker gave the woman a few details, which she wrote down. She took down the correct spelling of Parker's name and asked about the fire. The cameraman walked up with a decent size camera on his shoulder. He rotated them around until he had the backdrop he wanted and set up a tripod.

"Just look at me and not the camera when we're talking."

"Okay." She really should have put on makeup.

The cameraman told them he was ready anytime. Lisa, whatever her last name was, put the microphone to her lips and started asking questions.

Parker answered the questions as honestly as she could. When it came to safety, she made a statement about how the county had done what they could, but that her neighbors downstream needed to understand that it wasn't possible to tame Mother Nature. If they experienced any real rainfall, there would likely be damage and to take precautions.

When Lisa asked her how she came to that conclusion, Parker simply said, "There are miles of burned steep canyons back there and only a couple of ways for the water and mud to escape. The major artery runs right through my front yard. There are homes all up and down the wash that are a lot closer to the danger than mine is. If the media understands there's a threat, the homeowners need to do the same."

"Do you feel your neighbors are taking this threat seriously?"

Parker shook her head. "My neighbors downstream don't appear to have done anything to prepare for winter."

"Why do you think that is?"

"People wait around for someone else to save the day, but first responders can only do so much."

"You sound very passionate about this."

"I've been living it for five months. Tasting the ash every time I walk outside. Yeah, I'm passionate."

Lisa lowered her microphone and smiled. "That was great. Thank you."

Parker felt her shoulders relax.

The cameraman walked around a little more, took a few more pictures, and then took some film of Lisa talking with the canyon behind her.

Parker waved as they left the property and closed the gate behind them.

She turned back around and took in the vast, empty section of land that hadn't been empty since October. Well, empty except for the Porta Potty.

She called Scout over to her and knelt down to pet him. "Well, boy. It's just you and me again." Parker walked to where her driveway crossed the wash and sat, let her feet dangle where the culverts carried rainwater. "I really hope this works."

~

It was December fifteenth, exactly ten days before Christmas, when it started to rain.

Colin had called her that night, right as the first clouds moved in. "They're not predicting a lot," he told her.

"I know."

"It will take a little time for the basins to fill up."

They should. "I know."

"I can come over."

"I'm okay. Mallory and Austin are both here. We parked a car on the other side of the wash just in case the culverts clog up."

"Smart."

They talked a little longer. Colin flirted and took her mind away from the slow trickle of rain that splashed on the skylights. Even the wind chimes weren't impressed enough to make a lot of noise.

By morning, the sun was out and the sky was clear.

And the basins were full.

CHAPTER TWENTY-TWO

"I know how it looks, but the water will go down and all this will settle." Colin tried easing Parker's fears with facts.

The Porta Potty guy was loading the thing on the back of his truck while he and Parker stood on the banks of the wash.

The structures had held and were doing exactly what they'd been designed to do. What concerned him was that they'd had less than two inches of rain and there was already a week's worth of material to clean out. Even though he knew Parker didn't want to hear it, he kept it honest with her. "If the next rain dumps more, we can justify bringing everyone back."

Her eyes were wide. "I can't believe how much came down."

"As long as we get rain like we did last night, we should be okay. A little and stop, a little and stop."

"Like normal."

It's the microbursts that caused problems. Parker's home sat in the center of microburst central. Mountain ranges on all sides locking in clouds that dump and dump. In the years she'd been the responsible party at the house, that kind of weather condition hadn't happened.

He placed his arm over her shoulders. "This is normal. I promise."

She wrapped her arms around his waist. "I'm holding you to that."

"How is everything up at the house?" He only made it to the south side of the wash.

"A little runoff. Not a lot."

"The guesthouse?"

"So far, so good."

All good news. After he kissed the top of her head, he broke out of her embrace. "I'll be here at six to pick you up." They were going to drive to the crazy neighborhood that loved their power bills this time of year to look at Christmas lights.

"I'll bring hot chocolate."

"Is Austin joining us?"

She rolled her eyes. "He doesn't see the joy yet, he's seventeen."

"But Mallory is coming, right?"

"Yup. I was thinking of asking Erin to come, too. She doesn't get out much."

He'd noticed that about the woman.

"I'll see if Grace and Matt want to tag along. Maybe if Erin meets more of the family, she'll join us for Christmas."

He liked that idea.

~

"Come with us. I promise it won't hurt." Parker stood inside the guesthouse, insisting Erin go with them.

"I really don't want to intrude."

"Just grab a coat. I haven't seen you leave the property to do anything other than grocery shop." She pointed to the corner of the small living room. "And that tiny tree isn't festive enough for the season."

"I can see your lights from here."

"Erin, grab your coat. No one will bite."

Erin dropped her hands at her sides. "Fine."

Yeah, Parker knew what that meant. But she didn't care. She'd gotten her way.

First Christmas lights. Then Christmas.

She looked at her watch. "Colin should be here in ten minutes. Meet you in the driveway."

Right on schedule, Colin drove up. Mallory grabbed a scarf and gloves, and Parker followed suit. It wasn't very often that California gave you the opportunity to bundle up. At least not in their town. But the air was crisp after the rain, so Parker enjoyed the clothes she normally didn't have the opportunity to wear.

They met Colin in the driveway before he had the chance to walk up to the door.

He greeted her with a kiss. "Don't you look festive?"

"It's a scarf."

"A red scarf."

She laughed.

"With little bits of green splashed in."

"Fine," she giggled. "A festive Christmas-looking scarf."

Colin grabbed both ends of the scarf and pulled her toward him. "It's cute." He went in for a kiss.

"You two make me nauseous," Mallory teased.

Erin walked up the drive wearing a long coat that looked like it was made of some fancy material with puffy fur at the collar and cuffs.

Mallory beat Parker to a compliment. "I love that coat."

"Thanks. I've had it forever."

"Is that like saying, 'This ole thing?'" Mallory teased.

"Kinda."

"I'm glad you're coming with us," Colin told her.

"*Someone* was pretty persistent." She glared at Parker.

"Stubborn and persistent means you didn't stand a chance."

Colin opened the back door and ran around the car to open the others. His eyes landed on the driveway. "What's all that?" He pointed to the sandbags that had taken up most of Parker's day.

"The fence isn't holding all the mud back, so I'm sandbagging the driveway to try and keep it clear."

"You know you can ask—"

"Ask what? That you stop your day job helping thousands and just help me? Don't be ridiculous."

"Parker!"

"Colin!"

He knew she was right, she saw it in his eyes. "Fine."

"Okay, Miss Stubborn and Mr. Ridiculous, are we going or not?"

Parker wanted to hug her sister. "Yeah, the hot cocoa is getting cold."

They drove to the other side of town and parked down the street from where Santa and his elves threw up on the neighborhood. People were on foot everywhere doing the exact same thing.

They stood on the sidewalk while Colin texted his brother. "They're almost here."

Mallory looked up from her phone and searched the people walking by. When she started waving, Parker turned.

"Over here."

She thought she'd see Matt and Grace crossing the street.

That wasn't the case.

"Jase?" Colin asked.

"Yeah, I invited him." Mallory ran up and gave him a familiar hug.

Colin leaned close. "Did you know about this?"

"No idea."

Mallory introduced Erin to Colin's younger cousin.

"Hey, guys."

Parker turned with the sound of Grace's voice.

She greeted her with a hug and did the same with Matt.

Colin shook his brother's hand and hugged his sister. When they all pulled apart, Mallory looked over her shoulder. "Grace and Matt, this is Erin. She's renting my guesthouse."

Grace was all smiles and hellos.

Matt, on the other hand, seemed to have lost the ability to speak. He finally managed hello, but that was about it.

"Parker says you're a freelance editor."

"She makes it sound fancy. I promise you, it's not."

"You know what's the opposite of fancy? Being an engineer, trust me."

Matt found his voice. "The baby sister has the unfun job."

"I'm not sure about that. I dig ditches," Colin said.

"Is that what you call living in my front yard? A ditch?"

They were laughing.

Grace looked over at Erin. "Matt's the hero in the family."

Was Erin blushing?

Parker glanced Matt's way.

"You're a firefighter, right?" Erin asked.

Now Matt was a little rosy in the cheeks. "I have the fun job."

"Who has to work on Christmas so we try and do as much of this stuff together as possible before. Hope you don't mind that we tagged along," Grace said.

"The more the merrier," Mallory chimed in.

Colin grabbed Parker's hand in his. "Let's get on with it."

As they walked in front of their group on the sidewalk, Parker glanced over her shoulder.

She wasn't sure who distracted her more. Mallory and Jase acting like they'd been in contact this whole time, or Erin and Matt trying not to look at each other.

Grace seemed oblivious and walked between them.

"I think there's a little Christmas magic in the air," she whispered.

"I noticed," Colin whispered back.

~

The break room was filled with enough sugar and calories to feed small countries, but that didn't stop parents from bringing in more. It was the last day of school before the holiday break.

"I'm not even going to ask if you have anything fun planned for the break," Jennifer said.

"Waste of breath if you did. What about you guys?"

"We're going to my mom's for Christmas and spending a week."

"Enjoy it."

They both watched Janice walk through the room and waited until she was gone to continue talking. "Any more problems?" Jennifer asked.

"With Janice?"

"Yeah."

"She already cut me to four hours or less a day. The next step is to fire me altogether, but most of the aides don't want my job."

"Do you think it's personal?"

"I don't know. She's called me out anytime I've been so much as two minutes late." Even planning for the extra time to get off the property, sometimes there was a line of dump trucks ten thick going five miles an hour down the street.

"Maybe that's all behind you."

Parker was already done with her lunch and wadding up her napkin and the ziplock bags she'd used to package it all together. "It's supposed to rain through Christmas and into the new year. Which is fine, I'm home, but if that keeps happening, I'll have to call in. The few bucks I make in the couple hours I'm here isn't worth me coming in if I can't make it back home."

Her cell phone buzzed. Mallory's name popped up.

"Hey, sis, what's up?"

"My car won't start."

"What?"

"It makes a clicking noise, but that's it."

"Did you leave a light on or something? Is it the battery?"

Mallory huffed into the phone. "My car is old, but not that old. Everything turns off in a few minutes after I walk away. I opened the hood and looked."

Parker laughed. "And what? You thought you'd magically know what to do?"

"No! I called Jase and he said to look and wiggle the battery. I found a nest in there, Parker."

That caught her attention. "What kind of nest?"

"I don't know . . . mice, rats. The De Lucas have been complaining for months about a rat problem at their house. Ever since the fire."

That didn't sound good. "I'll be home in a couple of hours, maybe it's something simple."

"I have a final today. I have to get to school."

Parker squeezed her eyes shut. She'd forgotten.

"Come here and take my car." She could bum a ride home.

"Great idea, I'll just fire up the broomstick."

Right. Bumming a ride off someone in their neighborhood last minute wasn't going to happen. It would take twenty minutes for an Uber to get there minimum.

"It's a final. I can't be late."

Parker looked at her watch. She only had five minutes left on her break. She jumped up and grabbed her purse. "I'm on my way."

"Thanks, Parker."

She rushed an explanation. "Rats got into Mallory's car and it won't start. She needs mine to get to school."

If there wasn't any traffic, she could make it home in eight minutes. She rushed up the hallway, poked her head in Janice's office. "Hey, Janice. My sister is having a car emergency. I'm going to rush home and be right back."

Janice glanced at the analog clock on the wall. "The bell is in three minutes."

"It can't be helped. I'll be fifteen minutes." A stretch, but she could channel her NASCAR skills.

Janice sat both hands on her desk and glared. "Who is going to be out on the yard when the kids go to lunch?"

"Fifteen minutes, Janice. Maybe one of the teachers can—"

She pushed her chair back. "You know what, I'll take care of it. Fifteen minutes is almost half the lunch. Go take care of your sister."

Parker started to feel relieved.

"In fact, take the rest of the day off."

Okay, not so relieved. "I'll come right back."

"Hmm, right. I have it, Parker. Take the time on our holiday break to prioritize a few things. When you come back, be ready to work."

The *or else* was implied.

"Janice, I can—"

The bell rang.

Her boss scowled and walked past her and out the door.

CHAPTER TWENTY-THREE

"Looks like they got into the wiring." Colin dug a little deeper under the hood of Mallory's car.

"Can you fix it?"

"Sorry, hon . . . way out of my scope."

She dropped her head between her shoulders. She really didn't have a budget for these kinds of things. "I need to catch a break."

"I know a good mechanic that won't screw you over for repairs."

That was something.

"We'll have to tow the car there."

"That's a hundred bucks minimum."

Colin lowered the hood on the car. "I have AAA."

"What if you need to use the tow miles?"

Parker started to recognize "The Stare." The look where Colin pressed his lips together and lowered his head just enough to appear like he was looking over reading glasses. Only he didn't wear glasses. It was the best Mr. Ridiculous expression he owned.

"Fine."

He wrapped his arms around her before he could dial the number on the AAA card. "Progress."

She snorted, but hugged him back.

Thirty minutes later they followed the tow truck off the property.

~

"I appreciate the invitation, I do. But I'll be with my aunt and her family."

This was the first time Parker had heard of any aunt. "I thought you said you didn't have any family close by."

"She's in Arizona."

"Oh."

Parker couldn't argue that spending time with family on a holiday should trump time with friends. "As long as you're not going to be alone."

"Of course not. It's Christmas." Erin lifted the shovel in her hands and attacked the pile of sand. Parker held the bag open, and together they were quickly running out of bags to fill.

"So what do you think of Matt?" Parker asked.

"Matt?" Another shovel of sand went in the bag.

"Yeah, you know . . . the good-looking firefighter who was making you blush the other night?"

"I wasn't blushing. It was cold."

Parker grabbed a new bag, held it wide open.

"He was having a hard time spitting out words around you."

Erin grinned. "I thought that was just the steroid use."

She laughed. "He is a big guy."

"Too big for me," she said so low Parker almost didn't hear her.

Matt was definitely no stranger to working out. "He's a good-looking guy."

"I'm not interested."

That's not how it appeared when they were walking around looking at Christmas lights.

"Really? It seemed like—"

"Not my type."

On the fourth bag, they switched places. Parker took the shovel and Erin knelt down by the bags.

"What is your type?"

"Less . . ."

"Less what?"

"I don't know, just less." Erin closed the bag one shovel too soon and opened another one. "When will you get Mallory's car back?"

"A couple days." Another scoop into the bag. "Nice changing of the subject, by the way."

Erin looked up, briefly. "Sorry. I just don't need someone like Matt taking notice. I don't need that in my life."

Parker didn't press further. She was starting to feel like Erin was finally confiding in her and didn't want to screw that up. "So when do you leave?"

Erin closed the bag, grabbed the next. "Leave where?"

"Your aunt?"

"Oh, yeah . . . uhm, the twenty-third."

"I hope it's an early flight. We're expecting rain that night."

"Yeah, it's early. I'll be gone before you're out of bed."

"I'll have to go into your place and make sure there are no leaks if it rains hard enough."

Erin hesitated. "Uhm, right. Of course."

Parker felt her nerves. If anyone understood the desire for privacy, it was her. There really wasn't a way around invading Erin's space if she wasn't there to report any issues.

They filled the last couple of bags and stood looking at them.

"I've got it from here," Parker told her.

"Where are these going?"

"Behind your place."

"I'll grab the wheelbarrow."

"You've helped a lot already."

Erin started walking across the field to where she'd left the barrow the day before. "It's called exercise. My body can use it now that I'm sitting at my computer all day."

"If you insist." Because it wasn't like she could offer Erin a break on the rent.

She couldn't offer Erin a break on anything.

$\sim$

Colin stood up on the ladder, helping his father remove the spare tables his mother used at Christmas to seat everyone in the same space.

"You know we're going to get some rain in the next few days," his father said.

"Yeah, I've been watching the news."

"I don't need some overtanned network jockey telling me it's going to rain."

His dad had crashed his motorcycle at work over a decade ago that resulted in a broken femur and becoming the family meteorologist. When the barometer dropped, his dad felt it.

"You should take your show on the road, Dad."

Colin lowered the folding table to his father and went back for the second one.

"Your girlfriend is expecting some trouble at her house, right?"

He brushed aside a cobweb and reached over the dust-filled plywood and grabbed the edges of the table. "We're prepared."

"You be sure and check on her. My leg hasn't ached this bad since the accident."

"I will." He coughed as he unsettled a cloud of sleeping dust.

After climbing down the ladder, Colin helped his dad unfold the things and clean them up before taking them in for his mom.

"Is everything going okay with you two?" his dad asked.

"Me and Parker?"

"Is there someone else?"

His dad knew he didn't do that kind of thing. "We're great. Both busy, but—"

"You haven't tried to take over her life?"

Colin stood taller. "I don't try and take over people's lives."

"Maybe *take over* is an exaggeration . . ."

"Thank you." Colin found a towel and moved to the sink in the garage and turned on the faucet.

"On second thought, no. *Take over* is a nice way to say what you do."

"Dad!"

"It's a balance, son. Women want you to do for them, but they need to do for themselves, too. You like to go in and fix everything. That comes off as taking over."

"I learned from the best." In fact, all three of them could blame or give credit, depending on whom you asked, for their father's trait.

"So, are you?"

"No." He thought of the night he brought home her Christmas tree. He'd given Austin the money for the thing before Parker could notice, and Austin made up the deep discount and his boss taking it out of his check to avoid her arguing. The frustration that night over the stranger that walked in her yard . . . he saw red with the memory. The sandbags . . . the problems with her gate and the power outage. "She doesn't give me the chance," he finally told his dad.

"But you've tried."

"Not completely." He sighed.

"Your mom and I like this one. She isn't some delicate thing that needs you to function, and that's a good thing long-term."

Colin wrung out the soaked towel and moved to the table. "Sounds like you're already writing up a guest list."

When his father didn't laugh, Colin looked up. "Dad!"

"Your mom."

"We haven't known each other very long."

"I married your mom six months after we met."

"And I was born seven months later."

"You were premature."

Colin rolled his eyes. "Nine-pound babies aren't premature. But nice try."

"Is she on birth control?"

Colin stopped. "Are we really having this conversation?"

"You're right. It's none of my business."

Good!

He scrubbed the table hard enough to make the legs scrape against the garage floor.

"Does she even want kids?" his father asked after a few seconds.

"Since I don't know what her favorite color is yet, I couldn't tell you about her desire to procreate in the future." He couldn't tell his father if she was on birth control either. They'd used condoms like any respectable sexually active adults, so he hadn't asked. She hadn't volunteered either.

Colin finished with the one table and moved on to the other.

His dad folded the clean one and picked it up before going in the house. "Well, be sure and warn her about the rain. My leg is killing me."

Some days their family openness was over the top.

Today was one of them.

Yet as he was driving home an hour later, he kept asking himself if Parker wanted children of her own.

CHAPTER TWENTY-FOUR

Colin had left his brother's house around nine in the evening; an hour after the first sprinkles messed up his clean car. He'd been flustered by the conversation with their dad and needed a distraction. If he'd called Parker, he risked asking all the questions his father had posed to him and possibly scaring the woman off.

Matt reminded him of two important facts.

"Mom wants grandchildren and Dad hates not knowing all the facts."

Two things Colin knew, but wasn't focused on.

So they shared a beer while Colin refreshed the screen on his radar app on his phone. Bands of green, indicating rain, were moving in. Behind them were blips of red that may or may not make it over the hill. Either way, his morning would be busy.

He just hoped it wouldn't be on Parker's property.

Colin no sooner dropped his keys on the kitchen counter than his work phone rang. It was Glynn. "I just drove past the river site. So far so good."

"Have you been to Creek Canyon?"

"No. I wasn't sure if you were around."

"I'm not. Let me call Parker and let her know you'll be watching throughout the night."

"You're the boss."

He hung up and texted Parker. Are you still up?

Three dots flashed on his screen, answering his question.

I am.

Colin called her number and lifted the phone to his ear.

"Hey." Her voice was relaxed.

"You sound good."

"Mallory and I made some homemade eggnog. It's not bad. We may have poured the brandy a little strong."

He cringed. "Taking the domestic thing to a new level."

"Yeah, well . . . no one is out tonight so I don't have to stress about picking anyone up."

"I'm glad you're relaxing."

"I'm trying."

As much as he didn't want to be the one to bring her back to reality, he kinda had to. "Listen, Glynn will be in and out tonight, watching the wash."

"I heard the forecast. You think it's going to be bad?"

"It's going to be wet."

She laughed. "I parked my car on the other side of the wash just in case we can't drive over it tomorrow."

"Miss Practical. I like that about you."

She giggled. "Practical Parker stepping up."

Yeah, she'd poured the brandy a little heavy.

He wished he was there to see her smile. He heard Mallory laughing.

"I will leave you alone. I just wanted to let you know we'll be around."

"You mean Glynn."

"Yup. I'll be there sometime in the morning unless I get a call earlier."

"Okay." He heard her muffle the phone. "Just a little more for me . . . Sorry, Mallory is pouring us another drink." More scraping sounds over the phone. "Next time I drink this, you need to be here." She did a hoarse whisper thing with her voice.

"Why is that?"

She giggled. "It's making me horny."

It was as if his dick heard her. "I can come over," he teased.

"That would be way too obvious."

"I'm sure your brother and sister figured out the nature of our relationship."

Her voice was attempting a whisper . . . she failed. "Have you made love to a woman with your brother and sister in the next room?"

Now that she put it that way. "No."

"Okay, then!"

Parker was funny when she was drunk.

"Is that Kissy Face?" he heard Mallory ask.

Kissy Face?

"Look who's talking. 'Jase is so cute. Jase gave me a rose for our one-month anniversary. Jase is the best kisser.'"

Colin heard Parker and her sister teasing and wished he was there to witness it in person.

"He *is* the best kisser." Mallory sounded just as drunk as her sister.

"Colin probably gave him pointers." Parker's voice increased. "You gave him pointers, didn't you?"

"I can't take credit for my cousin."

"You're older. I'm giving you credit."

The level of ridiculous the conversation was going was right up there with reruns of *I Love Lucy*.

"Are you sure you don't want me to come over?" Testing the best kissing skills sounded good to him. He pressed the heel of his hand between his legs.

"My sister is right here!" She was back to whispering for the deaf.

He looked down at his lap, knowing he wasn't going anywhere. "You're right. Besides, I make it a rule to never sleep with drunk women."

"I'm not drunk." She laughed. "Maybe a little."

Colin really wished he was there.

"I'll see you tomorrow."

"Have fun."

"We are. Good night, Colin."

She hung up before he could reply.

~

Colin's phone rang at four thirty in the morning.

Startled from a deep sleep, he heard the rain pounding before he answered the call. "Yeah."

"It's Glynn."

"How bad is it?"

Glynn blew out a breath. "Fill the big thermos and wear boots."

Colin sat up, the blanket settled in his lap.

"I'll be there as quickly as I can."

Glynn hung up and Colin walked on autopilot to the shower.

Forty-five minutes later Colin stopped his truck at the intersection of Parker's street and the main road traversing the canyon. Under the bridge, water and mud flowed, but hadn't clogged up to the point where it was overflowing. He turned up the street, made it three-quarters of the way before he saw the problem.

Mud and rock were spread out on the street in all directions. This did not come from their project. He had a deep suspicion where it had before he pulled his truck to the side of the street and walked the rest of the way to Parker's gate.

When Colin started to climb, he spotted Glynn.

"Sutter Canyon broke free."

Colin flashed his light in the area between the De Lucas' and Sutters' homes. They knew the canyon they'd named Sutter Canyon because of its location would be a problem, but he hadn't predicted this. Four feet of mud and rock had careened down the canyon and flattened the chain-link fence where all the driveways intersected. Once the mud and rock hit the surviving manzanita on the side of Parker's driveway, some of the mud kept flowing toward the wash, but much of it detoured down the entrance to Parker's home and front gate. From there, it careened down the street, blocking everyone's ability to get in and out.

"Are the homeowners up?"

"Yeah, they heard it break loose."

Colin could imagine.

"How is our project?" Colin kept walking, Glynn beside him.

"Full, but working."

"Overflowing?"

"Yeah. Pretty sure we have repairs to make."

The rain had eased and the sun was starting to rise. He heard the water flow before he saw it.

Parker's bridge crossing had clogged up, and water ran over the top as it was designed to do. He glanced at her car parked on that side of the wash. Not that it would do her any good until they could clear the driveway.

He and Glynn walked to each of the choke points and watched the flow of water. The sound of rocks rushing together, and water crashing against debris was hard to talk over. "How bad was it at its peak?"

"I got here after Sutter Canyon opened up. I couldn't tell you what this looked like."

Colin pulled out his phone and started making calls. "I really hope everyone didn't run off for Christmas."

"I hear ya."

By six in the morning, Keith had arrived with his skip loader and was clearing the path through Parker's driveway. Colin had managed to get ahold of two of his subcontracted men who would bring their equipment back the next day. But most of the crew was gone until the twenty-sixth or later.

Mr. Sutter caught his attention and waved him over. "Our precautions weren't enough."

He could see that. What was four feet of mud on Parker's land was twice as much on her neighbor's. They walked together on top of the mud and debris to the Sutters' backyard.

Boulders sat in what was once a pristine swimming pool. Mud had taken over and pushed up to the backside of the man's home.

"Did it get inside?"

"Not a lot."

"I have another guy coming. This is our priority before the next swell comes through." He patted Sutter's back. "I'll do what I can."

~

"Parker. Parker!"

She rolled over, dragged a hand over her eyes. "What?"

"You need to come see this." Mallory's voice woke her.

"What? Did Santa come a day early?" She was half-asleep.

"No, the rain gods did."

Her eyes sprang open. "Oh, no."

Mallory was already in jeans and a jacket, her hair wet from the rain.

She shoved the blankets back and climbed out of bed and to her bedroom window.

"You can't see it from here."

Yeah, she saw water flowing where the driveway should be and mud on the far end of the driveway. But how much, she couldn't tell. "Give

221

me five minutes." She glanced at the alarm clock, saw that it wasn't working. "We don't have power."

"Nope."

"Great."

Mallory disappeared and Parker went into her bathroom. She emerged with her hair and teeth brushed wearing jeans and a sweatshirt. She grabbed her warm coat from the closet.

"Austin is already out here."

That was rare. Austin didn't emerge before ten most days he didn't have to go to school.

Scout followed them down the stairs and driveway.

Mud followed the path of sandbags, but overflowed onto their lawn. Not a ton of it, but enough to make a mess. She tried to take in the property in sections.

"The culverts filled up," Mallory told her.

That she could see. Water ran over the top, which would have made crossing the creek impossible. Except they had the footbridge. Parker sent a mental thanks to her dad, if he could hear her.

Scout sat on the north side of the wash as they walked over the bridge.

Parker looked upstream and heard the force of water rolling off the hill.

Mallory pulled her along.

Two white county trucks were parked where the county trucks had once lived. She heard the beep of a skip loader before she saw it.

"Holy shit." Mud was everywhere.

Her neighbors were up and milling about, shaking their heads.

Austin jumped down off a rock and walked over to them. "What a mess, huh."

She could see where a path had already been dug out, giving her the ability to drive on and off her property. "When did this happen?"

"Colin says sometime before four thirty this morning."

"This is crazy."

"We made out okay. The Sutters' backyard is ruined."

One of her neighbors walked in through her gate with a cell phone poised and taking pictures. "This is something."

"How does the rest of the street look?"

"There's mud everywhere," her neighbor told her. "But the county already cleared most of it off to the side."

The sound of a semitruck rolling up the street had them all turning around. One of the drivers with an excavator peeked around the corner. A Christmas wreath tied to his grille.

"Here we go again."

"Good morning, Parker." Colin's voice had her spinning around.

Not caring that anyone saw, she took several steps in his direction and wrapped her arms around his waist.

He embraced her, spoke softly in her ear. "This can all be fixed."

She closed her eyes and nodded against his chest. "I know."

"I'm going to get it all back to normal."

"I'm counting on that."

CHAPTER TWENTY-FIVE

Power had been restored by the evening, and the rain had reduced to drizzle and then finally nothing.

Colin had managed a skeleton crew until around three. They pulled everything out of the main driveway, putting much of the debris into piles until the cavalry arrived.

The mud hadn't penetrated the inside of the guesthouse, which was a blessing. The shed, on the other hand, wasn't faring as well. It was taking on water. So while Colin directed his crew on Christmas Eve, she was schlepping boxes from the shed up and into the garage.

By six that night, Austin was hibernating in his room and Mallory was in hers talking on the phone.

Parker turned on the news to try and catch the weather report.

She made the mistake of leaning her head back and closing her eyes.

For the second time that day, someone calling her name woke her up. She jumped.

Colin was slipping in the sliding door. "You were asleep?"

She rubbed her eyes. "Long day."

He kicked off his boots at the door and closed the distance between them.

"I wanted to check on you before I left."

She patted the space beside her.

"I'm exhausted."

"I bet."

She curled into his side. "You have to be, too. You've been up longer than I have."

"But I wasn't hitting the eggnog last night."

"Was that only last night?"

The lights of the Christmas tree flashed and reminded her of the date.

"Did you catch the weather report?"

She looked at her watch. "I missed it."

"My app says more by next week. By then we should have a fair amount of material moved out."

"So it can fill back up and do it again?"

He stroked her arm as he spoke. "And over, and over . . . until the rain stops."

"What a frustrating job you have. You get it all right, then Mother Nature messes it up, and you do it again."

"Public Works Flood Control Division. It's in the title."

"Is the gate still open?"

"Yeah. I think the motor took on some water."

"I have a guy I can call. He probably won't be here until after the new year."

"I can have one of my guys look at it."

She snuggled and yawned. "They have bigger fish to fry."

"Yeah, but closing that gate is a priority. You're back here alone. I don't want you having to chase anyone else away."

Parker found her eyes closing with the timbre of his voice lulling her to sleep.

"I'll put more signs up."

One minute she was talking about signs, the next she jolted because of a pain in her neck. She was on the couch, her head in Colin's lap, and he was sound asleep sitting upright. The clock on the wall said it was after midnight.

She patted his leg. "Colin?" she whispered.

Nothing.

"Colin?"

He hummed, moved, and placed his hand on his neck.

"C'mon. Let's get some sleep," Parker said.

"I should go."

"That's silly. It's after midnight."

"But your brother and sister."

She stood and reached for his hand. "We're just going to sleep. I'm too tired to do anything else."

"You sure?"

And that's exactly what they did.

~

"Merry Christmas, Miss Oakley." Colin slid up behind her in the kitchen the next morning and wrapped his arms around her while she filled the coffeepot. He pressed his lips to her neck and enjoyed the sigh that released from her lungs.

"Merry Christmas."

He kissed her, briefly, and released her so she could finish what she started.

"Is anyone up yet?"

"No."

Colin leaned against the island and watched as Parker's legs peeked out from under the short bathrobe she wore. Her tousled hair and sexy morning smile were almost too much to bear. "Should I duck out before anyone realizes I spent the night?" he asked.

She glanced over her shoulder while pouring the water into the coffee maker. "Like one of us is married and we were having an affair?"

He smiled. "I guess. Although I've never been married and make it a rule not to mess with married women."

"I'm sure Austin and Mallory realize what's going on between us."

He moved to the fridge, removed the creamer he knew Parker liked in her coffee. "I want to be sensitive."

She took the creamer from his hand, kissed him. "Thank you. But I think we're good."

Her ass snuck out from under her robe when she reached for the coffee cups on a top shelf of a cupboard. Much as he wanted to help her, he liked the view more.

Parker turned and hesitated.

When he looked up, he found her smiling. "Were you checking out my ass, Mr. Hudson?"

He licked his lips. "Yes, ma'am, I was. I didn't notice those red panties last night."

Damn if she didn't lift the hem of her robe and flash him a proper look at those panties from the front.

He lunged forward and grabbed her hips and pulled her close.

She giggled and tried squirming away.

"Oh, no, you don't."

He lifted her off her feet and put her on the countertop. Just like he liked her.

She gave up and into a much more satisfying morning kiss.

"I like waking up beside you," he said once she stopped kissing him back.

"Even if I hog the covers all night?"

He nodded. "You did hog the covers, but the fact that you were wrapped around me like a bun to a hot dog made up for it."

Her cheeks blossomed with color. "Sorry."

"Bite your tongue."

To make a point, she stuck that tongue out and did just that.

He made a biting motion toward her and she pulled back laughing.

If Colin could have a Christmas wish, it would be more moments like the one they were sharing right then. "I want to give you your Christmas present before anyone gets up."

"Like Santa?"

"If I knew I was staying the night, I would have wrapped up something nice."

Her eye narrowed. "I don't get it."

He pulled away from her and went to retrieve his wallet from her bedroom. He removed her gift from inside and walked back to the kitchen.

Parker had poured them both a cup of coffee and was stirring hers when he set the tickets on the counter.

She stopped moving, then lifted the papers. "Tickets to Cabo San Lucas?"

"Yep. Just you and me . . . five days of sunshine and margaritas. By the time your school has spring break, things here should be past the breaking point, and we will both be ready for a vacation."

"Colin . . . I don't know what to say. No one has ever done anything like this for me."

"Now someone has. Just tell me you'll come and pack a bag. I'll take care of the rest."

She tossed her arms around him in a hug worth every penny. In his ear she said, "All I got you was floor mats for your Jeep."

"I'll love them."

"Wait." She pulled away.

"What?"

She looked at the tickets and shook her head. "Nothing. This is awesome. Thank you."

Colin gave her butt a little tap when she turned back to her coffee. "I can hardly wait to get you alone for five days."

"Something tells me we may never see the beach."

He accepted the coffee she handed him. "I like that idea, too."

"Somehow I knew you would."

~

"There isn't anything to discuss. If we didn't remove the debris up that channel, the next rain will just wash it into our way." Two days after Christmas, Colin was in the office having a pissing match with his boss.

"The allocated money is for the main wash, not the side jobs." Ed was busting his balls.

"How about *we* engineer the structures right the first time so I have money in the budget to make sure the road is clear to maintain what we've built," Colin shot back.

Once the water level dropped and his men started the job of removing debris, giant holes where rocks crashed through the slotted structures proved the engineers wrong. Something Colin attempted to point out to Ed early on. His boss didn't listen.

Ed wasn't amused.

He also knew Colin was right.

"Dig it out, but if they want K-rails, the homeowner needs to buy or rent or whatever . . . we're not providing them."

Colin could work with that. Having gotten what he wanted, he turned to leave.

"And no special favors for your girlfriend."

He paused, kept his mouth shut, and kept on walking. "Asshole."

Colin chased problems all morning and into the afternoon.

It was after three when he walked up the drive to see if Parker was home. She wasn't answering her text messages, which usually meant she was busy outside.

He found her kneeling beside a hole next to the driveway, a shovel sat on the ground beside her.

229

"What are you doing?"

She looked up; her hair fell in her face.

Every time he saw her, she looked more tired.

"I woke up to water bubbling out of the ground."

He recognized the PVC pipes, Red Hot Blue Glue, and fittings. "You're fixing the sprinklers?"

"Yeah. This one's a bitch, though. The ground is hard, making it almost impossible to get to."

It appeared to be an offshoot from what was once her lawn, out toward the area where her barns once lived.

Now that he looked closely, he realized just how much damage that section of her property was taking on. The sandbags weren't handling the job, and three inches of mud covered nearly every manicured portion of the land. The section of pipe she was working on was in a designated water flow area that had obviously been undermined by the amount of rain they'd received.

"Damn it!"

He looked down to see her looking at her fingertip.

"What did you do?"

She wiped her dirty finger on her dirty shirt and stuck it in her mouth. "Cut."

Colin bent down beside her and pulled at the pipe she was trying to fit together. "I can help with this kind of stuff." The pipe hardly budged.

"And I can bake a pie, but we both have other things to do. This needs to get done so I can turn the water back on."

He stood and helped her to her feet.

"*Can* you bake a pie?"

She narrowed her eyes. "Of course I can."

There was a twinkle in her eye.

"Those Marie Callender's ones you pop in the oven for forty minutes are a cinch."

He laughed while she shook off the pain in her finger.

When he attempted to pick up the shovel, she took it from him. "Give that to me."

"I can—"

"Yeah, but it's personal now. I've been at this for two hours and the pipe drew first blood. It's mine."

He understood that emotion. "Can I give you some advice? I mean *strategy* for getting back at the pipe?"

"Sure."

"Dig out another foot around the whole thing. Under and around. Then you'll have room to work."

"I was hoping to avoid that."

He could see why, the earth was rock-hard.

"Then I hope your tetanus is up-to-date."

Her playful glare had him smiling. "Any more thought to New Year's Eve?" He'd broached the subject on Christmas Day after they'd eaten dinner and were playing cards with his family.

She shook her head and looked at the ground. "I can't, Colin. There's rain in the forecast and—"

"It's okay. I'll cancel."

"No! Don't you dare."

He had planned to go out to the desert with Matt and their cousin to camp and romp around to ring in the new year. It was a tradition any year Matt wasn't scheduled to work.

"I won't feel right if you're here alone."

"I won't be alone. Erin is sticking around. I don't think Austin is doing anything. Besides, Mallory is going out there with Jase, and I would love to know that you're there, too. Keep her safe."

"She's an adult."

"You're more adult than she is."

He laughed.

"Go, Colin. You made those plans before me and all my drama. Don't be the guy that gives up what he loves because of the girl."

"I want the girl to come with me."

"The girl would like that, too, just not this year."

"Parker . . ."

She stopped him with a hand to his chest. "I'm having a girls' night on New Year's, and you're not invited. So go hang with your brother and keep my sister from breaking anything. She doesn't know how to ride a motorcycle, and her experience with camping is about as much as mine. I don't think the firepit by the swimming pool and a tent in the front yard count."

He grabbed her hand and pulled her close. "Not invited, huh?"

She lifted her lips to his. "No. So kiss me and go away. I'm busy."

Colin made good on the kiss. Broke away. "I really can do this for you."

"You *really can* get your ass back to work."

"Ohh, I like the bossy part of you."

Parker was trying to keep a straight face. "Play your cards right and I'll bring the boss to the bedroom."

Damn if his body didn't hear her.

He pulled her back, kissed her hard. *Now who's boss?*

Yeah . . . she was speechless.

He liked doing that to her.

A playful slap to her butt and he released her lips. "Two can play at that game."

He walked away, stopped at twenty yards. "*Are* you good on your tetanus?"

CHAPTER TWENTY-SIX

Austin invited a friend over on New Year's Eve, and the two of them disappeared into the garage with a six-pack of beer. If two healthy hundred-and-seventyish-pound boys were limiting their New Year's to a six-pack, Parker was fine with it. She knew the boy's mom and they both had the same mentality. Be smart and don't drive.

On a normal night, Parker would be dressed for bed or already curled up in it. But she was so ready to kiss the year goodbye and start new. That meant staying up late and flipping 2016 the bird.

She and Erin had cooked a sinfully calorie-packed, cream-sauced pasta and countered it with a salad for dinner. They'd already polished off a bottle of wine and had opened up a second.

It was only ten.

"You never did tell me what Colin gave you for Christmas."

Parker squeezed her eyes shut and dropped the back of her head on the couch with a grimace.

"That bad?"

She shook her head. "A trip to Cabo."

"Why the long face?"

"Cabo is in Mexico."

"Yeah . . . and it's warm and *dry* and relaxing."

Parker lifted her head, brought her wineglass to her lips. "Mexico is a different country."

Erin nodded slowly and spoke even slower. "Yes . . . I'm aware of that."

"I don't have a passport."

Her smile fell. "Oh . . ."

"Yeah, oh . . ."

"So get one."

"Right. Easy." She shook her head. "I don't have a copy of my birth certificate. I looked. I have Mallory's and Austin's . . . not mine."

"Did your parents have it in a safety deposit box or something?"

"I emptied all those out a long time ago."

Erin shrugged. "So get the birth certificate and then the passport."

"Government agencies are closed until the third, then if I'm lucky, I will get the copy in two weeks. Then it takes six to eight weeks to get the passport."

"When did Colin book the trip for?"

"April."

"Okay, no problem."

"Except, I couldn't get an appointment at the passport office until mid-February."

"Oh, shit."

"I know! See my dilemma?"

Erin curled her legs under her on the couch. "What did Colin say about this?"

"I didn't tell him."

"Why not?"

She remembered the smile on his face when he showed her pictures of the hotel he'd booked for them, and how excited he was to get her away from the floods and the stress of Creek Canyon. "I didn't want to pop his bubble."

"How are you going to avoid that if you don't get your passport in time?"

"I don't know. I'm going to try and get things expedited. If that doesn't happen fast enough, I'll think of something else."

~

He was freezing his ass off. The clouds had blown in midday and sprinkled on them while they buzzed around the desert spitting up mud on each other for fun. Now it was almost eleven, the campfire was five feet around and still didn't keep him warm enough.

Matt loved this shit.

Colin was fine with admitting he tolerated it. More so when the weather cooperated. Less so when it didn't.

The beer they'd been drinking had long since stopped keeping him warm on the inside and kept making him walk away from the fire to pee.

They were determined to hold out until midnight when they could set off the outlawed fireworks, scream "Happy Fucking New Year," and then drop into bed.

He kept an eye on Jase and Mallory enough to know that the two of them would be knocking it out right then if they had a motor home to go back to alone. But they didn't. They were bunking with his aunt, uncle, and cousin, all three of whom had called it a night at ten. No one would be knocking anything out tonight.

Which made him miss Parker even more.

He wished she'd come. Would have rented his own RV and they could have skipped the *waiting for midnight* crap. He'd never wanted it to rain as much as he did now. Rain would chase them inside.

He shivered and told himself to stop being such a pansy. Colin stood and turned his ass to the fire to warm it up.

"Did anything crazy happen on Christmas?" Jase asked Matt.

"Bunch of medical calls and one kitchen fire that was out before we got there."

"At least there was a fire."

"I've never heard anyone say that," Mallory said.

Colin turned like a marshmallow, cooking all sides. "Matt makes his living with fires, and I make mine with rain. It's a sick family thing."

"I never thought of it that way."

"Too bad Parker couldn't join us," Matt said.

"She's probably out cold on the couch already," Mallory told them. "Maybe Erin will keep her up till midnight."

"Erin doesn't strike me as a party animal." Matt hadn't asked about Parker's tenant, and hadn't volunteered any information after they'd looked at Christmas lights.

"Yeah, she's quiet."

"I noticed," Matt said. "What's her story?"

Yup, his brother was interested.

"I couldn't tell ya. Parker knows her better, but she doesn't say a whole lot."

"You like the silent type," Colin teased.

"I like the type that doesn't bitch."

"Good thing Colin is dating my sister, then, and not you."

"Parker doesn't complain," he argued.

"To you maybe. Austin and I hear it all the time."

"You're her sister. That's normal," Jase told Mallory.

"She doesn't tell anyone her issues other than us."

"She talks to me." At least Colin thought she was open with him.

"Oh, yeah . . . did she say anything about your Christmas present?"

Colin turned his back to the fire again to look at Mallory.

"What about it?"

"What did you give her?" Matt interrupted.

"A trip to Cabo," Mallory answered for him.

"What about my trip to Cabo?" Now Colin felt prickles up his spine like he knew there was something coming he wasn't expecting. Parker had acted excited about a spring trip out of town.

"Does my sister appear to be the kind of woman who travels internationally?"

Jase laughed. "Mexico is hardly international."

Mallory snorted. "You need a passport to get there."

"Technically, you need a passport to get back," Jase argued.

"Jackass." Matt called their cousin out, humor in his voice.

When Mallory rolled her eyes, it reminded Colin of her sister. "What are you saying, Mallory?"

"Parker doesn't have a passport. None of us do. A vacation for us has been a trip to Disneyland or the beach."

He hadn't thought of that. He just assumed she had one.

"So now Parker is scrambling to get a copy of her birth certificate so she can then get a passport. But appointments at the passport office are just as hard to get as they are at the DMV. And I can tell by the look on your face Parker didn't tell you any of this."

No. She hadn't.

"If Parker didn't want to tell him, why are you telling him?" Matt asked. "Aren't you women supposed to stick together? Especially sisters?"

"Because this isn't like an ugly sweater someone gives you that you can say you love and never wear. It's a trip that she's going to stress over until she either has the passport and gray hair, or has to tell you she can't go at the last minute . . . with gray hair. I told her that if she just talked to you about her problem, you could both figure it out. Push the trip a few weeks, expedite the passport somehow . . . I don't know. Something."

"She could have told me."

"Yeah, but that isn't Parker. If you haven't noticed, she likes to fix everything herself. I'd hate to see her miss out because she's stubborn. I think we can all agree no one needs a vacation more than my sister. Besides, you're the best thing to happen to Parker. I don't want to see you screw anything up."

That didn't suck to hear. "I'll try my best."

"I'll be sure and tell you if you are. Austin might chime in, too. Seriously, Parker's been one big ball of nerves since our parents died, but since you came along, it feels like I'm getting my sister back."

"I guess that means you have the family approval," Matt teased.

"So take care of Cabo and bring her back loose as a noodle."

"You're just as bossy as your sister," he told her.

"Where do you think I get it from?"

They all laughed.

The wind kicked up and blew the smoke directly in Colin's face. "I'll fix it."

"Good. And don't say a thing about me telling you."

Matt moaned. "Oh, the games people play."

"I have to live with her. Don't you dare, Colin, or you won't get one more *get out of jail free card* from me."

"I won't say a thing."

A crack of light in the distance made Colin look at his watch. Was it midnight already?

Thunder rolled over them.

"Well, hell."

Then the sky opened up and they all scattered like ants.

~

They had fifteen minutes to go.

Parker was having a hard time keeping her eyes open.

The recorded images of Times Square filled the screen in the den.

Austin and his friend had already crashed. "It's midnight somewhere," he'd told them.

"I really want next year to be better."

"You and me both," Erin said, lifting the glass holding the champagne in the air.

Parker had stopped drinking when the first raindrops hit the sky-lights over the dining room. Erin, on the other hand, was going to feel it in the morning. "I know why mine needs to be better. Why does yours?"

Erin answered with a question. "Do you ever want to forget the past?"

Interesting question. "I sometimes wanted to *change* the past." Forgetting it would mean forgetting her parents.

Erin shook her head. "I just want to forget. Wake up with amnesia and chase the fear away."

The hair on Parker's neck stood up. "Fear of what?"

Her nervous laugh proved the liquor was talking. "Him."

"Your ex?"

"Yeah." And just like that, Erin realized what she'd said, sat taller, and put her glass down. "I shouldn't have said that. Forget I said that." Panic laced her words.

Parker took a slow breath . . . in . . . and out.

Erin looked as if she wanted to run away.

Parker folded her knees into her chest, wrapped her arms around her legs. "Six months after my parents died . . . I was sitting here, on this couch. I'd had a couple of drinks. I'd finally gotten Mallory to go to bed. She cried for our parents every night. Austin was angry, broody about it. I had had it. I was so busy taking care of them I hadn't even processed what had happened. I started taking big swigs out of the bottle of tequila I thought I could handle. Next thing I knew I'd tossed clothes in a bag and was sitting in my car."

Erin stared at her.

"I was just gonna leave. The pressure . . . I couldn't anymore."

"What happened?"

"I made it to the end of the driveway and stopped. I was drunk. I was willing to leave but wasn't willing to put my brother and sister through the pain of losing another family member."

Erin leaned forward, grabbed her hand. "I'm so sorry."

Parker leveled her gaze to Erin's. "I've never told them that story, and I'd appreciate it if you kept it between us."

"Of course." She offered a slight smile, narrowed her eyes. "My ex was very controlling. If I detoured from what he wanted, he forced me back in line."

"Forced?"

Erin looked like she wanted to be sick. "He was a big man. With a temper. The first time he hit me we were both shocked. Or that's how he played it."

Parker swallowed hard, placed a hand over Erin's.

"I should have run away then. But I didn't."

"God, Erin . . . I'm so sorry."

She squeezed her eyes shut. "I don't think I should have told you any of that."

Parker tried to smile. "I won't tell anyone," she promised. "If you need someone to talk to . . ."

Erin shook her head. "I've said too much already."

Yeah, Parker could tell Erin was regretting her admission.

"Three! Two! One!"

They both looked at the TV the moment the ball in Times Square signaled the new year.

Parker picked up her glass and handed Erin hers with a forced smile. "To a fresh new start for both of us."

Erin sighed. "I can drink to that."

CHAPTER TWENTY-SEVEN

Parker started the new year in the principal's office being scolded.

"I'm officially putting you on notice." Janice's humorless face held no compassion. "I've given this a lot of thought over the holiday break and feel I need to draw the line. Because mornings have routinely been difficult for you in your current situation, I've put you on lunch through afternoon pickup."

Parker tried not to take her reprimand personally. "I understand."

"I hope so. I'm not without compassion, Parker, I'm not. But we need to be able to count on you—"

"I understand," she interrupted.

"Good."

She stood, shook off the nerves the meeting created inside her, and left the office. Parker smiled at the office staff that looked away when she made eye contact.

Great, I've pissed off everyone.

Since she wasn't officially on the clock, Parker went to the empty break room and found a newspaper. She dug out the coupons and sat down at one of the tables. Her cell phone buzzed.

How did it go? It was a text from Colin.

I still have a job . . . Barely.

Hang in there. We should be done here in about a week.

Take your time. I feel better knowing you guys are there. When Parker hit send, she found it hard to believe that was actually how she felt. If Colin, Fabio, Glynn, Russ, Ray . . . so many names ran through her head. If any of them saw a problem, they would pounce on it. Arguably they didn't walk up to the house, but Erin was around most days and she had Colin's number to report any concerns.

You've come a long way, Annie. He ended his text with a winking smiley face wearing a cowboy hat.

That's Miss Oakley to you, cowboy.

The man made her smile. In fact, the man made her do a lot of things.

The water had receded enough that Colin's crew was back in the wash replacing broken boards and reinforcing the metal that held them together. Foundation rocks were being replaced, and dirt was being compacted along the sides of the wash again to keep it from being undermined in the next storm. Other than the never-ending job of digging out mounds of mud that was being piled up everywhere, there was nothing Parker could do to help.

Austin only had a five-and-a-half-hour day at school that started at seven in the morning. Now that the Christmas tree lot was behind him, he was putting in applications at different places throughout town. He liked the money. Mallory's schedule was virtually unchanged. Monday and Wednesday classes ten to two, and Tuesday and Thursday's from one to four. When she wasn't in school, she was waiting tables or studying.

Parker had marked up a calendar with their schedules on it to try and determine when they were all going to be home at the same time.

It wasn't often. And would be even less so when Austin got a job.

Still, they were determined to have at least one or two meals a week as a family. Something about spending time with the Hudsons over the holidays had shown them that was important.

Parker finished with the coupons and wrote up her list with the grocery store mailer at her side. She had managed to cut their food bill by 30 percent since her initial conversation with Nora. Parker was pretty proud of that.

Five minutes before the bell rang, she made her way to the auditorium that doubled as the lunchroom. When the kids started running in, Parker pasted on her smile and accepted hugs from the students that missed her.

She liked her job. The students, anyway. Yeah, once in a while she'd have to referee mean kids, but the little ones were always such a joy. Parker kept her eye on the positive and realized this was the last year she'd be with these kids. The summer would be dedicated to finding a new norm. A schedule of her own she could count on that would actually get her somewhere in her life.

"Miss Parker, can you help me open this?"

"Of course. Juice boxes are my specialty."

~

Colin loved having Parker over to his place. It was selfish of him to not want to share her, but he didn't care.

She was on her way over, so he'd jumped in the shower the moment he walked through the door.

Enough time had elapsed from his soaking wet desert trip over New Year's to now that he could bring up their trip to Cabo without clueing her in that Mallory had said anything.

Colin rinsed the shampoo out of his hair and turned off the water. He grabbed a towel after stepping out of the shower and rubbed it over his head. He stopped moving and listened through the open door to his bathroom.

Noise from his kitchen wafted up the stairs. "Parker?" he called.

"It's me. I let myself in."

He smiled as he pulled the towel over his hips and tied it in place. He was half tempted to walk into his kitchen like he was and see if he could entice her into some predinner exercise. It had been over a week since he'd gotten her alone and relaxed enough to get naked. Seven days too long. The only time he'd managed to spend the night with her had been Christmas Eve, and that had been a fluke. Neither one of them had the energy to do more than snuggle.

But he liked that, too.

In fact, it was the one part of their relationship they were both missing out on.

He hoped tonight would change that. It was Friday. The forecast didn't call for rain until Monday. He was hoping to convince her to spend the night.

Colin wanted to wake up with her. Make love to her when she was half-asleep and dreamy in the morning. He looked down, told his body to relax, and shifted his thoughts.

He quickly dressed and started down the stairs. He heard Parker laughing. At first he thought she was on the phone, then he heard another voice.

"Good thing I didn't come down here naked," Colin said as he walked in the kitchen.

"Yeah, nobody wants to see that." Matt stood at the island, a beer in his hand.

Parker raised her hand. "I do."

Colin pushed Matt aside. "Go away," he teased.

Matt laughed but didn't leave.

Parker met him halfway and lifted her lips to his. He kissed her briefly and smiled.

"Matt says Friday night is happy hour around here."

Colin grabbed a beer and joined his brother. "Yes, but normally he lets me know first."

"I texted. You didn't answer." Matt looked at Parker. "He's bad about returning his texts."

"I never have that problem."

"That's because you're a girl," Matt teased.

She nodded, looked down at herself. "The boob effect. I get it."

"Boobs over boys always win."

"Do you ever listen to yourself?" Colin chided his brother.

"Not if I have another choice."

"Neanderthal."

The front door opened, and the click of his sister's high heels sounded on the tile. "I saw Matt's bike."

Colin turned and faced Parker, mouthed the words *I'm sorry.*

Good sport that she was, she smiled and mouthed back . . . *It's okay.*

Grace waved a bottle of white wine. "I was hoping you were here." She walked over to Parker first and gave her a hug. "I'm tired of drinking beer, and that's all Colin ever has."

"You're complaining about my free beer?"

Grace came over to him and kissed his cheek. "No, I'm complaining that your free selection is limited to beer. There's a woman in your life, time to step it up."

Matt waved his finger at him. "The woman has spoken."

Grace looked in his silverware drawer, paused. "Wait, do you even have a wine opener?"

"Of course I do." *Wait . . . do I?*

He rummaged through a utensil drawer until he found one a girl he once dated had left behind. Colin took the bottle from his sister.

"I bought him wineglasses a couple of years ago, so I know he has those," Grace told Parker.

"The well-rounded bachelor."

Parker sat on one of the barstools at the island.

"How is the project?" Grace asked him.

"We're wrapping it up *again*. Pulled out another twenty-three thousand cubic yards."

"That's a lot of mud," Matt said.

"You're telling me. And the long-range forecast isn't showing any significant breaks over the next few weeks," Parker told them. "I think we can say that the drought is over."

Grace set the glasses down. "No one is screaming that yet. They wouldn't dare because that would mean lifting water restrictions in the summer and lowering rates from DWP."

Yeah, the Department of Water and Power was great about increasing everyone's bill, but sucked at lowering it.

"Well, I haven't seen the property this green in years. Too bad the hillsides look like crap," Parker said.

"I've been meaning to get over there." Grace handed Colin a glass to fill once the cork popped free.

"You're welcome anytime."

Colin handed Parker the wine, lifted his beer in the air. "To a night where we don't have to worry if Noah's ark is big enough to hold us all."

That had Parker laughing. "Cheers."

Grace took a seat beside Parker. "I bet you can't wait for Cabo."

Colin held his breath and looked at Parker.

She sipped her wine and Colin could see her wheels turning. "I'm looking forward to it."

His sister closed her eyes, smiled into a thought. "Sandy beaches, warm sun."

"No mud," Matt said.

Grace opened her eyes abruptly and turned toward Parker. "Wait a minute. Have you traveled to Mexico since they mandated a passport to come back into the States?"

Parker shook her head. "No, actually."

"Do you even have a passport?" Grace asked.

Colin looked at Matt, who was looking across the room.

"Actually . . ." Parker met Colin's eyes. "No. I don't. I'm working on it, though."

He opened his mouth to say something, Grace cut him off. "Cuz you have nothing better to do these days than deal with government agencies that love to make you wait."

"I assumed you had one," Colin said.

Grace waved him off. "Men never think everything through."

"Hey!" Matt yelled.

"When is the trip again?"

Colin told her the dates.

Parker revealed the day of her scheduled appointment at the passport office.

Grace took charge. "That's cutting it way too close, one week off and you're screwed. You need to push those dates back a couple of weeks, big brother."

"That's easy enough."

Parker's face brightened as if a weight had been lifted.

When Grace stood and moved behind Parker so she couldn't see her, his sister looked directly at him and mouthed the words *You owe me.*

Colin looked at Matt, who smiled and changed the subject.

God, he loved his siblings.

CHAPTER TWENTY-EIGHT

Heat swam up against her face, her hair whipped around with the force of the wind. She couldn't breathe. Everything was dark. She couldn't see them, no longer heard their voices calling out to her.

If only the smoke would lift so she didn't have to crawl.

She coughed and sputtered the ashes that fell into her mouth. Austin, Mallory . . . Where are you?

Only she couldn't scream.

All she could do was crawl.

Fear clenched her heart in a grip so tight it threatened to stop it altogether.

Austin!

Mallory!

Not again.

Her hand landed on an arm.

The arm didn't move.

Agony told her to look away.

She couldn't.

Colin lay there motionless, his eyes a blank stare.

Parker screamed.

"Wake up. Parker, wake up."

She jolted from her sleep, heart racing, with sweat beading on her brow. "Oh, God."

Colin wrapped his arms around her and pulled her into his chest. "Shhh, it's okay. Just a bad dream."

She couldn't stop trembling. "You were dead. The fire . . . the smoke."

"Shhh."

"I couldn't find them. It felt so real."

"Just a dream. I'm here."

Her breathing started to slow. "I thought I was over the nightmares."

Colin stroked her hair and pulled her back down to the bed. His room was dark, the digital clock told her it was after three in the morning.

"Do you have them a lot?" he asked.

"I did. They'd gotten better in the last couple of months. I thought I was past it."

"Do you want to talk about it?"

She closed her eyes, held him tight. "It's always the same. There's a fire. I can't see it, but I smell it, feel it . . . hear it. My mouth is full of ashes and I can't yell. At first, I hear Austin and Mallory, then I can't. I'm crawling and scared they've left me. That I'll find them. Only sometimes it's not them. It's my parents."

She felt tears in her eyes.

"I keep thinking I didn't get them out in time. If I'd only left sooner."

"Oh, Parker."

"My dream is so twisted, like an alternative reality of what could have been."

"Just a dream, hon. It can't hurt you."

"Why did all this happen, Colin?"

"I don't know. But I'm here, and it isn't going to happen again."

She felt him kiss the top of her head. "I'm sorry I woke you."

"Don't be. I'm glad I'm here to hold and calm you down. We got this, Parker. It's all going to be okay. Now go back to sleep so I can wake you in a few hours and make love to you again."

"M'kay." She closed her eyes to the feel of him stroking her hair.

~

She felt bad. Here it was on a Sunday, and she was working Colin's butt off. Another set of storms was due to roll in that week, and the guesthouse roof was showing signs of problems.

Matt had just gotten off of a twenty-four-hour shift, and he was up on the roof with Colin assessing the damage and securing a tarp.

The only joy in having the men on the roof was watching Matt trying to gain Erin's attention.

Parker and Erin were back at shoveling mud off walkways and talking in hushed tones. "It's so obvious he's into you."

"Not going to happen, Parker."

"I can tell you're attracted." The universe could see it from a galaxy away.

"Doesn't mean I'm going to do anything about it. I'm not ready."

A shovelful of mud made its way into a wheelbarrow. "The ex?"

"Yeah."

Parker wasn't going to push it.

Colin and Matt secured a tarp over the composite roof and worked their way off.

"That is a main priority by spring," Colin told her.

"The undercoat took on a lot of fire damage. Something you couldn't really see by looking at it. It's why the shingles are flying off in the wind." Matt smiled at the two of them, happy in his knowledge about fire damage and roofs.

"How much is that going to cost?" It all came down to money for Parker.

"They'd have to tear this down to the plywood since the paper underneath is what's shot. You're looking at six thousand, minimum, hired done."

Less than Parker initially thought. "I'd have to hire someone. I don't know the first thing about putting on a new roof."

"I can get a couple guys from the station, and Colin knows his way around a roof. We could knock this out in a weekend for what the materials will cost. Which is what, Colin . . . couple grand?" Matt asked his brother.

"About that."

"I couldn't ask you to do that."

Colin looked at his brother. "I didn't hear her ask, did you?"

"Nope."

"Guys, please . . ."

"Well, since you asked so nicely," Colin said.

"No. That's not what I meant. Please . . . as in *sarcasm*."

"The answer is still yes. We just need to wait for the rain to stop." Colin turned to Erin. "I'd like to see what happened on the inside, if you don't mind."

Erin balanced the shovel against the outside wall and walked them to the front door. Parker followed behind them through the open-concept living room and small kitchen to the bedroom. Very few personal belongings had joined what was already in the space when she'd rented it to Erin. No pictures, which struck her as a little strange. Everything was immaculate. Almost stale. There was water damage on an exterior wall in the corner where several shingles had blown off over the Christmas storm and then took on water over New Year's.

"Do you have a pencil?" Matt asked.

Erin smiled and nodded before walking out of the room and returning with said pencil.

Matt marked on the wall the outline of the water spot. "Chances are you're going to see this line since it's nearly dry now. But if the damage grows the next time it rains, then the tarp isn't working, and we'll have to get in here before spring or risk more interior damage."

Colin moved over to the switch on the wall. "Keep this fan going to dry it out. If you see any mold—"

"I'll tell Parker."

Matt handed her back the pencil when he was done writing on the wall. "We don't want you getting sick."

Erin was blushing.

"I'm going to need a drywall guy for this," Parker mused out loud.

"I can help demo," Colin told her. "But I'll let the professionals handle the new stuff, mud, tape, texture, and paint. And before you ask, I don't know exactly what that's going to cost. The damage we see on this side is usually twice as bad once you open the wall up."

"If it ends up being too much, have your insurance company come out and make another claim."

She'd already thought about that. Parker wasn't quite ready to make those calls yet, but it was coming.

Colin turned to walk out of the room.

Matt moved too quickly, and his foot caught the side of the dresser. He must have hit it hard because he jumped back and brought his fist up to his side to shake off what looked like pain.

At the same time, Erin took a giant step back and sucked in a breath. Her knees hit the back of the bed and she caught herself right before falling. Terror was written all over Erin's face.

Parker saw her start to tremble.

Matt froze.

Colin stood perfectly still.

Erin stood there paralyzed.

"When was the last time you ate?" Parker jumped to the first thing she could think of to take the attention off her friend and the fear in her eyes. She took a step and reached Erin's side and helped her sit on the bed. "She gets hypoglycemic," Parker lied. "Isn't that right, Erin?"

A numb nod was her reply.

"Colin, can you see if there's some juice or something in Erin's fridge?"

"Sure." Colin took off.

Matt lowered his hand slowly and stepped back. "Are you diabetic?"

Erin shook her head. "No." She looked at Parker. "Just dizzy sometimes when I don't eat."

Parker kept the lie going. "It was worse in the summer."

Colin returned with a glass of orange juice. "Here."

Erin's hands shook. Parker helped her bring the glass to her lips. A couple of deep breaths and some of the color returned to her face. "I'm better now. Thanks."

"You guys go on outside. I'm going to make sure she's okay." Parker directed traffic.

"You sure you're all right?" Matt asked.

"I'm fine."

Parker waited until after the sound of the door closing before taking the glass out of Erin's hands.

A rush of breath left her lungs. "Thank you, Parker."

She placed a hand over Erin's. "Anytime."

~

Colin walked with Matt up the side of the jobsite while Parker and Erin sat in the guesthouse.

"You saw that, right?" Matt asked him.

"Yeah."

"She thought I was going to hit her."

That was the exact feeling he'd gotten.

His brother was tensing up. "That fucking pisses me off. Who would hit her? Who hits a woman?"

"I don't know, little brother, but I'm pretty sure if you ask her, she'd deny it."

Matt stomped around the jobsite, the energy his anger created fueled him. Violence wasn't something the Hudsons understood. The only time their parents yelled at each other was right after their father's motorcycle accident when their mother tossed the keys to his bike in the neighbor's backyard.

The neighbor had a territorial pit bull at the time, and there was no way any of them were hopping that fence to retrieve the keys.

Love and fear fueled his parents' fight, and it ended in a closed bedroom door and the three of them turning up the television so they couldn't hear their parents *making up.*

The rules set by their father were simple. *"Don't hit girls. Ever! Defend yourself against boys, but never throw the first punch. If you see a woman getting hit, or someone weaker getting ganged up on and you don't step in, you'll have me to deal with."* Their father had a badge that said he was licensed to protect and to serve, but he told them both that they didn't need permission to do the right thing.

Colin understood the anger coursing through his brother. He felt it, too. Only his brother seemed to have a thing for Erin, and that was making this even harder.

"Talk me down, brother," Matt told him.

"Let's walk further up the creek."

CHAPTER TWENTY-NINE

"Why isn't Parker with you?"

Colin was starting to think his mom wanted to see his girlfriend more than she wanted to see him.

"It's raining," he told her.

Matt had his usual position on the couch with their dad watching a game. "Parker is afraid she's going to melt," Matt teased.

"She doesn't like leaving her house when it's raining. She's too afraid she won't get back in," Colin explained. He'd spent a half an hour on the phone with her the night before trying to talk her into dinner with his family. She wouldn't have it.

"Does the wash flood that much?" Nora asked.

"It does."

The sound of the front door slamming was familiar. Grace walked in, her tennis shoes squeaking on the tile floor. "Sorry I'm late. People don't know how to drive in this town with a little rain."

"And you do?" Matt teased.

Grace whacked him on the back of his head, kissed their father, and then turned to Colin and their mom. While she was hugging him, she asked, "Where's Parker?"

"She melts," Matt and their father said at the same time.

Grace caught Colin's eye roll. "Everything okay with you two?"

"Couldn't be better." If he were honest, he'd like it if she were a bit more accessible.

"I know that look," Grace said.

"What look?"

She waved a finger in his face. "That one. Where something is eating at you but you're keeping it in."

"Nothing is eating at me." He sat on a high stool at the kitchen island and popped a chip in his mouth.

His mom stood quietly behind the counter cutting vegetables for the salad.

Grace stared at him, saying nothing.

Even the commentary from the sports bar section of the house was silent.

"I can count on one hand the amount of times I've gotten Parker off her property since we've been dating," he told them. "It doesn't matter how much I assure her that I can get her back in and that there isn't anything she can do to stop the mountain from sliding off and into her yard, she won't leave."

"She's scared," Grace said.

"I get that. I just wish she'd believe in me."

His mom picked up the cutting mat filled with food and dumped it in a bowl. "I don't think this has anything to do with you."

"I want it to. I want her to know she can count on me."

Grace grabbed a bottle of water from the fridge. "You can't tell a woman that, you have to prove it over time. Especially with someone like Parker. She's like a single mom. She has the house, the kids, the responsibilities, and no man to help with any of it. She's been doing it on her own her way, and so far it's worked."

"That's just it. She doesn't have to do it all alone. I'm around."

Grace shook her head. "You're dating, Colin. Not married. Women are alone until they're not. We start depending on a man and that's when they disappear and leave us floating in the water without a life preserver."

Seemed like Grace just tossed a suitcase of her own baggage out there for everyone to see.

"And that right there is why I won't date single moms." Matt had moved off the couch to join the conversation.

Their dad turned down the volume on the TV.

"The older you get, the less of a chance you're going to find a woman without kids of her own," Nora told him.

Matt reached into the chip bowl. "It's like you always said. Don't date someone you can't see yourself falling in love with."

"I said that in reference to profession. I dated your father and spent thirty years worried he wouldn't come home from work."

"I came home every night," Emmitt told her.

None of them brought up the time he'd taken the spill on the motorcycle and was in the hospital for two weeks.

"And if I remember right, I told you that when you started to date that flight attendant."

Colin remembered her. "The blonde." She was model hot and knew it.

Matt smiled. "She was fun."

Grace nudged Matt and brought him back to the conversation. "The point is . . . blondie would have been off all over the world, and your jealous personality would have gone crazy over that."

"Your sister's right," Emmitt said from the couch.

"I'm not that bad."

Colin grinned. "You're not going to win that argument."

Matt waved a chip in the air. "How did this conversation get turned onto me? This is about Parker and Colin."

"Parker isn't a flight attendant, or a cop."

"Or a single mom," Grace added.

"She might as well be," Matt said.

Colin shook his head. "Doesn't matter. I'd date her anyway."

"Then be patient with her," his mom told him. "She's been through a lot. She'll let you know when she needs you to step in. Just be there when she does."

~

"I think we all need to park our cars on the other side of the wash tonight." Parker dangled her car keys in her hand.

The app Colin had shown her was displaying orange and red bands in the storm headed their way. With her job on the line, she wasn't about to miss work because her car wouldn't pass over the wash.

Austin and Mallory were sharing dish duty since Parker had cooked. "My keys are on the desk in my room," Austin told her.

"I'll move mine once I'm done."

Parker retrieved her brother's keys and grabbed a sweater. It hadn't started to rain yet, but it was still cold.

She drove his car to the other side of the wash and parked it outside of the gate and out of the danger zone. His car was way too low to the street to manage going over any rocks. Her and Mallory's cars could take a little more abuse. She locked the car tight and took note of her neighbors who had done the same thing. Pitch-black and quiet, the night held an ominous feeling that something was coming. The air smelled like rain.

Parker enjoyed the quiet as she walked back to the house. She opened the gate in a locked position and grabbed a garbage can and laid it down next to the motor that ran the gate. She hoped her effort would deflect mud and rocks that would likely wash down Sutter Canyon during the night. Either way, she was doing whatever she could to avoid an expense later on. She propped the "Authorized Personnel Only" sign on one side of her driveway, and the "No Trespassing" sign on the other.

Colin had two of his crew coming in the morning to try and keep her culverts clear. It had taken hand crews several days to loosen the rocks wedged inside the pipes that ran under her driveway. Backbreaking work that no power tool could make easier.

Four pieces of equipment stayed behind when the bulk of the guys moved on to other jobs once they'd cleaned the basins out. It was comforting to see them there. She was hopeful they'd be able to stay on top of the mess Mother Nature was bound to throw their way.

She walked on top of the Arizona crossing and leaned on the split rail fence that was more decorative than functional. Water flowed under her. The sound was peaceful since it had been several days since the last rain. She closed her eyes and imagined it was a river . . . a real river and not a wash that only funneled runoff from the hillsides. She'd always thought she'd want to one day have a small home on an open piece of land where a river ran three hundred sixty-five days a year. Now when she brought up those images, she saw walls of fire with no way to escape.

She supposed the need for a therapy couch was in her future. But it would have to wait for another day.

Parker took a second trip down the driveway with her car, parking it inside the gate, but out of the danger zone. By the time she had to leave for work, one of the crew would be there, and she was confident they'd be able to get her out.

Mallory was pulling her car out as Parker walked up. "I parked Austin's car down the street a ways. Lots of neighbors did the same," she told her sister. "How early are you leaving in the morning?"

"Study group, so early."

"You might wanna park outside the gate, then."

Mallory gave her a thumbs-up and drove off.

She walked over to the guesthouse and knocked on the door.

Erin was already in her pajamas. "Sorry to bother you."

"No worries."

It looked like she'd been crying.

"Are you going anywhere tomorrow?" She reminded her about the parking situation, but Erin shook her head.

"I'm hibernating. Getting some work done."

Parker offered a smile. "You all right?"

"I'm okay. I am."

"Well, you know where I am if you need me."

"Thanks, Parker."

She turned and walked away.

Once inside the house, Parker went around turning off lights.

Mallory bounced up the back stairs from the garage and rounded the corner.

"All set?"

Mallory nodded and paused. "Thanks, sis."

"For what?"

"For taking care of everything around here. I know it's not easy, and I don't thank you enough." Mallory took a step forward and gave her a hug.

She squeezed her sister hard. "That means a lot to me. Thank you."

"I love you."

"Love you, too."

Mallory disappeared down the hall to her bedroom.

Scout was nowhere in sight, and Austin's bedroom door was closed.

Sushi meowed at her feet and looked at the door.

"Oh, no, you don't. Not tonight."

Her cat complained for ten minutes about not being let out, but then got over it and joined Parker on the couch.

She looked at the picture of her parents over the fireplace. For the first time in a long time, she spoke to them.

"Can you believe Austin's almost out of high school?"

They stared at her, their smiles frozen in time.

"He's a great kid. Reminds me a lot of you, Dad. He has your sarcasm. I thought I was witty, that boy has a comeback for everything. I'm not sure what happened to your culinary skills with me, Mom . . . but Mallory seems to have caught on to some of them. I try, but I suck at it. Nora's helped me out with that. I think you'd like her. I think you'd both like the whole family." She sighed. "Colin is amazing. He puts up with me and all my drama."

She found her eyes swelling with tears. "It's been really hard this year. I keep asking what you guys would do. But it's hard. I hope you're both up there keeping things going on whatever path it is we have to have. No derailing."

Sushi jumped in her lap, circled twice, and then sat down.

"Just keep them safe, okay? Watch over them. Together we're going to be fine. We made it after you, we'll make it after this."

She wiped the tears that fell down her cheeks.

Her phone buzzed with a text message.

Everything is going to be fine tonight. I'll be there tomorrow after the morning meeting in the office.

Her belly warmed. Did you bug the house? Are you spying on me?

Ha! I don't have to spy on you, I know you're nervous. Whatever happens, we'll fix it.

You're a great guy, Mr. Hudson. I haven't figured out why you're still single. She was all smiles.

I'm not.

She wasn't expecting his words, which made them all the more powerful.

I'll see you tomorrow.

Good night, Miss Oakley. Get some sleep.

Parker looked up at her parents again. Couldn't help but feel they were smiling a little brighter. "Did you make him happen?"

They didn't answer.

"I love you," she told the quiet room.

~

She didn't fall asleep until after two in the morning. Rain started to fall, and every gust of wind kept her from rounding that last counted sheep to a blissful night's sleep.

Sushi jumping up on her bed woke her. The sun was up, barely.

Scout sat beside her bed, his nose rested on the edge as he scoffed at her.

"What are you doing?"

His whole body moved with the shake of his tail.

Austin must have left already. The clock said seven.

At least they still had power.

She padded to the window to see a soggy day.

From her view, she saw her car parked on the other side of the wash, and one car that belonged to someone on the crew. No white county trucks in sight.

She looked to the sky. Dark and dismal. And nothing that couldn't wait for a cup of coffee and a hard-boiled egg.

Scout whined at the door, so she opened it and let him out.

He was smart enough to stay away from raging water. The dog didn't even like jumping in the swimming pool after a ball.

Mallory had brewed a pot of coffee before leaving for school, so all Parker had to do was pour herself a cup.

Within five minutes Scout asked to be let back in, and she obliged.

She clicked through a few e-mails . . . nothing important, and finished her coffee.

After dressing in the jeans from the day before, a sweatshirt, and a raincoat Mallory had bought her for Christmas, she ran a toothbrush over her teeth and made her way outside.

Parker forced the dog to stay inside. There was no real way of knowing what was going on out there until she was in it. With only a couple of hours to do a damage report before she needed to get ready for work, Parker walked out of the house.

One step on the driveway and she knew today was going to be different.

Mud and rocks flowed from under the burned fence she'd left in place to hold back the hillside behind it. A look over the fence and Parker's eyes grew wide. No less than three feet of mud climbed up behind it, forcing much to escape and run across her driveway and into what remained of their manicured yard. Water rushed, but not to the point where she couldn't walk through it, over the entire field that once housed the barns. The chain-link on the east side of the property held back rock, but not water and certainly not mud. It was everywhere . . . but spread out, as much of it rushed to the lowest point.

The wash.

She walked over the dip in the driveway. The water level was rising, and the culverts were clogging up, but had yet to hit the saturation point. The noise from above was deafening. She heard rocks slamming against the structures and the roar of the water.

The sound of a skip loader beeped outside her gate. She recognized the driver who worked to push the escaping mud from Sutter Canyon as it fell.

Her neighbors were all outside. One was on his personal tractor trying to keep up with the mud. His son had a shovel in his hand and was pushing water away from the fence.

As much of a mess things were, the waterways were somewhat under control. Her neighbor Tracy walked up to the gate. "This is crazy."

"I'm over it."

She could see from her face, her neighbor was, too.

"What's it look like up there?" Tracy indicated the main wash with a wave of her hand.

"I haven't looked yet."

Together they walked along the high end of the property as a cloud overhead let loose.

Tracy carried an umbrella, where Parker didn't bother. A raincoat was good enough. Besides, she'd take a shower before going to work, so there was no reason to stay completely dry now. Not that staying dry was possible. Wind blew the rain in all directions.

They walked past the first structure that had reached the brim and was starting to spill over. The second structure was bowing under the force of water behind it.

"I don't think this will last the afternoon," Parker told her.

"It doesn't look like it."

Band-Aid on a hemorrhage. Water rushed off the mountain like anxious kids on a slip-and-slide. All Parker could think was she hoped the people downstream had prepared. If the dam burst, homes could be lost.

By the time they walked back by her driveway, Keith had positioned the backhoe portion of his skip loader by her culverts. Rocks were threatening to clog it again.

Parker waved at the man and kept walking beside her neighbor.

A shout from the Sutters had them both turning. There had to be eight people, all with shovels, working against time.

Water flowed off the back hillside and straight toward their house.

Seeing the need, Parker rushed back to her house and grabbed as many shovels as she could before joining the fight.

"The back needs more hands." This from the homeowner.

Parker ran to the back and started pushing mud and rock away from the house as it flowed toward them.

No matter how hard they worked, the mud kept coming.

So far, they were staying on top of it. Even when the sky opened up and rain pelted down on all of them, they managed to divert much of the mud. They grabbed bigger rocks and created dams. Pots from the garden and plywood they'd bought as a precaution.

Parker lost track of time.

The rain kept coming.

It took a bolt of lightning to make her snap out of the fight.

She looked at her watch. She had to go. Didn't want to.

Parker handed her shovel to someone who didn't have one. "I need to check on my house."

"Go."

Almost jogging down their driveway, and then past her gate, Keith stopped her.

Rain poured in buckets. "Your bridge is gone!"

"What?"

"Gone. Your bridge is gone."

Her nose flared. "You mean I can't cross over the wash?" She assumed he meant the culverts had filled up. But that she expected. So why was he wide-eyed and serious?

"Your footbridge."

Chills ran down Parker's back.

And not the good kind.

She ran around the corner and lost her ability to speak.

Not only were the culverts filled up, but water was hitting the side of her Arizona crossing with such a force that the wave it crafted was fifteen feet tall. The split rail decorative fence was annihilated, and the footbridge had been swept away as if it had never been.

"Oh my God."

She walked closer.

"Oh my God!"

She stood on the high side of the water flow, outside of the danger zone, and watched as the water gushed by.

Her heart slammed in her chest. Seeing her home, completely cut off from her reach, made her want to scream.

The roar of the water made it impossible to hear her own voice. Boulders the size of smart cars bounced in the water.

Once she caught her breath, she walked up the length of her property. Water rushed over the K-rails Colin and his crew put in place. It was obvious that the structures had gaping holes in them because of the amount of water that rushed through sections of the structures meant to hold them back.

The next time she looked at her watch it was a half an hour after she was meant to be at work.

Not that it mattered.

The keys to her car were in the house, and she couldn't get over the water to retrieve them.

She stood at the water's edge, chest heaving for several minutes, and mourned what would be the end of her job with the school district.

Janice would fire her.

And Parker didn't care.

She walked off the high side of the wash and back to her neighbors who were struggling to save their home.

This was more important.

This was where she needed to be.

CHAPTER THIRTY

Colin turned up Creek Canyon to see a police car backing down. Full-on reverse, lights flashing.

"Holy shit."

Mud was flowing down the street, bringing rocks with it. Not something normal cars could handle.

Colin turned the flashing light on his truck on and pulled to the side. He lowered his window and waited for the sheriff to pull alongside him.

"We're locking this down," the sheriff yelled between the cars.

The water in the wash had swelled to street level and was billowing out of its banks.

"I have equipment coming."

The officer nodded. "We need to keep this clear for emergency vehicles."

"I'm on it." Colin rolled up his window and slowly made his way up the street.

He called in to Ed, put him on speaker. "We have a situation here. I need every available piece of machinery and man to run them at Creek Canyon."

"I already got a call from the sheriff's department. Did the structures hold?"

"I'm not even there yet." Colin stopped his truck by one of the Arizona crossings that traversed the wash. Water was flowing so fast it was hitting the sides and spilling over the cross streets, directing the mud to run down the center of the road.

"Keep me updated."

Colin hung up.

Two of his crew were busy chipping away at what looked like a losing battle by Parker's and her neighbors' gates.

He pulled his truck to the side and jumped out.

Keith cut the engine to his skip loader, making it possible to hear him.

"I need you to sweep down the road, keep it clear enough for emergency vehicles."

"Got it."

"How does it look up there?"

Keith shrugged. "A shit show, but nothing we didn't expect."

"Help is coming. Let's give them a path."

Keith fired up his loader and moved it down the street.

Colin slid back into his truck and drove the rest of the way in. His guys managed to keep Parker's drive somewhat clear. From the big stuff, in any event.

The crossing over the creek was unidentifiable. It took him a minute to realize that Parker's footbridge was gone. He noticed her car and wondered if she was inside the house watching. His two texts to her earlier hadn't resulted in a reply. He checked his phone again. Still nothing. He'd bet money that she was freaking out.

The rain was slowing down, and according to his app, the heavy bands were behind them. Although clouds often got stuck in mountain ranges, and microbursts brought a gush of crap with them.

He parked his truck and walked the high bank of the wash.

Both structures took on some damage, he could tell by the way the water swirled and moved. Both were completely overwhelmed and spilling over. The amount of water was simply too much for their capacity.

There was nothing anyone could do about that.

Two of his hand crews turned into the drive.

"Pull the chain-link back. Keep this clear." He pointed at the fence between the properties. The fence they'd replaced already. There was no point in letting the mud pile up behind the fence and block the neighbor's drive. Mud was going to go where it wanted to and take out whatever was in its path. And since there wasn't a structure at risk, Colin would just as soon clean it up when it was done.

"You got it, Boss."

From there, Colin stopped where he found reception on his phone and started calling everyone in.

He tried calling Parker, but she didn't pick up.

Worry creeped up his spine.

De Luca waved him over.

"How is your place holding up?"

"I have a year's worth of cleanup, but the house is okay so far."

"Good. Any chance you've seen Parker?"

"I saw her at the Sutters' about an hour ago."

Colin felt marginally better knowing she'd been spotted.

Trucks started showing up along with the media. Much as he wanted to keep them away, he really couldn't.

Colin found Parker halfway up the Sutters' driveway, shovel in her hand.

The smile on her face surprised him. "Nice of you to show up." Her voice was teasing.

He laughed. "I had that manicure scheduled for a month."

She opened her arms and he hugged her hard. "How are you holding up?"

"My bridge is gone."

"I saw."

"I'm stuck on this side of the wash."

"I figured that out."

"I'm going to get fired."

He squeezed her harder for that one. "There will be other jobs."

"No one died."

Sometimes death was the barometer. "Great attitude, Miss Oakley."

With a shrug of her shoulders she said, "It is what it is . . . What are you going to do?" Her question was rhetorical.

I love you.

The words sounded inside his head, and it took him a minute to realize he hadn't said them out loud.

His smile grew.

Yeah . . . he loved this woman.

When had that happened?

~

The rain had stopped, and behind it the sun started peeking through the clouds. The rainbow arching over the property made Parker smile.

She'd given two interviews for two different stations and then sat back and watched all the activity. Every possible county public works truck had descended on her property. There were three fire engines parked in the yard; one was from Matt's station, the other two were from the station up the street. Squad cars buzzed in and out.

Erin stood on the other side of the wash, bundled into a fur-lined coat.

"What a mess!"

"It's crazy everywhere." Parker shouted across the noise of the water and the trucks buzzing around. "Do we have power?"

"Yeah, but no water."

"Ah, damn." Parker spun around. "Don't go anywhere."

Matt walked over to her, waved across the creek to Erin.

"What's wrong?"

"Erin says the water is off. Do you know if it's a wide problem?"

"I haven't heard if it is."

There was only one working valve on that side of the wash, and it had been hit twice with debris down Sutter Canyon. Parker walked over to the PVC pipes sticking out of the ground, fresh with blue glue from the repairs they'd made a couple of weeks before. She opened the valve, and water gushed out.

The good news was, it wasn't a city problem.

The bad news was, it was hers.

Matt stood beside her. "It's on here, which means it's broken somewhere between this point and the house."

They both looked up at the same time.

"That has to be at least seven hundred feet."

Parker twisted the valve off.

Back at the bank of the wash, Parker called out to Erin. "Turn on the hose bib under that tree."

Erin waved and walked over to the hose and turned it on.

Nothing.

"I'm going out on a limb here and suggesting the break is in the wash."

"Let me guess, you're the smart one in the family," Parker teased.

Matt rolled his eyes.

"I have a fork for the main at the street, but it's inside the garage." The fork was a special tool needed to shut the water off.

Matt signaled one of the crew over.

Parker showed the man where the main connected, which was outside the gate and down the joint driveway two hundred feet away.

"I need to get on the other side of this," Parker told Matt.

"Why?"

"To close the valves at the junction box and avoid the house pipes backflowing."

Matt narrowed his eyes. "What does it matter if they do?"

"The whole house has a fire sprinkler system in the ceilings. When those pipes backflow, the alarm goes off and you guys are called." She patted his arm. "And since there won't be a way to fill the pipes back up until I figure out where the break is—"

Matt started to nod, understanding her problem. "Where do the main valves live?"

"They're inside the water heater room. Right off the sliding glass doors of the den. I'd tell Erin to do it, but if you turn the things the wrong way you empty the system. There are a lot of shutoffs in that room."

Matt patted her on the back. "Okay, I'll get over there."

The water in the creek still raged. "How?"

"Big boys have big toys." Matt walked away, and the next thing she knew, one of the fire engines pulled alongside the wash. When she saw one of the ladders being extended, she smiled.

"What is he doing?" Erin asked.

"He's coming over. Show him where the water heater is."

Matt climbed onto the ladder and crawled on top of it until he was able to jump down on the other side.

A crowd watched, and at least one news crew caught it on film.

"Is my brother showing off?" Colin walked up to her.

She explained the water problem as they watched Erin and Matt walking up the driveway.

Colin twisted around a couple of times, ran a hand through his hair. "That's a long distance to find a break."

In this, Parker felt a little more confident. "Sadly, I know way too much about plumbing."

"Oh?"

"There is a main up at the house, the one Matt is shutting off now. Another shutoff lives in the sprinkler box at the bottom of the drive. That big wooden box under the oak tree. There is another shutoff over by the swimming pool and guesthouse. Another one over here." She pointed to the one they tested from the street. "And the final resort is the one where we connect to city water at the corner."

Colin's eyes grew big. "Why so many?"

"Because it's a big freaking property and sadly, whoever put the main in originally didn't know what the hell they were doing. We've had constant breaks throughout the years. Each time we dig we find pipes with lots of purple connections."

"Purple?"

"As in primer. Whoever connected the pipes used the primer and not the glue. Unlike any normal house, the water main is buried so deep because it needed to go under the wash that we don't even know there's a problem until we get the water bill."

"Damn, Parker, that sucks."

"I know. With each break, my dad added another shutoff to isolate the break and work around it while he fixed it." But no matter how you looked at it, there was some serious digging in her future.

Colin draped an arm over her shoulders. "You're holding up remarkably well."

"The alternative would be falling apart, and that doesn't do anyone any good."

"You're something else," he told her.

"That and five bucks will buy me a Starbucks."

He laughed.

She leaned her head into his shoulder for a brief second.

Colin sighed. "Primer?"

Parker closed her eyes and shook her head. "Dipshit."

CHAPTER THIRTY-ONE

Colin's mom met them at his front door.

Inside, the house smelled savory. Whatever his mother had cooked, he could hardly wait to dig in.

"Look at this motley crew," she exclaimed.

Everyone took their shoes off at the door and left them on the front step.

"Hi, Mrs. Hudson." Mallory hugged her first, Austin followed next.

"You all look exhausted."

Colin waited until Parker and Erin filed inside before closing the door behind him.

"It's been a long day." Parker hugged Nora. "Thank you for cooking."

"It's the least I can do," she told them. "You must be the roommate I've heard so much about."

Erin smiled and shook her hand. "Tenant, actually. Erin," she said.

"*Tenant* sounds so impersonal. I like *roommate*. Call me Nora."

Parker gave Erin a half hug, agreeing with Nora.

"Where's the shower?" Austin went straight to the point.

Once the rain had stopped, the crews had dug out around the crossing in the wash enough so they could drive a truck over to the other side. But without running water, there was no way for any of them to wash off the day's grime.

Colin invited everyone to stay the night, but Parker nixed that. "The gate is wide open. We've been all over the news. I can't leave the house for long until all this dies down."

As much as Colin wanted to argue, he didn't.

"I'll show you where the one is down here," Nora said.

Colin waved for the girls to follow him upstairs. He showed Mallory and Erin the guest room and dragged Parker into the master bedroom with him.

Her shirt came off the moment the door was closed. "I can't wait to scrub this day off."

"I'll give you a two-minute head start and then I'm joining you," he told her.

She gave him a half-cocked smile. "Your mother is downstairs."

"I was talking about saving hot water, but if you wanted to linger for a while, I'm sure you can talk me into it."

"You're bad, Colin Hudson."

"Terrible, I know."

She turned her back to him and disappeared into his bathroom. He heard the toilet flush and the water turn on.

He stripped out of his clothes, waited until he heard her sigh under the warm stream of water before joining her.

Damn, she was beautiful. Water running down her hair and sticking to her eyelashes. "Room for me in here?"

Parker took a step to the side and smiled.

She'd brought her flower-scented shampoo with her and reached for it.

Colin took it from her hands and did the honors. "Turn around." He poured a generous portion in the palm of his hand and rubbed it into her hair.

She moaned and reached for the tile wall to steady herself. "God, that feels good."

The more pressure into the scalp, the more she moaned.

The more she moaned, the harder it was to tame his body to not get aroused.

"You're hired."

He would do this every day if she let him. "I have many talents I've yet to share with you."

"Oh?"

His fingers traced her neck, letting the soap run down her back. With liquid soap helping his quest, he massaged the stiff muscles in her shoulders and back as he washed away the reminders of the day.

"Ohhh."

His palms ran up her arms and down. Slid over her back to the curve of her hips. And because he was more than a little turned on, he reached around and made sure her breasts were squeaky clean.

Parker leaned back, her body flush with his. No hiding his erection.

"This was a bad idea." Her words were breathy.

He flicked one nipple to attention. "Tell me to stop and I will."

No, the opposite of stop came by her grabbing one of his hands and leading it to the space between her legs. So wet . . . she pushed against his hand as he moved his fingers inside of her.

Colin kissed the side of her neck. "More?" he questioned.

She nodded. "Faster. Please . . . make me . . ."

He found the nub of her clit and felt the cues her body sent him. He alternated pressure until he felt hers build, until she let her hand join his and moved faster. "I've got you," he whispered in her ear.

She let go and buried her cry in his arm.

He held her while she caught her breath.

"Your turn," she said, twisting around.

"You don't have—"

Her fingertips surrounded his cock. Never mind. He didn't have it in him to stop her.

She found the conditioner, the only reason he had it in the shower was for this very reason. But damn, it was better with her small hands taking charge. What he really wanted was to bury himself deep inside her, but he'd settle for this.

He thrust his hips into her hands, felt the swell of an orgasm rising to the surface.

With her body flush with his, her hands between them doing the work, he pushed her against the tile.

"Don't hold back," she told him.

There was no way he could.

Her fingers squeezed, her hands pumped . . . and he exploded in waves.

Colin held her against him, his orgasm evident on her belly.

They both started to laugh at the same time.

"We're so bad."

"Horrible."

"God, I needed that," Parker sighed.

"Me too."

They washed off quickly and managed to get out of the shower before the water turned ice-cold.

He couldn't stop smiling as she brushed out her wet hair, a towel wrapped around her body. Her butt peeked out from under, and he couldn't stop himself from giving her a playful pinch. She returned the favor by pulling his towel off completely. Unaffected, he shrugged and continued to brush his hair naked.

"No shame," she teased.

"Not around you."

Their eyes caught in the mirror. "Don't look so satisfied. Everyone's going to know."

He tried to frown.

"Forget it."

Oh, no . . . he wouldn't be forgetting any of that anytime soon.

~

Nora had the news on when they all showed up in the kitchen for dinner. She'd set the table that was part of Colin's great room and stacked plates by the stove. When Parker and Colin joined them, Austin was already sitting at the table shoveling food in.

Erin had brushed her wet hair back in a ponytail, and Mallory was still in the shower.

Apparently what Parker thought was a long shower with obvious outcomes, no one seemed to be wise to. "This looks amazing, Nora. Thank you."

"My pleasure, hon."

Colin gave his mom a hug. "Thanks, Mom."

"Everyone's talking about the flooding," Nora told them.

Erin took her plate to the table. "It was hard to believe."

"How long will it take to clean up?"

Parker didn't want to think about it.

"It has to stop raining before I can give you an estimate on that," Colin told his mom.

Colin walked behind Parker, ran a hand around her waist.

She smiled up at him. "I think we're going to be battling dirt all summer long," Parker said.

"Really?" Nora asked.

"The county project won't be active all summer. What I think Parker is saying is the runoff on their land," Colin said.

"It's everywhere," Austin chimed in. "Like two feet of mud . . . everywhere."

"Oh, I'm so sorry. And no running water?"

Mallory walked in the room, like all of them, her hair wet but her disposition brighter because of the shower.

"I'll get on that tomorrow, hopefully find a temporary fix to get the basics going."

"If the break is under the wash, we can't get to that until the water stops flowing," Austin said.

"We might be able to when it slows down," Colin said as he took a seat at the table.

Parker sat beside her brother and dug into the roast Nora had made. She moaned. "This is perfect."

"Brilliant," Erin added.

"So glad you're enjoying it."

They decompressed from the day by talking about it throughout their meal. At one point Austin pointed to the TV that was playing in the background. "Look, we're on the news." He jumped up and found the remote, turned up the volume.

"Creek Canyon was ravaged by wildfires last summer and is now suffering from devastating mudslides that are threatening homes throughout the area. Parker Sinclair lives at the epicenter of activity and had this to say."

Parker saw herself on the TV, larger than life. "The force of the water running off these hills needs to be respected. It doesn't abide road signs and speed limits. If you see it coming, get out of its way."

"Well said," Erin told her.

The news flashed to a car stuck in another wash downstream where the driver didn't heed the road signs that said "Flooded." Then the camera came back to the point where Matt's crew lowered the ladder over the wash so he could turn off the water at the house.

"Look, it's you, Erin."

Parker looked over to see Erin's smile fall. "This is local news, right?"

"Is that Matt?" Nora asked.

"Yeah. Baby brother manages to get air time on my project."

Austin tossed more food in his mouth. "Upstaged again, eh, Colin?"

They were all laughing, and Erin looked like she wanted to throw up.

Parker looked at the TV again. The footage showed other sections of their valley before moving on to a new story.

Colin pushed back from the table. "I'm going to pack a few things to bring over," he told them.

Parker looked at him. They hadn't discussed him spending the night.

"You guys don't mind if I stay over, do you?" he asked anyone who listened.

"I don't care." This from Austin.

"Whatever," Mallory said, her eyes glued to the TV.

"I think it's a great idea."

Parker turned to Erin, surprised by her words.

"It's settled, then."

Colin kissed the side of Parker's cheek before leaving the table.

"Let's help clean this up, guys."

"No, no. I got it. You all have enough to do. Just relax," Nora told them.

Parker took her plate over to the sink, ran it under the water before putting it in the dishwasher.

Erin walked behind her. "It's okay, isn't it?" she whispered.

"That Colin stays over?"

"Yeah."

Her head bobbed like a doll's. "Good. We're bound to get trespassers."

Parker didn't want to remind her that trespassers were better off with Colin than they were her.

"Why don't you stay in the guest room for a couple nights? Until we get the water back on at least."

"I think that's . . . yeah. I like that idea."

"Good." Parker smiled.

Some color returned to Erin's face.

CHAPTER THIRTY-TWO

Parker cradled the phone in her shaking hands. She'd dreaded this moment for months, knew it was coming . . . but that didn't stop her insides from turning to mud.

"Hello, Parker."

"Good morning, Janice."

"You received my e-mail?"

Yes, the one that told her to call before showing up the next day. "I did."

"You know what I'm going to say."

Parker swallowed. "The mudflow was impassable." She looked up to see Colin watching her from across the table, coffee in his hands.

"I'm sure that's what you would say. Our other staff managed to make it in."

Your other staff doesn't live at the epicenter! The words screamed in her head. "It wasn't possible for me. If I'd left first thing in the morning, I would have made it. By the time my shift started, the police couldn't even make it up the street."

Colin reached out and took her hand in his.

She smiled at him, felt her nerves settling.

"Then there's your answer. You could have made it had you left earlier. But you didn't." Janice sighed as if the noise was an exclamation point.

Parker refused to grovel.

"Nothing else to say?" Janice asked.

What could she say? She was sorry? She wasn't. That it wouldn't happen again? She couldn't promise that either. "No."

"Okay, then. Your final paycheck will be available at the end of the day. If you have anything here, I would appreciate you clearing it out."

Parker closed her eyes, blew out a breath. "Okay."

"Okay, then. Goodbye, Parker."

Janice hung up before she could say the same.

Parker placed the phone on the table, and Colin grasped both her hands in his.

"Well?" he asked.

She shrugged. "I pick up my check later today."

Colin shook his head. "That's ridiculous."

"It is what it is."

"The same water washed right by the school," Colin argued for her.

"Doesn't matter. She warned me."

He lifted her hands to his, kissed her knuckles. "You okay?"

She did a quick head to toe. Realized she was no longer shaking. The unemployment line had been hanging over her head for months. Now that it had finally happened, no fault of her own, she was actually relieved. "I'm sure I'll freak out later. Right now, we need to get some water flowing in this house."

She pulled away and stood.

"You're something else," he told her.

"Glad you think so. You're now dating an unemployed deadbeat."

He stood with her, pulled her close. "Unemployed, maybe. Deadbeat . . . never."

~

The way Parker's mind worked was genius.

She initially filled buckets with pool water and dragged them into the bathrooms in the house so they could flush the toilets. She stocked up on baby wipes and hand sanitizer along with paper plates, plastic utensils, and rolls of paper towels. But when she strung a series of garden hoses from the working valve by the gate, across the span of the wash, and to the nearest working hose bib and bypassed the section of land where the break had to be, Colin knew she was the right woman for him.

"That's gonna work?" Fabio asked her.

"Are you doubting me?"

Colin shook his head and Fabio nodded.

Sure enough, she managed to turn the shutoff valves on and boom. Running water in the house.

She stood over the sink, water flowing, and smiled. "Pressure sucks. It's one shower at a time around here and laundry only when nothing else is running . . . but we can flush a toilet."

Her accomplishment showed on her face. Hard to believe that the day started off with a call from her boss telling her she no longer needed to show up for work.

That was it. Parker didn't cry, rage, or anything. She jumped right into getting the water limping back into the house and managed it before noon.

Colin went back to work and so did Parker.

Every time he looked up, she was on a different part of the property shoveling mud or filling a sandbag.

One of his drivers leaned out of his truck and pointed across the property. "Your lady works harder than any woman I've ever seen," he told Colin.

"She sure does." He really liked that Parker was being referred to as his.

He stayed three nights before Parker pushed him out and told him to go home.

Three nights of holding her when she fell asleep and waking up next to her early in the morning.

He liked it. All of it.

"Absence makes the heart grow fonder," she told him as he stood by his truck, reluctant to leave.

"Or forgetful."

Her jaw dropped. "You're going to forget me by morning?"

"That would be a little hard since I'll be here in the morning."

He leaned against his truck, his arms around her waist as she stood between his legs.

"You need to sleep in your own bed and water your plants."

"My plants are fake."

"Happy hour with your brother and sister."

"Okay, okay . . . I get the hint."

She kissed him briefly. "Besides, if you go home now I won't feel guilty about asking you to come back over the weekend when it's supposed to rain again."

He kissed the tip of her nose. "You've proven you can handle the rain."

She glanced toward the guesthouse. "Yeah, but we have to pull the fence back and open the gate."

Lights from inside the guesthouse glowed across the pool. "That makes Erin nervous."

Parker started to nod and stopped herself. "It makes all of us uneasy."

"But especially Erin." Colin looked over his shoulder. "Why is that?"

"I'm not entirely sure, but if I did know, I wouldn't tell you. So please don't ask."

He really did appreciate someone who could keep a secret. "You're a rare find, Parker."

"Loyal. In fact . . . once things settle down I'd like to see about getting an alarm system inside the guesthouse."

"You mean like the one you have inside yours that you don't use?"

"Touché. In my defense, I'm a better shot than Erin."

"Kinda hard to miss with a shotgun."

She grinned. "It's on my short list of things to do around here."

His thoughts moved to his brother. "Matt installed the system in his house."

"Really?"

Colin nodded. "He's gone for days on end with his job sometimes. I can ask him to take a look and see what it will cost." Doing something for Erin would make his day.

"I can't ask—"

"You don't have to. I will. It's quiet back here at night, isolated. I see why your parents installed your system and would like to see you using it. I'll ask Matt to look at yours and figure out what it will take to put one in the guesthouse."

Parker leaned into him from knees to chest. "I'm depending on you way too much."

"God, I hope so."

"Why do you say that?"

"The sooner you depend on me, the sooner I can pull you into my web and never let you go."

Confusion swept over her face. "I don't know what to say to that."

"Too much?" he asked. Because it wasn't too much for him.

"I don't know."

She shifted in his arms, but he didn't let her go. He tried to calm her unease. "Would it be easier if I asked you to be my girlfriend?"

"I thought I already was."

"*Exclusive* girlfriend?"

Her smile fell completely. "I thought I was that, too."

"Glad we're on the same page, then." He loved getting under her skin.

She narrowed her eyes. "You're teasing me."

He kissed her nose. "I'm defining our relationship so there is no misunderstanding. If I thought you'd let me, I'd go all Neanderthal and lay my claim on you right now."

That had her smiling again. "What does that look like?"

"I don't know, but I'll come up with something."

She was laughing now.

He kissed her and set her aside before his body got the wrong idea. "I'll see you tomorrow."

As he drove down her driveway, and saw her turning to walk inside the house, Colin had a strong desire to turn back. Every time he left her side it felt wrong. Even calling her his girlfriend felt weak. The image of him picking her up and tossing her over his shoulder was the perfect amount of Neanderthal for him. Something told him she might not be into the over-the-shoulder toss.

Yet.

~

The next morning Parker's toilet didn't flush.

She panicked. "What the hell is it now?"

A note on the refrigerator door told her Austin didn't have water when he'd left.

She tossed on yesterday's clothes and bundled into a coat.

Halfway down the driveway she paused, looked at her breath in the cold winter air.

Small puddles of water were iced over on the driveway.

Instead of walking to the shutoff valves, she stepped through what was left of the ice plant that once lined the driveway to the garden hose that replaced the water main. She lifted it and squeezed.

Frozen.

Relief washed through her and she started to laugh. "I never thought I'd deal with frozen pipes in Southern California."

When she returned to the house she texted her brother and sister. The hose froze. The water is fine. From now on we fill a bathtub and have water to flush on cold mornings.

Austin texted back immediately with a toilet emoji.

You can just pee outside, she told him.

I did. You're welcome.

She'd been kidding . . . but whatever.

Mallory texted back. TMI, Austin.

Jelly, big sis?

The whole conversation made Parker smile. The fact that they'd all gotten back to the brother and sister roles took weight off her shoulders. Austin hadn't relapsed into his rebellion once. God knew he had every excuse if he wanted to. Even though Parker kept the pace as gatekeeper to their family, it didn't feel like she was playing mom and dad any longer. And that was huge.

She moved through her morning, missing Colin in a way she hadn't seen coming.

He woke up before she did and brought her coffee in bed. In fact, he had insisted she lie there while he prepared her coffee the way she liked it, and then curled up next to her and drank his first cup of the day with her.

She loved that.

They brushed their teeth alongside each other, and when they were done, Colin picked her up, placed her on the bathroom counter, and kissed her to check how well she'd done the job.

She loved that, too.

He ate whatever she cooked, even if it was a little burnt, without complaint.

That was weird.

And adorable.

She finished her coffee and had a bowl of cereal before going outside to find a shovel.

~

"Matt will be here in an hour," Parker informed Erin. She'd already talked to her about an alarm system, which Erin not only wanted, but was willing to pay for. "I thought I'd give you a long enough warning so if you wanted to peace out, you could."

The property buzzed with men of all shapes and sizes, religions, and races . . . but the only one Erin seemed to fear was Matt.

Unfounded as that may be, it was a reality, and Parker was going to shelter her friend from that fear if she could.

"I'm pathetic."

Parker stood outside of the guesthouse, her boots caked with mud or she'd invite herself in. She'd been hard at work with her power washer that was doing a fabulous job of taking the final layer of mud off the hardscape throughout the property. Well, maybe not the whole property, but the space closest to the house, pool, and guesthouse. Anytime those spaces could be kept clean, the less time Parker spent vacuuming and scrubbing inside.

It felt as if she'd given up her day job to become a full-time housemaid, gardener, plumber, and cook. And that was okay. It was taking control of what she could. While it didn't bring in a paycheck, it did bring some satisfaction.

"You're not pathetic. You're entitled to your feelings."

Erin wore a stylish pair of jeans and a long sweater. She looked girl-next-door fresh, clean of makeup with her hair pulled back in a simple clip. Parker envied the look. It was expensive without looking fake.

Most of all it was clean.

Parker forgot what that felt like.

"Thanks," Erin said.

"Matt would just as soon cut off his right arm than give you a reason to fear him."

Erin nodded. "I'll stick around."

That made Parker happy.

"But if I need to, I'll make excuses and go."

She could work with that. "Right, you have that appointment . . . What was it, dentist or something?"

Erin's smile reached her eyes. "You're the best."

"I'm making chicken tacos for dinner. Colin is staying the night so I invited Matt to stay for dinner. You're welcome to—"

"One hour at a time."

Parker placed both hands in the air. "Got it."

Fifty-five minutes later, Matt pulled his truck up Parker's driveway and parked next to Erin's car.

She walked across the section of her lawn that hadn't been affected by mudflow only because it was downstream from her house and protected by it.

Matt waved as he started toward her. He stopped at the garden hose water line and looked down on it. "Is this really your water supply?"

"It works."

"The firefighter in me is having serious issues with this."

"Because my house is going to catch fire anytime soon? Take a look around, it's like Ireland around here." Everything that wasn't covered in mud was bright green.

"Didn't you say there is a junction box closer to the house?"

She waved him over and walked alongside him to the location he mentioned.

He looked inside the box, rubbed his chin a couple of times. "Do you know how the water main runs?"

"I'm not completely positive. There's no map of it on the property plans, and it's been modified over the years with each break." She walked the property with Matt and pointed out where she thought the line ran. So far only a couple hundred feet of garden hose did the trick. On nights like the one coming, she'd turn the water off, unhook the hose over the creek, and wait for the water to recede to hook it all back up.

They walked up to the junction by the gate. It sat behind where the picnic benches had lived for the crew to take their breaks, and right in the path of the Sutter Canyon mudslides.

Colin saw them and walked over. He shook his brother's hand. "What's up?"

"Matt's looking over my hillbilly water main."

"What is the likelihood of this pipe breaking again?" Matt asked Colin.

"Ninety-nine point nine percent."

That had Parker frowning. "Really?"

"It's sticking out of the ground and has been hammered twice."

"When it happens again, I say we move it," Matt told his brother.

She shook her head. "This is all working for now. Let's focus on alarm systems today, shall we?"

CHAPTER THIRTY-THREE

"It's not going to take much," Matt told Parker and Erin after he poked around the guesthouse for about thirty minutes. "Having the phone line is key, and that's already in."

"Will it be possible for this system to tell me if the gate has opened, like it does up at the main house?" Erin asked.

"That I don't know."

"The gate was installed long before the guesthouse was built," Parker said.

"If there's a way to link the line down here, I'll do it." Matt was trying so hard to keep a distance from Erin. She, too, was hanging back and avoiding eye contact.

"How soon can we get started on this?" Parker asked.

"I don't see any reason to wait, unless money is an issue."

Erin jumped in. "Money isn't an issue. I'm paying for it."

Parker shook her head. "That doesn't seem fair, Erin."

"You never promised me a security system."

"No, I promised you a quiet home with lots of privacy, and I've failed on epic levels with that." Not that she had much of a choice, but still.

"I insist."

Parker wasn't going to argue in front of Matt, so she dropped it.

Matt walked around the backside of the guesthouse. "What about security lighting? The kind that pops on when there's motion outside."

Erin's eyes lit up. "I like that."

"I have two up at the house," Parker said. "I have to warn you, they go off all the time. Between the wind blowing the trees and coyotes playing tag at night, motion lights might be more nerve-racking than they are a comfort."

"We can dial them in a little," Matt offered.

"I really like that idea."

Matt's smile grew. "I can run over to Home Depot and pick up a couple right now. They aren't hard to install."

Erin turned and started back inside the guesthouse. "I'll get my wallet."

"You can come with me," Matt offered.

Erin didn't turn white as a sheet with the suggestion, but she did get a little pasty.

"Don't you have a dentist appointment or something?" Parker asked.

"Oh, yeah . . . that's right. I almost forgot." Disaster averted. "Can I just give you some money? Or you can tell me what to buy and I'll pick up the lights myself."

Matt waved her off. "I'll buy them and tell you what they cost after."

"You sure?"

"Absolutely."

Erin smiled at him, and Parker thought he was going to spark a fire from his eyes with how they beamed. "Thank you, Matt. It means a lot to me."

"I'm a fan of brownies or white-chocolate macadamia-nut cookies. In case you're thinking about how to repay me."

That had her laugh. A rare thing when in the presence of a man. Parker liked it.

"Noted."

"I'll get going, then. When is dinner?" he asked Parker.

"Sixish."

Matt looked at Erin. "Will you be joining us?"

"Uhm, yeah. I was going to . . . ah, yeah. I'll be here."

"Great." He backed up grinning. "See ya later, then."

He damn near tripped over himself before he made it to his truck.

Once he was out of hearing range, Parker said, "You twist that man up in knots."

"I can tell."

Parker patted Erin on the back. "You better get to that appointment of yours. Don't forget to brush your teeth before you come back."

They both laughed.

~

It ended up being the four of them. Mallory was out on a date with Jase, and Austin was out with friends.

They were on weather watch once again. Parker had gone around filling bathtubs and sinks to wash hands since they'd be unhooking the hose before they went to bed. But for now, they were drinking beer and wine and listening to Colin and Matt tell stories of their less graceful moments in high school. They were sitting around the formal living room, a coffee table separated Matt and Erin while Parker and Colin sat close to each other on the couch.

"Matt was always the player."

"Dude, don't call me out like that." Matt tried to look offended and failed.

"It's true. You never took the same girl to high school formals twice."

"I was picky," Matt told Erin.

"Mom stopped paying for pictures, said it was a waste of money since she couldn't keep the picture hung on a wall for more than two months."

"I have a hard time seeing that. You haven't dated anyone that I know of since Colin and I met."

Matt placed a hand to his chest. "I saw the error in my ways."

"You mean you got caught cheating?" Erin asked.

"In my defense, I thought college was all about nonexclusive dating."

"Only if you're both on board with that," Parker said.

"I thought it was nonexclusive until otherwise stated. But Misty didn't see it that way."

Erin laughed. "Her name was Misty?"

"Don't look at me, I didn't name her."

Colin chimed in. "Misty was a tomboy. Didn't match the name at all. There was all kinds of ugly when she found out you were dating that other girl . . . What was her name?"

Matt placed a hand to his cheek. "I don't remember. I do recall how she slapped me when she found out and how grateful I was she hadn't thrown a punch."

Erin's smile fell. "She hit you?"

He nodded several times. "She was hurt. I get it."

Parker felt Colin's knee tap hers. It dawned on her that the conversation sparked something inside of Erin. "What did you do when she slapped you?"

"I backed away so she couldn't do it twice. I apologized, told her I didn't mean to hurt her." He looked at Erin and paused. "I'm a nice guy, honestly. I stopped dating two different women at the same time after her. I figured it was better for my overall health."

"What about you, Erin? Did you ever play the field?" Colin asked.

"No! I wouldn't know how."

"Me either," Parker said. "I had friends in college that used dating apps and found lunch dates, coffee dates, and happy hour with three different guys on the same day. It's almost expected these days."

"Did you ever use a dating app?" Colin asked her.

"When would I have had time to do that? I've been taking care of teenagers."

"Do you feel like you've missed out?" Matt asked Parker.

"On dating apps? No."

"On life?" he clarified.

"I had a life before my parents died."

"What about after?" Matt asked.

"Some times were harder than others."

Colin brushed his fingers over her shoulder.

"Do you think you'll ever want kids of your own?" Erin asked.

"No. I don't think so." She'd been asked that question ever since Mallory had graduated from high school; her reply was always the same. "Kudos to adoptive parents who take in teenagers. Austin wasn't even driving yet, and Mallory was a hormonal seventeen-year-old when our parents died. I went from awesome older sister to dictator overnight. Austin was a nightmare. Getting him straightened out took years off my life. It nearly broke me. Now that I see light at the end of the tunnel, the last thing I want to do is jump back into that fire." She huffed. "Pun intended."

Parker looked over at Erin, noticed her forced smile directed at Colin.

It was then she realized the impact of her words on him.

"It's easy to see how you'd feel that way," Matt finally said.

Parker slowly turned her eyes to Colin.

He, too, wore a strangled smile.

Because she couldn't stop herself, she asked, "Do you want kids?"

"I always thought they'd be in my future."

She swallowed. Heartache sat in her chest.

A gust of wind rattled the silence growing in the room.

Matt stood and walked over to the window overlooking the property.

Colin shifted and stayed silent.

"It's really coming down out there," Matt said.

Colin patted her shoulder and got up to join his brother. "If you're leaving, you might want to. The culverts fill up fast, and you won't be able to get over the wash until I bring someone in tomorrow."

"I need to shut off the water and disconnect the hose." Parker unfolded from the couch.

"We'll take care of it," Colin told her.

Matt found his raincoat on the back of the kitchen stool.

"Thanks again for installing the lights," Erin told him.

"My pleasure. I'll get back to you on the alarm system."

Parker and Erin stood back while Colin and Matt bundled up to go outside.

"Thanks for dinner," Matt said as he opened his arms for a hug. Parker stepped in and returned the gesture.

"Drive carefully."

"Always do." He looked at Erin, smiled, and waved. "See ya later, Erin."

"G'night."

They opened the door and Scout jumped from his curled up position on the floor.

Parker held him back. "Oh, no . . . I don't want to wipe you down again tonight."

She waited until the men walked out to let the dog go with a long sigh. "That was awkward."

"I saw. Colin didn't know you don't want kids, did he?"

"We never talked about it."

"God, I'm sorry I brought it up," Erin said.

"It's not your fault." Only now what?

~

Rain pelted the hood of the truck as Matt drove them down the driveway to the point where Colin could run out, turn off the water at the two valve points, and disconnect the line. Then he'd roll it to the side so it didn't get caught in the current when the wash started to flood again.

But before he did that, he and his brother sat in the car while the windshield wipers kept a heavy-metal beat.

"You didn't know about the kid thing, did you?" Matt asked him.

"No."

"Damn, Colin. I'm sorry."

His mind couldn't stop hearing how fast she'd said the word *no*.

"Is it a deal breaker?" Matt asked.

"I-I don't know," he answered honestly. "Maybe she'll change her mind."

Matt sighed. "And maybe she won't."

A life without kids? Was he willing to do that? *Be careful who you date, you never know who you were going to fall in love with.*

"Fuck. I don't want to think about this right now." Colin jumped out of the car and rushed over to the water line and went to work.

CHAPTER THIRTY-FOUR

A cloud hovered over them, figuratively and literally. How had a simple conversation about Parker's past resulted in the wedge that had somehow come between them?

Colin didn't like it. At all.

Matt left, and Erin went down to the guesthouse, leaving them alone.

He wanted to talk to her about it, but needed to work out his own feelings first.

Unlike any other night he'd spent at her home, he sat in her bed waiting for her to finish in the bathroom and stared at the walls. The room was nearly twice the size of his. The bed was a queen. He liked that. His bed gave her too much room to move away.

The door to the bathroom opened and she stepped out. The nightgown she wore stopped midthigh and wasn't something he'd classify as sexy, but Parker made up for it.

"I have some bad news," she said as she walked to her side of the bed.

"What?"

"I started my period."

Now he was really confused. She didn't want kids . . .

She must have figured out where his mind went because she quickly clarified. "No fooling around tonight."

"Oh. Sorry, I'm a little slow." He pulled the blankets back for her. "I'll enjoy holding you just as much."

Parker turned off the lamp and curled in beside him. "Just as much?"

"Ninety-nine point nine percent as much."

She looked up, reached her lips toward his.

His heart pounded in his chest a little harder as if it were trying to tell him something.

When she broke away, she smiled before resting her head on his shoulder. "I'm glad you're here," she told him.

"I am, too."

"Good night."

He kissed the top of her head. "Good night."

Only his mind didn't turn off. Couldn't turn off. He'd never dated a woman where he even cared to know about her view on kids. What was different with Parker?

He closed his eyes, tried to slow his breathing down and rest his mind.

Parker was different because he loved her.

Everything about her was completely unlike anyone he'd dated before. She was independent and often unwilling to accept his help. When he'd push to do something for her, she'd push back equally hard to do it herself. He wondered if that was to prove to herself she could . . . or to him? It was endearing . . . annoying, too, at times, but appealing all the same.

Her breathing started to even out, and the arm she had draped over him felt heavier.

He saw this woman in his future. Wanted her there.

Matt's question sang in his head. *Is it a deal breaker?*

God, he hoped not.

~

"We haven't had lunch in forever." Jennifer sat across the booth from her in one of their favorite places.

"Thank goodness for half days. How is everything at the school?"

Jennifer sipped from her iced tea. "The flu is going around and the kids are stir-crazy with all the rain. How are you and Mr. Wonderful?"

"We're good. Real good."

Jennifer's smile fell. "Oh, no . . . What's wrong?"

"Nothing."

"I call bullshit. You were all giggly and blushing the last time we talked about him, now you've got a frown. What's going on?"

She picked at the salad in front of her. "He wants kids."

Jennifer practically spat her tea out.

Parker handed her the extra napkin sitting in front of her.

"Warn me next time, will ya? Kids? What the heck are you guys talking about kids for?"

"I don't know, it just came up."

"How long have you been dating?"

"Couple of months."

Jennifer shook her head. "Two months and you're talking about babies? Call me old-fashioned, but didn't you miss a step? Like living together, at least."

"We weren't talking about now, more of a general thing. Either way, Colin wants to be a dad."

"Did he say he wanted you to have his children?"

"No." Parker explained the conversation the weekend before and how strained they'd been ever since. She chalked it up to being hormonal, but now that her cycle was fading, she realized it wasn't completely that.

"Do you love him?" Jennifer moved right to the point.

"I don't know. I mean . . . I like him a lot. There isn't a day we don't talk."

"His day job is your front yard, that isn't hard."

"We *talk* talk. Emotions and problems and solutions. He gets me."

"But you don't want kids."

"I want to live a little. Playing parent to two grieving teenagers and not being able to cry myself was awful. I still see the bags under my eyes when I look in the mirror sometimes. I've been doing what I have to do for so long, having the option to do something else is liberating. Having kids changes all that. You're a mom, you know."

Jennifer nodded. "I completely agree."

"See." Parker stabbed at her salad as if it cussed her out.

"I wouldn't change it for the world."

"Ugh. You're not helping."

"Listen, I'm not saying you should or shouldn't have kids. I think if more people realized they didn't want them before they had them, there would be less screwed-up kids out there. But you didn't say you didn't want kids because you didn't like them, that you didn't understand them . . . that you don't love even the lil' shits that cause the biggest problems on the playground. You said you didn't want them because you wanted to have a life. So tell me what that life looks like to you."

That was easy. "Get a real job, go back to school. Maybe take a trip somewhere."

"Like Cabo?"

The question smacked her upside the head.

"Yeah."

"What kind of real job? And what kind of school?"

"I don't know. Court reporters make good money. Maybe I'll get a paralegal degree."

"You see yourself sitting in an office?"

"Maybe. I don't know."

"Every time I've asked you this question you've given me the same answer. *You don't know.*"

She was starting to feel less than adequate as the conversation moved on.

"What about Colin . . . Do you see him in this ambiguous future of yours?"

"I want to. It's hard to see beyond what's right in front of me right now. Day by day, hour by hour."

Jennifer shook her head. "You've lived like that for as long as I've known you."

"Yes, but more so since the fire."

"I'll give you that. My guess is you know Mallory and Austin's next moves on the chessboard of life while you sit on the sidelines in a constant state of flux."

Parker opened her mouth to argue, realized she couldn't, then shut it. "I don't think Colin lives that way, and I don't want to be the one to drag him down with me." Her life felt a little like quicksand these days.

"Someone is feeling sorry for herself. It doesn't sound like you're dragging Colin anywhere. He saw your crazy train coming and jumped on board with a backhoe. Why don't you stop stressing about what might be tomorrow and enjoy today? If he has a real issue with the kid factor, he'll let you know. Until then, stop letting it mess with your head."

"You don't think I'm misleading him?"

"You told him you don't want kids, he told you he did. No one is misleading anyone. Enjoy life for a few minutes, Parker. Enjoy having someone to lean on. That's the difference between what you've been doing the last few years and what I've been doing. Sam is my rock. Raising kids is a ton easier with a husband. I don't think I could do it without him."

"You could," Parker said.

"You're right. But God willing, I won't have to."

"Thanks, Jennifer."

"You're welcome. Now, tell me about the circus in your yard. Do you have running water yet?"

She closed her eyes and whined. "Noooo . . ."

~

The weather eased up for exactly three days, allowing Colin enough time to set his crew in motion to help get the main water line attached through the wash. They were fighting the clock . . . another set of storms was set to roll in.

He had crews filling the rocks around the structures with a form of shotcrete in hopes of keeping them in place instead of breaking loose and becoming part of the problem. So far, the structures themselves had been repaired twice and now had twice as much metal wedged on the down side to keep them in place. Each passing storm, while devastating, was holding back and stopping right at the breaking point.

Parker was off the property, and he was hoping to have the water main turned on before she got home. He and four of his crew were in the wash working as fast as they could. They'd dammed up the water but only had a short window of time before it overflowed. The massive pipe they buried the main in should hold, or so he told himself. He had one of his best operators backfill with large rocks to stabilize the thing. Ten minutes before he saw Parker drive in, he'd turned the water on and tested it.

She stopped on the north side of the wash in the middle of her driveway and jumped out. "Is that what I think it is?"

"It's in."

His men were all grins.

She jumped up and down like a ten-year-old getting a pony for Christmas. She ran to him with open arms. "Thank you, thank you, thank you!"

Parker then turned to the crew and hugged them all, too. "You have no idea how happy this makes me."

"I might have a clue," Colin teased.

She laughed. "I meant everyone else." She looked down at the pipe. "You sure that's going to hold?"

Every single one of them shrugged their shoulders.

Colin was a little more confident. "It's not going anywhere."

"You sure?" The other guys weren't so convinced.

He shook his head and then ended with a shrug. "Who the hell knows?"

Parker laughed. "I won't place any bets, then. Maybe the worst of the storms are behind us."

Yeah, he wasn't banking on that either. He did accept her final hug and kiss.

"How about tacos for lunch tomorrow? I'll put the order in now and have them delivered."

"You don't have to do that."

"You're right. I want to. Just tell me how many guys will be here for lunch and I'll get it here."

"Okay, but only because it seems to make you happy."

She winked. "Lots of things make me happy."

One of the guys made a whoop noise and abruptly turned away when Colin looked at him.

She pulled his arm so he could walk with her. "Thanks again, guys."

A chorus of *you're welcome*s followed them as she walked toward her car. Once out of earshot, she started talking.

"Mallory texted earlier, wanted to make sure Austin and I were going to be home tonight and that you weren't going to be here."

"Did I forget something?"

"No. We didn't have plans . . . it's a strange request. Is anything going on with Jase that you know of?"

"I have no idea."

"If you hear of anything . . ."

"I'll let you know."

She kissed him, quickly, and opened her car door. "I have laundry to do."

"I've never seen a woman so happy to do laundry."

"Don't get used to it."

Damn, she made him smile. "I won't."

"Let's get back to work."

CHAPTER THIRTY-FIVE

Parker asked Erin to be on standby with emergency wine should Mallory be delivering crazy news. Her sister had never been so cryptic in the past. All she was praying for was for her sister to not be pregnant.

Which was the first thing that went through her mind.

Why else would she want to have a *family meeting* and make sure Colin wasn't there? Maybe she was breaking up with Jase and didn't want Colin to know . . .

The suspense was killing her.

Austin had come home from school and wanted to rush off. Parker cut him off before he got too far.

"Your sister has something important she wants to talk to us about, so I need you to stick around for a while."

He moaned. "When is she getting home?"

"Anytime."

He rolled his eyes. "If she's not home in an hour, I'm out of here."

Parker was folding laundry in the den when she heard the gate signal her sister was home.

A few minutes later she heard the garage door open and close and her sister running up the back stairs.

"Hey!" she said as she tried to skirt on by.

"Whoa, wait . . ."

"What?" Mallory said.

"What do you mean *what*? You asked for a family meeting."

"Yeah . . . give me a minute to put my things down."

Parker took a deep breath.

Mallory made it two steps.

"Just tell me you're not pregnant." She held her breath.

Mallory turned. "I'm not pregnant."

Relief flooded through her. "Okay, go. Grab Austin on your way back. He wants to go out and is waiting for you."

Ten minutes later they were sitting in the den waiting for Mallory to tell them whatever was eating at her.

"You know how I've been dating Jase."

"Yeah, so?" Austin wasn't amused.

"Well . . . it's been getting serious."

"Two months, Mallory . . . How serious can it be?" Austin asked.

If anyone knew how a couple of months could be in a relationship, it was Parker. "You're too young to get married."

"Oh my God, Parker, I'm not pregnant and I'm not getting married."

"I'm sorry. I'm jumping ahead."

"Yeah, you are."

"Sorry. Go ahead."

Mallory took a deep breath. "I'm moving out."

Of all the things that could have come out of Mallory's mouth . . . *I'm moving out* was not what Parker saw coming.

"You're what?"

"During spring break. Jase and I have been talking and—"

"I get Mallory's room." Austin didn't miss a beat.

Parker waved her brother off. "You hardly know him."

"I'm practically living with him now with all the flooding and drama around here. We want to take the next step."

"You're still in school."

"I'll still go to school. My college fund has provisions for me to live on campus, so I'm going to move out. Jase has a job, I have a job . . ."

"We had plans on how to make it work around here," Parker argued.

"Yeah, and now you won't have to worry about me. I'll take care of myself."

Something inside of Parker broke. Shattered in a million pieces.

"If it doesn't work out, I'll be back." Mallory was staring at her.

"I still get your room."

"God, Austin, you can have her room. Let it go," Parker yelled at him.

Mallory tilted her head. "I thought you'd be happy."

She was devastated. "I'm shocked."

"You had to know that I'd move out eventually."

Yeah, she did . . . but that *eventually* wasn't supposed to be for a while longer.

"Our original plan was for us to go our separate ways after Austin was out of high school . . . You remember that, right?"

"We changed that plan. After the fire."

Mallory stopped smiling. "I know. But this is something I want to do. Knowing you're keeping the house means I just have to work a little harder to make it happen. I can do that. If Mom and Dad were still alive, I wouldn't have money from the sale of a house to rely on. So I won't rely on it now."

All kinds of emotions ran around inside her like screaming kids on a playground. The bottom line was Mallory wanted to do something different in her life than what Parker thought she'd do . . . and who was she to stop her?

She tried to think like her parents . . . What would they say? How would they react?

The photograph of them on the wall stared down at her.

It pained her to voice the words running through her head. "I think it might be a mistake for you to rush into living with Jase—"

Mallory started to talk, but Parker cut her off.

"But . . . I'd rather you rush into living with him than get married or anything else equally as permanent."

Mallory slowly started to smile. "So you're okay?"

"Nope." *Nowhere near okay.* "But I get it. And you have a home to come back to if it doesn't work out."

Mallory lunged off the couch to hug her.

Tears threatened to spill in big, ugly waves.

Then Austin opened his mouth. "If you move back in, I still get to keep your room."

Parker picked up the pillow on the sofa and tossed it at her brother.

~

Someone was pounding on Colin's front door.

Had he locked it without thinking? Both his brother and sister had a key and they were the only ones who knocked on his door after work.

"I'm coming . . ."

He hustled down the stairs and yanked on the front door. "Did you forget the . . . Parker?"

She was in tears. Launched herself at him as soon as he opened the door.

"Hey?" He wrapped his arms around her and pulled her inside. "Honey, what's wrong?"

She sucked in a breath like a bad cartoon character, bottom lip flapping in shuddering waves and blowing out in big sighs.

Colin started to panic. He'd never seen her like this. In everything he'd watched her go through, never once had she broken down. He didn't like it. "Parker?"

Just her name had her squeezing him harder.

"I got you, okay. Whatever it is we'll get through it. I'm right here."

Her shuddering sobs went to staccato breaths.

Slowly she started to calm down.

"Come on." He led her into his den and sat with her on the couch. "Tell me what's going on."

She blinked several times until she gathered enough courage to speak. "Mallory." Another big breath. "M-Mallory is m-moving out."

"Okay." He waited for the punch.

Parker stared at him. "Of the house."

He got that. What was he missing?

"You're upset about Mallory moving out of the house." Please let her clue him in to the problem.

"She told us tonight. She's moving in with Jase over spring break." The tears started to return.

Colin swiveled around. He didn't have tissue boxes close by. He was a guy; the sleeve of his shirt did in a pinch. He jumped up and rounded the sofa and into his kitchen. He grabbed a paper towel and brought it back to her.

Parker blew her nose, wadded the paper towel up, and did it a second time.

He waited until she'd gained some control before he spoke. "Parker, honey . . . I'm trying really hard to not be a clueless boyfriend here. But you're this upset because your sister is moving out of the house?"

She nodded.

"She's not pregnant or anything . . . right? She and Jase didn't elope or something like that."

Parker shook her head.

Swallowed hard.

"She's just moving out."

Her eyes pitched together. "I know . . . I shouldn't be this upset." Again with the tears.

Colin reached for her and pulled her into his shoulder. Now that he knew nothing catastrophic had happened, he started to relax.

He held her while she cried for a good ten minutes. If the day ever came that he truly understood women, he'd write a book and become a millionaire.

"It's been a hard time for you."

"This hit me."

"I can see that."

She sniffled against his shirt. "All she wants to do is live her life."

"Yeah."

"Jase is a nice kid."

There was that little pot-smoking time he had in high school, but Colin thought maybe now wasn't a good time to bring that up. Besides, he was pretty sure that was behind him. "He'll never treat her bad. And if he does I'll kick his ass. Family or not."

That got a tiny chuckle out of her.

She pushed off his chest. "Why does it feel this way?"

"I don't know."

"She's my sister. It's not like she's moving to Syria or anything."

"Does anyone move *to* Syria?"

"Right . . . it's not like it's that," Parker said. "She isn't joining the military or running off to war . . . or anything dangerous. She's just moving out." She held her chest like it hurt.

Then it hit him. "Because she isn't *only* your sister. You helped raise her."

Parker stared at him. "So what, I'm empty-nesting? I'm only twenty-six. I can't empty-nest. I'm not old enough."

He remembered his mother's tears when he moved out. Never mind that he was twenty-two . . . she had cried. "It's a state of mind and not an age, hon."

Her lower lip still stuck out.

He had a strong urge to kiss it.

"You've been under a serious amount of stress. I mean, c'mon, look how excited you were about doing laundry today."

That got a smile.

"I'm being stupid."

In epic proportions. "No. Emotional."

"Stupid emotional."

He couldn't help but laugh. "Damn, I love you."

Her smile faded.

Oh, no . . . Had he said that?

"It's not fair," she said. "I'm going through an empty nest and you haven't had the children you want. This is so wrong." She tried to get up, but he gently pulled her back down.

"Okay, stop. How did you make that jump?"

"I'm not loveable. I'm a mess. Look at me."

"I am looking at you. Loveable mess that you are."

Her face went stone-cold. "I don't know if I can ever give you what you want."

He wanted to assure her it didn't matter.

"Good thing we're old enough and young enough to figure that out." And the fact that she'd run to him for support was all he needed to lay hope to their future. Maybe he'd finally earned her trust.

God, he hoped so.

CHAPTER THIRTY-SIX

Mallory started spending the weekends at Jase's apartment and called only to say she wouldn't be home until Monday after school. The plan was for her to move out completely after the rain and flooding stopped. Parker was fairly certain her sister felt guilty for leaving in the middle of chaos.

"It doesn't bother you?" Parker finally asked Austin.

"Nawahh. I mean, eventually I'm going to want to move out, and now that she's pulled the Band-Aid, it won't hurt as much when I do it."

"You want to move out, too?"

"Hell no. I don't want to work that hard. I'm not stupid. Someday, though."

Parker breathed a sigh of relief.

They were watching the news on a rare Saturday night when Austin was home.

"That doesn't look pretty," he said, indicating the TV.

"I don't ever remember getting this much rain in one winter."

One of the newscasters who had interviewed Parker twice spoke from a location a good five miles from her property with the Santa Clara River behind her. "We're expecting a one-two punch here in the southland. Officials have declared the drought over even before next week's storms descend upon us. The valleys can expect an inch of rain on Tuesday with as much as three to five inches in the mountains and burn areas. The authorities are advising residents to stay away from known areas of flooding and to keep an eye on the weather reports throughout your area."

"No cameo tonight?" her brother teased.

"They like to come after things get real." She turned off the TV once Austin got up to go to bed.

"I'll go out tomorrow and fill the gas cans for the generator and do some grocery shopping. If you need anything, put it on the list."

"You got it."

"Fill your bathtub. I'm not convinced the water main is going to make it." It had been in for almost a week. She was pretty sure the next storm was going to test it.

He stopped and looked at the picture above the fireplace. "Do you ever look at this picture and feel sad?"

"All the time," Parker said.

He turned to her. "Then why do we leave it there?"

What was up with her siblings making her want to cry? "It felt wrong to take down."

He shrugged, in true Austin fashion. "My vote is to take it down. Maybe in ten years we can put it back up and not feel like we're missing out."

The back of her throat started to thicken.

"I love you, Austin."

"Love you, too, sis."

~

The wind chimes smashing against each other woke her from a dead sleep.

The clock said four a.m.

She rolled out of bed, every muscle felt the ache of the day before . . . and the day before that.

"I'm so over this!"

Her bladder called, so instead of turning her pillow to the cool side, she forced her legs out of bed and walked to the bathroom. On the way, she glanced out her bedroom window. The outdoor emergency lights were on by her driveway and over by the guesthouse.

The wind howled.

She used the bathroom and fell back in bed. For the next hour she pretended to sleep. Finally she gave up and padded out of bed and into the kitchen.

Parker started a pot of coffee while looking at the weather app on her phone. When it rang, she jumped.

It was Erin.

"Are you awake? I thought I saw the lights go on."

"Yeah, the wind is awful."

"I know . . . I couldn't sleep." Her voice was strained.

Parker woke up faster. "Are you okay? You sound scared."

"The lights went on outside. I, ah . . ."

"Come up . . . have some coffee with me. I'll turn on the floodlights."

"You sure?"

She was freaked out. Parker could hear it in her voice.

"If it's okay."

Parker walked over to the switch for the floodlights and turned them on. Light shot on and illuminated the entire lawn area of the property. Most nights when the coyotes were restless, the lights alone would scare them away. She opened the sliding glass door, shivered, and walked to the edge of the patio where she could see the guesthouse. With the phone in her hand, she waved. "I'm here."

"I'm on my way."

She almost turned to go into the house and decided to wait.

Bundled in a big coat, Erin ran around the pool and up to the house on the steep path connecting the two. Once she climbed the final steps, they both jogged into the house.

"Damn, it's cold out there."

Erin was white as a sheet.

Parker went over to the thermostat and turned it up two degrees. "I don't know about you, but I'm getting tired of this crap."

"Yeah . . ." Erin stood by the window looking over the property.

"I told you the lights would go on when the wind blew."

"I thought I heard something, then the lights popped on and didn't go off."

Parker filled the coffee maker with water. "The wind is nasty without a storm."

"Yeah . . ." Still Erin stared outside.

Erin had cracked the door open into her past enough for Parker to give it a little push. "You really are frightened that your ex is going to come here, aren't you?"

Erin looked over her shoulder. Ever so slowly, she started to nod. "He said he'd find me." Her voice was flat.

The only noise in the room was the coffee maker percolating and the sound of the wind and rain that pelted the windows.

When Erin didn't elaborate, Parker offered the only solutions she had.

"When things calm down around here, you and I are going to the range. Not that I think I could ever actually shoot someone, but it's empowering. Maybe we can take a self-defense course together. And on nights like this, you can take Scout down to the guesthouse with you. He may not bite a stranger, but he will bark and let you know if it's the wind or a person. Or you can come up here and sleep in the guest room. Your call."

"It doesn't scare you?"

"That your ex is scaring the hell out of you based on something he threatened? No. It pisses me off. I don't know enough to be scared. Maybe when you trust me enough for the whole story I'll feel your fear, but for right now, I want to punch him."

Erin blinked several times. "Some men punch back."

Parker walked over and put an arm around her friend.

The coffee maker beeped.

As Parker poured two cups, Erin said, "I trust you. It's him I don't trust."

"Answer me this . . . Does this ex live anywhere around here?"

"No. Oh, no . . . he lives really far from here."

"Washington?" Where she said she lived before her move.

"I-I'd rather not say."

"Not in California."

She shook her head.

"Okay, then." That was good enough for her.

She turned on the faucet to rinse off the spoon she used for her creamer, and all that came was a trickle of water.

"Son of a bitch."

~

All Colin could do was watch while Mother Nature raged.

Parker had called him at first light and told him his water-main fix had failed. She couldn't be bothered with emotions. All he heard was defeat in her voice. When he got on-site, he saw why. One-ton boulders were being tossed around like popcorn.

Only a few of his crew were on-site. No need for anyone else to come in until the rain stopped. The structures were holding and the cleanouts up and down the street had given room for this storm to dump more mud downstream.

He stood on the opposite side of the wash from Parker, and yelled over the rain.

"How does it look at the neighbors'?" she asked.

"So far so good. The channels are working. How are you guys?"

"We have everything we need."

"I doubled the amount of trucks coming tomorrow. We'll be starting at first light. They're predicting the next storm as a category four."

Parker lifted her arms to the sky. "What the hell does that mean? Sounds like a hurricane."

"It means my guys are working overtime to get as much crap out of here tomorrow."

Rain splashed the side of her face, her hair was plastered to her cheeks. "I'm going to need a month in Cabo instead of a week once this is over."

"I'll see what I can do."

There it was . . . the smile that kept him warm when she wasn't with him.

"Go inside. There's nothing you can do out here."

She blew him a kiss and turned to walk up the muddy span of her driveway.

CHAPTER THIRTY-SEVEN

They named the storm Lucifer.

They either had a sick sense of humor, or were trying to send a message to anyone listening.

Parker wanted to know who *they* were.

By the time she emerged from the house the next morning, the sky was blue with only a few scattering white clouds. The whole lot of emergency vehicles was once again on the property. It was hard hats and vests and no time for donuts and pizza.

Colin had cleared in front of her culverts enough for some of the water to flow under.

"I'm surprised my crossing is still here."

"Me too," he told her.

"Do you know who those people are?" she asked, pointing to a man and a woman who looked like they could work for the city. There had been times on days like this where office staff came in to check things out.

"No idea."

The couple stopped on the side of the wash to watch.

"I got them. You go back to work."

Colin kissed her. "Bossy woman."

She winked and walked over to the trespassers. She played dumb this time. "Hello?"

The woman was all smiles. "Hi."

"This is something else," the man said.

"Are you with the city?" Parker asked.

"Oh, no. We're neighbors."

She didn't have the energy to yell.

"Great. Do you have a phone?"

The man looked at her. "Yeah."

"Pull it out, take a picture, and move along. These trucks and this crew don't need to work around lookie-loos while they're desperately trying to save all the houses downstream from flooding with tomorrow's storm. Every minute counts."

The woman had the good sense to be embarrassed. "I told you we shouldn't have walked in."

"You live here?" the husband asked.

"I do. And you're welcome." She smiled, despite the irritation she felt.

The wife pulled the husband away.

Parker saw another gawking bystander, marched up, and was less kind.

With the trespassers dealt with, Parker walked off the property and over to her neighbors'. Deliveries of straw bales from a local feed store were stacked up along the fences. Friends, neighbors, and a crew of firefighter explorers were working together to prepare the homes in danger as much as they could.

Parker pulled her work gloves out of her back pocket and went to work.

While all emergency crews were on her property, she spent the entire day helping others. As tired as she was, she smiled when Austin, Mallory, and Jase grabbed shovels and helped.

"We're either going to laugh or cry," Tracy said.

"I can't believe the storm is named Lucifer," Mallory said.

"Better than being taken out by a storm named Betty Ann." Austin's wit always came through.

"He has a point."

Parker looked over to find that Erin had joined them. She wore an oversize jacket and a baseball cap on her head.

Parker walked over to where she was helping fill sandbags. Media buzzed around filming all the chaos. "You don't have to—"

"I couldn't sit around and do nothing." She glanced at a news van.

Parker smiled, waved her to the back of the house away from the spotlight.

Two local sheriffs walked over to each set of people working. "Who lives at this house?"

Mr. Sutter lifted a hand.

"Evacuations are being advised after nine o'clock tonight," one of them said.

"We've already made arrangements to leave," Mr. Sutter told them.

Parker couldn't blame them. Of all the houses not along the wash, theirs was at the biggest risk of being buried. Which was why they were surrounding the place with plywood and straw bales.

The officer then asked who lived in each of the other homes, writing down names.

The De Lucas weren't going to leave. Neither were Parker and her household. Even the sheriff agreed that her home wasn't at risk. When he informed her that the wash might be impassable, she laughed. If that was a reason to evacuate, she'd have left in December and not come back until May.

The police didn't argue, they just advised and made a note of who was staying and who was going.

"You realize it may be impossible for rescue crews to come in to save you."

"We wouldn't expect that you do. There is no one in my home in poor health. We have food, water, and gas for the generator," Parker told them. "Most of us in this part of the neighborhood do."

The officer she was talking to smiled. "Good luck, everyone. We'll see you in a couple days when it's all over."

"Thank you, Officer."

A handful of them watched the police leave, then went right back to work.

"You think it's going to be that bad?" Austin asked.

"I have a deep and unwavering respect for Mother Nature these days."

"So that's a yes."

Parker started to laugh. "Yes, Austin. I think it's going to be that bad. How bad? I couldn't tell you. I'm amazed we still have a gate to even close." She waved at the dump trucks that were lined up and moving through their property. "They have less than three inches on both sides, and not one of them has so much as tapped the rock pillars. The driveway is hammered. Every time they unbury the crossing through the wash, I don't think it's going to be there. The structure is undermined everywhere. Our sprinkler system is already shot, half the Malibu lighting died with the fire, and the rest was taken out with the first flood. We don't have running water. I don't want to tempt fate, but for us, there isn't much more that can happen." She took a breath. "So when it stops raining, Colin will bring his crew in and dig us out. And I'll call the insurance company. No amount of home repairs is going to fix all this."

She turned to look at the Sutters' home. "We don't have to worry about losing our home. The Sutters do."

"Let's get back to it, then."

She gave her brother a half hug and picked up a sandbag.

～

"I can't believe how much debris you guys cleaned out of there in one day."

Colin stood beside Parker on the high spot overlooking the basins. Pride in his crew was a smile on his face. "They were in rare form today."

It was dusk and the crews had parked their equipment out of the known danger zones for the night.

"I wish you'd reconsider and bring everyone over to my house tonight." He was going to be out with his crew throughout the night keeping watch, so he couldn't stay on the house side of the wash to be with her.

"You know I'm not going to do that."

"Miss Stubborn."

She leaned into him. "I like Miss Oakley better."

"She was stubborn, too."

"You of all people know we're safe inside the house. If it takes a week to dig me out, we're good."

"It won't take a week. Even if the bridge completely washes away, I'll find a flatbed off a truck, get it in there, and give you access."

"Won't your boss be unhappy with that?"

He laughed. "He can be as unhappy as he wants. The homeowner had the brains to put it in writing that we make sure she can get in and out of her land. Ed can't say shit."

"Smart homeowner."

They started back toward the house. "Mallory is home tonight?"

"Yeah. She didn't want to leave with all the crazy going on. We're all going to watch movies and bet on how many inches we get tonight. Then probably go to bed early."

"You've got to be exhausted."

"I'm running on fumes."

He took her hand and kept her steady on the slope of the hill. Once they were back at his truck, he pulled her into his arms. "This weather can't last forever."

"I know."

Colin lowered his lips to hers, enjoyed the feel of her for a little while longer. "I'll be in touch."

"Be safe tonight," she told him.

He stepped over the garden hose water line she was back to using and around to the driver's side door.

As he drove down the street, several homes were already dark. Gates were open for emergency crews to come in, or to avoid mudflow and rocks accumulating behind them.

The sheriffs were on a constant rotation. Only residents were being allowed in the canyon. Which made the jobs of all the first responders easier.

He really hoped the storm was all hype. The kind of thing forecasters screamed about and then skirted over with a whimper.

Either way, he felt good about the project. He wanted to give his entire crew a raise. Overtime . . . a bonus, something.

Colin first went to his house to shower, then headed out to his parents' for dinner. Matt was working, so it would just be his parents and Grace . . . but he welcomed the company since he couldn't spend it with Parker.

Once he walked in his parents' home and kissed his mom and sister, he sat beside his dad, who had the news on.

"Well, Dad . . . what is your leg saying about this storm?"

Emmitt looked at him, grinned. "I hope you have your raincoat with you."

CHAPTER THIRTY-EIGHT

Lucifer came in low and was hitting hard by nine in the evening.

The news became a source of angst, so Parker suggested a board game. As tired as they all were, no one felt like going to bed yet.

They could hear the wash as if it were directly in front of the house. The crossing already impassable. Status quo for this year, Parker found herself thinking.

No one had anywhere to go for a few days, so she'd enjoy the family together time for as long as she could. Who knows . . . maybe she'd look back on this time and smile one day.

One day fifty years from then.

They set up a game of Life, and instead of picking a gender based on who they were, they closed their eyes and pulled a peg from the bag. They gave each other different names and spun the dial.

About halfway through the game, the power popped off.

"Oh, man . . ."

She thought about going out and turning on the generator but hesitated. "Let's just light some candles and enjoy the quiet."

Using their cell phone flashlights, they went through the house and gathered candles.

Parker walked out onto the porch to the water heater room to grab a three-hour log to put in the fireplace.

The creek roared.

As she turned to walk back into the house, a high-pitched hissing noise drew her attention. It sounded as if it were coming from the other side of the wash.

She opened the sliding door and called inside. "Hey, guys . . . come here."

Austin and Mallory rushed over, Erin took her time.

"Do you hear that?"

They all held their breaths while they listened.

"What is it?" Austin asked.

"I have no idea," she said. "You hear it, though, right?"

Erin shrugged.

"It's way over there, whatever it is." Unimpressed, Austin walked back into the house.

Back inside, Parker placed the log in the fireplace and opened the flue. She waited for Mallory to finish lighting a few candles before taking the lighter from her, when her phone rang.

"Hey, Colin . . . how is Armageddon out there?" she teased.

"You've got to get out of there."

Parker lost all levity with his tone.

"What's going on?"

"Are you by the front door?"

"Yeah." She moved back to the slider. Austin took the lighter from her and went to the fireplace.

"Do you hear that noise?"

"Yeah, we can. What is it?"

"Jesus, Parker. I knew you should have come home with me."

Now she was starting to panic. "What is it, Colin?" Her voice grabbed everyone's attention in the room.

"The gas main between the Sutters' and the De Lucas' busted. The noise you hear is gas escaping."

Parker looked up and saw the lighter in Austin's hand. "Austin, no!"

She ran over and grabbed it.

"What is it?" Colin asked.

"We were just about to start a fire. The power went out."

"No fires. No generator. We need to get you out of there."

Parker took a deep breath, walked over to the candles Mallory had just lit, and blew them out. "Find some flashlights. The noise outside is a gas main break."

Erin's eyes widened.

"Oh, shit," Austin said, his eyes moved to the fireplace.

"Parker, are you listening to me?"

"I hear you, Colin. But we can't get over the creek. And even if we could, I wouldn't run toward a gas leak."

"Gas main explosions take out blocks, Parker."

She'd watched enough of the news to consider that.

"It's an all-electric house. No line is connecting us to the break."

Part of her panicked, but the practical part of her took a deep breath.

"Damn it, Parker. I can't lose you."

He was scared to death, she heard it in his voice.

"I don't need you losing it, Colin." She put the phone on speaker so she could use her hands and talk at the same time. She started shouting orders. "Close all the shutters like we did for the fire," she told Mallory and Austin. "Grab a case of water and take it downstairs," she instructed Erin.

"What are you doing?" Colin asked.

"Remember when I told you the house was built like a bomb shelter? That the basement was completely underground? I'm taking everyone down there until I get an all clear from you that everything is safe." She walked into her bedroom and pulled the comforter off her bed.

"I don't like this, Parker."

"We're a thousand feet away. I'm not climbing mountains that are washing away to die in a mudslide to avoid a gas main explosion. C'mon, Hudson . . . you're smarter than that. I'll text you in ten minutes. Cell phone service downstairs is spotty." She grabbed cushions from the sectional and started tossing them down the stairs.

"Ten minutes."

"Let the gas company do their job. Don't make me worry about you out there."

"I will. I love you, Parker."

She stopped what she was doing, looked at her phone. "I love you, too, Colin. Although I didn't see this as how I was going to tell you that for the first time."

"God, I hate this."

"Ten minutes, Colin. I need to get everyone downstairs."

"Go. Be careful."

"You, too."

She hung up the phone, tucked it in her back pocket.

"Blankets and pillows . . . let's move!"

~

The police sectioned off the street. They went house by house, pounding on doors and evacuating all who hadn't already left.

All Colin could do was watch from the side. Rain dripping down his frame.

It gutted him.

Three fire stations, including Matt's, had their trucks on the street and standing by.

"Did you get ahold of them?"

"They're safe," he told his brother.

"All of them? Is Erin with them?"

"Yes. They're holed up in the basement."

Matt nodded several times. "Good, okay. Smart." He spun around. "Son of a bitch . . . When do they think they can get it turned off?"

"I heard a couple of hours."

"That's too long."

"It's a main, Matt. Not a simple switch."

For two men who were first to jump in and help, sitting back and watching was no easy task.

Colin channeled Parker's calm. "They're going to be okay."

His phone chimed with a text.

It's a slumber party in the basement. We're fine. Don't worry.

Colin waved his phone at his brother. "Don't worry. She told me not to worry."

Matt rolled his eyes and stepped off the street as a squad car rolled by.

They really had no choice but to sit back and wait.

∼

"This is crazy." Austin took up one corner of the room, the flashlight illuminated his face. "Overkill, don't you think?"

"Remind me in the morning to show you videos of houses exploding and taking out everything around them from gas leaks," Parker told him.

"We're farther away than a normal neighborhood."

Scout settled his head in Austin's lap as if to tell him to mellow out.

"I agree, but I don't see taking any chances. We have a bomb shelter, we might as well use it."

"Parker is right," Mallory chimed in. "Jase says the whole street has been evacuated."

Colin had told her the same thing, but she didn't really want to freak everyone out. Apparently her protecting Austin was making him feel like there wasn't any danger.

Truth was, she'd been wringing her hands in her lap ever since they settled in the basement. Unlike when the fire blew through, this wasn't a matter of *should they leave*. They absolutely should. They just couldn't. "I'd suggest we hike up and out of here on the back hill if it wasn't washing away."

"Think of it this way, Austin," Erin started. "You'll have a story to tell to your friends in the morning."

Parker's phone buzzed. How are you holding up?

Austin is whining and Mallory is texting Jase. What's it look like out there?

Three ring circus. The neighbors are bitching they have to leave. The police are everywhere. Gas company is running around. And the media just showed up.

Parker pictured lots of red flashing lights and men bumping chests to take charge.

Matt is here. Asked about Erin.

Parker nudged Erin's shoulder with her own and showed her the text.

"Is everything okay?" Austin asked.

"It's fine. Colin says everything is under control." What's a white lie between brother and sister?

Austin put in his ear buds. "Whatever. I'm going to sleep. Wake me up when the shit show is over."

Parker started to text. Tell him she said not to worry.

"Don't encourage him," Erin chided.

Parker ignored her friend and hit send. "Too late."

~

There was no way Colin could sit in his truck. People were everywhere. Matt had suited up, and he and his unit were closer to Parker than he was.

Damn it . . . Why didn't I become a firefighter?

Rain was coming down so hard, he couldn't imagine anything igniting, but it wouldn't take much with the volume of gas escaping from the main.

Fabio stood at his side, both of them wore rain gear, but both of them looked like something fished out of the ocean.

"Let's hope Sutter Canyon doesn't let loose again."

Yeah, Colin had thought about that. "I warned Matt and told the gas company to keep an ear out."

Even though the noise from the main was loud enough to hear from half a mile away, the sound of a flash flood was hard to miss when it was barreling down on you.

"How long has it been?" Fabio asked.

Colin looked at his watch. "An hour and a half."

"How is your lady holding up?"

"Like she's made of steel."

Fabio patted him on the back. "They'll have this off in no time."

Yeah, and now he had his girlfriend and his brother to worry about until they did.

~

Scout curled next to Austin, and between the two of them, filled the room with sounds of snoring.

Mallory had put in her ear buds and was quietly texting Jase until she gave up and lay down.

Parker sat with her back against one of the walls and waited for her sister to fall asleep. One small flashlight shined against the door of the room. "I need to chat or freak out," Parker finally admitted once her brother started snoring.

Erin reached out, squeezed her hand. "Tell me what you used this room for."

Good. Something that wasn't about fire, floods, or disasters. "When we were kids, our parents set this room up as a playroom. It was perfect. We could make all kinds of noise and it didn't bother anyone. Slowly the forts and toys went out and it just sat empty unless we were having a slumber party."

"Just like we are now," Erin said.

"Minus the popcorn, chips, ice cream, and pictures of boys."

"I already know what Colin looks like. So you can keep your phone in your lap," Erin teased.

Parker looked around. "I never thought I'd use it for an actual bomb shelter."

"At least you have it."

"I feel safer, and I know Colin is breathing a little easier."

Erin stretched her arms and yawned. "It's nice to have someone to worry about you."

"Matt is worried about you," Parker pointed out.

"Matt is being polite."

"And you're being blind. But that's okay." Parker looked at her sleeping brother and preoccupied sister. "A discussion for a different day."

Something upstairs made a loud enough sound to make Scout lift his sleeping head from Austin's side.

Austin and Mallory didn't budge.

"What was that?" Erin asked.

Parker felt herself holding her breath as she listened for anything to indicate what the noise was.

All she heard was silence.

She pushed out of her sitting position.

"Where are you going?" Erin asked in a hoarse whisper.

"To check it out." She grabbed one of the flashlights and started for the door.

"Be careful."

"It's probably nothing." But the basement did a great job of sheltering them from the sound outside, so if something had exploded, she wanted to know.

She walked down the hallway of the basement, rounded the corner, and started up the back stairs of the house. The flashlight barely chased the shadows from the walls once she got to the top. Since the shutters were down on all the windows except the big bay one in the dining room, the only window in the house that didn't have shutters, Parker headed toward it.

She saw flashing lights beyond the wash and could still hear the hiss of the gas. No evidence of anything exploding, or any real progress on shutting down the main. Not that she could see much from her vantage point.

So what was the noise?

She turned to go back downstairs when Sushi darted out under her feet, scaring her within an inch of her life.

"Damn cat."

She caught her breath and the flashlight landed on a metal vase that looked like it had fallen on the floor. "Damn cat," she said again in case Sushi was listening.

By the time Parker made it back downstairs, Erin was up and pacing.

"Well?"

"The cat is having a party up there."

Erin sighed, her shoulders slumped.

Parker found herself consoling her friend. "It's okay. The gas isn't turned off yet, but it's okay."

Erin shook. "I thought maybe he found his way in."

Parker grabbed both of Erin's hands. "If there was anyone in the house, Scout would be barking his head off. It was the cat. Your ex isn't here."

"I know that." She shook her head. "I hate that he makes me afraid even now."

In a room with her brother and sister, the last thing Parker was going to do was pry. "You're okay. He isn't going to hurt you here."

Erin opened her arms and Parker gave her a hug.

The screen of her phone lit up the room at her feet.

She broke off the hug to look at the message.

They shut off the line.

She blew out a breath, showed Erin the text from Colin.

"Yes," Erin said.

Parker replied. Thank God. That's a relief.

This has been the longest night of my life. Colin texted.

I've had better, too. I'm exhausted. We all are.

Go to sleep, honey. You're safe now. I'll be back at first light.

She smiled. Thank you for looking out for us.

The three little dots flashed for quite a while before Colin's last text came through. Be warned, Miss Oakley. I'm going full-on Neanderthal on you the first chance I get. Love you.

Her heart warmed, despite the chill in the room. Love you, too.

Parker lowered the phone and looked at her sister and brother. "Should we wake them up?"

Erin shook her head and sat down. "It's been a long time since I had a slumber party."

Parker joined her. "Me too." She pulled a blanket up to her chin, shoved a pillow under her head. "I'm too tired to talk about boys."

"Another night, then," Erin said.

Before she closed her eyes, she heard Erin say, "Thanks for being here, Parker."

Parker reached out, and grabbed Erin's hand. "If he ever shows up here, I'll kick his ass for you."

CHAPTER THIRTY-NINE

Lucifer was still sputtering, but the bulk of his wrath had filtered east.

It was nearly eight o'clock in the morning and Colin had yet to hear from Parker. Which was completely unlike her. The woman was up before he was.

He stood outside his truck as misty rain continued to fall.

The wash was an inferno.

But his structures held.

The mudflow that had seared off the gas line and caused the night's chaos had built up against a retaining wall between the Sutters' and their neighbors to the west of them. Somewhere in the night, the wall gave way and took a chicken coop and a shed with it.

The houses still stood.

Two of his men were on skip loaders clearing the driveways, while Russ sat in his excavator waiting for a break in the rain to start digging.

Matt showed up with Grace, and right behind them his parents drove through the gate.

"Holy cow, son. You weren't joking about the scale of this project." His father greeted him with a hug.

It was the first time his dad had been to the house.

His mom hugged him long. "How are you holding up?"

"I'll be better once my eyes land on Parker."

"She isn't answering her phone?" Grace asked.

"No."

"Call Mallory."

"I don't have her number." Colin would fix that before the day was over.

"I know who will have her number," Matt said as he put his phone to his ear. "Hey, Jase, it's Matt. Are you in touch with Mallory?" Matt nodded a couple of times. "Ah-huh . . . tell her to wake her up and get her butt outside so Colin can stop sprouting gray hair." More nodding followed by a smile. "Thanks."

"She's on her way."

"She was asleep?"

"They all were, apparently."

He spotted the dog first. Scout darted down the stairs and ran to a tree and lifted a leg. One by one, all four of them walked into view.

Colin's chest rose and fell with thankful breaths.

"You brought the whole family?" were the first words out of Parker's mouth when she got within shouting distance.

"You can't keep us away," Nora shouted.

"I was starting to worry again," Colin told her.

"My phone died. And there are no windows downstairs, so we didn't notice when the sun came up."

He shifted from foot to foot.

"Is it safe to—"

He turned his ear, still didn't quite make out what she was saying. The beeping of the loaders behind them made it even harder.

"The gas line . . . generator . . ."

"I think she's asking about the generator."

He nodded. "Yes."

Behind them, Russ turned over his long reach excavator.

Colin grinned and walked toward the man.

Russ leaned out of the cab of his rig. "Mornin'."

"I need you to get me over to the other side."

"You got it."

Russ moved the equipment, and Colin walked to the edge of the wash.

He looked over to his mother. "Mom. Don't watch."

"What are you doing?"

Matt grinned.

Colin stepped into the jaws of the arm and held tight as Russ tilted it so he wouldn't fall out. He crouched down and held on.

Russ extended the arm of the excavator the span of the wash and slowly lowered Colin to the ground.

The second his feet touched the mud, Parker was there with fire and brimstone. "You crazy son of a . . . was that payback for last night?"

He didn't answer, he just picked her up in his arms and held her as tight as he could without squeezing the air out of her.

"You can put me down now," she laughed in his ear.

"Nope. Not done yet."

She giggled. "You're crazy."

He set her down just so he could kiss her.

When he let up, he held her face in his hands. "Last night is never going to happen again."

"I hope not—"

"No. It's not. I'm staying with you, or you're coming with me. I can't do that again."

"Okay, Colin. I won't fight you on that."

He kissed her again. "And another thing . . ."

"Yes?"

"I'm redefining our relationship."

"You are?"

He looked up and saw his family watching them, but was fairly certain they couldn't hear what he was about to say. Not that it mattered. They'd figure it out soon enough. "When two people love each other, they don't stay boyfriend and girlfriend for very long. They acquire new titles."

The silly smile on Parker's face started to slip.

"I'd get down on one knee right now if I had a ring . . ."

"Colin?"

"The only way I can prove to you that I'm not going anywhere is to give you my name and make you mine."

Her hands clenched to his chest. "I come with a lot of baggage."

"I knew that going in, Parker . . . And you know what? It's part of what I fell in love with. All the things that put you in my life, from your parents' accident, to the fire and all this flooding, all of it paved my way to you."

"What about kids?"

He placed a hand on her cheek. "Let's get the teenagers out of the house before we have that conversation."

"And if that doesn't happen?"

"I love you. Your desire to have or not to have children is not a deal breaker for me. I don't know what the future holds except that we're in it together. Don't let all that you've been through be in vain, Parker. Let's redefine what we're doing here."

She was smiling now, the mist plastered her hair to her face. "Turn something negative into a positive."

He ran his fingers into her wet hair. "Tell me yes."

"You didn't ask me anything yet." Her smile was radiant.

"Tell me you'll say yes when I ask." Because he'd be damned if he was going to propose to this woman standing in six inches of mud.

She lifted on her tiptoes, put her lips next to his. "Yes, Colin. I will say yes."

He picked her up again and spun her around.

EPILOGUE

A breeze blew the wind chimes into a soft, welcoming song.

Colin handed Jase the last box from the pile of Mallory's personal possessions.

Parker tilted her face to the sun and sky and wondered if her parents were watching.

It had been nearly a month since the last rain, and Colin's crew was cleaning up what they all felt was the last of the muck for at least another year.

Parker had called the insurance company back and was waiting on checks before they started digging the new path for an entirely new water main. The fire hose setup Matt had helped put together was better than a garden hose, but still not the real thing.

In the end, it was all stuff. Stuff that broke . . . stuff that needed to be fixed. And mud to be shoveled and taken away.

Colin placed an arm around Parker's shoulders and held her.

"That's the last of it," Mallory told them as she walked out of the house to join them.

Parker felt her eyes swell with tears and did everything she could to hold them back.

"Don't go doing that," Mallory chided.

"I'm not crying." Parker held her arms open for her sister to hold her.

Out from the garage, Austin walked holding a paint roller. "Last chance, Mallory."

Mallory broke free of Parker's arms and moved to her brother. "You dork. Give me a hug."

Colin once again held Parker, kissed the top of her head. His support was everything she needed to get through each day. Although he hadn't yet asked her the question that she'd already promised to say yes to, they both knew it was coming, and that somehow made everything about them complete.

"It isn't like she's moving out of state," Jase told them.

Parker raised a finger in the air. "Don't you dare!"

Mallory broke free of Austin and stood in front of Colin. "Keep her from going crazy, will ya?"

"I'll try."

They hugged.

"Remember, dinner on Sunday," Parker called out when her sister jumped in the car.

"I haven't even left yet."

Jase got in his car. "I'll meet you at home," he told Mallory.

Her sister was all smiles as he drove off.

It was nice to see her so happy.

She turned over the engine and hung out the window. "I left you something in the living room."

"What is it?"

Mallory didn't answer, she just blew her a kiss and then drove away.

"If you need me, I'll be de-chick-a-fying my new bedroom," Austin exclaimed as he strutted back into the garage. Scout barked and followed Austin inside.

"One down, one to go," Colin teased.

"Don't get your hopes up, Austin is turning Mallory's bedroom into the man cave."

"I'm just giving you a hard time."

They started back in the house. "I talked with Ed this morning."

"How did that go?"

"Like I thought it would. It's a conflict of interest for me to be the point man on this project if I'm living here." Colin hadn't completely moved in. But he stayed over more days than he spent in his own home.

"He took you off the job." It wasn't a question.

"No. He kept me on the job."

Parker narrowed her eyes. "I'm confused."

"I think he wants me to screw up so he has an excuse to demote me. I had a conversation with Fabio, and he's up for double-checking any and everything."

"You think that will keep you out of trouble?"

Colin opened the door for her and stepped inside the house.

"It can't hurt."

A large, brightly wrapped box sat against the wall in the family room. Mallory must have put it there after they'd all walked outside to say goodbye.

"What did she do?"

"No clue."

Parker picked up the box and brought it to the sofa. A folded card next to the bow had a message.

Time for a new chapter.

Parker unwrapped the gift to find a box. She ripped off the tape holding it together and reached inside.

Her fingers fell on a frame, and before she could even get the picture free, she knew what it was going to be.

Parker, Mallory, Austin, and Scout stood huddled together. The picture hadn't been staged, no one in their right mind could think otherwise. It had been taken the day after the fire. They'd been dirty, hair sticking up, clothes a mess. But they were all smiling. So happy that they had a home to get back to.

It was perfect.

The tears she'd held back from saying goodbye to her sister were flowing now as Parker looked up at the image of her parents looking down over the fireplace.

Colin walked up behind the couch and leaned over, wrapped his arms over her shoulders and looked at the picture with her. "That's awesome."

"Yeah." She sniffled. "It is."

He kissed her cheek.

"Would you mind putting it up?" she asked.

Colin glanced up at her parents. "You sure?"

"Yeah. It's time to move on."

And when Colin had removed the old family photo and placed the new one, they both looked at it and smiled.

"Next year I see you up there in a white dress and me in a tux." He held her close as he spoke.

"I need a ring first," she said, chuckling.

"Patience, Miss Oakley . . . patience."

NOTE FROM THE AUTHOR

On July 22, 2016, the Sand Fire erupted from the side of the 14 Freeway in the Santa Clarita Valley. Southern California was in its seventh year of severe drought. The cause of the fire was never made official, but it is widely believed that it took one careless smoker tossing a cigarette from a car to spark the fire that obliterated over fifty square miles of land. By the time the fire was out, two lives were lost, and eighteen buildings were destroyed. One of those structures was counted on my property.

This fire was by no means the biggest, the worst, or the deadliest in California history. But it was personal to my family and me.

My home and five-and-a-half-acre property for twenty years escaped complete destruction because of the heroic efforts of the firefighters from LA County Fire, Cal Fire, and LA City Fire. Putting my hands on my home that I was sure I had lost was one of the single most grateful days of my life.

Once the fire was out, and the damage had been assessed, it became horrifically apparent that should California's drought end, my property and that of my neighbors would be in serious danger from mudslides and flooding. Thankfully, the Los Angeles County Public Works Department and the City of Santa Clarita joined forces and expedited a collaborative effort to help reduce any damage Mother Nature might inflict upon us. Three months following the fire, the County Public

Works Department showed up at my gate and seemingly never left until spring.

Mother Nature decided to dump 200 percent above normal rainfall in the winter and spring of 2016–2017. I caught most of it on video. Search my Facebook archives, dear reader, you'll find it.

I knew one day I would write a book where I could show the world what it feels like to live through such hardship, but more importantly, to shine light on all the heroes involved. My heroes wore fire gear and carried water in the beginning and then wore hard hats and drove backhoes in the end.

This story is a work of fiction. Arguably the backdrop is not. But the characters and their actions are their own. I am comfortable to admit that some of Parker's personality may resemble the author's. All names have been changed to protect the guilty . . . or innocent.

ACKNOWLEDGMENTS

So, dear readers . . . here is where I want to list the names of everyone I can think of as my way of thanking them for everything they did to protect, serve, and care for me and my family in ways I never saw coming. If I missed your name, I am truly sorry.

The firefighters of LA County Fire, Cal Fire, and LA City Fire. I don't have all your names, or all your station numbers, so to avoid messing up, I will thank your departments as a whole. My respect for you is immeasurable. Thank you for putting your lives on the line each and every day you clock in. Thank you for keeping us safe, but more to the point, for saving my home.

My sons, Jeremy and Joshua. I love you both so much and am so proud of how you handled everything. I cannot imagine what it would have looked like to not have you by my side during all the chaos.

My father, Tom Kemmer, for ignoring me when I told you the fire wasn't going to reach us, and rushing to be by our side when it did.

Jeff and Sheri Davidson for all your support before, during, and after the fire. I love you like family! And your little dogs, too.

Ed and Josie Chow. Nothing like having your own police escort to get back home!

Santa Clarita Sheriff's Department for keeping us safe.

Future firefighter Troy Leidholdt for packing cars and being there when the fire raged toward us.

Farmers Insurance and agents Bryan Kreuzberger and Bryan Gros for taking some of the pain out of the situation.

Sharon Meyer . . . lady, you held my hand and drank lots of wine with me for months. Your support will never be forgotten.

The City of Santa Clarita. Thank you for pushing to make this happen.

Kurt at Kurt Bohmer Plumbing, and your staff. Thank you.

Now for the long list: The men and women of LA County Public Works Department on and behind the scenes along with the subcontracted talent that saved our neighborhood.

First on this list, and the man I dedicated this book to, is Superintendent Paul Melillo. Paul . . . I can't type this without tears in my eyes. You and your team were by far the best thing that could have ever happened after the fire. Your unwavering strength and resolve that everything would be fixed in the end was often the only thing that kept me sane. Thank you from the bottom of my heart. Enjoy your retirement, my friend, and bring the family for a visit in San Diego anytime.

Next we have the supervisors, Martin Lemus and John Rice. I'm pretty sure you both thought I was a piece of work when this project started. And in the end, I confirmed it. John, I wish you the best of luck filling Paul's shoes. I know you're rocking the superintendent position. I hope you love your forever nickname.

Area Engineer: Ken Swanson. Assistant Engineer: Laren Bunker. Secretary: Lindsey Bennett.

Crew Leaders: Andy O'Callaghan, Luis Montes De Oca, James Young, and Emilio Nieves. Thank you for the late nights and early mornings.

Employees in no particular order: Eric Mendibles, Jade MacDonald (RIP), Francisco Mayorga, Ryan Kiefer, Mark Robinson, Gavin Pugh, Dan Moreno, Tom Miller, Adan Cano, James Martinez, Geraldo Alcala,

Darrin Livingston. Thank you all. And if I never saw you walk out of the Porta Potty pulling up your pants . . . thank you twice!

Welders: Jeff Rupe and Dwayne Meyers. Jeff, I will cherish my CB welded horseshoe yard art forever. Thank you!

Design/Engineer: Amir, Araik, and Mike.

The men at Northwest Excavating: Ken (Rodeo Tractor Guy!), I will never forget the look on your face when the footbridge crashed downstream. Julio, Rob, and Jack. Thank you!

Robby from Kirby Excavation.

Kip Construction: Hawkstone and Mike.

April from April's Trucking. And all fifty trucks and their drivers who drove through day in and day out FOREVER! Oh, and thanks for never hitting my gate. Serious skills there!

Tommy and Angel from Isco.

Lastly:

My neighbors: Joe and Lorinda Graziano, John and Philippa Gunner, Jeff and Debbie Habberstad, John and Roni Richardson, and Kara Franklin. I feel like we went to war and back. It's when the chips are down that your true colors are seen. And we came through pretty damn good. Thank you for the showers when we didn't have running water, advice when I was at a loss as to what to do, and hugs when there was nothing *to* do but cry. I love and miss you all.

Thank you, Montlake, for understanding all my delays and missed deadlines.

As always, thank you, Jane Dystel, for not only your professional help as my agent, but more importantly being there as my friend. You were in contact constantly, and always believed I would overcome.

A million thanks to all of you.

Catherine

ABOUT THE AUTHOR

Photo © 2015 Julianne Gentry

New York Times, Wall Street Journal, and *USA Today* bestselling author Catherine Bybee has written thirty-four books that have collectively sold more than seven million copies and have been translated into more than eighteen languages. Raised in Washington State, Bybee moved to Southern California in the hope of becoming a movie star. After growing bored with waiting tables, she returned to school and became a registered nurse, spending most of her career in urban emergency rooms. She now writes full-time and has penned the Not Quite series, the Weekday Brides series, the Most Likely To series, and the First Wives series. For more information on the author, visit www.catherinebybee.com.